Boot

Boot

A SORTA NOVEL OF VIETNAM

by Charles L. Templeton

www.charlestempleton.com

ISBN: 978-1-7340997-0-6

Permissions and Acknowledgements

My wonderful wife, Sandra, who has been my muse and my inspiration and continues to be my primary source of new and compound profanities.

The enigmatic Eleanor Roosevelt who said, "The Marines I have seen around the world have the cleanest bodies, the filthiest minds, the highest morale, and the lowest morals of any group of animals I have ever seen. Thank God for the United States Marine Corps!"

Fearless and undaunted, Bill McCloud, for providing poetic interludes in the Boot. Bill's words define ideas and display emotions like a razor slicing through a vein. Specifically:

'I Think I May be Dead'
'The Smell of Death'
'Eating Glass' from his book 'The Smell of the Light' published by Balkan Press
'Mail Call'
'I Don't Want to Die'
'That Hill has a Name'
'Wall Shadow'

Several of these poems and many more about his experiences in Vietnam can be found in his book, 'The Smell of the Light', published by Balkan Press.

William Bernhardt, author of over forty books and friend, for his inspiration and for performing a literary colonoscopy on the Boot.

The folks over at Sony/ATV Publishing for allowing me to use:

Rocky Raccoon
Words and Music by John Lennon and Paul McCartney
Copyright (c) 1968, 1969 Sony/ATV Music Publishing LLC
Copyright Renewed
All Rights Administered by Sony/ATV Music Publishing LLC
424 Church Street
Suite 1200
Nashville, TN 37219
International Copyright Secured All Rights Reserved
Reprinted by Permission of Hal Leonard LLC

Friends, from my writing group, who served as beta readers and who had to sit and listen to me read from Boot, every Monday for over two years, without the benefit of marijuana: Dan Morris, Tom Gorsuch, Wendy-Taylor Carlisle, and Verne Rudebusch.

Beta readers who provided much sought after input and critiques, without whom the Boot would have been completed years ago: John and Jane White, Todd Simpson, Jim Wilson, Janie Rohr, Al Larson, Will Morris, Jeanna Whatley, and J.J. Huntz.

Jennifer Chandler and the folks over at Elite Authors (www.eliteauthors. com) who helped guide me through the self-publishing process. From line editing through cover design they were challenging and awe-inspiring and managed to find a novel in my hallucinations.

Table of Conents

Washington, DC 20 February 1989

George sat on the steps of the Lincoln Memorial, gazing at the Reflecting Pool, lost in his thoughts. He was back from a mission for one of the many alphabet organizations that crowded Washington, DC. *Make a decision. Are you going to look at that damn Wall, or are you going to di-di[1] back to Georgetown?*

He squinted into the pool's reflection. His face was a mask hiding his shadows. *Christ on a crutch. What is the matter with me?* His heart raced and his brain whirred, like an old-time nickelodeon, speeding up and slowing down as he cranked the handle, replaying images from his tour in Vietnam forever camped in his memory. They had been hidden away on the shelf where he kept his nightmares.

Why would I want to think about that crap anyway? That was then; this is now. How young and unschooled he'd been and how hard he'd believed in serving his country like his father, his uncles, and both his grandfathers. Hell, he still had some 1918 letters one Marine grandfather

---

1 From the Vietnamese *di-di-mau,* meaning to "Go, go quickly!" Borrowed by the American Military during the Vietnam War.

wrote home from France. He'd been serving with a Marine in the Seventy-Third Machine Gun Company and had sworn he'd heard the legendary gunnery sergeant Dan Daly say, "Come on, you sons of bitches, do you want to live forever?"

This same grandfather told him before his enlistment, "I hear the fishing in Canada is pretty darn good. Wouldn't mind visiting up there." The look he gave his grandson as he put his arm around him said, *Hey, everything is all right. Whatever decision you make, the family will stand behind you.*

When he returned from boot camp, he noticed the pride reflected in his grandfather's eyes. But now, in the water of the Reflecting Pool, he saw the image of a headless North Vietnamese regular. Some creative grunt had pinned a note on his blouse that read, "I just wanted to get ahead in life." At the time, he lost his lunch. These days he chuckled about the grisly scene.

He could also see the faces of the Vietnamese orphans at the Catholic home where he helped build a school. He could see the CH-46D helicopter eat itself on the flight deck of the *Iwo Jima* as it rolled over the side of the ship into the South China Sea. Unbelievably, every crew member survived. Going blind on gin and chocolate milk. Weird and insane images kept popping up in his mind. Flying through a perfectly circular rainbow in the Quang Tri province. Private Hakim with a K-Bar between his teeth. Mooning the Republic of Korea Marines out of the back of his helicopter. *It was so surreal. Will these images never leave me? Can they be changed? God knows alcohol and drugs did not help. Maybe if I just go back to the beginning, maybe I could make some sense of it...*

Chapter One

The Kootchie Is Undefeated

George Orwell Hill planned the perfect sexual coup de grâce. After eons of pleading, begging, arm-twisting, and out-and-out groveling, he convinced the object of his lifelong affection to bed him. All he could think about was getting laid. The objective of his desire—Prudence Amaryllis, true Diana—decided to end the chase. Proo captained their high school drill team, the Steppin' Fetchits, and also played a forward position on their half-court basketball team. A thick mound of dirty blond hair cut short framed her angelic face. A face that hid her ambitions and desires. Her eyes were as blue and deep as the South Texas sky. G.O. felt like she could look right through him. While G.O. was headed to the Marine Corps, Proo was headed to Trinity University in San Antonio.

Ah, Prudence,
Princess Loving Fox,
Mother of the Horned Dream,
Scintillating lady with the 1956
Cadillac tits.

◆ ◆ ◆

Proo, relinquishing her sanity, decided to spend G.O.'s last night of freedom with him. Actually, she detested Georgie Hill...but it was his last night in America, he was a soldier, and he had been in love with her since they were in Miss Ernestine Sneed's third-grade class. *God*, she thought, *I could almost justify it based on how long he chased me.* But she knew the real reason she had consented. She secretly coveted the promiscuous thought that Georgie might be a little light in his loafers. Because, she reflected, why else would he grow his hair out like that? George was over six feet tall, and he was lean, like most of the young men in South Texas. He possessed a flowing, unruly mane of auburn hair that he had grown to extravagant lengths. George told her it was his last attempt at being rebellious before leaving for the Marine Corps. She thought differently. Tonight she would find out.

♦ ♦ ♦

Ordinarily, the Hogg-Legg drive-in movie was not the scene of idyllic romance. This night would be no exception. G.O. had been in heat for three days and three lonely nights. In quiet moments, prior to a full moon, G.O. found he resembled the fabled unicorn. Now, stretched out on the back seat of his brother's 1964 candy-apple-red Mustang, reality became an erection of Pythagorean proportions. G.O. endeavored to suck Proo's lower intestinal tract through her esophagus until she became transparent. Ah, but that devil sphincter would not yield. Each breath amplified, added a nebulous texture to foggy minds and foggy windows, manifesting mysterious journeys to lands known only to the Virgins of the Dupont Chemical Gods.

The Mustang stood alone on the back row. His brother had lent G.O. the car, feeling that it was the least he could do for the poor Marine about to leave for Vietnam. Plus G.O. had promised to buy him a case of Lone Star beer. His brother had been deferred by the local draft board because he possessed a fractured hangnail. And because he was employed by the president of the local draft board, who happened to own the Eichenberry-Jones Funeral Parlor and Indoor Miniature Golf Course. They had a reasonable layaway plan, and play was always halted on the back nine during funerals.

Before leaving to pick up Proo, G.O.'s brother had taken him aside and offered his best brotherly advice. "You just remember one thing, Fantan, the kootchie is undefeated. Always has been, always will be."

The "Yellow Rose of Texas" blared through the speaker, Rock Hudson crashed through the blue-plate special, and kaleidoscopic colors reflected a myriad of images through the pasty windshield as the backseat bacchanal progressed. Clothes strewn. Proo half-in, half-out of her bra. Breasts heaving. Voluptuous mounds swelling under G.O.'s maniacal gaze. Oh God!

Good evening, ladies and gentlemen, and welcome to the Rose Bowl. It's a beautiful night for football, and if you haven't noticed yet, we have two Goodyear blimps here tonight. For those of you who would like an up-close look at these magnificent aircraft, they will be on display at the Los Angeles International Airport all week between the Lips of George Oliver Hill.

Oh-h-h-h no-o-o-o! thought G.O. *It can't be.* A lone hair stood defiantly near the top of the color-splashed breast. *Oh well, the price one must pay,* and he zeroed in on the Promised Land, already moist with a glaze of perspiration.

Sweet Proo's persimmon panties had been adroitly manipulated by G.O. They had traversed the length of her legs and formed a hobble around her equine-like ankles.

G.O. held Prudence steadfastly in place while he balanced precariously between her thighs.

Marshal Dillon stepped into the street and ran his fingers caressingly over the hand-tooled leather holster as his steely-eyed gaze sized up the challenger. This was to be his most formidable opponent yet. Stories had preceded the red-headed stranger into town, and Matthew certainly felt some apprehension. Doc, Chester, Kitty, and Bilbo

Baggins (played by Burt Reynolds) stood quietly at the doors of the Longbranch, feeling Matt's trepidation from afar. Matthew and the stranger stood but a few feet apart now. Suddenly, with the swiftness and agility of a one-legged short order cook, G.O. had his fly open and his pride in his hand. He had outdistanced the marshal by a full three inches. Miss Kitty was his. Bilbo could hold the ring. Chester could hold the onions. And Doc...Doc could kiss a fat baby's ass.

G.O. managed to struggle out of a pair of reluctant blue jeans and free the Maroon Harpoon. His Majesty swung gently back and forth. The deadly cobra, ready to spew its venom.

The crowd roared! G.O. was on the one-yard line about to penetrate the best defense in the Milky Way.

"George," Proo whispered.

George caught Proo's eyes in his best insincere French actor's gaze. Her face was uncommonly placid, like the sea after a tempest. *Shit*, G.O. thought, *there hasn't been any fucking storm!*

"What is it, Proo?"

"George, please don't, someone is watching."

George reacted by raising straight up, head ricocheting off the head-liner. George stifled a condemnation of all that is holy in the Baptist Church as he glanced quickly around. Then with a quizzical look, heavy in disappointment, G.O. looked at Prudence and queried, "What? There's no one looking."

"Oh yes, there is, George. God's watching."

Instant impotence.

That night as G.O. lay alone in bed and rubbed an old football injury he received playing a game in his dreams, he looked quietly at the ceiling. Flashes of Prudence implanted themselves permanently in his mind as the fan above him whirred gently around. G.O. whispered a solemn private prayer. His first in many years. "Lord, please don't let me get a calcium deposit in my penis."

Chapter Two

The Sojourn Begins

G.O. remembered, but the closeness of the dream moved inexorably away from him. As he gazed into the rust-corroded urinal at the Hue-Phu Bai Airport, the dream became so clouded it seemed distant and receded into the smoky recesses of his memory. G.O. was shaken from his lascivious thoughts as a cockroach tried to escape the urinal by struggling up to the rust-stained enamel and crawling precariously out. Alas, the poor cockroach never had a chance. G.O. hit him with a stream of urine, knocking him from his perch. The cockroach fell haphazardly into the urinal and grasped a cigarette butt as George relentlessly maintained his target practice.

> *Shee-it!* the cockroach thought. *Mother Justice ain't blind...the bitch is fucking crazy. I hope his aim is this good when the bad guys are shooting back.*

G.O. found a ride to the Marine Corps' side of the airfield in the back of a passing six-by-six truck. Ordinarily, G.O. felt little affected by being alone in a strange place, but now an odd feeling came over him. Like the time he rode from Alice to Dilley for the greater glory of the god of itinerant farmers, Amun Ra, in the back of a pick-up truck loaded with Mexican Americans. *The tacos were tasty, but the conversations were a wee bit loaded. All those Tejanos talking Spanish and me noddin' in English.* The language had been no barrier. One of his lesser loves, in between dreams of the fabled Proo, had been the daughter of a nomadic Hispanic family. She was nine. G.O. was ten. When alone, they would stare into each other's eyes with childish innocence. G.O. first glimpsed infinity in those large charcoal eyes. The absolute pronounced reflection of the immortality of the soul. The essence of which was ostensibly concealed on that nine-year-old face. She had moved away, and G.O. had lost something special. Try as he might, he had never been able to recall those visions, to feel as deeply, or to be as self-assured. It had been stolen from him by a demon from the land of Prester John. Cataloged and stored by a renegade bureaucrat in the hidden recesses of George Hill's mind. *Too much Freudian nonsense for this white boy.* G.O. jumped off the back of the truck as it lurched to a halt in front of a large crimson and gold monolith. It read, "Marine Air Group 36 First Marine Air Wing."

"Adios," the driver hollered.

"Hasta luego, puta!" G.O replied under his stale breath.

Pere Goriot Gonzales smiled as he put the truck in gear and erupted in a cloud of dust. *Stupid gringo*, Pere thought. *Doesn't even remember riding from Alice to Dilley in that dilapidated old truck with me. I suppose all jawbreakers look alike to that stupid gringo.*

◆ ◆ ◆

Pere recalled standing barefoot in the sun in front of the Dulceria. He was admiring, with orgiastic pleasure, a jar filled with jawbreakers. Each one a glorious entity bathed in a myriad of colors. A waterfall of saliva-producing sweetness. Each jawbreaker had its own personality, and Pere had given each a name. He also held the most intimate conversations with them about the sublime pleasures they might bring into his cloistered life.

"Here comes that pesky little fart again," said the Blue Jawbreaker.

"Yeah, poor little fella, actually thinks all Jawbreakers are different," replied the Orange with Green Speckles Jawbreaker.

"But we are different, brutha," chimed in the remarkably arrogant Green with Yellow Flashes Jawbreaker.

"Jackass," said the Blue. "It's no medical secret that all Jawbreakers are inherently formed the same way and serve the same basic function."

"Well, ain't you the literate muthafucka," replied the Green with Yellow Flashes. "Anybody can see you be you and I be me."

"He's right," cried the predominantly Purple Jawbreaker. "We are different simply because we look different."

"That's ninety-nine percent pure horse pucky," the Blue retorted. "You look different to keep the suckers who admire you from dying of boredom. The color is merely therapeutic. Something to entice the taste buds and tantalize the gluttonous section of mind. The color is only a stimulus for tongue erection, nothing more."

"I've noticed how the less fortunate, that is, less beautiful Jawbreakers, seem to take great pleasure in believing all Jawbreakers are the same," the Gray with Red Spots that looked like little griffons said to the Green with Yellow Flashes Jawbreaker.

"The Lord works in strange and mysterious ways," replied the Pious White Jawbreaker that had been ravaged by a one-eyed cockroach named Lomax.

"When the great class struggle is over the bourgeois Jawbreakers will finally recognize the equality of the proletariat," cried the Marxist Pink Jawbreaker, who rested uncomfortably in the bottom of the jar that contained the Jawbreakers.

"Who gives a crap?" sighed the Newly Married Middle-Class Conservative Jawbreaker, who had recently been purchased by an anxious youth. However, in the youth's haste to consume his new treasure, he was unable to coordinate his jaw muscles, and the Jawbreaker shot across the floor of the Dulceria. The shopkeeper, being a kind old man who remembered the failures of his own youth, gave him another. The old man wiped off the Newly Married Middle-Class Conservative Jawbreaker and replaced him in the jar.

The argument developed into mayhem with each Jawbreaker expressing his views on whatever it was that started the row.

"Quiet!" screamed the Fuchsia and Lemon Jawbreaker. As Pere approached, the Fuchsia and Lemon continued, "Pere, tell us, are all Jawbreakers the same or are they different?"

Pere, who was only six years old on this planet, replied, "All Jawbreakers are different, of course."

"Ah-h-h-h-h-h!" sighed half the Jawbreakers.

"Oh-h-h-h-h-h!" sighed the other half.

"Who really gives a big honk?" said the Semi-Dirty Newly Married Middle-Class Conservative Jawbreaker.

Suddenly, the Fuchsia and Lemon lit up and became an even more brilliant hue as a thought strobed his mirrored mind. "But, Pere, are Jawbreakers different because of their color?"

Pere replied, "Oh-h-h-h no-o-o-o! Color has nothing to do with the difference!"

"But if we were all the same color, there would be no argument," cried the Marxist Pink.

"Maybe not, but you would still be different," said Pere.

The Jawbreakers became deathly still. Aristotelian logic had confused the anal retentives. Lomax, the one-eyed cockroach, broke the silence. "What the hell does a kid know?"

The other Jawbreakers agreed, and pandemonium broke out.

◆　◆　◆

As Pere motored down the road in the truck, the thought returned. *Stupid Gringo cockroach, he sees all Jawbreakers with the same jaundiced eye.*

Chapter Three

A Quixotic Diversion

G.O.'s eyes were glassed over. Filling out some two million forms in trip-licate can be tedious and time-consuming, even though this task is the true measure of a Marine. What happens to all the forms, of course, is still as mysterious as the great Cheops pyramid. *Recycled*, G.O. thought.

◆ ◆ ◆

At a Shell station near Milhaus, Mongolia, a very ancient Genghis Omar Hill tied up his Hertz rent-a-yak and ambled slowly toward the People's Room. Ambled back to get the key. Take two: G.O. ambles slowly back to the People's Room. G.O. Picked out a hygienic-looking piece of porcelain and situated his well-worn, well-kicked, and heavily nibbled-on posterior in a comfortable position. It had been nearly half a century since G.O. had used such a device. He had almost forgotten the comfort of such luxury as he glanced at the brown stains on his heels. For the first time in years, G.O. felt a twinge of pain from the scars left by the wooden teeth of Gunnery Sergeant G. Willis Peabody.

The door opened abruptly and the wind blew the original Sea Hag through the door, mizzenmast flapping. The ancient creature coughed, and the disposable flannel toga she was wearing fell from her wrinkled body. Corpus Uglius (-a, -um). She lightly creaked down on the center throne, cocked her ancient head, raised a piece of skin that once claimed the distinction of being an eyebrow, and inhaled deeply on some home-grown herb. On a signal from the hag's brain, her cheekbones would elon-gate, then shorten and become fat. Unseemly bitch. She studied G.O. for a moment, then rasped through beetle-nut-stained teeth, "Why the hell you taking a crap in the sink?"

"I'm fond of cockroaches," *G.O. replied, studying the hag through va-cant eyes. A trick G.O. had learned a half century earlier in a high school history course. The old professor had told G.O. that if he had no thoughts visible under an electron microscope, then he should stare into space and say things like,* "Ontogeny recapitulates phylogeny, Hank Crampton." *The old professor assured him that those around him would nod their approval and cry,* "Hear, hear." *However, G.O. had found in his life experi-ence that most folks just looked at him and said,* "Get a fucking life, man!"

Glancing again at the hag, G.O. thought, No self-respecting under-taker would touch that body. *Of course, G.O. did not know that the tribe of self-respecting undertakers had died out right after the advent of per-petual care cemeteries. G.O. checked out his dangling manhood and was relieved not to be an ancient Indian cobra, with two dangling manhoods. Then Isis, protector of bi-penid mammals, smote him with thought.*

"Do you have a pencil?" *G.O. queried the hag.*

"Of course," *the hag replied.* "Who do you think is writing this insipid part of your life story?" *Without changing her expression, she reached into a purple-and-green argyle sock, retrieved a pencil, and tossed it to G.O.*

G.O. grunted his thanks and began to scribble a message on the wall.

"There is nothing so overrated as good sex

And nothing so underrated as a good healthy dump."—Ed Norton

G.O. leaned back and admired his work. Ah-h-h-h, *he thought,* the wisdom of the Orient.

Toe-Jam
Bearer of Confucian Blues
Renderer of yak-butt lard
Flatulator of the red, white, and fuchsia Manchurian
Sunset
Of thee I sing...

G.O. tossed the pencil back and asked the hag if she would mind terribly to throw him a roll of toilet paper.

"Of course not," she replied. "Just say the Word."

"Logos."

"Locust?" the hag quizzed. "I thought you were fond of cockroaches?"

"Oh, I am, more ancient than me, but only if they're in the John."

G.O. checked out the roll. Luxurious Papyrus. Black military stencil. Made in Beijing. He opened the roll and tore off a few sheets. Ah-h-h-h-h, another luxury. G.O. glanced at the paper and could not believe his optical nerves were decoding correctly. Evidently, there had been some type of malfunction in the machinery that processed the TP. At some point in the manufacturing process some industrious German technician had screwed up. The paper, on which the TP had been prepared, still revealed the original manuscripts. There was Bobby Dylan's original hand-scribbled version of "Rainy Day Women", a partial picture of the Mona Lisa, Hitler's orders to begin operation Barbarossa, the Gettysburg Address, an order blank for a Popsicle T-shirt, and an edict from the Spanish Inquisition to remove the left breasts of all Hebrew women to be sold as money pouches in order to raise money to get Queen Isabella's jewels out of hock, which she originally pawned to get her Italian lover out of town.

"Holy snail sperm," G.O. gasped as he came upon the forms he had filled out a lifetime ago. Maybe ontogeny does recapitulate phylogeny, G.O. mused. He remembered that he had filled out the forms in a country that now existed only in World Books printed before 1984. He leaped from the sink and started out the door.

"Wait!" the hag yelled. "Do you never think of anyone else's arse?"

G.O. reeled off fourteen sheets of Terry and the Pirates and explained that it was Woody Wilson's plan for world peace, which was rejected by a Senate of right-thinking armadillos that thrived on dead young things.

G.O. swung through the door and rushed to tell Mao-the-Yak that he had proof that another civilization had actually existed and was not some wild tale spread by the wandering yaks of Outer Mongolia. Mao listened to G.O.'s ravings. Mao farted.

◆ ◆ ◆

"Hill, George O.," the lieutenant called through expensively capped teeth without moving his lips.

George looked around the room, headquarters for MAG (Marine Aircraft Group) 16, and saw that it was empty except for the lieutenant and himself.

"I believe he stepped out, sir," a diaphanous Hill, George O. said. "Something about an errand to Outer Mongolia."

"Had to take a leak, huh?" the lieutenant said. Thus, showing the deep insight and understanding required of neophyte officers in the corps. The lieutenant had evidently attended a consortium of New England schools to develop the ability to speak through his teeth. Shiny gold wings stood out on the lieutenant's sunken chest, indicating that he had either matriculated from naval flight school or waited tables for the Hell's Angels.

"Well, when he comes in tell him to report to the admin hut of HMM two-six-five."

"Yes, sir," G.O. replied.

G.O. rose in a bumbling manner and began limping toward the door of the hooch. Hill had limped ever since a yak had kicked him in the right knee while hauling cannonballs to the front during the Crimean Police Action. Probably some ambitious lieutenant had decided to lead a cavalry charge into several batteries of Russian cannon. The end result had been a knot on the knee for G.O., forget the pseudoheroics of the fat red egos going up against insurmountable odds. The lieutenant waved G.O. to a halt with a crossword puzzle in hand. He had been succinctly working on the puzzle while G.O. had triplicated all manner of forms (to be later recycled as toilet paper).

Chapter Four

To Bee or Not to Bee

"Hold up a moment, Marine," the lieutenant squealed from an emaciated 125-pound frame. "Would you happen to know a six-letter word beginning with a C and ending with an E, meaning 'a group of chiefly tropical herbs of the caper family'?"

"Cleome," G.O. said as he glimpsed a familiar face through an open window. The body attached to that face was conveniently relieving itself in an odd-looking contraption sticking up from the ground.

"Right, C-L-E-O-M-E," the lieutenant spelled.

"Is that how it's spelled?"

"Yes, it is," the lieutenant replied cautiously as one of his eyebrows cocked near its zenith. "You know, Corporal, one should be proud of one's spelling. Being able to spell correctly enhances one's opportunities, breeds confidence, and broadens the intellectual capacity. Correct spelling is a sign of professionalism."

The lieutenant's eyes softened as he remembered his grandfather reciting those same prosaic lines to him before he entered the National Spelling Bee in Herodotus, Vermont. The lieutenant reached down and pulled a small rectangular plastic container from his bloused trousers. G.O. remembered he had not had a smoke in thirty-seven seconds and reached for the small rectangular plastic container he kept in *his* bloused trousers. The lieutenant, however, pulled a copy of *Roget's Semi-Pocket*

Thesaurus from his container. G.O. stuck a finger in his ear, scratched a molar, and quickly slid the embarrassing pack of smokes into one of the large thigh pockets on his jungle trousers. G.O., feeling a twinge of guilt, remembered the time he had been caught playing pocket pool in Miss Annabelle Loop's American history class. G.O. glanced up at the lieutenant to see if he had been caught about to transgress the invisible boundary between officers and enlisted men by not humbly seeking permission to "light the smoking lamp." The lieutenant saw only the National Spelling Bee.

◆ ◆ ◆

"Lobotomy," the reader called.

Lobotomy, *the young Chesterfield Rinehart thought,* now is the time. *The young Rinehart remembered the night before in his Washington, DC, hotel room. He had been tucked comfortably into bed and left alone to watch John Wayne take a platoon of Apaches up Mount Suribachi to win the Battle of Winnipeg Bay. Suddenly, the door to his room was kicked in, which disturbed him greatly. There before him stood the vision of his childhood dreams.*

There stood Magdalene Swartzrock, winner of the Greater South Carolina Regional Spelling Bee. Beautiful and full of grace. Eyes popped open. Sweat beaded on his forehead. The young Rinehart stared at the undernourished figure of Magdalene, shadows dancing through the flimsy Sears-Roebuck nightgown. The light from the hallway revealed a shapely Ichabod Crane-ish figure through the polyester nightgown with the picture of Raggedy Ann on the front. Chet, as his grandfather affectionately called him, lay perfectly still.

"You asleep?" Maggie asked.

John Daddy-Daddy Wayne was telling the boys how necessary and vital it was to kill every stinking slanty-eyed yellow bastard in existence until the world was safe for the Good Guys.

"Yes, I'm asleep," Chet replied, *thinking he might fool this uninvited apparition into vacating his space. After all, Grandfather would not approve.*

Old Glory waved as John Daddy-Daddy continued his recitation on the dangers of the Route 61 being occupied by the nips.

Maggie moved seductively close to Chet's ear and whispered, *"Are you sure you're asleep?"*

Sweet Jesus, *Chet thought,* what's happening to me. Penis, P-E-N-I-S, *Chet spelled. A habit Chet had picked up was to spell any new word he encountered which was unfamiliar to him.*

Chet replied, *"Un-n-n-n-n-n-h!"*

Maggie stumbled around, then perched herself on the edge of Chet's bed and began slowly stroking Chet's stomach. A massive electric bubble formed in Chet's groin and moved slowly to his throat. She started sobbing as promises cascaded from her tiny mouth. She would do anything, if Chet would only misspell a word in tomorrow's finals

Misspell, *Chet thought,* M-I-S-S-P-E-L-L...Misspell. *Chet was absolutely appalled.* There is not enough root beer in the world to get me to throw a contest. *He began explaining to Maggie that there was just no way; he was a warrior, and warriors compete. What would have happened if John Daddy-Daddy Wayne had capitulated to the slopes? What would his grandpapa think?*

Maggie stared disbelievingly at Chet for an infinite minute, then stood abruptly and left the room. The maroon harpoon frowned, then wilted. Chet sighed. Chet lay awake. Baffled as never before. Life is simple when all you have to do is spell it, *Chet thought.* Life...L-I-F-E...Life. *Should he or should he not throw the contest? Chet lay awake the rest of the night, his mind reeling from his desire to chase after the promises of Maggie.*

Suddenly, the door opened and his grandfather appeared. Looking grimmer than ever. His game face plucked from a French pimp. Menacing as ever. Finally, from the caustic mouth, his grandfather said, *"Chet, before we go down to the competition, I think we should have a little talk."*

Oh God! *Chet thought.* Here comes the old crap about doing your best, the Lord loves a winner, climb every mountain, piss in every creek, win one for the Gipper, you can hang by your balls for five minutes (if you've a mind to), and Jesus never quit routine.

"Chet, I'm not going to give you the old crap about doing your best, the Lord loves a winner, climb every mountain, piss in every creek, win one for the Gipper, you can hang by your balls for five minutes (if you've a mind to), and Jesus never quit routine."

Chet's eyeballs ricocheted around in their respective sockets. Eddie Cantor move. Grandpapa went out of focus as the room whirled around him.

"No, sir, young fella. This is the real world. A world full of assholes and worse assholes. I know and you know that it would be easy for you to take this contest today, eh? But, I think now is the time that you begin to think of someone other than yourself. If you want to be a really top-notch, first class award winning asshole, now is the time to show the world what kind of man your generation represents. I was looking into the background of the contestants last night to see what kind of competition you would be up against today. They are all total horse shit, Chet. I mean a bunch of lowlife numb-nut losers. However, there was one young lady among them whom I thought might be most deserving. She grew up on the dark side of Charleston. Poor as a Hittite church mouse..."

Hittite...H-I-T-T-I-T-E...Hittite, *Chet mused...*

"Pay attention, boy, and quit staring out into space! This child's father ran off when she was two, and her mother died just this past Christmas. She's living with her blind aunt right now. Winning this contest would mean something to her that you could just never imagine, Chet. Her name is Magdalene Swartzrock."

Chet's mind whirled as he said, "But, Grandfather, wouldn't that be cheating?'

"It ain't, son, if it's helping another." Then in his best Irish brogue, he said, *"That's the way Jaysus sawr it, laddie, yep, that's the way. What Jesus would want you to do is throw the contest and help this poor lost lamb find her way in this rough old life. Now, do think you might be able to look past your own selfish instincts and your unhealthy desire to win, and perhaps, see your way to throwing this contest?"*

"Well, I suppose so...for you...

"Not for me, boy, not for me! For the good of humanity! I could not be more proud of you, Chet, unless of course you decided to join the navy like your old granddad. Come on, now, let's grab some breakfast and get on over to the contest."

Now is the time, *Chet thought.*

"Lobotomy...L-O-B-O-T-O-M-E...Lobotomy."

"Oh-h-h-h-h-h!" The assholes who could spell sighed as they empathized for the young man.

"A-h-h-h-h-h!" The worse assholes who could not spell sighed as they thought about the young man losing.

Chet walked all over Washington that evening, thinking about what his grandfather had told him, and even though the thought of helping someone else put him at ease, he could not figure out why he should not feel more invigorated and alive. Should he confront his grandfather? Or not? Maybe the Old One could explain why his virtuous act did not make him feel better. Chet felt better having made the decision to confront his grandfather about his feelings. As he was riding the elevator up to his grandfather's room, the elevator stopped at the twelfth floor. An old scraggly-looking fart walked into the elevator, carrying a lantern. The Viejo had one of those Abe Lincoln beards. Probably trying to look older, *Chet thought.*

"Did you lose something?" Chet asked politely.

"No, I think I've found it," old olive breath replied.

The elevator door opened on the twentieth floor, and Man and Boy emerged. They looked down the hall and saw old Granddad drop a six pack of empty root beers and stumble through his bedroom door, carrying young Maggie Swartzrock. The old man with the lantern scratched his ass, shook his head, and climbed back in the elevator.

♦ ♦ ♦

G.O. grunted. Lieutenant Rinehart's eyes rolled counterclockwise around his head several times and came to rest on opposite sides of his nose.

Still doing the Eddie Cantor thing. Son of the proverbial slot machine. Jackpot. The eyes rested on G.O. and became heavy. G.O. shuffled some Shing-A-Ling feet and slid through a doorway where none existed.

Chapter Five

Locker Gallo

Outside, G.O. trudged through the sand, dragging a somewhat lumpy seabag. G.O. stopped alongside a strange-looking contraption protruding from the ground. It appeared to be a round galvanized aluminum tube. It was. As a matter of fact, it was a tinhorn used by farmers all over South Texas to prevent roads over drainage ditches from being wiped out by the bicentennial rainstorms. It had been planted in a vertical position so that one end stood a foot above the ground and that end was covered by screen wire. Evidently, this was the Seabee equivalent of a urinal. *Notably,* George thought, *since a Marine was relieving himself into the tube.*

"Say, pard, I don't need to drain the old lee-zard right now, but you won't mind if I pull out just to be on the sociable side, will you?"

The young Marine who had been urinating into the streets of Sidney, Australia, via the mystical tinhorn, looked quite startled and accidentally splashed G.O.'s trousers. Neither of the two were really paying much attention.

"Jee-e-e-ez," the young man blurted. "Ya scared the crap outa me. G.O., man, when did you get here?"

"Just this morning, sunshine."

"Have you been assigned yet?"

"Marine Medium Helicopter Squadron Two-Sixty-Five, pard."

"That's really bitchin', man, that's my squadron."

Locker Gallo had been in Hue-Phu Bai about a week longer than G.O. and possessed a noticeably richer tan. The tan only enhanced Gallo's boyish good looks. Locker was a little shy of being six feet tall but was extremely well proportioned. He grew up in California and spent most of his time either surfing or skiing, which engendered an excellent sense of balance in him but not one of accuracy. When Locker's hair wasn't "high and tight" (Marine slang for buzz cut), it was curly and blond. Locker and G.O. had become great friends when they had been stationed together at New River, North Carolina, across the river from the Camp Lejeune conglomerate. Both tried their hands at influencing the cabbage market but found the rigors of playing the commodities market to be an exasperating economic experience. Bet Adam Smith never dreamed about commodities.

Two Vietnamese women with Joan of Arc haircuts and black satin pj's strolled down the elevated roads arm in arm, which ran beside the outdoor facility. G.O. and Locker looked up about the same time. While Locker merely turned and shook his one-eyed Willie at the giggling blossoms of Southeast Asia, G.O. almost committed self-circumcision trying to holster his schlong. His zipper caught the skin, and G.O. momentarily froze as the pain shot throughout his entire being.

"Ah-h-h-h-h-h!" G.O. screamed.

"You OK, man?" Locker asked, as he saw G.O. trying to extricate his penis from his fly.

"You know, G.O., if a mortar round went off, you could get a Purple Heart for that thing."

"Shut the fuck up and give me a hand."

"You just gonna have to bleed to death, old stick. I ain't touching that ugly thing. You should have had that taken care of a long time ago. How you ever gonna be a good Jew with all that skin hanging off your schlong?"

"Oh, man, I'm dying."

"Come on, puss, your pecker's a good two feet from your heart; you ain't dying. But if you're gonna continue to act like you're dying, I'll show you how to get to sick bay," Locker said with an impish grin.

"I don't think that will be necessary; those assholes will probably just wanna take some pictures."

"Yeah, right, like they could find the damned thing."

The problem with Marines is that you cannot and never will be able to get in the last word. Better to just change the directions of the conversation.

"You'd be surprised where they might find the damned thing. Say, you wanna see some naked pictures of your mama?"

"I already have plenty, man. Wanna walk over to the squadron and get checked in? We're really hurting for qualified crew chiefs right now."

"Can't think of anything better," G.O. replied.

"How about some Budweiser and popcorn?" Locker winked.

"Oh, come on man, you're not gonna start with that fantasy about the guy that stuck his penis in the box of popcorn at the drive-in movies so when his girl went for a handful of popcorn, she would come up with a handful of head. Really, not that one."

"No, G.O., it's a real story. I know the guy that it happened to."

"You mean you know the guy that told the story."

"No, the guy said it was gospel. Swore on his mother's grave and everything. It's gotta be true."

"Locker, man, did you ever hear about the girl that took too much Spanish Fly and then screwed herself to death on the gearshift of a car?"

"Man, how do you know that story? The guy I heard that one from lived in Anaheim."

"It is just a *story*, Locker. It's not *true*! I heard the same story in Texas."

"Well, man. It has to be true if it made it all the way to Texas."

"Jesus, Mary and Joseph the poet, lad, you are hard headed. It's just a friggin' story. Do you think it happened in California and in Texas?"

"You mean it happened in Texas, too?"

"OK, let's start over. Did you hear the story about the New Cadillac that was advertised for ten dollars in the paper and everyone thought it was a misprint…"

"Yeah, except for this guy from San Jose who called the lady, and she sold it to him. She was getting a divorce from this son of a bitch and he was only gonna get half..."

"Exactly, only when I heard it, it was in the Houston paper."

"Now that really is coincidental, G.O. Three things just alike happening in California and Texas."

"Ah-h-h-h-h-h-h-h-h-h..."

"What? What is it, man?"

"Do you remember the car lot that sold a new 'Vette for a hundred dollars because someone died in it and the car lot couldn't get the smell out?"

"No, man, I haven't heard that one. But why would anyone want a car that smelled like a dead guy?"

"OK, how about this story? A guy takes his grandmother on vacation to Mexico..."

"I know this one dude, grandma dies, they won't embalm her in Mexico, so he had her boxed up and strapped to the top his station wagon..."

"Then before he crosses the border in Laredo..."

"It wasn't Laredo, man, it was TJ...you know, Tijuana..."

They looked at each other, then both said simultaneously, "Someone stole the box."

"What I'm trying to get across, Sir Gallo, is that these are just modern folktales. They didn't happen. They are just made up."

"Why would anybody just make up those stories? Surely, there has to be some small particle of truth in them."

"Christ on a crutch, I don't know why people make up stories; maybe there is some truth, and maybe they are just exaggerated to make better stories. Maybe some scriptwriter out in Hollywood made 'em all up so he could put 'em in the movies."

"Exaggerated? You mean like when you're talking about the size of your Willie?"

"Whachatalkinbout? Don't mess with a man that can stand flatfooted and shit in the back of a dump truck."

"Who-o-o-o-p, I know one story that you will have to admit is true."

"What's that Locker?"

"That night in Jacksonville, when we picked up that Westpac[2] widow. You remember?"

"Ge-e-e-ez, how could I forget?"

♦ ♦ ♦

G.O. lay wide awake on the floor with a blanket pulled up around his shoulders, trying to stifle the noises coming from the bed where Locker and the barfly they had picked up earlier in the evening lay and giggled. They didn't have enough money for two motel rooms, and the damned motel only had a room with a double. So G.O. ended up on the floor. Moral: Never pick up a woman when you're with a guy that looks like a blond Paul Newman. She kept telling Locker that she wouldn't do anything because his friend on the floor might hear. Locker kept telling her that G.O. was asleep. Finally, Locker said, "G.O., man, you asleep?"

"Yeah, I'm asleep."

"Are you sure you're asleep?"

"Yeah, man, I'm asleep!"

"See, honey, I told you he was asleep."

"Let me ask," the honey responded.

"Go ahead," Locker said.

"G.O., are you asleep?" the honey asked.

"Yes, honey, I'm asleep."

"Well, if you're asleep why are your eyes open?"

"Because my dick is so hard I don't have enough skin left to close them!"

Locker must have told this particular story a thousand times. Probably end up in a movie, too. *However*, G.O. thought, *there was a second part of the story Locker didn't know about.*

---

2 Military abbreviation for *Western Pacific*. A Westpac widow would be a woman who had lost her husband in the Vietnam War.

Later in the morning, G.O. thought he heard some sniffling and got up to look around. Locker was cutting Zs in the bed. But the honey in the bathroom was crying. G.O. went to the door and whispered, "Hey, is everything OK in there?"

The door cracked a little and the honey said, "No, not really, it's just, well, you know, Locker doesn't seem to like me."

"Oh no," G.O. said. "That's not it; he really does like you. It's just, you know, private stuff."

"What is it, G.O.?"

"Well, he has the clap and doesn't wanna tell you."

"A-h-h-h-h-h-h-h," *the honey screamed and bolted from the door and the motel and the town and the country and the universe.*

At last, *G.O. thought,* now I can get some sleep *and crawled into bed with Locker. Locker never awoke from his drunken lovemaking stupor. Later, in the morning when he woke up, G.O. was in the bed, and she was gone.*

"G.O., man, wake up! The honey's gone."

"Yeah, she left in the middle of the night, man. Said she had to get home to get her six children off to school. Oh, and she asked me to tell you that you have the smallest pecker she's ever seen."

"In your dreams."

Chapter Six

Gunny Peabody

Gunnery Sergeant G. Willis Peabody stood defiantly in the line shack, staring at the squadron coffee pot. The ferret eyes, set in the apple-shaped head, challenged the temperature light to signal the completion of the magic which transpired in the urn. The one-eyed urn. The urn that stared unblinkingly through a dull maroon lens challenged the Gunny to draw a cup before its time. Gunny G. reached up and flicked a particle of sugar-coated glaze from his perfectly groomed Boston Blackie mustache. The Gunny rubbed the flat side of his hand up and down a large protruding middle, which showed all too well the physical effects of lifting too many Filipino San Magoos. The CPA hands, golf glove–textured, moved lithely, in midstroke, from his overtaxed paunch to the sacred Top Shelf. Only officer's cups were allowed admittance to the Top Shelf. Woe be to the lowly enlisted puke who drank from a cup removed from the Top Shelf. Houdini hands moved unnoticed to the mystical Top Shelf. Blackstone fingertips danced flamboyantly along the Top Shelf under the Gunny's spell of invisibility. The Gunny's mind transmitted Svengali incantations to his fingertips allowing him to penetrate the barrier that separated officers from enlisted.

Black from white.
Penis from Clitoris Magnus (-a, -um).

All Hail, Vishnu
Protector of the thick of head
Breeder of superstition

Creator of the White-trash limbo
Curator of the Museum of Unnatural Stupidity
Banish thyself from the King's Garden of Cups

Insubordinate old bastard. The Gunny grasped the cup of Captain Charles D'Amato, just as G.O. and Locker stumbled into the line shack. The Marine answer to government housing. The Gunny's large asshole slammed shut on an unsuspecting hemorrhoid. Sepulchral grimace. Then momentary ecstasy. Fantods. That was not the way Captain Chucky D. usually stumbled in, but damn close. Only the Coupe deVille fart was missing. The Cadillac of all flatulence. Chucky D.'s odoriferous calling card.

G.O. and Locker walked between the two counters. Behind the counter to their left was located flight line personnel and administrative staff under the guidance of Gunny G. To their right was quality control, QC. Various and sundry folk stood lurking at the two intruders through predatory eyes. Most were staff NCO's and up. Lifers. Flies. Maggots full grown. Food for snakes and toads and other smooth-skinned mysterious-looking reptiles that hang around places where raw sewage is dumped. Lifers. Known throughout the corps for their insatiable desire to consume inordinate amounts of chickenshit while causing a mountain of controversy over minute, immaterial, totally irrelevant events. All equipped with the uncanny ability of passing the buck. Making sure the shit continues to roll downhill in the proper military fashion. Definitely flies. The double Yo's turned and faced Gunny G.

G.O. pierced the Gunny with eyes that drew upon twenty-one years of empirical visual memory. The Gunny's face remained enigmatic. Unreadable by the Sage of Southeast Asia. Sphinxian riddle. Locker merely let his jaw drop a little. Another James Dean mutant mysteriously arrives on the planet. The Gunny looked back at G.O. with eyes that had not yet been blinded by years of trivial demeaning tasks, farcical political games, and degradations known only to his species. Line shack flies. The prostate section of the Gunny's mind began releasing old dreams. Dreams of the young warrior. Sons of Mithras. Sons of Thor before him. Resplendent creatures primed for combat. The asshole part of the Gunny's mind, from whence these dreams escaped, seemed to revel in the sensuousness of the dreamlike fantasy. The Gunny saw something in Hill and Gallo that reminded him of his own dreams of being a warrior. The elasticity of the moment transcended space and time. The Gunny drank deeply of the indescribable essence flowing from the two young boots standing before him. In the depths of their eyes lurked the devil. Der Teufel. Doubt. The Gunny reeled. The value section of the Gunny's mind, the Sphincter, immediately started squeezing off the dreams it found so difficult to cope with. Especially after eons of training by the corps. The sphincter had become rigid in its line of reasoning. Green or gone. My corps, right or wrong. If you don't like it, then get the fuck out. *Children of Kronus*, the Gunny thought, *do you think I would actually swallow you up? Do you think I am one of the flies? A goddamn Lifer, for fuck's sake. No, children, I love this shit. Warriors don't get to choose their character; they're born to it. I, too, was once a warrior. Ooh-rah.*

The sphincter tightened. The old windmill slumped.

♦ ♦ ♦

"Don Quixote, do you actually think it wise to attack the beeg windmill?" queried a shaky Sancho.

"Is nothing, thou of pants endowed with lard cheeks. Hand me the lance, and we will slay this ugly monster...this blight on humanity."

"But, Señor, he will whack you on your head of emptiness."

"The lance, Sancho, the lance, and I will pierce this malignant growth!"

♦ ♦ ♦

"Gunny G.," Gallo erupted, "this is George Hill. We flew together back in New River. He just arrived, and I thought I would show him around. If that's all right with you, Gunny?"

"Your daddy a senator, boy?"

"No, sir," Locker replied.

"Did you ever attend Copyle Lincoln Institute for the Terminally Ignorant?"

"No, sir."

"Do you think you're in the fucken navy?"

The hint of a smile passed briefly across G.O.'s face as the disjointed dialogue continued between Locker and the Gunny. *Insipid old fart,* G.O. thought. *Ought to have been a census taker.*

"Did the goddamn Commies train your ass to be so goddamned stupid before they sent you here to fuck up the best squadron in Southeast Asia?"

"No, sir."

"Uh-huh! I thought you was a Commie-looking sumbitch first time you set foot in my line shack, and what's worse they didn't even take time to train your dumb ass. I bet you're the one that boosted the insides of the coffee pot. Did you have to get drunk first? Everyone knows what chickenshit drunks the Commies are."

"Uh-h-h-h…"

"Well, speak up, you goddamn coffee-pot-stealing, drunken Commie bastard!"

"No, sir."

"Would you let a coffee-pot-stealing, drunken Commie bastard show you around, Hill?"

"Well, I—uh, I'm really not sure, Gunny."

"Not sure! Not sure! Everyone hear that?" the Gunny bellowed. "The only people that I know that aren't sure are goddamn fags. You a goddamned fag, Hill?"

"No, sir," G.O. replied.

"Then get in contention, you wishy-washy bastard, and make a simple goddamn decision. Do you or do you not want a goddamn coffee-pot-stealing, drunken Commie bastard showing you around?"

"No, sir."

"See how easy that was, Hill? You've only been in country five minutes and already you've made several mind-bending decisions. You ain't a fag. You don't like drunken Commie bastards. And...you would not, under any circumstances, fuck with the squadron coffee pot."

"Yes, sir." G.O. chuckled.

The Gunny's face underwent a sudden mystical transformation. The subtle laughter that had danced upon the crow's feet at the corners of the Gunny's eyes faded as quickly as they had appeared. *Goddamn*, G.O. thought. *The man is not your typical Lifer. Definitely not a fly.* G.O. felt the edges of his soul burn and turn to ash under the Gunny's cold iron stare. Immutable Hephaestian stare. No doubt, the Gunny had never used these eyes until now.

"Those were the easiest decisions you will have to make while you're here, Hill. Well, since there is no one available with any goddamn intelligence in this goddamn line shack, I suppose I'll have to let you go with this coffee-pot-stealing prick." Heads turned in quality control. Frowns. Daggers. Papers shuffling loudly to muffle inaudible curses. "Well, what are you standing here for? The bus quit running a year ago. Get his ass checked in pronto, Gallo, and when you two birds get back, we'll schedule a check ride, and you, Corporal Hill, will explain why you had a naked man in your car in North Carolina."

"Yes, sir," piped the magpies.

♦ ♦ ♦

The old windmill looked defiantly down upon the twin lunatics that dared to challenge his ancient and revered structure. Boldly, they rode. Into the jaws of the Chthonian animal. Protector of medieval ways, prepare to die! Fucking idiots, the old windmill thought. Then with all the swiftness and dexterity of most windmills his age, the elder statesman of the

Pythian Way raised a wrinkled and dilapidated side and cut loose with one of those transcendental grist-mill farts. Don Quixote and Sancho were blown into the next county. As they lay in a twisted pile of recycled cuspidors, lances broken, dust settling, Don Quixote raised one eyebrow very slowly, and then a small slit appeared between the lids. Sancho groaned. Don Quixote rolled an eyeball in his direction.

"Sancho, my friend, I thinks we have been undone by the weather."

"Don Quixote, meaning no deezrespecks, is there no easier way to get to Kathmandu?"

"We could always fly, my burro-brained friend."

◆ ◆ ◆

Chapter Seven

God's House

Directly behind the hangar stood a large Neolithic concrete block structure. Gallo led G.O. toward the Gothic architecture. Corbusierian afterbirth. Norte Dame du Garbage. Golden mean gone mad. Totally arrogant in its immenseness it was the most massive structure at Hue-Phu Bai. Larger than the hangar that they had just left. The high ground, which it occupied, gave it a domineering appearance. Some ingenious bastard had welded together parts from the helicopter wreckage of some poor unfortunate bastards, to form a life-size crucifix that stood unwillingly in the shadow of the pseudobuttress. The first born-again helicopter.

"Is that a goddamn church?" G.O. quizzed aloud.

"Yep, our first stop," Locker replied.

"Locker, old pard, why don't you just sign my check-in sheet right here where it says 'Chaplain,' and we'll bypass this holy edifice."

Locker whipped around quickly and momentarily disappeared. Locker was the only person G.O. had ever met that could move so fast that he could become momentarily invisible.

"G.O., you are going to see the chaplain!" Locker said with some finality. "It might do your ass some good…besides, it's the only air-conditioned place on the base."

"Well, why didn't you explain it that way the first time? Let's go."

The two shuffled through the molten sand to the gates of Dixon Ticonderoga's Palace of Human Degradation. Each expecting the hand of God to squash their young not-so-angelic asses, in the same manner he might squash a young not-so-angelic cockroach. Pooh-pooh the thought. The Big G was actually spending a leisurely afternoon punching holes in Cheerios. The twin warriors entered the massive doors of the chapel undetected by the Lord's good eye. Cool air greeted the pair. They walked the length of the opulent structure. G.O. was quite amazed at the vainglorious accumulation of wealth in the middle of a war. *Hokey smokes*, G.O thought. *No wonder the bad guys tried to burn Tom Dooley's fucking mountain.*

Locker Gallo walked along as if on nails.

As they reached the Chaplain's office at the back, Gallo said, "I'll wait here, G.O., go on in." Gallo immediately laid his butt down on the most comfortable pew and set sail for the Strawberry Fields.

On the side of the pew was a sign which read: Donated by the VFW, Post 112 San Francisco. Hill mused, *Nothing too good for our boys.*

♦ ♦ ♦

The referee sent Muhammed Ali to his corner. Locker peered up from the canvas through swollen eyes. Coughed up his mouth protector. The ring Zebe stood over him.

"Eight!" the Zebe cried and pointed accusatorily at Gallo.

Must be a garage mechanic, *Locker thought.* Dirt under his nails.

"Nine!"

'And the goose drank wine...'

"Ten!"

Winkyn, Blinkyn, and Nod.

♦ ♦ ♦

G.O. heard someone chuckling inside the revered pastoral chambers. G.O. knocked lightly on the door. The door opened, and a young man with a sheet draped over him beckoned G.O. to come in. The chaplain, Commander Dixon Ticonderoga, peered over the rim of his reading glasses.

"Come in, Marine, come in. Is there something I can do for you?"

"Er—uh, yes, sir," G.O. mumbled, eyes riveted to the young angelic cherub dressed in the white robe. "I just arrived, and I need you to sign my check-in sheet."

"This isn't standard jungle dress, Marine," the chaplain said as he looked at G.O.'s papers. "We're getting ready for the First Annual Hue-Phu Bai Christmas Pageant."

"Yes, sir," Hill mumbled.

G.O. glanced at a cheap print of Matthias Grunewald's *Crucifixion* nailed to the wall behind the chaplain's desk. Gibbon arms stretched almost endlessly from the body of Christ. Lacerations poured forth the blood which kept the Pooh forever damned. The Da Vinci muscles were taut with pain and seemed to scream their defiance to the Father that would bring such torment to his only Son. King of the Lumpenproletariat.

◆ ◆ ◆

Why, Father? Why invoke and inflict such discipline on me? Was I such a bad Son? Or was it because I fought against the injustices and the improprieties of the Pharisees? Was it because I didn't want to be a goddamn carpenter? I tried. God knows I tried. Don't hand me all that crap about doing it to save the world from sin. We both know that's a lot of hype to keep all the little troublemaking Jews from fucking with their daddy's wishes. Hell, if you had just given me one more year, I'd have had enough followers to kick the Romans' asses all the Appian Way back to Rome. Then I could've gone back to building tables for the officer's club. Good tables. Tables for thirsty men. Tables for the Brotherhood of Avid Drinkers to use. Why do this to me? Your only begotten Son? Hell, if I screwed up the tables, why not just tell me! Shit, I'll even take a Jim Walters's building course. After all, I'm only a simple deity; you're the creative one.

♦ ♦ ♦

The dirt-encrusted features of Grunewald's Christ seemed to draw G.O. deeper into his reverie.

The Chaplain grinned. "Yes, it's an interesting piece, isn't it." The big Dixon of Ticonderoga had noticed G.O.'s magnetized stare at the *printus cheapus* (-a, -um). "You can almost feel the texture of the Lord's limbs, torn and bleeding." The chaplain's fingers played a ragtime tune on the desktop while he thought back to his ordination.

♦ ♦ ♦

A young Dixon Ticonderoga sat in the back of the Aragon Ballroom alone. Wifey had risen for to pee. Dixon slid his paw secretly under the napkin which he had so neatly laid across his lap. Family jewels intact. Cock behold! A game of pocket billiards was soon underway. Root, root, root for the home team.

"Yousa, yousa, yousa..." Rudy blared through the megaphone. The young chaplain broke into a sweat. Nerve endings pulsated with excitement as Rudy broke into the ultimate crowd pleaser, "My Time Is Your Time." Wiforus returned and noticed from across the room the feral look in the young recently ordained padre's eyeballs. Christ, she thought, he's at it again. *Rabbit incarnate. Thumper at the harehouse. The poor dumb bastard can't even keep a decent beat.*

♦ ♦ ♦

"You know my son, Jesus hung on that cross so that we mortals might go on doing the same stupid things we've always done."

G.O. was still mind traveling and he could not take his eyes from the print. G.O. was lost in the nether world. A slave bound to the Kyrie tree. Encompassed by monumental agony G.O. became the print. Muscles and sinew were slowly being ripped from his numbed limbs. Scylla and Charybdis pounded ferociously at his temples, as the thorns grew tighter from the swelling. When the pain neared its apex, it would momentarily subside, and then return with such clarity and crispness that all previous pain was forgotten. Yet nothing He experienced physically could compare with the pain of His father's rejection.

> *Here I hang from this high tree,*
> *Fetus of the Last Checkmate.*
> *"Hi, Mom!*
> *Say hello to Pete and all the guys."*
> *Do I become you now, Pop,*
> *Or have I always been?*
> *Will I return again like that Egyptian dude*
> *Osiris?*
> *Thanatos approaches,*
> *Steel-tipped spear in hand.*
> *Love me*
> *And*
> *Set me free.*

"Have you been listening, Hill? Have you heard anything I've said?" the chaplain asked. Once again breaking into G.O.'s thoughts.

"Yes, sir."

"Well, here's your papers. Do you have any questions?"

By this time, G.O.'s butt cheeks had grown numb and were sorely anxious to move. Mind ablaze. Seeking something a little more relaxing and a bit more mind manifesting than a religious dialogue in the middle of Vietnam with a chaplain some would consider to be a little light in his loafers.

"Well, I do have one question...You reckon Hey-Zeus ever fucked Mary Magdalene, Padre?"

◆ ◆ ◆

"What the fuck is the chaplain yelling about, G.O.?" Locker asked through sleep-filled eyes.

"The man's insane, Locker. Doesn't believe I'm the Son of God."

"Are you, really?"

"Well, only partially. On my momma's side, I think, yet my cycle is not yet complete."

"You're right; the man must be a complete imbecile not to believe that *You* are not the true Messiah."

"I can see God rejecting me, but the chaplain? Go figure."

"Rejection is a bitch, brother Cain."

"It sho' be, brother Abel."

Exit the Palace of Hue-Phu Bai. Hastily. Godspeed. Back door and all. Right into the amphitheater. The outdoor amphitheater had not yet been completed but the Seabees were working fast and furious to see it to its completion before Christmas. Immediately in front of the Dynamic Duo, a bulldozer strained to push earth to a different location. Other imperialist Yankee dogs carried helicopter blades to the embankment and shoved them into position. They would serve as seats for the five-hundred or so imperialist Yankee dog assholes, that would sit painfully through the First Annual Hue-Phu Bai Christmas Pageant. The assholes would suffer collectively for a solid three hours through a barrage of kaleidoscopic sights and sounds representing the birth of the world's first cockroach. Special event. Three wise entomologists from the East would come bearing zithers from Sears-Roebuck. Made in Korea. Little wooden instruments with the telltale hand-painted rose petals shining brightly on the keyboard. The wise ones would think the young cockroach was making way too much noise for one his age. Existentialists arise. Twenty billion insects can't be wrong. Long live the cockroach! Death to the fly! Eschatological nonsense. Heaven and Hell syndrome. After all, we know that insects don't actually have what it takes to get to that Big Anthill in the Sky. They are way too busy sitting around food preparation areas trying to deconstruct the Ontological Arguments proving God exists.

Chapter Eight

Mother Earth

"Wait up a sec, G.O.," Gallo howled above the roar of the dozer...

G.O. looked confused as Gallo mounted the side of the mammoth bulldozer and startled the driver.

"Say, man, you know what you're doing?"

"Huh, what? The driver yelled as he eased back on the throttle, a procedure that allowed G.O. to hear the ensuing dialogue.

"I repeat," Gallo said, raising his voice, "do you know what you're doing?"

The beleaguered driver removed the muddy sunglasses from his face, though the sky was overcast, and looked piercingly at Gallo.

"Well, suppose you tell me. It's obvious you don't think I do."

"You are fucken your mother!"

Pregnant pause here as the driver made the determination not to emasculate Gallo.

"Quite possibly. I suppose that is one perception not bound by any discursive ratiocinations."

The driver returned the sunglasses to his face, the throttle groaned, and Gallo jumped from his precarious perch.

Gallo shook his head in a negative fashion as he and G.O. proceeded their march toward the enlisted barracks.

"You know, G.O., you just can't teach an ignorant Seabee mother-fucker to argue."

"Locker, my man, there are some motherfuckers unaware of how they are affected by the disease of Oedipus."

"Oh, I forgot, you think all men are motherfuckers!"

"You've got me all wrong, brother Gallo; *all* men are possessed by the beast. But only those who refuse to recognize the creature actually become one."

Locker was scratching his head as the two started up the raised road. G.O. could hear the faint melodic tunes of the Beatles falling softly on his ears.

Perched high above them a lone figure hung precariously from a utility pole. Three-quarter time smoke danced its way up G.O.'s nostrils. Funk on a telephone pole. Laced with paregoric.

"Who is our small friend in suspended animation?"

"We call him Pogo, but his real name is Daniell," Locker replied as the two came to a halt directly beneath the telephone pole.

"Dan-yell!" Gallo hollered up the pole. No response. Turning to G.O., he said, "Pogo's a little Frenchman that got his ass drafted. Stays fucked-up on something most all the time. Says it eases his mind."

"Dan-yell! Locker hollered again. Again, no reply.

"Shit, man, give up your insidious screaming, it vexes the soul, and obviously Pogo is not a man of this planet."

"Right," Gallo replied and headed for the crapper located directly across from the barracks.

G.O. followed Locker into the little wooden structure. Dismal affair. A three-holer. Quite unlike the palatial six-holers built in officer's country.

Now we know how many holes it takes to fill the Albert Hall...

Evidently, the brass had been reading their Bibles. The idea of the "Holy Trinity" did serve an institutional purpose, however. Gallo seated himself on the far end, and G.O. seated himself next to the door. Leaving an empty hole between the two. Had there been no hole between them, they may have felt somewhat uncomfortable. Gethsemane. Scene of idyllic constipation. People no longer had to say they were stepping out to pray. They said, "I'm gonna take a dump." The space between the two brought spiritual peace to their machismos but kept them comfortable in the same womb. Blessed Virgin. Cult of Mary. Hand me your tit. Please, not the leaky one. Three-holers were meant only for strangers, there should be no shame or embarrassment amongst human beings.

◆ ◆ ◆

The terminal at Dallas Love Field was sparsely populated. A normal Sunday evening. In the men's room, G.O. strode toward one of the urinals. Fifty, count 'em, folks, fifty gallant white urinals stood against the wall waiting to relieve the urine-filled travelers who refused relief thirty-thousand feet above Butte, Montana, for fear of dousing the red-headed stranger. G.O. stepped up to the most profound looking monolith of the bunch. The door opened and in walked a rather distinguished looking gentleman. Got his start in life imitating a Lox in a Cousteau special about the pitfalls of fucking a Sea Bass. The stranger to blue water looked at the remaining forty-nine urinals and walked over to the one beside G.O. and whipped out. Goddamn, G.O. thought, he could have found another pisser. *G.O. glanced subtly at the poacher's business.* "What the fuck is that?" *G.O. queried as he noticed the sickening sore on the stranger's Gossamer Albatross. It resembled the inside of a grape skin. An old Hindu trick. Popping a diseased Sea Bass between takes.*

G.O. barfed.

The stranger went to work for the CIA claiming the disease had actually started in his mind.

◆ ◆ ◆

G.O. grinned and glanced at Gallo in the middle of a genuine de Gaulle strain. Clamorous gorilla fart. Hummingbird whiz. Sonorous thump as Locker's turd hit the empty steel drum. An etude to stool. G.O. heard a scraping noise and glanced between his legs. Asshole drawn up real tight. A secret compartment at the rear of the crapper had been opened and cast a tumultuous ray of sunshine across the drum. *Wonder of wonders,* G.O. thought. *The only place the sun shines in this dismal country is the crapper.* A small head then appeared through the opening and turned upward. Yakking a yak G.O. did not understand. *It's hard to find good help nowadays,* G.O. thought as he peered down into the tiny eyes. Two slender arms followed the head through the opening and removed the metal drum to return to Mother Earth that which She lends us on a temporary basis. *Must be trying to start a Reggae Band,* G.O. thought.

G.O. looked at Locker and queried, "Do you think Jesus ever took a shit?"

Chapter Nine

The Game

A gloomy funk permeated the wooden barracks as G.O. and Gallo entered. Greens, grays, and browns all blended in a smoky haze. Grotesque shadows danced beneath the cheap lights that dangled from frayed cords. A strong odor of mildew from clothing and flight suits that hung haphazardly from the bunks. Giant spiders spread themselves helter-skelter across sleeping bodies. Innocent countenance was trapped by a deathly pallor. Time froze momentarily for G.O. Immeasurable loneliness closeted his mind. His mind set sail for the fabled land of the Cimmerians, somewhere beyond the stream of Okeanos, where no mortal soul ever sees the sun, no taste, no color, no tears, no testicles, oh no! Only the shadowy imitation of life on this earth. Fantods. *Got to give up all this trans-Okeanic backpacking*, G.O. thought.

G.O. tried hard to swallow. Halfway down disaster struck. He was greeted by a loud wall-fart. Hiroshima magnitude. No mean feat. The swallow never had a chance. No one would ever know the fate of the swallow. Tales would be told and songs would be sung lamenting the fate of the swallow. Long live the swallow.

G.O. never blinked.

G.O. reached into his sporran for a sunflower seed.

At the end of the barracks G.O. could hear a cacophony of voices.

Several large metal wall lockers had been arranged to create a semi-private gaming room. A poncho liner splashed with some industrious advertising executive's idea of the colors the jungle should be, hung between the lockers, forming an entryway. Gallo pushed the poncho liner to one side and walked triumphantly into the room.

"Greetings, O Bearer of the Torch..."

"How goes it fuck-face..."

"Where's the money you owe me, Locker?"

"Shit, motherfucker, close the Goddamn door..."

"You grow another asshole, Gallo man?"

"Naw, dude, this is G.O....I flew with him back in the USSR."

"No shit?"

"No shit."

"You in or out Sugar Bear?"

"I'm in...if you'll tell me why you always deal with one hand."

"So's I can rake in the money with my free hand, brother Bear."

"Honky muthafucker."

"Don't start with that ratio shit."

"J-a-a-a-a-ck..."

"Pour the injun another drink, Bear man."

The Sugar Bear reached down to the floor and found a bottle of Jack Daniels and handed the bottle across the makeshift poker table. Six would-be Ho Chi Minh hostages sat and played a game of chance. G.O. and Gallo pulled up a footlocker and wedged themselves in between the Sugar Bear and the Bugman. The prattle remained effusive and garrulous as G.O. became familiar with each of the players. To G.O.'s right was the Sugar Bear. An impish little black man. From what G.O. could discern from his conversation, the Bear had recently escaped from a Lilliputian bordello where he was being held captive by a group of spank-enthusiasts. G.O. figured this to be Detroit. Sugar Bear kept one hand on his crotch. To Sugar Bear's right sat Andrew Jackson Redfeather. A genuine Flathead Indian from Idaho. He was called either Jack or Chief or some slur regarding his ancestry. The only word Jack had said since G.O. had sat down was, "J-a-a-a-a-ck." When the Sugar Bear heard "J-a-a-a-a-ck," he would fill up Chief's cup, even though it was never more than half-empty. To Jack's right sat Scrotum. Definitely from New Jersey, although he kept telling everyone he was from Philly. Had this weird eye, à la Jack Elam. Kept humming "Hey Jude." Different keys. Different tempos. *Obnoxious twit*, G.O. thought. To the Scrotum's right sat Duck Butter. Duck for short. Or Duck-man. Duck wore little rose-colored John Lennon glasses. A .357 Magnum on his hip. Smooth-jawed and small-boned. Well mannered. *Why the fuck is he carrying that big-ass gun?* G.O. thought.

To his right sat Barf. The Barfman. Red-headed. Freckles grape-shotted over a pale countenance. Recently returned from filming a number of toothpaste commercials. Eyes glazed. Kept spilling his drink and dropping his cards. Real Hollywood type. *Brush it, brush it, brush it,* G.O. thought. To the right of Barf sat the Bugman. Escapee from the Afghanistan Special Forces. Front two teeth missing. Sleeves cut out of his jungle utility blouse. On his upper left arm was the proverbial tattoo. It was a tat of Jesus on a Triumph motorcycle with this huge cross strapped to his back. The tattoo read, "Prince of Peace—MC" Substantial deposits of grease under his fingernails. Not Jesus, the Bugman. *Possibly a Tennessee ridge-runner,* G.O. thought.

"J-a-a-a-ck!"

"Fuck, Chief, why don' you jus' pass out so the rest of us can get serious 'bout this game?"

"Shit, something is swimming in my drink..."

"Don't scare the little motherfucker maybe it'll swim to the top..."

"Christ on a fucken crutch, Chief, you are a slave to the fucken grape..."

"I'm not drinkin' this shit till the motherfucker swims to the top..."

"Keep your fucken cards up, Barf."

"More guapo for the Flathead..."

"Shit, Chief, you winnum plenty wampum, buyum white squaw?"

"Fuck Barf, you spillin' that shit all over me!"

"Quit makin' fun of da injun..."

"Who's making fun, the motherfucker's got most of my money..."

"Keep your fucken eyes on your own cards Duck, or I'll stick that god-damn pistola up your skinny little ass...'"

"Promises, promises ..."

"Ante up, Bear ... we're waiting for your slow fucken self ..."

"Fucken honky muthafucker, how many times I gotta ante?"

"Bettum, Ace..."

"Aces ass, Chief...the Bugman's showing a pair..."

"Keep your fucken cards up Barfman, or you'll be looking at 'em outa one eye..."

"Bettum, Paregoric..."

"Paregoric bets one Victor Charlie Ear, recently brought back from the front by Chesty-by-God-Pullyum..."

"It's Puller, you dumb Tennessee fuck..."

"What the fuck are you? A black Funk and Wagnall's?"

"You got the black funk right..."

"Fuck, who's calling this shit...I ain't putting up hard cash against a fucken ear..."

"Yeah, how we know you didn't take that off of some white boy back in Tennessee?"

"J-a-a-a-ck!"

"Shit, call..."

"Keep your cards up Barf..."

"You callin'..."

"Call..."

"Call, muthafucker..."

"Is that all you got...a goddamn pair? Beats me."

"Fuck, I'm out..."

"Yeah, beats me..."

"Kiss a fat baby's ass..."

The poncho liner suddenly whipped open and three of the most un-likely characters entered, singing, "We Three Kings of Orient Are." One carried a large metal pot, commonly referred to in corps vernacular as a sea-pot. Generally used for cooking large amounts of vegetables or soup or a myriad other indistinguishable, foul-smelling, sewer-tasting dishes universally accepted as "chow" in the corps. His two compadres were carrying boxes of grapes.

"Yo, Blaze Man..."

"What the fuck's up with the pot and the grapes?"

"We're going into the wine-making business, dudes and dudettes... look out, Barf...you're spilling your drink..."

"Great, when do we start?"

"You white dudes don' know nuthin' 'bout making wine..."

"O-o-o-o-o-h, Sugar Bear, now there's a real racial comment..."

"Nuthin' racial 'bout it, muthafucker...I was jus' commentatin' on the fact that if we added all the IQs in the room and multiplied by two, you'd still have zero."

"Who's the new guy?"

"Oh, that's G.O....he's one of Locker's friends."

"He CID?"

"Locker's friend? I don't think so."

"He flew with me back at New River," Locker explained. "He's safe."

"Nobody's safe in this fucken country," and with that he set the sea-pot in the middle of the makeshift card table and extended his hand. "Blaze Dawson," he said. "The one on the floor that looks like he's trying to shit himself is Wacky Wayne and this innocent looking fuck is the Gerber Baby."

"G.O. Hill," G.O. replied and extended his hand. The first sign of sanity G.O. had experienced in this God-forsaken place. The Gerber Baby was an easy one...he looked just like the picture on the baby food jar. Blaze was a little more difficult...he looked like a miniature Sumo wrestler and really didn't move all that fast. Opposites, maybe? G.O. couldn't fathom Wacky Wayne, either; he seemed to be quite mellow. It would be later in Subic Bay that G.O. would come to understand the full meaning of that namesake.

"Why's the Gerber Baby taking off his shoes?"

"To stomp the grapes."

Bugman started unlacing his boots, and when he pulled off his first boot, it was evident to everyone in the room that not only did they not want his feet in the pot, they didn't want to be in the same room with him.

"Goddamn, Bug…didn't yo' mama teach you to wash yo' feet?"

"Hell, you only been in country two weeks, Bugman, surely you washed those nasty fuckers since then?"

"Hadn't had the time."

"Shit, Bugman, you could sell that shit growing on your feet to Cal-Poly or MIT for some big bucks."

"Fuck you one and all."

"I ain't drinkin' the wine if that red-necked Tennessee muthafucker is allowed to put his feet in the pot."

"Shit, I guess if you and the Gerbs is gonna stick yo' feets in…then so will I."

Vat 69 began to take shape. Eleven pairs of feet began squashing the grapes in the sea-pot. Because of its size, several members of the group had to wait until one or more of the stompers had tired, and then take a turn in the pot. The Italian wine-stomping song sounded a lot like Steppenwolf's "Born to Be Wild." About this time a pair of marijuana-laced eyes peered through the side of the poncho liner.

"Daniell, just the one we need…"

"Yeah, Pogo ought to know somethin' about making wine…"

Daniell put down the portable Japanese tape player he carried and looked at the appalling ensemble and their work in progress.

"God, thees iz some foul-smeeling sheet…"

♦ ♦ ♦

The Mayflower *rested peacefully at anchor, while the first boatload of Pilgrims unloaded and scouted around the beach. From the bush appeared eleven hearty Indians and one smaller one.*

John Alden and Captain Jones gathered the Pilgrims in a defensive position around the small boat in which they had rowed to shore.

"Good God, look at the bloody harpoon on that savage, John! 'Ave ye ever seen such a tool, man?"

"No, Captain, cannot say I 'ave, not since I left Ingersoll-Rand, anyway. What's in that bloody pot they be carrying? The odor offends my sensitivities."

"Who gives a damn about your bloody nose? We need to board ship and set sail for a more desolate area. There'll be no livin' with the women folk after they lay eyes on them bleedin' cocks!"

♦ ♦ ♦

Daniell Nadal. Pogo. Drafted six months after he entered the United States. While standing in line for a physical, one of those silver-throated Marine recruiters convinced him that a tour in the corps would bring him health, wealth, happiness, a coupon booklet for a week in TJ, and no combat duty. Daniell heard no combat. He joined the Marine Air Wing for four long years. Now, after only a year and a half in the corps and two weeks in the Republic of Vietnam, his mind frantically searched for a glimpse of the real. Mind-expanding drugs and mind-numbing alcohol only served to distort his sense of reality. *Would he ever hear a word of French again? Would he ever feel the warmth of the sun on his shoulders as he stood in his grandfather's vineyard? Or smell the fresh bread rising in his grandmother's wood-fired oven? Who are these strangers in my life?* Why, God, am I here? Daniell felt his breath quicken as he entered the world of the absurd. Paranoia closed in on the Pogs. Perceptions amplified and mangled. The lights, the loud noise, the smell, the stink. Daniell's mind reeled from the myriad stimuli bombarding his brain. The herb that Daniell had been toking only moments before, only served to exacerbate the situation. Pogo threw both hands up, palms out, fingers spread, as if to say *"Stop!"* Like the little metal policeman that used to stand in crosswalks at most elementary schools throughout the United States. The one that some kid named Butch always kicked in the ass on the way home. The metal cop would always go down, but he would always pop-up again. Good Samaritan Syndrome.

"Fuck's wrong with him?"

"He's a puss..."

"He's no puss, Bugman, he's French..."

"He's fucken stoned..."

"J-a-a-a-a-ck!"

"Goddamn, we're outa whiskey!"

"Beer?"

"Gone, too."

"Club closed?"

All eleven stared at each other for a moment. The Chief screamed and ran head first into the metal wall locker. The others left through the poncho liner while the Bugman loaded the Chief into his rack. G.O. looked back as he exited the cubicle and saw that the Bugman was tying the Chief's hands to his bunk. *Guess that's to keep him from masturbating,* G.O. thought. *Cruel. Only a Baptist could be that cruel.*

Chapter Ten

Gunz and Drumz...

G.O. and the motley crew stumbled laughing and cursing into the make-shift club and ordered up a round of rusted Ballantines. *Especiale.* Ten centavos apiece. A little overpriced for a Ballantines, but what the hell; it's war. Thirty-six beers later, G.O. and some of the mob had gathered around a wooden picnic table enraptured by the poignant war stories of the Antoninus of Southeast Asia, Daniel D. Dupree. Gunz, as he was known throughout the I Corps. G.O. preferred D Cubed, but Gunz would cast suspicious glances at him when he said, "D Cubed." So G.O. stopped. Danny D. was carrying a product of the Smith-Wesson family. Danny D. had also been in country for almost a year, and he was a short-timer incarnate.

> *Mr. Entertainment*
> *Son of Narragansett*
> *Bearer of the Rhode Island Cross*
> *Divine Dancer*
> *Rise O' Dionysus*
> *Bring forth the Spring*
> *Tell the Tale of the Lotus*
> *And the powers granted to you by mighty Khepera*
> *Mystic Son of Antoninus.*

Open a Chili-One
And sing the song of the
Mysterious Albino WaterBoo

"Another shit sandwich like the one today, and I'll quit this fucken flying," Gunz lied.

"What happened, man?" the unsuspecting straight-man, Duck, asked.

"Sheeee-it, you wouldn't fucken believe it! We're flying along, see. A fucken milk-run. We were delivering some gedunk out to Vandy and we were on our way home. You know, I'm sitting in the jump seat looking out the door and smoking a butt wid one hand and playing a little pocket pool wid the other. You know it's a real conundrum…which hand do you hold your pecker with while you're smoking? So, I'm sitting on the jump seat and I'm checking out some grunts walking down the fucken road. Fucken mine sweep I'm thinking. Really stupid fucks, grunts. I mean they're gonna be out doin' the same stupid fucken shit in the morning, right? Well, anyway, I hear this goddamn fifty open up and the goddamn grunts are scattering everywhere."

"Hey, man, how you know it's a fifty?" Sugar Bear interrupted.

All eyes fixed on the Master.

"*Whump*, man. A fifty goes *whump, whump, whump*. A thirty cal goes *pop-a-pop-a-pop-a*, you know?"

"Oh yeah, man, I knew dat. The pigs in Detroit carry them fucken thirty cal muthafuckers."

"Well, anyway, this fucken truck blows, I mean K-goddamn-boom. Fucken disappears. Nothing but smoke. Then the bad guys see us pokin' the fuck along, enjoying the show, you know, and decide to open up on our asses. Sheee-it, we were lucky to get the hell outa there. So, we get back and what happens? The goddamn metal-fucken-smiths throw this wild-ass fit. They were whining about having to stay up all night to fix all the goddamn holes. I mean shit, like it was their asses getting shot off. I mean it's enough to make a basket case outa your ass."

G.O. and Gallo sat transfixed. Listening. Magnetized. Spilling one beer after another while they drank up one phantasmagorical story after another. Danny D. was on a roll. War at its most glorious. Fought around the foam of rusty Ballantines. G.O. glanced around at the other tables. Same stories. Told by different salts to different boots. Would G.O. live to tell the FNGs how to survive in the land of Boom-boom? G.O felt a wave of Nausea sweep over him. That sudden feeling of an explosion about to erupt. G.O. stood and stumbled toward the door, muttering, "Gotta drain the lizard, Kemosabe..." G.O. did his best to hold down the impending explosion, for the sake of embarrassing himself. Danny D.'s gaze followed him for a moment and then he turned to the Duck.

"What's wrong with him, Duck-man?"

"I-ahhh-urrgh..." And the Duck fell off the bench onto the cement floor. Gerber Baby and Wacky Wayne rushed to pick him up. Danny D. began banging an empty can on the table demanding that one of the rookies get another round before the club closed up its womb for the evening.

Gallo caught up with G.O. heaving his guts up outside beside the elevated roadway. "Hey, Pard, you want me to get a bucket? You can save some of that crap for breakfast."

"Oh, dear Jesus, Mary, and motherfucken Joseph...ahhh...urrrgh..."

"Easy, man, they'll think the bad guys are coming over the wire."

"I didn't want those guys to think I was a FNG...urrrrghhhhh...fuck..."

"No one really gives a shit, Pard. None of those fuckwads have been in-country for longer than two weeks. Hell, that makes all of us Boots. Except for Danny D, of course. I think he was born here."

"For real?"

"Yeah, for real, you doofus (-a, -um) come on man, you need a shower."

G.O. and Locker stumbled into the showers. It was one of those screened in affairs with six spigots arranged around the interior of the showers. Only one temperature. Whatever came out of the tap. Locker managed to shove G.O. under one of the shower-heads and turned on the flow of water. G.O immediately starts to rally. He looks up and reads one of the signs in the shower. "Nonpotable, what the fuck is nonpotable?"

"It means don't drink the shit," Gallo replied.

At about this same moment in time, Wacky Wayne and the Gerber Baby came in carrying the Duck singing, "If the ocean were whiskey and I was a duck..." The Duck remained relatively peaceful until the water was turned on him. Never turn nonpotable water on a peaceful, unsuspecting drunk. Luckily, Wacky and the Gerbs had the foresight to take away the Duck's sidearm. The Duck was having none of it. The Duck strips off, squats, and defecates on the floor.

"Good God, would you look at the size of that fucken man biscuit?"

"Wacky, you think we ought to find the Blaze, he won't believe a Lincoln Log that size could come out of a man."

"Oh shit, G.O. let's di-di..." Locker says as he tries pulling a perplexed Hill from the shower.

"Wha...?"

"You got that right..." Duck screams, "Here's some shit for you!" And starts hurling shit at everyone in the showers.

A couple of Butterfinger bb's splatter next to G.O. on the wall, just as Pogo makes his appearance in the shower. "Merde!" he says.

"Yeah, eat shit and die, you frog-looking, crapaud motherfucker," screamed Duck.

"*Mangez la merde et mourez*, Duke," Pogo shouted as he scooped up part of the Duck's chocolate loaf from the shower floor and hurled it back in the Duck's general direction.

"Why does he call the Duck *duke*?" queried the Gerbs as he took aim at Pogo.

"It's short for dookie," Wacky explained as a short round caught him on the arm.

"Oh, that eez some foul sheet," Pogo said wiping some brown grumpy from his splattered head.

"Smells bad, too." Wacky grimaced as he sniffed his hand and looked up to find the Duck.

◆　◆　◆

On a farm in Mississippi, Mrs. Hunter slowly and nervously opened the official-looking envelope from the Defense Department. "We regret to inform you," it read, "that your son Wackorus (–a, –um) Wayne Hunter was mortally wounded in a shit fight. The shit fight occurred in shower number four at the Hue-Phu Bai Marine Compound. Because of Wayne's valiant defense of his fellow Marines, he will receive the corps' lowest award, the Shit from Shinola Medal."

◆ ◆ ◆

G.O. and Locker fled the showers.

"You in for a swim?" Locker quizzed.

"In for a penny…"

Locker led G.O. to a humongous rubber tank suspended in the air by a wooden derrick–looking structure.

"This is the storage for the nonpotable water for the showers. It's open at the top; all we have to do is climb up and dive in."

G.O. and Locker climbed the structure and then jumped into the large rubber water storage bin. The water tank was only about 6 feet deep, so G.O. and Locker were able to hold onto the sides when they were not swimming.

"Hey man, you gotta light?" G.O. asked.

Locker swam over to his jungle trousers hanging over the side of the water tank and fished around in about ten different pockets until he found his trusty Zippo, then swam over to where G.O. was clinging to the side of the tank.

When G.O. fired up his Marlboro, he noticed something swimming on the other side of the water tank. "Whatthefuckwaszat?" G.O. blurted.

"What are you talking about, man?"

"Over there," G.O. said, while pointing across the tank.

"Hell," Locker said. "Those are just some Republic of Vietnam Class A Rattus Rattus (-a, -um) rodents. Asian black rats. Pretty much harmless, they're just up here for some skinny dipping like us. Don't be such a puss, man."

G.O. and Locker simultaneously turned toward the ladder as they heard the Sugar Bear's calling card, "Can't get enough of that Sugar Crisp, Sugar Crisp..."

"Please tell me I didn't hear two white motherfuckers talking 'bout black rats," Sugar Bear called out as he climbed up to the edge of the tank.

"Bear, man, come on in, the water's nice and one more black rat won't hurt."

"I ain't breaking up no love affair, am I? I know how you white dudes can be," Bear said as he glided over the edge of the rubberized water tank. "Damn, who you white boys gonna satisfy with them itty bitty peckers?"

"*Me!*" G.O. and Locker chimed. Then all three laughed as they splashed around the pool.

A one-eyed cockroach sat on the edge of the makeshift pool and pondered life, death, and the undagondalated[3] advantages of the doggy paddle.

---

3 Invented word used by Marines during the Vietnam War. Meaning ominous or filled with sorrow in a unique and marvelous kind of way. Also, used as an adjective to describe to describe any type of unknown and/or indescribable feeling a Marine might have. E.g., 'We wandered around the undagondalted boondocks for about a week.' Also, "He was overcome with the undagondalated fantods when he heard the twig snap."

Chapter Eleven

The Artists of Dong Ho

Xin Loi was completely at ease. It had been a hard year for Xin and his comrades in his regiment's scout platoon. The scout platoon had lost twelve of its fifteen members in the central highlands over a year ago where Xin had been wounded when an American helicopter caught them unprotected crossing the Song Thu Bon (Thu Bon River).

If they had crossed the day before like their Viet Cong guide, Hung, had suggested, then they might not have been caught out in the open. The Huey gunships had rained fire and death on Xin's platoon.

The only three survivors had been Xin; the scout, Hung; and their platoon leader, Little Minh. Little…there was not anything little about Phouc Minh. He was the largest Vietnamese that Xin and Hung had ever laid eyes upon. He resembled the laughing Buddha in his girth and the inscrutable Confucius in his demeanor. He even tried to mimic the wisdom of Confucius with his provincial aphorisms like, "Don't go down trail that smell like Winston cigarettes; you come out with smoking ass," or "Helicopters in sight, comrades take flight" or his most famous, "rainy season make everything wet." Little Minh. Fucken Loser. Had to have been some kind of political appointment.

Phouc Minh thought it would be good for the scout platoon to take a day off after humping sixty days from their staging area southwest of Hanoi. Mostly at night to remain undetected by American aircraft. While the rest of the platoon splashed and played along the banks of the river, Xin and Hung found a fairly well-protected spot up river and cut some fishing poles from a stand of bamboo. When the helicopters unleashed their rockets, Xin and Hung momentarily froze. The loud explosions and the pink mists in the geysers of water seemed to be in slow motion. Cam Troung, a fifteen-year-old from Xin's village in the North, stood naked with both arms raised at the helicopters in a posture of supplication one moment…and the next…he was a pink mist…and the next…Troung's bleeding body parts hung from the tree branches stretched out over the river.

Xin and Hung grabbed their weapons and ran to the riverbank as the Hueys made a gun run along the river. The hailstorm of 7.62 mm bullets lashed the water and mud around them as they continued to run toward their comrades. Then the unexpected happened. One of the rounds found Xin and spun him around as another round found him and spun him back. Xin closed his eyes and thought, *So this is what death is like.* Then Xin felt hands under his arms. It was the Viet Cong scout, Hung, pulling him from the river into the jungle.

> I think I may be dead
> there is no pain
> just a sense of loss
>
> Someone is calling me
> but to return?
> or to go forward?
>
> Things are devolving toward
> a great sense of nothingness
> but I want so much more

When Xin awoke he was in a people's hospital in a Binh Tram, one of the way stations on the Ho Chi Minh Trail. In the bed next to him was Hung. "Well, Hung, how you hanging?"

"You decide to wake up, Sleeping Dragon?"

"Yeah, where the hell are we?"

"We're in a Laotian Binh Tram waiting to be transported back north when they can find porters to carry us. Usually they try to find someone from your village. But since I'm from outside Hue City, I didn't think that would work, and I couldn't remember where you told me your village was."

"Who else made it out?"

"Just that idiot, Phouc Minh."

Later, after Xin and Hung were transported back north to Xin's ville, Dong Ho, they were allowed to rest and recuperate. These two heroes of the People's Army of Vietnam. Xin's village was well known for the beautiful art produced by many of the families in Dong Ho.

The art consists of a family making its own paper and its own colors for the woodcuts used in printing the art. The woodcuts are engraved by hand, usually one for the outline and then separate woodcuts used for the design the artist is making. Many of the woodcuts were in the same family for generations. The paint was applied to the woodcut and then pressed onto the paper. The process is repeated until the artist is satisfied with the colors and the painting. Since the Ly Dynasty, the villagers of Dong Ho have prepared paintings for the celebration of Tet, the Vietnamese New Year, usually celebrated between January and February.

During the day, Xin would slip off to the nearest fishing hole and spend the day reliving the disaster in the "Jungle of the Screaming Souls." Exactly what he was fishing for, he couldn't explain. Although the village had been depleted of most of its young men, there were plenty of the opposite sex who cast meaningful looks Xin's way. Looks he largely ignored, even though he tried to remember a time of young love and happiness, before the war and suffering had warped his soul.

Hung, on the other hand, had no problems with the young ladies of Dong Ho. Hung had also fallen in love with the art of Dong Ho. Hung's village was a farming community, and he had never before experienced the creativity and intricacies of an art village. Hung spent most of his day in Mr. Cua's studio/gallery. Partly to observe and learn, partly because Mr. Cua had three beautiful daughters in their teens. Mr. Cua welcomed Hung as a son. Mr. Cua had lost seven sons to this War of Reunification and had only his daughters left. Mr. Cua had lost brothers against the French and had himself fought at Dien Bien Phu, and he remembered the brutality of the Japanese who occupied his country when he was a small boy.

Xin Loi felt utterly at ease. Surprising him, his comrade from the south, Hung, sat down beside him on the bank of the stream.

"What brings you outside on a beautiful day like this? Mr. Cua's daughters go to Hanoi for the day?"

Hung gave Xin a questioning look. "What, are you writing pamphlets for the party now?"

"No, just curious how an ill-mannered peasant from the south could win over an entire northern village in a little over two months. Please tell me you are not screwing Mr. Cua's daughters. You have been a good friend, but you would miss your itty bitty plaything if Mr. Cua found out."

"Itty bitty! Bah!" Hung looked between his legs and said, "Do not take offense, Fat Rhino. The Fat Rhino and I feel it is our duty to provide the seeds for a new generation of warriors. The party demands it of us. To go forth and spread our seed and grow a new crop of warriors. Even Mr. Cua wouldn't deny the wishes of Chairman Ho."

Xin shook his head slowly. "You know, the Americans would love your name, Hung Dong, because it is so fitting in their barbaric language."

"What do you mean? In Vietnamese we both know my name means Breaking Dawn. What does it mean in American?"

"It means you have a large manhood."

Looking between his legs, Hung said, "Ah, you hear, Fat Rhino! I knew there was something good about the Americans! And what, pray tell, does Xin Loi mean in American?"

"My name doesn't mean anything in American."

"Oh, sorry about that, Xin Loi."

"No problemo, Fat Rhino. What takes you away from your art lessons today?"

"Mr. Cua thought I needed some time off. He said it would give my hands a chance to remember what he has so patiently taught them. I tell you, Xin, if your village would have me, I will gladly come back here after the war and work for Mr. Cua. His art is exquisite!"

"Really, and what makes you think the war will ever end?"

"Well, it will end for all of us one way or another. Still, dead or alive, this is where I would want to be. It is heaven on earth."

Xin could not help but smile. He clapped Hung on the back. "Then you will be my guest, friend Hung. Now tell me, what is your favorite piece of Dong Ho art in Mr. Cua's gallery?"

"Oh, that would have to be the satirical piece done by his family after World War One. Where the Vietnamese are dressed up like Frenchmen and strutting around like peacocks thinking they are better than the peasants. It reflects both the realities and dreams of the peasants and the colors! My God, the colors are so magnificent and the woodcuts are excruciatingly intense and elegant..."

"Oh, Hung, the warrior-artist! You are now a slave to Dong Ho, my friend."

No sooner had Xin spoken than one of the children ran up to them and began to speak in a very excited manner. "Xin, Xin, and Master Hung...the political commissar has arrived from Hanoi and wishes to speak with the two of you. He is waiting in Mr. Cua's shop."

After arriving at Mr. Cua's gallery, Xin and Hung were both astonished to discover that the new political commissar for their province was none other than Phouc Minh!

Minh smiled benignly at the two, then said, "You seem somewhat surprised at my promotion, gentlemen. But I am not the only one who has received a promotion or decorations for valor in the 'Jungle of Screaming Souls.' My superiors do not know the anguish and sorrow I feel for having led my platoon into an ambush. They only see the sacrifice of our platoon as something noble and the bravery of those of us who survived. It seems as though our comrade Xin Loi has been noticed by the party and has been promoted to lieutenant of a scout platoon. I am sorry for you, Hung, but the Central Committee in Hanoi would not allow me to promote or decorate a southerner, but they said you could choose your next assignment."

Both young men stood frozen for a few moments before Hung said, "Commissar Phouc, it is my wish to remain with Lieutenant Xin. He has allowed me to remain with him in his village to recuperate from our wounds, and I owe him my life."

Xin Loi paused a moment and thought, *You may have come here as an act of contrition, Comrade Phouc, but you will receive no forgiveness from me for your stupidity at the Song Thu Bon.*

Then Xin said, "Thank you for this great honor, Comrade Phouc. I will endeavor to bring honor to my village and the People's Army of Vietnam!"

After much genuine celebration, the party officials from Hanoi had left. Xin, Hung, and Mr. Cua were left alone in the gallery. Mr. Cua looked at the two and shook his head. "Did you think you would not be called back, Xin? And you, fathead Hung, what in the world were you thinking? I have trained your hands well, but obviously, I have not had much effect on your brains!"

Stunned, Hung asked, "What...what do you mean?"

"What he means, my friend Hung, is that you could have asked to be at one of the Binh Trams, or you could have asked to be a guide for porters moving south or any other number of meaningless jobs that will not involve getting your peasant ass shot off. But no, you had to stick your patriotic neck out. Were you trying to impress Mr. Cua or Phouc Minh? Do you really think you owe me a life? Then it would be my wish for you to remain here at Dong Ho and become a Dong Ho artist of Cua's caliber. That, my friend, would be real courage. Risking your life does not show real courage. Anyone can get shot at, and everyone will die. I mean even Phouc Minh can be a hero. I'm talking about the courage to live. The courage to open your mind and stretch your thinking. The courage to raise a family and to go to work each day, day after day, week after week, year after year. The courage to incorporate new ideas into your art and risk your beliefs for them, the same way Mr. Cua's family did with their famous World War One prints. That, my friend, is the kind of courage that will win this war."

"Enough, young men! The die has been cast. It is your duty to survive this war and come home to your village. Especially you, my young friend Hung, you have much to learn, and you will have three new responsibilities when you return. All three of my daughters are pregnant. Your castration will wait until you return…that is, if the Americans don't cut it off first."

Chapter Twelve

The Smells of Southeast Asia

"Wakee, wakee, motherfucker," an effervescent Locker prodded G.O.

G.O. opened one eye, then the other. His body was sore and stiff. "Where the fuck are we, Locker? It's not even fucken daylight! Oh God...I feel like I been ate by a wolf and shit over the side of a cliff."

"We are in the belly of a Forty-Six-D, old stick, where you have slept soundly for the past two hours. No, it is not daylight, yet, dude. And *you*, being the FNG, have to go to the armorer's and pick up the fifties and then preflight this baby and be ready to fly by six in the a.m. I've already cleared it with the Gunny for you to fly with me today. Any questions?"

"Yeah, how did we get here? Things got a little fuzzy after the Sugar Bear showed up with the brews."

"Well, let's say you enjoyed yourself quite a bit, even made friends with the rats, but you left the Bear with the impression that you might be a little light in your loafers."

"What?'

"Yeah, you kept talking about his 'black snake' and how you never saw a wahrule[4] that big. You told Bear that he could get a job as a tow truck when he got back to the world. Yeah, told him he could use his prick

---

4 Another slang term for penis.

65

to pull semis out of ditches. But none of that was as bad as you making racial remarks about the Bear."

"No, man, don't tell me that. I didn't really, did I?"

"Sorry, dude, I can't speak for the Bear. I can only tell you what it sounded like to me. You kept talking about his *black* snake, and if he put some horns on the thing he would have a *black* dragon, and everything was just about *black* to you. What does that sound like to you?"

"Well, I suppose—"

"You don't have to answer; that was a rhetorical question, dumb ass. For somebody that prides himself on his thoughtful, rational approach to life, you have all the empathy of a sea slug."

"Oh man, I think I need to talk with the Bear. Let him know—"

"I think you should quit thinking for a while. You need to just cool out and start thinking about today's mission. I'm headed to the line shack for today's briefing. While I'm away, you get this bird ready to fly the friendly skies of South Vietnam, and I want at least three cans of ammo for each fifty. Have the damn thing ready for preflight when I return."

"Oh yes, sir, General Gallo, sir. And a cheery aye-aye to you, motherfucker."

After hauling two .50 caliber machine guns and six cans of fifty ammo to the furthest revetment on the flight line in a mere three trips, G.O. had the aircraft unbuttoned and ready for preflight by the pilots. All of the aircraft's inspection panels were open and the ramp down, when he saw Locker coming across the flight line with Captain Chucky D. and...what the fuck!...Lieutenant Rinehart from admin. *Oh jeez,* G.O. thought, *this should be exciting.*

"Fuck, son, it looks like you been ate by a wolf and shit over a cliff," Captain Chucky D. greeted G.O.

"Got in with a bad crowd sir, the kind my granddaddy warned me about."

Daggers from Locker and a quick shake of the head. The shake that says *Shut the fuck up.*

Without taking his eyes off Hill, Chucky D. said, "Lieutenant, why don't you and Lance Corporal Gallo preflight the top, and Corporal Hill and I will preflight the bottom half of this bird."

"Roger that, sir," replied Lieutenant Rinehart without moving his lips as he began climbing the stub wing to the upper aft rotor head.

"Anything I should look for, G.O.?" queried Locker.

"You might want to check that aft rotor head carefully."

Locker began climbing the stub wing, mumbling some ethereal denigrations under his breath.

"Two things, Hill," stated a serious Captain D'Amato. "First, are you going to have trouble taking directions from a crew chief you clearly outrank? And second, what was all that nonsense about the aft rotor head?"

"Sir, when Locker and I flew together back in the world, he trained with me and was my first mech until he managed to get his own aircraft to crew. So, clearly I do not mind Lance Corporal Gallo giving me orders; I know who trained him. And the aft rotor head, sir? It is nothing really, sir. Back in the world Locker and I used to keep each other on our toes by screwing with each other's aircraft prior to take off. If you found where your aircraft had been screwed with, well then you got a free beer. If you didn't find the screwup, well then, you bought. It made us focus on the preflight, sir. You know, take it more seriously, we felt like if you never let it become boring or routine, it might possibly save your life. Once Locker left a dead skunk in the number two engine exhaust of the aircraft I was crewing and once I polished his pilot's windscreen with a Hershey bar. But we never left Mother Earth without letting each know what needed checking. Sir."

"So I take it that was what checking the aft rotor head was all about?" responded Captain D'Amato.

"Yes, sir, he should start bitchin' about how some ignorant blind-assed idiot safety wired a nut backward on the aft rotor head any moment now."

"G.O.!" Locker yelled from the top of the aft rotor head. "Would you get me some safety wire and some pliers? Some blind-assed idiot has safety-wired a nut backward on the aft rotor head."

Chucky D. gave G.O. a crooked grin.

G.O. reached into a pocket on his flight suit and came up with a roll of safety wire and safety wire pliers and underhanded them up to Gallo.

"Is she ready to fly, Hill?"

"Oh yes, sir!"

"Button her up, Locker. We're going flying!" Captain D'Amato yelled to Gallo.

"But, Captain, we haven't finished our preflight," Lieutenant Rinehart responded.

"Rinehart, I know you like crossword puzzles, so tell me...what's a five-letter word for a group that wants to join together to protect its rights?"

"Union, Captain?"

"That's right, Lieutenant. Do you belong to some kind of fucken union?" Chucky D. queried.

"Uh, n-n-n-o-o-o-o, Captain," Lieutenant Rinehart responded shakily.

"Then get your ass up in the cockpit and light up the auxiliary engine, we're burning daylight, son." Then the captain put his weight on his left foot, raised his right leg slightly, and cut loose one his notorious Coupe de Ville farts. Chucky D. then proceeded to the cockpit whistling something that vaguely sounded like Bob Dylan's "Blowin' in the Wind."

Ten minutes later the air in the aft cabin was still a little green as the crew of EP-21 taxied to the runway at the Hue-Phu Bai air base. As they taxied, Captain D'Amato went over the flight plan with the crew over the Aircraft Intercom System (ICS).

"Today should be a milk run," Chucky D. assured the crew.

Milk run, G.O. thought. *Isn't that what Gunz Dupree warned them about last night?*

"This morning we fly up to Quang Tri to pick up some parts and then we fly up to Vandy and sit on the runway there as a standby aircraft. Should be a nice boring ass day, gentleman." With a second click on the pilot's cyclic stick, Captain D'Amato engaged a different set of radio frequencies. "Tower...this is Echo Papa Two One call sign Highboy One Eight, requesting permission to depart runway nine. Over."

"Highboy One Eight cleared to depart runway nine, I say again, you are cleared for departure...runway nine. Over."

G.O. leaned over to Locker and, in a voice loud enough to be heard above the jet engines and rotor blades, said, "Highboy, our fucken call sign is Highboy? I think I'm going to love this squadron!" G.O. sat on a toolbox and stared out of the port-side hatch where he had mounted a fifty earlier in the morning.

Locker came over and yelled in G.O.'s hardhat, "Since we're flying up the coast, there won't be much to see until we start back to Hue-Phu Bai."

No sooner had Locker spoken than the radio chatter picked up.

"Highboy One Eight we are located at the following coordinates..."

"Be advised Tango Four Bravo we do not have a chase aircraft and cannot fly into an unsecured zone."

"Highboy One Eight, our zone is secure, repeat secure. This is just an extraction, over."

"Roger, Tango Four Bravo, we can be in your area in five mikes."

"Roger that Highboy One Eight, five mikes, over."

"You boys get all of that?"

"Most of it, sir," Gallo replied. "Where is this extract taking place and how many?"

"Just down the road from Con Thien, crew chief, an APC (armored personnel carrier) was ambushed and they would like for us to pick up four KIAs and remove them to VCB (Vandegrift Combat Base). Does that fit in with your luncheon plans, crew chief?"

"Excellent, sir."

"I want your asses on those guns when we fly into the LZ...those damn grunts would tell Jesus their LZ was safe."

G.O. pulled back on his fifty's bolt handle and released it, then squeezed the butterfly trigger on the fifty and fired off a short burst into the South China Sea. "Jesus, Mary, and a cuckolded Joseph, this is some awesome shit!"

"Good shooting, Hill...you certainly riddled those insurgent communist waves...Say, Lieutenant...what's an eight-letter word meaning to shit one's self?"

"Defecate, sir?"

"That would be correct...so, Hill, next time give us a little warning before you crank that damned fifty up...unless of course we're taking fire, and I feel sure the lieutenant will already have airbrushed his flight suit with one of those chocolate man biscuits...so, Lieutenant, what's a five-letter word for when your skin draws up real tight..."

"That would be pucker, sir."

"Right, Lieutenant...that's what your ass is supposed to do when you hear gunfire...so since you are new in country, you are going to get a little stick time, Lieutenant...you are going to land this beast in the LZ...and Hill...you don't get off so easy. You will be the lieutenant's eyes for the ass-end of this bird as we land..."

"Roger..."

"Roger..."

"Roger..."

"OK...here we go...Tango Four Bravo...we are in your area...have visual on smoking APC on the side of the road..."

"Roger, Highboy One Eight, we have visual on you coming in due east of our pos...we have not had recent incoming fire...would you like smoke?"

"Negative smoke Tango Four Bravo...there's mucho coming off the APC...beginning descent..."

"Take over, Lieutenant...try not to shove the struts through the stub wings..."

Highboy One Eight began its descent and spiraled in smooth tight circles down to the roadway and settled gently into the middle of the perimeter established by the grunts.

Hill dropped the ramp at the rear of the helicopter and he and Locker walked to the back to assist with casualties. There were no wounded, just KIAs. Four of them. In body bags. The grunts struggled up the ramp with the body bags. Locker was busy showing the grunts where to stash the body bags while G.O. bent the grunt sergeant's ear. After the grunts had cleared the helicopter, G.O. said, "We are good to go back here, sir."

"Roger that, lifting off now…"

♦ ♦ ♦

As soon as they were airborne, G.O. started back to his gun. He saw Locker trying to unzip one of the body bags.

"What the fuck you doing, Locker?"

"Well, it's like this, G.O., I promised my granddad I would send him a pair of bona fide Marine-issued binoculars from the land of boom-boom, so I thought I would go through the body bags and see if any of these recently departed young men might have a pair. You going to stand and gawk at me or you going to lend a hand."

The first bag the dynamic duo unzipped contained a Marine burned beyond all recognition. FUBAR. The smell hit G.O.'s nostrils like he had just been baptized in ammonia. *Oh my God,* G.O. thought as he reeled from the body bag, head spinning, eyes clouded and watering, *Oh God, no.* The sulfurous odor of burned hair clung to the inside of G.O.'s nose, and he started to gag as Locker moved an arm…and burned rotting flesh fell from that arm. Locker began a meticulous search of the burned Marine, but evidently some industrious bastard had already removed anything of value from the burned Marine.

"Well, fuck," Locker complained, "the goddamn, self-righteous, ground-pounding grunts have already robbed their very own crispy critters. I mean, go figure?"

"Well," G.O. responded, "isn't that what we're doing?"

"See, dude, once again, your perception is highly skewed. We are *not* stealing from the dead; we are trying to secure very select war trophies for the edification of future Marine folklore to be passed on from generation to generation. Each generation will be consumed with the need to create its own mythology by gathering its own symbols of courage in combat. This will ensure the Marine Corps has plenty of cannon fodder for future wars. The cycle never ends. Death on a pogo stick. Population control at its finest."

"You are a sick fuck, Gallo, my friend."

"G.O., we are all on our way to the last wipeout. We are all going to eat it, dude. Just like these poor pukes. If you want to get philosophical on me ask yourself if these dudes had the courage to share the music that was in each of them or did they keep it inside, did they have the courage to really live life at all? Did they bring joy or sadness to the world? What dreams did they have? Were their lives fulfilled? Hell, we will all be fertilizing daffodils some day and the only lives we have any control over are our own. And if we are not courageous, we don't have a hell of a lot of that. Now get over here and bring a little joy to my *sick* fucken life by helping me to find some binoculars. OK? We will check one more body bag then call it a day."

"Roger that, old son."

Gallo and Hill no sooner opened the next body bag than they both received an intense blast of the very distinctive sulfurous, coppery, metallic stench of another burned-beyond-recognition Marine. Only this one was not entirely connected. The burned head of the dead Marine rolled across the floorboards to the starboard bulkhead. G.O. made it to a window on the port bulkhead and started calling to the Ralph the Assyrian God of Stomach Ailments. Goodbye, Ballantines. And to think…the sun was barely up.

Captain D'Amato keyed their mics. "What the hell is that godawful smell? Damn, and I have to ride up here with a lieutenant that hasn't even been potty-trained…you boys better not be back there desecratin' the dead…"

"Oh no, sir…one of the body bags wasn't secured, and a head rolled out…I'm securing the head now, sir."

"And you boys just thought my farts smelled bad."

Chapter Thirteen

A Shau Valley

The early morning mist covered Xin's mind like it covered the mountain. Xin and Hung had traveled south after spending an indeterminate amount of time in a staging area not far from Hanoi.

Of the original twenty members of their scout platoon, seventeen had completed the trip. Two were lost to disease, and one was taken in an unexpected bombing mission in Laos by the American B-52s. Xin never foresaw the day when he would lose more men to disease than to enemy gunfire. He wondered if the Americans were afflicted with the same problems.

They had traveled during the rainy season, which was just now coming to an end in their area of operations, that part of the A Shau Valley that runs through the Quang Tri and Thua Thien provinces. Still, they had to deal with the wet. Everything was wet. The wetness went all the way to your bones, and you were damp and chilled all the time. Only in the past week had the sun managed to burn the mist off the mountains before nightfall, but then would come the evening rains and the fog. The fog and the mist brought a strangeness to the war.

Xin thought he could hear the ghosts of his former platoon chatting late at night and often thought he saw their shadows among the triple-canopied jungle. Especially Cam Troung. But he could not see Cam's face, only the pink mist he became. The only respite the platoon had was when they went into one of the tunnel systems for a short period to dry out. These periods did not last long because one of his superiors was always wanting new intelligence about the whereabouts of the Americans and their intentions. *Just once*, Xin thought, *I would like to tell my superiors the Americans intend to kill us!*

Hung continued to be his jovial self as well as an asset in training the young members of his platoon. The platoon had a hard time dealing with the fact that their commander was so close to a peasant from the south. Lieutenant Xin and Scout Leader Hung would eat together and laugh together and always consult together about the best course of action to take when scouting the Americans. It was unbecoming for Commander Xin to never confer the other members of the platoon. Although there may have been many complaints by members of his platoon, they were never given voice to either Xin or Hung. The members of the platoon knew their best chances of success and survival were to listen to Lieutenant Xin and follow his directions explicitly.

It had been some three long years since the Marines had landed at Da Nang in any sizable force and their numbers just continued to grow. Xin's masters in Hanoi had not figured out how to stop the air war. Wherever the Marines found the People's Army, there were bombs and rockets and strafing by jets…then the helicopters. Helicopters loaded with well-trained Marines ready to seek out and destroy all members of the People's Army.

They will dance on our graves, Xin thought. So far Hung was the only one Xin had met who had an original idea about how the Americans might be defeated. "We just keep killing them until they leave," Hung had said. After the terrible losses suffered by both the Viet Cong and the People's Army in last February's Tet Offensive, while Xin and Hung recuperated in the north, the American media had portrayed it as a loss for the Americans. All the Americans had lost were soldiers.

The North had lost all the gains it had made in three long years and was struggling to maintain its position in the south. Slowly inroads were being made. The thousands of miles of tunnels in the south bringing troops and supplies from the north were not detectable by air. *We must choose our battles wisely,* Xin thought.

◆ ◆ ◆

Xin was snapped out of his specter filled contemplation by Hung.

"What? Are you thinking about fishing again? In this rotten-assed weather? It will give you nightmares, comrade. Best to think about our village, Dong Ho, and the beauty that awaits us there. Ah...there...a smile, I knew you capable."

"Comrade Hung, I was just thinking what a pleasant evening it would be for you to take out a patrol and set an ambush for any wayfaring Marines that happen upon us."

"In this weather? No one will be out in this, except those damn mosquitoes that can pick up a water buffalo. Surely you do not mean tonight?"

"Orders, Fat Rhino, from on high. I don't think the mosquitoes will be interested in your skinny ass. They would probably get high off all the *Rosa canina* you have been smoking."

"Oh, my friend, I don't smoke that stuff to get high. I smoke it because it allows me to see my three wives back in our village. Mr. Cua's daughters were so beautiful that I sometimes forget what they look like. But when I smoke *Rosa* or marijuana, I can see them so clearly it makes my heart full."

"That's fine as long as you don't smoke it on patrol. Now, pick five of your comrades to go with you, *di-di mau*!"

"Well, I will take Water Boo—"

"I don't care, Hung, take whomever you will...just go!"

Hung beat a hasty, intelligent withdrawal. Sometimes he just didn't understand Xin, but he did understand the pressure he was under from command. They might not be able to defeat the Americans but they could keep them tied up until they were ready to leave. The Americans had no stomach for this war. Most of them were only here for a year, and could not wait to leave. *Yes, I will take out a patrol and set up a small ambush... where there are no American soldiers, where we can sit and dream. I know this is what Xin wants even though he can't voice it. But if any stumble upon us, we will destroy them*, Hung thought.

Later that evening, Hung and his five scouts exited one of the secret tunnels midway down the mountain. Xin was there to wish each of them luck. The platoon had been together now for over six months, but Xin still refused to get close to the men after what had happened at Song Thu Bon. Xin was still haunted by the death of Cam Troung, one of the scouts from his village. Xin had a terrible premonition about this patrol but felt that Hung would keep the young men out of harm's way.

"Tighten those straps, Water Boo, do you want the enemy to hear you coming?" Xin said using the nickname for Nguyen Tuan. *He could not have been more than fifteen, but he was big for his age. This must be why Hung calls him the Water Buffalo, which the troops shortened to Water Boo,* Xin thought.

"Yes, Comrade Lieutenant!"

The merry band made their way silently down the mountain until they came to a small grove of bamboo on a small ridge set above a meandering stream. On the other side of the creek was a clearing that an animal trail ran through. After placing the scouts in among the bamboo, Hung left to check the path. After satisfying himself that the trail had not been used in quite some time, Hung returned to the patrol and told them to settle in for the night. "No noise and no movement. If you make a sound it will be your last, I will personally cut off your itty-bitty peckers!" Hung warned his men.

A thick fog set in interspersed with a fine mist. The water drip, drip, dripping from Dong's bush hat set up a quiet rhythm. Ghostly shadows moved through the night. Dong would have sworn he saw men from his and Lieutenant Xin's old platoon marching single file beside the stream. *It is just the* Rosa canina *slowly wearing off,* Hung Dong thought to himself. *It will pass with the dawn.*

Dong's ears pricked up as he thought he heard a whisper of a footfall. It was ever so quiet. Then a very low growl…then a thrashing noise. The sounds of a predator feeding early in the morning. He must congratulate his men for keeping noise discipline on ambush. Surely, they had been as frightened as he was. Then through the slots formed by the bamboo, Dong could make out the form of a tiger stealthily pulling one of his men by his pack straps through the dense foliage. *My God,* Dong thought. *It's the Water Boo!* Hung Dong did not know if Nguyen Tuan was alive or dead, but he certainly was not making any noise. *What noise discipline!* Hung thought. Hung Dong crawled after them, not knowing what to do, but knowing he could not leave one of his men behind. After about fifteen meters the tiger backed underneath a huge tree that had fallen in the jungle. But the Water Boo would not fit underneath the tree. The tiger tugged and tugged and snarled her dissatisfaction. Finally, she let go of Tuan's straps, looked at Hung Dong with yellow eyes, turned, leaped over the fallen tree and silently fled into the undergrowth. Dong crawled quickly over to Tuan and grabbed his face in both his hands. Tuan looked into Dong's eyes and smiled. Then they both laughed. Long and hard they laughed.

◆ ◆ ◆

On Hill 881, about ten clicks away (a click being one thousand meters, or in this instance, 6.2 miles), a Marine sentry was reporting to his sergeant that he had heard laughter. After a thorough reaming from his sergeant, the Marine told his squad what had happened. Of course, although none of them believed a word he said, they all empathized with him for the ass chewing he took. "Get some sleep, you shitheads. I don't want you hearing things on patrol today!" the sergeant yelled in their bunker. Later that morning a tired group of young Marines checked each other's equipment before they started out on their patrol.

"Heard any more laughter, Santiago?" the sergeant queried.

'No, Sergeant," Santiago sheepishly replied.

"Don't worry about it, son. Some of these guys have reported hearing all kinds of shit late at night, while the LPs set outside the perimeter don't report a damn thing. This mist and fog plays tricks on our senses," the sergeant replied as he cast knowing glances at the some of the other squad members.

"OK, listen up, our squad has the point today. We will go down the mountain and find the stream that runs toward the Da Krong River. We will follow the stream to any sizable open area and then clear it for a helicopter insert if needed. I'll keep you informed as the mission progresses.

"We have heard that Mr. Charles is in the area, so we will keep noise to a minimum, and I expect all of you to keep your eyes and ears open. We do not want to be the reason for a medevac, I shit you not!" After sharing those thoughts, the sergeant got his squad underway, and they proceeded cautiously down the mountain.

◆ ◆ ◆

Of course, no one else in Hung's patrol believed his and Nguyen's story about the tiger, but they thought it was a good story and should be repeated. Hung Dong was wondering to himself when should they start back up the mountain toward the tunnel since dawn was beginning to break, when he received several panicked hand signals from different members of his squad. He quickly responded in kind for them to go back to cover.

All he could hear was the stream as it coursed down the mountain. But there was a smell. A smell that preceded an American patrol. It was the smell of American cigarettes. But this American patrol was different; there was no music blasting, and no loud noises being made. As they lay camouflaged in their bamboo shelter, they counted twelve Marines as they crossed over the stream into the open area beyond. The Marines spread out as their sergeant radioed in their position.

No sooner had the first group of Marines spread out than another squad of them passed by and joined the first group. Then a third group crossed over moments later from a different direction. Hung Dong knew they would not be able to report back until the Marines had left his area, so he would gather what information he could while his squad waited.

The clearing itself was not that big. It was an irregular oval shape about ten meters in length and about five meters wide. The Marine sergeant reported to his lieutenant. "Sir, I have one man running about a hundred and five degree temperature, and I think we should have him extracted."

"You sure you are not just looking for a decoy sergeant? You know if there are any gooks in the area, they'll take a shot at a helicopter, which will save us a lot of time trying to find their sorry asses."

"Never crossed my mind, sir," the sergeant replied with a sly grin. "It's the new guy, Santiago, sir."

"Same guy who heard the laughter last night?"

"That would be him, sir."

"Very well, call it in. Let's see if we can get a chopper in here to hoist his dumb ass outa here. In the meantime have the men spread out into a larger defensive perimeter. I don't want any surprises."

"Roger that, Lieutenant."

Chapter Fourteen

Panty Porn

As soon as the crew dropped off the KIAs at Vandy's graves registration and refueled, they were directed to an empty revetment and shut the aircraft down. Captain D'Amato came through the hatch from the cockpit first. He looked at Locker, then G.O.

"What the hell is wrong with you son? You're as white as a fucken sheet."

"Nothing sir, the smell back here just got to me and my breakfast came surging up. I swear when I was heaving out the port side, it kept coming back and hitting me in the face."

"Hah!" roared Chucky D. "That wasn't *your* puke hitting you in the face, son...that was Lieutenant I-got-my-MBA-at-Yale Rinehart throwing up out of the copilot's window. That was what was hitting you in the face, son. Shit, what a crew. Hell, Gallo, you and Hill get some water and get this flying coffin cleaned up. Goddamn! It stinks back here."

"Aye-aye, sir," the magpies chirped.

Lieutenant Rinehart came through the hatch next and without looking up, followed Captain D'Amato off the aircraft, like the whipped puppy he was.

G.O. and Locker sat on the ramp smoking a couple of C ration ciga-rettes. Locker had a Chesterfield, and he had one of the fabled Philip Morris cigarettes, probably from the second World War. *It tastes like crap, but it smells better than those bodies we were hauling*, G.O. thought. The morning mist had all but burned off, and Phoebus Apollo had begun making his way across the sky. *I just hope Phaeton doesn't get ahold of the reins,* he mused as the sky changed from a deep aubergine to a mild apricot. After his smoke, he found a bucket and filled it with water and returned to the scene of the epic regurgitation and began washing down the side of the aircraft that he and Lieutenant Rinehart had managed to camouflage with their breakfasts.

As expected, another helicopter from their squadron taxied over to the revetment next to them and began shutting down. It was the Sugar Bear's bird, the infamous *Cloud Nine.* One of the more creative metal-smiths had painted *Cloud Nine* on the side of the Bear's aircraft right below a picture that resembled the Bear smoking a roll-your-own and blowing out a colossal psychedelic cloud with a little CH-46 hovering above the cloud. Only the Bear could get away with that. The Bear and the Bugman came over and sat down on the ramp next to Locker.

"Shit, man, what's Hill doing?" the Bugman asked.

"G.O. is washing his puke off the side of the aircraft. Couldn't handle the dead bodies we were hauling this morning."

"Why don't you give him a hand, Bugman?" the Bear suggested.

"Fuck you and the Shetland pony you rode in on, Bear. He chunked it; he can wash it."

Unexpectedly, a small man with four different cameras around his neck came walking up to the back of the aircraft.

"Hey, fellas," he squeaked. "Y'all seen any action today?"

"Damn, son, anybody ever tell you you look exactly like Wally Cox?" the Bear said.

"Wally who?"

"Cox, man. You know, Mr. Peepers," the Bear informed.

"Oh, him...yes, I have heard that more than once, soldier."

"Soldier?" the Bugman exploded. "Soldier? Do I look like a goddamn soldier, you four-eyed fuck? What the hell are you doing here if you don't know a soldier from a Marine? Are you looking to have your emaciated little ass kicked?"

"Bugman!" the Bear intoned. "Back off, man, you intimidatin' Mr. Peepers here. Don't pay the Bugman no mind, Mr. Peepers, he get a little riled when you reporter types don't know sic 'em from come here."

"I'm s-s-sorry," Mr. Peepers said.

"Sorry? Sorry comes right between shit and syphilis in the dictionary, son. You fucken pansy reporters, you got no business here. You won't kill nobody, what good are you?"

"Well, I was hoping that I might be able to tell the story about what it's like to be a soldier...I mean, a Marine, in Vietnam."

"Can't nobody do that but a Marine, son," the Bear said.

"Yeah, the Bear's right on that one," Locker agreed.

"If I don't like what you write, I will tear your fucken arm off and beat you to death with it," the Bugman growled.

"And my name is not Mr. Peepers; it's Carlisle Jones. I'm with the *Washington Post.*"

"Too late," the Bear said, "from now on, you is Mr. Peepers."

"That's right, Mr. Peepers." The Bugman sneered, flexing his Prince of Peace M.C. tattoo.

G.O. appeared from around the side of the helicopter. "G.O., this is Mr. Peepers," Locker told him. "He is a reporter with the *Washington Post.* Doing a story on the Marines in Vietnam." Locker gave Hill a wink. "Would you like to enlighten him about keeping a clean machine?"

"Well, I could go on for quite a while on the ramifications of allowing your aircraft to fall into an irreparable condition if you would care to hear about it, Mr. Peepers. Did anyone ever mention that you look exactly like Wally Cox?"

"Only four times this morning."

"Mr. Peepers," the Bugman said as he put his arm around Carlisle's neck, "you're not being sarcastic, are you? Marines don't like sarcasm in their reporters, and you are about to cross the line."

"Come on, Bugman, let him go. He about to shit hisself."

Pulling away from the Bugman, Mr. Peepers said, "Actually, I was wondering if I might go flying with you boys."

"Boys?" all four said simultaneously.

"I'm s-s-sorry...men?"

"Shee-it, son, there are not enough R's in the world to spell how sorry you gonna be if you call anybody else a boy," the Bear warned.

The reporter walked up onto the ramp of the helicopter, grimaced, and said, "God, what is that smell?"

"That, Mr. Peepers, is the smell of death.

The smell of death
combines the scents of
almonds
fish
garlic
roses and
shit and also
something undefined
An aroma of uncertainty
A fear of the future

Come on in and breathe deeply. That's a smell you should try writing about, but I don't think it can be captured with a pen. It just might, however, make you stop and think about what you are getting into. Because if you go flying with us today, you may be the one that ends up smelling like that. You got the balls for that, Mr. Peepers?"

Walking toward the helicopters were Captain D'Amato and the other pilots. "Let's get 'em buttoned up, *boys*! We got us a bona fide mission."

"Aye-aye, sir," Locker and the Bear replied.

G.O. tilted his head and looked at Mr. Peepers. *That's right, only a Marine officer can call us 'boys.'*

"Sir, this gentleman here from the *Washington Post* would like permission to go flying with us."

"Goddamn, son, anyone ever told you that you are the spittin' image of Mr. Peepers?"

"For a fact, Captain."

"Well, you can fly in the chase plane with Lieutenants Abramovitz and Kelly. You won't mind will you, Lieutenant?"

"No, sir, not at all. You got an extra hardhat, Bear?"

"Yes, sir. I'll get him checked out."

◆ ◆ ◆

Fifteen minutes later both aircraft were airborne and headed toward the A Shau Valley. The pilots had received a request to pull a heat prostration victim from the jungle near the Da Krong River. Locker and G.O.'s aircraft would be the lead aircraft on the extract, while Cloud Nine would be the chase plane.

"Highboy One Eight this is Alpha Six X-ray...over."

"Alpha Six X-ray, this is Highboy One Eight...we are in your vicinity. Would you pop a smoke? Over. Roger, Alpha Six, I have purple smoke at my three o'clock, over."

"This is Alpha Six, roger purple smoke. The perimeter is secure, no enemy contact...I say again, no enemy contact."

"Roger, Alpha Six. This zone is too small for a CH 46. We will drop a hoist cable to you."

To G.O. and Locker, Captain D'Amato said, "OK, boys, get the hell-hole opened and get ready to drop a cable to the grunts down there... And you better pray they know how to hook that damn harness around him...or one of you unlucky bastards will have to cable down there and do it for them."

"Roger that, sir."

G.O. took turns going between the guns and checking out the jungle canopy while Locker opened the hellhole in the center of the aircraft. Locker ran out the hoist cable and attached the harness to the end. Captain D'Amato came to a hover above the small open area around which the grunts had set up a perimeter. Locker tossed the cable out of the hellhole and continued to reel the cable out until it reached the grunts. It was about sixty-five feet to the ground.

The grunts were looking at the harness, not quite knowing what to do, when a corpsman, a sergeant, and some guy with his equipment off and white as a sheet, started walking toward the harness. They strapped the Marine in the harness and then gave a thumbs-up.

"What the hell's going on back there, Gallo? You need to talk to me...I can't hover this big bastard forever."

"Roger that, sir. Our medevac is strapped in and on his way up. I'll let you know when we have him secured in the aircraft...I might need you to give me a hand, Hill."

"Roger, that."

Hoisting someone through the hellhole was not the best way to retrieve a Marine on a hoist cable. A special hoist was built for the CH-46 that fit securely in the front hatch. The hatch was removed and the hoist arm extended from the side of the helicopter directly behind the pilot's seat. This enabled the pilot to see much more clearly what was taking place on the ground and on the hoist cable and to keep a steady hover.

"He's almost here, sir...give me a hand getting him in the aircraft, G.O."

◆　◆　◆

Discipline, men, Hung thought. *I know that the party offers substantial rewards for shooting down helicopters, but keep your discipline. Do not be tempted to fire on the helicopter and give away our position.* It might be too late. Hung could see the Water Boo lining up the aircraft in his sights as it hovered over the clearing. *Why is it taking them so long?* Hung wondered, *Please go, before one of my men can no longer wait and starts randomly shooting at your helicopter.* The Water Boo could no longer resist and began firing at the helicopter. The firing was infectious as the rest of Hung's squad began nervously shooting at the helicopter. *They use their weapons like fire hoses,* Hung thought. *They do not look for targets; they just spray the sky hoping to hit something.* The Marines on the perimeter of the clearing began firing blindly also, while they searched for targets, then the guns on the helicopter opened up on them. Suddenly the aircraft nosed over and started picking up speed as it hurriedly left the area.

The firing had stopped almost as soon as it began. The top of Nguyen Tuan's head was missing, they must change positions immediately before the Marines found them. Hung grabbed Nguyen's dog tag and signaled for his troops to follow him, they would come back later for the Water Boo, if the Marines didn't find him first.

◆ ◆ ◆

G.O. went to help Locker as Private Santiago reached the aircraft. "We have him in the aircraft, sir." Santiago was bug-eyed and had that scared-shitless feral look about him. In the next few moments, all hell broke loose. In the blink of an eye, the interior of the helicopter looked like a thousand small bits of matter as Sir Charles opened up on the aircraft.

"This is Highboy One Eight, we are taking fire…I say again, we are taking fire."

"Oh God," Rinehart screamed into a keyed mic. "God and Jesus help us…Oh God, God, *God!*" Calm and collected, Captain D'Amato reached over and slapped Lieutenant Rinehart's hand off the cyclic stick where he had pressed the ICS and engaged his mic. At the same time, the captain nosed the helicopter over and raised the collective and started to gain airspeed. D'Amato looked over at Rinehart, keyed his mic, and said, "Radio discipline is a sign of professionalism."

G.O. and Locker had reached their guns by this time and opened up on the trees, the sky, and in all probability, the grunts, too. When in doubt, close your eyes and pull the trigger. Locker, once again, moved so fast he disappeared. *Damn*, G.O. thought, *If I'm going to be in this country very long I must learn that trick.*

"Anybody hit back there?"

"I don't think so, sir. You OK, G.O.?"

G.O., heart pounding and eyes wide replied, "Yeah, I'm good. What about our medevac?"

Both crewmen looked to the rear of the aircraft and sure enough, Santiago was bleeding profusely from his forehead. G.O. and Locker made it to Santiago and raised his head up for a better look.

"It looks like a piece of shrapnel might have cut the medevac's fore-head open, sir...G.O and I will get the bleeding stopped."

Locker reached down into the bottom leg of his flight suit, where most mechs kept some type of rag, to wipe up the usual oil and grease spots that were part of the charm of the CH-46 D. But what he came up with surprised even Hill. It was a pair of black lace panties. If Santiago had not already been in shock, he would have just been pushed over the edge.

"Christ, Locker, you carryin' some fancy rags nowadays!"

"Shit, it's all I've got."

"It'll do, my friend...it'll do. And you can explain how those got in your flight suit later." And with that, G.O. took the panties and placed them on Santiago's cut and gave him a kind of "what the hell" shrug, then took Santiago's hand and placed it on the panties. "Hold that on real tight; it's just a small cut...And don't try them on. They're not your size."

Locker and G.O. went back to their guns as Chucky D. made for Vandy.

"Hey, I think I might have taken some shrapnel in my leg, Gallo...come up here and take a look, would you?" Captain D'Amato called back.

"Yes, sir," Gallo replied and went forward to the cockpit.

"Take over, Rinehart...here, cut the pant leg on my flight suit with my K-Bar and take a look."

"I don't see any blood, sir, but there are some red marks...It is pos-sible you were hit." Old Marine Corps axiom, when an officer is trying for a Purple Heart, don't stand in his way.

When they returned, they dropped Santiago off at the medical aid station, then hopped over to the tarmac and shut the bird down in the revetment they had occupied earlier. The chase plane taxied in and shut down next to them. Pilots and crew stood around the aircraft looking for entry and exit holes to see if there was damage that would prevent them from flying the bird back to Hue-Phu Bai. It was Lieutenant Abramovitz, the aircraft commander of *Cloud Nine* that spotted the holes in the forward rotor blades.

"Well, hell, Lieutenant…looks like we'll be flying back with you guys. Gallo, you and Hill will remain with the aircraft. Where the hell is Mr. Peepers?" Captain D'Amato asked as he looked around.

"Well, he threw up all over the side of Sugar Bear's bird when the shooting started, so the Bear's making him wash it off while the Bugman supervises," Abramovitz responded.

"Hope the Bear gets a picture of that. It will look great in the squadron history book. Right next to the photo I took of Rinehart!"

As the pilots walked over to *Cloud Nine*, Chucky D. looked back at Hill and Gallo and winked, then raised his right leg just a little as they stepped up on the ramp.

Chapter Fifteen

Cabbage Patch Dolls

G.O. and Locker had returned to Hue-Phu Bai and Locker had explained how the panties had been situated in his flight suit before G.O. had sniffed them out. A story that G.O. had found both amusing as well as unbelievable. G.O. also found it humorous that the wounded grunt they had extracted in the A Shau Valley had kept Locker's black lace panties. *Damn grunts could steal the tires off a moving bicycle,* Hill mused.

Gallo and Hill had walked over to where the metalsmiths had begun work on Locker's bird. They had suspended string from the incoming rounds' entry points to the exit points. It was a ritual they went through to make certain they left no unrepaired holes in the aircraft.

When G.O. and Locker walked up the back ramp, it looked as though they had entered a giant cave that had last been inhabited by spiders. The string forming a giant cobweb. G.O. expected a giant tarantula to climb out of the cockpit wearing a hardhat. It was remarkable that the only person in the aircraft that was hit was the medevac, even though he would not be the only one getting a Purple Heart for that mission.

G.O. stood by the hatch where his gun had been, in the same position he thought he had been in when he had started firing. There was string under his arms, between his legs, and on both sides of his head. G.O. looked over at Locker who was doing the same thing.

G.O. and Locker walked across the tarmac toward the line shack. "So, G.O., you think you might want to make a trip out to the Cabbage Patch tonight?

"Fucking-A," G.O. replied. "What does this adventure entail?"

"Getting permission from Gunny G. shouldn't be a problem."

"Let's go for it, then."

◆ ◆ ◆

"What part of *no* do you two idiots not understand?" Gunny G. responded. "You tell me you want to go into the ville to find a new coffee pot for the squadron, but I know what you two are really up to. You, Locker, are going to take Hill here to the Cabbage Patch and get him laid. Hill returns to base and two days later he's at sick call because his pecker won't quit dripping, and he has this burning sensation every time he takes a leak until it gets so bad, he will go to sick bay and beg for them to cut Mr. Happy plumb off."

"Well, Gunny, wouldn't it be worth Hill getting the clap, if the squadron got a decent coffee pot in return? That seems like a justifiable trade-off."

The Gunny stared at the ceiling of the line shack for a moment, then at the sock hanging out of the coffee pot, then at the two magpies in front of him. *I guess a night in the ville won't hurt these two dildos after the shit they went through yesterday, hell, any neurosis they might develop can be cured with a blow job.* He rubbed his chin, tugged on one end of his mustache, and patted his stomach. "OK, you two…you are hereby authorized to go into the ville to secure one coffee pot for the squadron. But you are not, I say again, are *not*, under any circumstances, to be in the Cabbage Patch, for any reason. Am I clear?"

"Yes, sir, crystal," piped a cheery Locker.

"And Hill…"

"Yes, Gunny…"

"If you so much as come back with even one tiny microscopic crab, I will lock your ass up in a Conex box for the duration of this fucken war, I shit you not."

"Yes, sir."

"And woe be to you, son, if you come back with the gallopin' crud… for verily, I will send you off to the Island with No Name. That's where the Marines send all of their species that come down with the Black Syph. *Intiendo*, cocksucker? I will send you where people's arms drop off as a matter of quotidian routine. Where pus and blood are shared at every meal and the stink of rotting flesh is more than any mortal can bear. We clear, Marine?"

"Yes, sir, crystal."

"And, Hill, you still owe me an explanation about having a naked man in your car back in North Carolina."

"Sorry about that, Gunny…seems like I just forgot. I'll explain it all to you in the morning."

"You goddamn right, you will! Now, I've got you scheduled to fly with Gunz Dupree tomorrow, be on the flight line at zero four thirty with an explanation for your dear ol' Gunny. And your pecker had better be dry."

"Yes, sir."

"What about me, Gunny?"

"You, Lance Corporal Gallo will have a cup of coffee waiting for your dear ol' beloved Gunny at zero four fifteen, it will be at the perfect temperature, made in the squadron's new coffee pot. It will smell so good, that one whiff will give the CO a hard-on so stiff that a mountain lion couldn't scratch it. And I, your grateful Gunny will be the first to drink from it, and it had better be done correctly or you might find your ass sitting next to Hill on the Island with No Name. Now, both of you commie bastards get the hell out of my line shack."

Yes, sir," the magpies intoned.

Out in the ville, while Locker searched for a large coffee urn, G.O. tried on a variety of holsters. G.O. had noticed that all of the pilots had shoulder holsters, probably for comfort while driving the aircraft, and the crew chiefs all sported these nifty fast draw holsters. G.O. mused, *Perhaps to look good in photos being sent home.*

◆ ◆ ◆

Oh, Mama, would you just look at our little Brucie! He seems like such a manly man with his manly sidearm hanging down in front of his itty-bitty penis.

◆ ◆ ◆

Yeah, it's to look good, G.O. continued to think as he rifled through a variety of leather holsters.

Locker came running up to G.O. "I found one!"

"You have got to be kidding. Where is it?"

"Oh, the mama-san told me we could pick it up in four hours...she said it was at the warehouse...whatever that means, so we have some time to kill, kemosabe."

"What you mean, *we*? You got a mouse in your pocket?"

"Come on, G.O., man, you know what I mean, the Cabbage Patch awaits."

"We told Gunny G. under no circumstances would we visit the Cabbage Patch..."

"Yeah, but the mama-san told me that's where we would have to pick up the coffee pot."

"Do you have any condoms?"

"Sorry, pard, I only ride bareback."

"Well," G.O. said, "I'm afraid I am going to insist on a triple X sheepskin Trojan before I climb on anything I haven't ridden before. I'd rather spend a year in a Conex box than be sent to the Island with No Name."

"Come on, man, the mama-san told me these girls were so clean you could eat your ham and lima beans right out of their kootchies."

"Yeah, like that Westpac widow back in Jacksonville? The one that had you screaming and trying to rip the pipes out of the head at two in the a.m., if I remember correctly? I ain't riding bareback, Locker. Either we find me an English riding cap, or I split back to the compound."

"OK, OK, don't get your panties in a wad. You can be such a tight ass, dude...we'll find you some condoms."

"Trojans."

"OK, Trojans, for crying out loud. And some wire to safety wire the damned condom onto your itty-bitty."

♦ ♦ ♦

The farther they progressed into the ville, the more dilapidated it became. The smells that reached their noses were unfamiliar and exotic. One of the scents was most perplexing to G.O. He just could not decide what it was. "OK, Locker, I give...what is that awful smell?"

"That aromatic, titillating, pleasant fragrance is the Balm of the Cabbage Patch, old son. That is *nuoc mam* fermenting in all these lovely clay pots you see standing in front of these priceless homes."

"God, it smells like a fish that washed up on the beach...a week ago!"

"Well, you see, G.O., the Vietnamese try to not waste food. They are very unlike us in that regard."

"Yes, very."

"So, when they sit down to eat, they come outside and skim some *nuoc mam* sauce from the clay pot. They use it to season their rice or fish. Actually, they use it to season most everything. So, when they finish eating, guess what happens to any leftovers?"

"It goes in the *nuoc mam* pot?"

"Ding-ding-ding! Give that man a cigar! Yes, it goes in the *nuoc mam* pot to continue fermenting and creating the fragrant aromas you keep smelling. Well, well, well...I think we are here."

♦ ♦ ♦

Locker and G.O. walked up a stone path through a well-manicured garden to what looked to be one of the larger houses in the neighborhood.

They were greeted at the door by one of the loveliest Vietnamese women G.O. had ever seen. She was wearing a sheer black baby-doll negligee with black lacy underwear. Light and laughter were emanating from the room along with the harmonic tunes of the Temptations.

Then G.O. looked into the room and saw the Sugar Bear sitting on one end of a sofa, with three Vietnamese women surrounding him. "Gallo," Bear called, "get your skinny ass over here and extract me, man. I'm taking too many hits."

"Yo, Bear man, looks like you have the situation under control. I'd be careful with that Vietnamese herb, though. That shit will bring you down, Bear man. Who you with?"

"Oh, I'm with the Duck...he in the back with the lovely Yellow Jade Python."

"How did you get off base?"

"Well, Gunny wanted me to come into the ville to keep an eye on you and Hill, and he sent Duck to keep an eye on me. Hell, he probably be here hisself in a little while. Anyway, Duck and me got tired of following y'all's asses around and decided to come on down to the Cabbage Patch to see what Mama-san had cooking, I figured you'd be along, Locker, dragging that crazy Texan with you."

◆ ◆ ◆

As the evening grew late, Hill and Gallo were sitting around in their birthday suits having a brew and talking with a couple of the house favorites when in walks the Duck and the Bear, both inebriated and buck naked. "I see you white boys are enjoying the fruits of Vietnam," the Bear intoned.

G.O., who was feeling no pain at this time, managed to mumble, "Oh, hell yeah, my black friend."

"I'm going to let that go, G.O, being as you is mentally impaired...even when you ain't drinking."

"Oh shit, I say something wrong?"

"Look at my skin, G.O...does it look black to you?"

"Well, no, not really...it's more of a dark caramel color."

"That's right, and is your pink ass really white? Do I say, 'G.O. my white-ass friend'? or how about, 'G.O. my some kinda shade of ivory friend'? Or does that Vietnam tan change your skin color even more? And how about little Lotus Blossom here?" Bear said while placing his hands on the young Vietnamese woman's shoulders. "What color is she, she sure ain't yaal-loww, you dumb Texas redneck? You might say she is a beautiful light cocoa-colored girl. There are a million and one shades of brown and from those shades, there are another billion combinations. All beautiful, if like the man says, beauty is in the eye of the beholder. So, you can call me Bear, or Sugar Bear, or Sir Bear, or I hope...friend. But you are not to call me black under any circumstances because I am not black; I am a beautiful mahogany-colored African American man. Now, to be clear, there are some men who like to call themselves 'black,' so you have to be careful, Hill. You sho' don't want to call some Black Panther an African American...Hah-hah-hah! Look at his face, Locker. I think G.O. about to shit hisself."

"I'm really sorry, Bear, I thought that you negroes wanted to be called black."

"Why do you need a name for us nee-grows, Mr. Hill, suh? Is it so's you can continue to classify me as something other than a human being, something less than a man? Or is it just so's you can have someone you feel like you is better than? Is your pecker that small, Hill?"

"Well, I know it ain't because my pecker is small. Ask Lotus Blossom here," a drunken Hill offered.

"Oh he beeeg, he very beeeg! Numbah one!" A deranged Duck laughed, pointing at Hill's peckorus (-a, -um).

"Oh, for crying out loud, Hill," Locker said. "You really don't get it, do you? What matters to you, Hill, when you pick a gunner to go flying with you?"

"What are you getting at?"

"What matters, asshole?"

"You know as well as I do, Locker, you want someone competent, someone cool that doesn't panic under fire, someone that won't desert you when things get a little rough, someone—"

"You haven't mentioned what *color* you want them to be, Hill."

"Oh-h-h-h-h..."

"Right on, Brother Locker...I thought I was going to have to hit the Texan upside the head with a brick, but you 'splained it to him pretty good. Mm-hmm, that's what I'm talkin' about."

"Why is Duck here, anyway? He's not going to find anything he likes," Hill asked, trying to change the subject.

Both the Bear and Locker looked at him like he had a turd on his head, while the Duck just sat there grinning.

"You is one dumb fuck, Hill. Now you going to get down on the Duck because he like boys better than girls? You jus' can't leave it alone, can you, Hill? You just have to be better than someone, don't you? And you think you is born better than people who is different from you, just 'cause you is a straight white Christian man? Let me ax you, Hill, who is the better crew chief, you or Duck?"

Lomax, the one-eyed cockroach, peeked out of the rusty Ballantine's can and shook his head. *God, why do I get stuck with the thick-headed?*

"Dude, you have led one sheltered-ass existence. If you look in Yellow Jade Python's panties, you might be in for a surprise!" Locker chimed in.

Before G.O. had a chance to respond to this new accusation, Duck jumped in and began a rather slurred explanation, "I will tell...(hic)...why Gunny G. sent...(hic)...me. He wanted me...(hic)...to keep an eye on Hill...(hic)...cause Gunny thought Hill...(hic)...might be a little light in his loafers."

"What? You don't mean that, Duck? Do you?"

"O-o-o-o-o, shoe on the other foot now, Hill."

Locker could not stop laughing at the absolutely shocked and confused look on Hill's face.

Suddenly, Mama-san came running into their room. "Hide...hide... Marine must hide...shore patrol, they close...very, very, close." The girls were quick on their feet and had a panel open in the wall and were tugging on the crew and pointing at the wall. Sugar Bear went in first, then Duck, then Gallo, and lastly, Hill. After the four had arranged themselves in the false wall, things quieted down. There was light coming through the wall where the boards had not lined up precisely, and Hill could see a small, slender portion of the room as the girls hustled back and forth hiding all of their paraphernalia. Mama-san came into the room with two Marine SPs, trying to explain that business was slow and there were no Marines here tonight. The SP sergeant looked around, then scratched his head and wondered why the Gunny over at HMM-265 had called and told them to check on the whorehouses out in the Cabbage Patch.

G.O.'s eyes followed the dust particles that played in the light and followed them down to his penis. He noticed that there was a nail point about an eighth of an inch away from Mr. Happy. *Oh God,* Hill thought, *please don't let me get shipped off to Island of Crucified Peckers.*

Chapter Sixteen

Groundz for Divorce

PART A

Xin Loi could hear much of the battle over the regimental radio that was tuned into the channel the Americans were using. He listened as the aircraft was directed to the LZ, then was shocked to hear AK-47 gunfire erupt. After that everything became very confused on the radio. The American infantry were calling in airstrikes as well as artillery strikes. The helicopter had managed to leave the area unscathed. Xin did not believe this to be Hung's squad. If this had been Hung's squad, there would not have been a firefight. Hung's team would have maintained scout discipline. The battle did take place in the area Hung was supposed to have been scouting, however, and this perplexed Xin. After he listened for about thirty minutes, the gunfire and artillery explosions seemed to be more intermittent. Xin Loi went to the regimental canteen deep in the mountain to await news of Hung's team.

Early the next morning, Xin Loi was awakened by one of the scout team, Hung and the members of his team who had survived were waiting in the radio room. When Xin entered, he could tell that Hung Dong was being questioned about the patrol by the regimental commander while the political commissar listened.

"Who broke discipline and fired on the American helicopter, Scout Hung?"

"I did not see Comrade Colonel, like I told you before, we were spread out in the bamboo thicket above the stream. I could not see any members of my team."

"Yes, but you knew their positions, correct? So you could guess as to the area the firing began, yes?

"Yes, sir, I should be able to make an accurate guess, but because of our location and the echoes in the jungle, it would just be a guess."

"You say you lost one of your scouts, comrade. Was he the one who broke discipline and fired? And maybe you are just trying to protect him?"

"Oh no, Comrade Commissar, that would be incorrect. I would gladly tell you if I knew."

After the interrogation was finished and Hung was unable to provide command with any more useful information, he was dismissed to go with Xin Loi. Xin and Hung stopped in the canteen and found a quiet spot for themselves.

"Well, friend Dong, tell me all that happened. There may be lessons to be learned that will help us in the future. Here, look at this map," Xin said as he unfolded a map on the table, "and show me where you set up your observation post."

Hung looked at the map and pointed to the area where they had set up. "It would have been here, by the stream. There was a large bamboo thicket above the stream before it became jungle. We would have visuals in all directions during the daylight, except for the jungle. After I settled the men, the strangest thing happened. You will not believe this."

"Try me, friend," Xin responded, trying to get Hung to relax.

"Well, I heard some noises late in the evening and tried to find who was breaking noise discipline. But it was not the scouts; it was a tiger. Yes, my friend, a tiger! The tiger was pulling Nguyen Tuan through the bamboo! You can imagine my surprise. I was at a loss as to what I should do. But I was proud of the Boo for maintaining noise discipline. I don't know if I could have done the same. So I decided my only course was to follow them. Well, the tiger got the Boo stuck trying to pull him under a fallen tree. When Tuan wouldn't budge, the tiger looked at me, then fled into the jungle. I asked Tuan why he did not yell out. He said the straps the tiger had dragged him by went across his throat, and it was impossible for him to make any sound at all. Hah! We had a good long laugh at that!

"Later, after getting back to the scouts and explaining to them what had happened, we repositioned and decided to wait until dawn to try and move back to the tunnels. But by dawn it was too late, an American patrol came down from their firebase as you expected and crossed the stream to the clearing. Two other patrols also found their way to the clearing, and they formed a company-size unit. It was at this time that I told the scout patrol that our mission became one of observation only.

"When the American helicopter appeared and began removing one of the Marines from the clearing, I prayed that the scouts would maintain fire discipline. They could not. It was Nguyen Tuan who fired first, then the rest of the team opened up. Then the Americans began spraying gunfire at everything, the trees, the rocks, even the sky. Then the helicopter opened up on us. By this time our firing had stopped and the scouts were going to ground as we trained them to do. When I got to the Water Boo, it was too late. I have his dog tag here." Dong handed Nguyen Tuan's dog tag to Xin. "We spent the rest of the day hiding in the jungle while the Americans continued to pound the area with artillery, and finally, when I thought it was safe, I brought the rest of the patrol back to the mountain."

"You did very well, Hung, my friend, very well indeed. Are there lessons here for us?"

"Well, we must teach our men to hold their fire. When they are ready to fire they must have a target, they cannot simply pull the trigger and wave their weapons around and hope to hit anything. Finally, we must shadow their infantry until they send for their helicopters. Then we can concentrate our fire to bring them down. We must plan our escapes so that if the Americans follow us, it will bring them more pain and death."

"I will pass this on to the commissar, Hung. Thank you again, my friend."

◆ ◆ ◆

PART B

A sleepy G.O. had mounted the fifties and secured the ammunition on Gunz Dupree's aircraft, *Groundz for Divorce*, when he heard a loud boom and screaming coming from the line shack. *Damn Locker, must* not *have made the Gunny's coffee just right.* G.O. grinned. In a few minutes, Gunz showed up at the aircraft.

"Hey ya, Hill, got everything ready to go?"

"Yeah, this baby's ready for preflight. What was all that brouhaha coming from the line shack?"

"Oh, that! Seems like your friend Locker bought a coffee pot, but it didn't have the insides! So, he was trying to explain it to the Gunny and the Gunny pulled out his forty-five and threatened to shoot Gallo right on the spot. Well, the Duck walked in about that time and thought he would get in on the joke, and so he says, 'Here, Gunny, use my gun. It's bigger.' So the Gunny looks at the three fifty-seven Magnum that the Duck is totin' and says, 'OK, that might just give Gallo a bigger asshole than he already has. Hand me that damn hog leg, son.' Well, Duck pulls his pistol out and *bam!* A round goes through the roof of the line shack. Sheeeee-it! You should've seen the lifers ducking for cover and Gallo...he liked to have shit himself, swear to God. Funniest damn thing I've seen since I been in the 'Nam. Except for the albino water buffalo just outside Da Nang, maybe."

"You saw an albino water buffalo?"

"Yeah, you been here as long as me, Hill, and I shit you not, you will see some strange shit. Hell, you were in the Cabbage Patch last night. Did you check out the schlong on Yellow Jade Python? There's something you don't see every day!"

"Well, I think the Duck saw it. Actually, he might have been screwing her, er, him?"

"So what, Hill? You have a problem with the Duck's sexuality? You afraid to bend over in the shower, maybe? Hell, G.O., next to the Bear and me, he's the best damn crew chief in the squadron. Who cares if he goes out on a limb? Hah! I made a joke, get it, 'Goes out on a limb.'" Danny couldn't help but laugh at his own joke.

Hill, however, was still mystified. He was brought up Southern Baptist and believed that homosexuals were deviants, no ifs, ands or buts. Hell, he had even read that in a psychology book! And here these guys were treating the Duck like he was not only some kind of normal guy but some kind of gifted mechanic to boot. But, then again, Hill remembered that he was also taught that blacks and Mexicans were also outcasts and less than human, but he admired and respected the Bear. And his first love, before he knew about misogyny, had been a young Tejana girl. *Hell,* G.O. thought, *this ain't right. Everything I've been taught seems like a lie. I wonder if five moderately sized armadillo penises still equal an inch?*

Captain D'Amato and Lieutenant Kelly came walking up to the aircraft. "Damn, I got to fly with you two magnet asses today? And on an aircraft named Groundz? Every time I think I'm going to get a milk run, I end up flying with some magnet ass...but today, I get two of you!" Captain D'Amato laughed.

"Shit, Cap, don't tell me you don't like the action. Hell, you live for this!" Danny shot back.

"As long as I get back every night and find a warm place to shit, you can shoot at me all day long, son, all day long. Now have you got this bucket of bolts ready to fly, Dupree?"

"Yes, sir. Just waiting for you to preflight her."

"Hill, we gonna be needin' a car wash today?" Chucky D. cut his eyes at Hill and grinned.

"No, sir, not today."

"Well, that's good. Very good. Did you hear about your young friend Gallo in the line shack this morning? What a hoot! Blew a damn hole in the line shack roof so big you could fly a 46 through it, swear to God. Gunny's got him on the roof now trying to repair the hole before he goes on mess duty. Play your cards right, Hill, and you may get to crew Gallo's aircraft until he comes off mess duty."

"When will that be, sir?" Hill asked.

"Could be the end of the war or it could be when the Gunny needs another crew chief." Captain D'Amato smiled.

Well, G.O. thought, *someone has got their story screwed up. I guess this is how American folk legends get started.*

◆ ◆ ◆

Hours later, *Groundz for Divorce,* and her merry crew were busy flying supplies to different mountain-top firebases. Their last stop before Vandy was the Rockpile. A notorious piece of property that resembled Gibraltar. It was a large karst outcropping that jutted up about two hundred meters. It had a commanding view of five different valleys that led from North Vietnam into the South. Positioned on the Rockpile were 105mm Howitzers and several different types of mortars that could be called upon for fire missions by grunts in the field, forward observers, and American and Vietnamese aircraft. The North Vietnamese could fire rockets and mortars onto the Rockpile, but it was virtually unassailable by ground troops. As they landed on the remote hilltop, the grunts came up the ramp and began offloading boxes of C rations. Danny D. always kept a supply of Kool-Aid on board to give the grunts on the offloading detail. He had told G.O. that the grunts loved it because the potable water tasted like warm piss without it. One of the younger troops looked like he might be new to the country. Like G.O., he had no tan. Unlike G.O., he had curly blond hair and appeared to be about fifteen. Blond peach fuzz covered his jaws. What was so compelling about the Marine was that he had one blue eye and one green one. It gave G.O. the willies. The kid had a tattoo on his right shoulder of a bulldog in a helmet smoking a cigar. It read *Devil Dogs* on top and *Death before Dishonor* on the bottom. It was definitely San Diego tacky 1968. G.O. reached into his flight suit and came up with a package of lemon-lime-flavored Kool-Aid and tossed it to the kid. The Marine looked at G.O. with this wild, vacant stare, then at the Kool-Aid, then back at G.O., then back to the Kool-Aid, for what seemed like one orbit around Mercury.

Finally, the young Marine said, "Thanks, man! This is some righteous shit." Turned and left the aircraft. G.O. and Gunz looked at each other, then shrugged like *What the fuck was that?*

"I think that motherfucker has been sniffin' the gun barrels on them one-oh-fives a little too long," Danny reflected.

"Hell, if the Marine Corps is having to recruit spaced-out fifteen-year-olds, we are in some serious shit," G.O. replied.

"It don't mean nuthin', G.O.. It don't mean nuthin'."

"OK, listen up back there..." Captain D'Amato's voice came over the ICS. "We've got a call to pull a recon team out of a shit sandwich on Tittybong Knob...seems like the bad guys have been chasing them for two days running...and they are ready for an extract *muy pronto*...so you boys get on those guns...we got us a bona fide mission!"

Jeez, Hill thought, *who names these damn hills? Tittybong Knob?*

Danny had G.O. put his bulletproof vest on the floor by his fifty so he could stand on it when they approached the LZ. "Sir Charles is gonna be shootin' straight up, Hill, not straight *at!* Better to have the protection under you; besides, that damn vest weighs sixty pounds."

As *Groundz* circled the hill, the chase plane flew above them at about two thousand feet. "This is two-three zebra...we have a visual on two CH-46s in our vicinity...I say again, two CH-46s...we have not taken fire in forty-five mikes, but Charlie is close. I say again, Charlie is close..."

"Roger that, two-three zebra, LZ is secure for now...how many are we extracting today?...over."

"We are five, I say again, five in number...one severely wounded...The rest are walking wounded...we are popping smoke now...over."

"Roger that...we have purple smoke on the southeast side of your pos...over."

"Roger that...purple smoke."

"This will be dicey, Dupree," Captain D'Amato said through the ICS. "We are going to have to balance the ass end of this baby on the steep side of that hill...when I give you the word, Dupree, drop the ramp...you are going to have to herd that recon team on board...The sooner, the better, so we can di-di before the bad guys arrive."

"Roger that, sir."

The helicopter spiraled into the side of the knob and with expert flying ability, Captain D'Amato set the tail end of the 46 meticulously on the steep slope. The minute they touched down, Chucky D. told Dupree to drop the ramp. The aft rotor blades were only about four feet off the hill, but there was still plenty of room for the grunts to crawl under them or just go around. Three grunts came out of their cover and started sliding down the slope of the hill. Two of them were dragging a third member of the recon team in a poncho liner. When they came to the aft rotor blades, they stopped. Danny D. disconnected his headset and started out the back of the helicopter and up the slope to the grunts.

Pandemonium erupted on Tittybong Knob. The bad guys started walking mortar rounds down the hill toward the aircraft. "What the hell is going on back there, Dupree?" Captain D'Amato calmly asked.

"Danny left the aircraft, sir. Went to speed the grunts up!" Hill responded as he looked for targets out of both sides of the helicopter.

Danny D. had pulled the wounded grunt in the poncho liner under the rotor blades and had convinced the two grunts to crawl under them. As they started to the ramp of the helicopter, the last two grunts came flying out of their cover and started sliding, crawling, and tumbling down the slope. The distinct sound of AK-47s could be heard in the tree line above them. G.O. could see rounds following the grunts down the gradient. Because of the location of the bad guys in relation to the aircraft, the fifties could not be brought to bear. Danny grabbed an M-16 from the back of the helicopter and went out and started firing at the tree line while the last two members of the recon team made it on board. Danny came running up the ramp as a mortar round went off at the exact spot where the grunts had hesitated moments before. G.O. was excitedly telling Captain D'Amato they could leave. "Everyone's on board sir. Let's get the fuck out of here!"

"Radio discipline, Corporal Hill, radio discipline."

The 46 lifted off the side of the mountain as the ramp came up. G.O. had moved to Danny's fifty and started to return fire on the tree line. Two more mortar rounds went off as they gained altitude and speed. The small arms fire was then directed at the 46. As Danny D. reconnected to the ICS, G.O. heard him call out, "Oh, shit!" as he went down in the middle of the helicopter cargo bay. "Captain D'Amato," G.O. said, "I think Danny has taken a round...I'm moving to him now." Both the pilot and copilot were busy flying the aircraft and monitoring the radios as air strikes and artillery had been called in to pulverize Tittybong Knob.

As G.O. made it to Dupree, he asked, "Where did you get hit, man?"

"In my fucken leg, man!"

G.O. looked down and saw that a round had gone through Danny D.'s flight suit pant leg, and his muscle was hanging out of one side. He went for his K-Bar to cut off the pant leg.

Danny started screaming, "No, man, don't cut off my fucken leg... Don't cut off my fucken leg!...Please...it ain't that bad, really!"

One of the recon members came over and stuck a morphine syrette in him and held Danny down while G.O. cut off the flight suit pant leg. As soon as he had cut it off, the muscle fell out on the floor. G.O. tried to put the muscle back in Danny's calf, but blood was shooting everywhere. G.O. and the grunt decided to wrap the muscle to Danny's leg and try to stanch the blood flow.

Slowly Danny D. descended into semi-consciousness. He thought back to the time when he was really young. Maybe four or five. He remembered being in school. He was outside riding his new tricycle that his pops had brought home for his birthday the previous weekend. Danny's mom had told him not to go down the driveway because it was too steep. But it looked like fun, and he could go really fast. About halfway down he got his foot caught in the spokes. God, the pain. And the terrible feeling that shot up his leg when his knee came into contact with the asphalt driveway. Like when you are standing on the edge of a cliff in your dreams...and suddenly...the ground gives way. He remembered waking in the hospital with the doctor talking to his mom and pops. *Well, he may lose the foot, but we are doing everything we can so that that does not happen.* A single tear left his eye and rolled gently down his cheek.

"The closest triage is Vandy...but the hospital ship *Repose* is just off the coast...we are headed for the *Repose*...get the troops ready, Hill," Captain D'Amato barked.

"Aye-aye, sir."

"Hey, Hill," Danny mumbled as he held tightly on to Hill's hand. "Thanks for not cutting my leg off, man." His eyes rolled back, and Morpheus took him.

Chapter Seventeen

Intelligence

As Hill walked into the line shack, he was met by a concerned Gunny G. "Well, Hill, is it True?"

"What's that, Gunny?"

"Well, I heard you tried to amputate Danny D.'s leg with a fucken K-Bar, true or not?"

"Not true, Gunny," a thoroughly surprised Hill exclaimed. "I was trying to cut the pant leg off the bottom of his flight suit so we could get the bleeding stopped."

"Who is 'we,' Hill?" As Hill started to explain, the Gunny ran through his mental list of symptoms for neurosis. Hill looked and acted fine now, but Gunny G. knew that eventually the gods of combat would extract a heavy toll from Hill.

"Me and one of the recon guys. Thank God the recon guy had a morphine syrette, or we might never have gotten Danny to quiet down. But when we finally got him to calm down, we were able to cut off the pant leg and get the blood flow stanched. Then most of the recon team were so shot up Captain D'Amato decided to fly straight out to the hospital ship *Repose* and drop them off. Say, where did you hear this? We just got back from the *Repose* and the pilots headed over to the ready room."

"Well, one of the nurses out on the *Repose* called in and said that one very spooked crew chief was screaming that some asshole tried to cut his calf muscle off with a K-Bar, and I figured there was another story. Fucken Navy. Don't know 'sic 'em from come here. Shit, if you put that fucken nurse's brains in a bumblebee, it'd fly backward," the Gunny mused as he rubbed his chin and contemplated what to do next. "I'll take care of this, Hill. You don't need to worry about it."

"Well, thanks, Gunny, but I wasn't worried."

"That's your fucken problem, Hill; you don't worry enough! You been flyin' twice, and you got shot up twice. When I was your age, Hill, I worried about every goddamn thing there was." *Jeez,* the Gunny thought, *maybe I'm the neurotic.*

"I don't understand, Gunny."

"Well, I can explain it to you, but I sure as hell can't understand it for you. Reach over there and hand me that box of Christmas lights."

"Uh-h-h, sure, Gunny, which box would that be?"

"Well, if you are not one sad fucken Looney Tune…the one marked 'Christmas lights,' for crying out loud!"

G.O. couldn't help but chuckle at Gunny G.'s ungainly and ungraceful movements when he was trying to do anything with his hands except hold a coffee cup. Gunny G. had these really thick fingers that weren't much good for anything except making a fist to knock out some poor sailor. G.O set the box of lights on the counter of the line shack, and the Gunny started pulling lights out of the box the same way a gorilla might go through a produce stand.

"Here, Gunny, let me help you get those lights untangled. You act like you're trying to put socks on a rooster."

"Goddamnit, Hill, you are now HMFIC"—Head Mother Fucker in Charge—"of Christmas Lights. I want these bastards strung up around the line shack before the change of command ceremony next week."

"That's only a couple of weeks before Christmas, Gunny. I didn't think command was changing before January," G.O. responded.

"Hill, do you think someone in the Marine Corps hierarchy gives a shit what you think, or are you just another numbnuts trying to pass himself off as knowing more than the Gunny?"

"Er...ah...I really don't think the Marine Corps cares about us numb-nuts trying to act like we know more than a gunnery sergeant."

"You fucken straight they don't, douche bag. If the Marine Corps wanted you to think..."

"I know, Gunny, they would've issued me a brain."

"Well, hell, Hill...I believe you are already getting smarter just being around me. Now, get those fucken lights strung!"

"Aye-aye, sir."

◆ ◆ ◆

For the next week, things were busy around the squadron as they prepared to send their Commanding Officer, Colonel Blue, back to the states and welcome their new CO, Lieutenant Colonel Van Meter, to the squadron. G.O. had been scheduled to fly every day, so he had been able to keep out of the way. The squadron had a formation every morning, and those not flying or excused were required to attend.

The executive officer (X.O.), Major Bridger, was not only irritated but actually offended that he was not offered the position of squadron CO. Of course, none of the crew chiefs cared for Major Bridger because he found every excuse he could not to fly into a hot LZ when he flew lead aircraft, and because he flew so goddamn high, you could not see the earth when he was flying the chase aircraft.

G.O. had never flown with him, but the Gerber Baby, Blaze, and the Scrotum all swore he could fly a piano through a keyhole. They claimed he was an excellent pilot. At this time, Major Bridger was being a major pain by inspecting everything to make sure that the squadron was perfect before Lieutenant Colonel Van Meter arrived. Even had Pogo painting all the three-holers on the compound.

Colonel Blue kept pretty much to himself. Colonel Blue was a diminutive man whose greatest love was birding. Both he and the squadron's Sergeant Major went on birding expeditions every week and now that the squadron was getting a new CO, they were gone damn near every day. And the day before the change of command was to take place, they had flown to Marble Mountain because they had a report that a Red-Footed Booby had been spotted there. *Jeez,* G.O. thought, *I wouldn't mind finding a couple of those Red-Footed Boobies.*

✦ ✦ ✦

About all that Hill could find out about Lieutenant Colonel Van Meter was that he was a Phantom driver before the Marine Corps moved him over to 46s and gave him a squadron. The only rumors that he had heard was that Lieutenant Colonel Van Meter had augured a Phantom in on an approach in Beaufort, South Carolina, and somehow survived it. G.O., in his full-tilt James Dean mode, didn't really care. Still, there was a lot of anxiety going around the squadron about what kind of commander he would be.

After the formation held to welcome the new C.O., the troops were supposed to retire to the soccer field and have some brews in celebration. Somehow Major Bridger had secured a whole trailer full of iced-down beer (beer, yes! But iced beer...who'd believe it in the land of boom-boom?), and the Marines of HMM-265 could not wait to be dismissed to party.

✦ ✦ ✦

The day of the change of command ceremony, G.O. had been sent to Quang Tri with the Scrotum to pick up some spare parts. The Scrotum, being from New Jersey, and G.O., being from Texas, quickly got on each other's nerves. It wasn't just that the Scrotum blatantly lied; he lied about crap that was transparently a lie. *If Scrotum lived in the South, he would have to move if he couldn't lie any better than that,* G.O. mused, *but if he had grown up in the South, he could lie a whole lot better than he's been doing.* Scrotum had just finished telling G.O. that his dad took him to Rome to meet Pope Paul VI, and what a swell guy he was as they both walked over to the Quang Tri supply depot from the flight line.

"Lemme tell ya, Hill, da Pope had this awful fucken ax-cent, and I cudden unnerstan' a fucken woid. I mean fuhgeddaboudit!"

He's not the only one, G.O. thought.

"Wha' da fuk issup witch yew, Hill? Yew ain't hardly said a fucken woid since we got heah."

"Oh, haven't had a lot to say, Scrotum, man. How about you go on over to the club and I'll pick up the parts and meet you over there?"

"Yeah, sounds gud, all dis fucken tawking is wearin' me down. I cud use a couple a beeahs!"

"Fuhgeddaboudit."

"Fuk, Hill, I'm startin' to unnerstan' youse."

G.O. walked on over to supply depot, triplicate forms in hand, and was met by one of the myriad clerks that exist in the Marine Corps whose primary goal in life is to make the lives of other Marines miserable. Of course, they have a variety of weapons at their disposal that could be just as deadly as the fifty caliber Hill used on the 46. But the clerks didn't destroy you physically, just mentally. In the corps, the clerks were referred to as Remington Raiders. They could change your entire life with a few keystrokes on their Remingtons or could misplace your pay voucher in their unique filing system or could cut surreptitious orders for you to be sent to the Island with No Name. Clerks were not to be trifled with.

"Excuse me, Corporal," G.O. said to the clerk as he worked judiciously at his typewriter.

The lance corporal looked up and stopped typing. "I'm a *lance* corporal, were you talking to me?"

"Well, you won't be a lance corporal long," G.O. responded. "Someone is bound to notice your speed and efficiency on that typewriter before long."

The lance corporal stood, adjusted his pink-rimmed Marine Corps glasses, and came over to the counter that G.O. was standing behind.

"Something I can help you with, Marine?"

"Oh, I'm sorry to interrupt. I didn't mean for you to stop typing. I was just enjoying the air conditioning and was amazed at your dexterity on that typewriter!"

"Thank you, Marine. You know, some people just don't appreciate how difficult it is to be a clerk in the Marine Corps. We get all the navy's worn-out old equipment, and half the typewriters we do get are missing keys. It's just very, very difficult to be a clerk. It is so nice to meet someone who understands."

Later, at the Quang Tri E club, G.O. told a very tipsy Scrotum how he had not only been able to get all the parts they needed, but also had managed to get them delivered to the aircraft and loaded.

"What? Didja have ta blow da fucken clerk?"

"No, I told him you would let him be a door gunner sometimes when we were up this way."

"Naw, you din'int?

"Fair trade, Scrotum, we can get back in time for the beer bash, now. All we have to do is find the pilots and tell 'em we are loaded and ready to boogie."

"Fuk, Hill, ya know a deal can gitya killed in Jerzee."

"Hey, pard...do you think it's safe where we are now?"

"Yeah, yeah...point taken."

On their way out of the club, Hill and Scrotum headed toward Officer Country to find their pilot and copilot. As they started toward the O club, they heard the first explosion.

"Hey, this way, Scrotum, there's a bunker over here!"

G.O. and Scrotum started running madly toward they first bunker they saw as they heard the second and third explosions.

As the two orangutans burst through the entrance of the bunker, they were met by two rather large, foreboding Marines toting M-16s.

"Hold up, Marines!" One of the guards ordered. "You are going to have to leave. This is the S-2 Bunker, for Intelligence personnel only, and you are not allowed in here."

Explosions four and five. "Hell, we ain't going back out there!"

From the far end of the dimly lit bunker, G.O. could make out a large map table with three officers standing around it. One of them, a colonel, had a pointer in his hand. The three were staring at G.O. and the Scrotum.

Explosions six and seven.

Finally, the colonel spoke. "They can stay, Sergeant, just put them somewhere out of the way and tell them to keep quiet. We are trying to work here."

"Aye-aye, sir. OK, you two can sit in the corner over there," the sergeant said, pointing to a corner of the bunker by the map table.

G.O. and Scrotum, feeling about as welcome as the breeze from the outhouse, sat on the dirt floor of the bunker and listened to the explosions and the discussion that ensued around the map table.

The colonel walked down to the far end of the map table and pointed at a position on the map. "Well, gentlemen, my best guess is that Charlie has mortars placed somewhere in this area, to be hitting us with this kind of accuracy."

"Sir," the major said, "the explosions we are hearing sound more like rockets, but I'm not sure. What do you think, Captain?"

"I think the major is right, Colonel. They do sound like rockets."

More explosions. Getting closer.

The colonel turned to a radio operator nearby and said, "Have you heard anything from our observation posts, son?"

"No, sir, no communications at this time."

"Well, gentlemen, you may be the two dumbest intelligence officers I have ever known. Those are goddamn mortar rounds if I've ever heard one."

"Yes, sir, after listening more closely, I believe the colonel is correct," said the major.

"I'm in complete agreement with the colonel's assessment," said the captain.

"Now, I'm not saying those are mortar rounds; I'm saying they *sound* like mortar rounds," the colonel clarified.

"Yes sir, we are in agreement with the colonel," said the major.

"Excuse me, sir," said the radio operator, "I'm receiving communications now from one of our forward observers."

"Well, go on, son, what's he saying?"

"He says they have identified the position that the rockets are being launched from and are calling in artillery now."

"Rockets? Did the FO say Rockets?" the colonel asked.

"Yes, sir. He said rockets."

"Distinctly?"

"Yes, sir, distinctly."

"Well, that's exactly what I told you gentlemen, rockets. It is just like Charlie to have developed rockets that sound just like mortars."

"Yes, sir," said the major, "they are devious little bastards."

"Roger that," said the captain.

"Did the forward observer tell you the position of the rockets, son?"

"Yes, sir he gave me these coordinates," the radio operator said as he handed the colonel a sheet of paper.

The Colonel looked at the coordinates then walked to the opposite end of the map table. The major and the captain followed along.

"Just as I thought," said the colonel, and pointed at the coordinates given to him. The major and the captain nodded sagely at the colonel.

G.O. looked over at Scrotum who just shrugged and mouthed the word FUBAR.

G.O. grinned and nodded his agreement with the Scrotum's observation. *Jeez, I've come all the way to Vietnam to die in a command bunker where no one has a clue about what's happening. Story of my life.*

The rocket attack was over almost as soon as it had started. G.O. and the Scrotum couldn't wait to get out of the bunker and back to the flight line to see if their aircraft had any damage.

When they arrived, the pilot, Lieutenant Abramovitz was walking around the aircraft looking for damage.

"Didja find any damage, sir?" Scrotum asked.

"No crew chief, but you and Hill might want to have a look around while Lieutenant Kelly and I get the aircraft preflighted. We want to get back for the squadron party ASAP."

"Aye-aye, sir!" the happy duo responded.

Chapter Eighteen

Of Cabbages and Kings...

Hill and Scrotum made it back to Hue-Phu Bai with time to spare. After refueling and shutting the aircraft down, Hill picked up a bag, and then he and Scrotum strolled to the line shack to see what kind of maintenance problems the pilot had left on the bitch sheet. As they walked in, Gunny G. greeted them with his usual bark. "Where the fuck have you two been? Did you pick up the parts that were ordered? How'd you get back so damn quick? Did you have to blow one of the clerks?"

"Jeez, Gunny," Scrotum began, "we wuz jus' followin' orders. The pahts are in da aircraft and I don' know if Hill blowed da clerk up dere at Quang Tri...but I'm kinda suspicious."

"Well, Hill?" the Gunny asked, "what kind of deal did you have to make?"

"Not much Gunny, Scrotum has to take the guy flying next time he's up Quang Tri way. But I do have a little surprise for you," G.O. said as he set the bag he had been carrying on the line shack counter.

"What's this?" Gunny G. asked as he opened the bag. "Well, I'll be goddamned, parts for the inside of the coffee pot! That's genius, Hill, pure genius. I've been pissing up a rope trying to get parts for that damn coffee pot for six months and a goddamn commie bastard managed it in one trip. How did you do it, Hill?"

"Well, when the clerk took the forms to supply and I was waiting for him to return, I noticed they had a coffee pot just like yours, so I..."

"Enough!" the Gunny barked. "I don't want to hear about any kind of theft, no matter how warranted it might have been. It would make me an accomplice to petty theft and I might be locked up with your genius ass in a Conex box. Let me add...how delighted I am that you were able to talk a supply clerk into *legally* issuing our squadron the insides of a coffee pot...clear."

"Clear, Gunny."

"Now, you have been here, what? Two weeks? I would say you are checked out enough to have your own bird. So tomorrow you start crewing Dupree's old aircraft, *Groundz*. We clear?"

G.O. couldn't help but smile. "Clear, Gunny."

"Well, what the fuck you standing around for? You two idiots have a squadron formation to make in fifteen minutes, so get the hell out of here and get your boot asses squared away before Major Bridger sees you. For crying out loud, you two look like you were in the shitter when lightning struck."

◆ ◆ ◆

G.O. and Scrotum made it back for the squadron formation on the flight line with time to spare. The Gunny called the squadron to attention when the CO, the XO, and the sergeant major marched up to the front of the formation. The CO and the sergeant major were both diminutive men in their physical appearance. *The odd thing,* G.O. thought, *is that I have never seen their faces, just like today. They have shadows covering their faces. And I have never heard them speak. Odd.* Major Bridger, on the other hand, was a rather large presence wherever he was. *Christ,* G.O. thought, *if he ever has to haul ass, it'll take him two trips. Dumb fucker blames everything on a lack of discipline. Like he knows what that is. He ought to try pushing his big ass away from the chow line. Idiot, couldn't knock a hole in the wind with a bagful of hammers.* Major Bridger stepped out front and began haranguing the troops in his high tinny voice.

"Let me tell you, gentlemen, this is the shabbiest Marine formation I have ever seen. Attention! Dress right, *dress*!" The squadron straightened up even more and right arms shot out to the shoulder of the person on the right, then looking to his right, that person aligned himself accordingly. "Ready...front!" Arms came down and heads snapped back to the front. "The new CO, Colonel Van Meter, is still delayed in Da Nang and will not be reporting in until later in the week. Colonel Blue thinks that because of all the hard work you have put in this past week that we should go ahead with the squadron party."

From the back of the formation came a tremendous roar as though Major Bridger had just scored the winning touchdown. "Goddamnit, you are at attention! There will be no yelling and screaming when you are at attention. You are the most undisciplined group I have ever seen. I've been here six months and you just get worse. No one in this squadron ever gets a haircut. You are the shaggiest bunch of Marines in the I Corp. And those uniforms. God, but you are a disgrace, I can smell you a click away...and those boots! Christ almighty! No discipline. It as plain as the nose on your face...No discipline! Well, that shit is about to change, gentlemen..."

As Major Bridger was getting wound up, the CO whispered something to the sergeant major. The sergeant major grabbed Major Bridger by the sleeve, and the major stopped in midsentence and went over and huddled with the sergeant major and the CO. After a subdued argument, a red-faced Major Bridger came back to the squadron. "Squadron," he bellowed to a formation already at attention, "when you are dismissed you will report to the soccer field where the squadron party will commence immediately...Dis-s-s-s-missed!" There were a few indistinct "aye-aye, sirs," but many more replies of "who does that motherfucker think he is?" spoken softly and out of the major's hearing range. The irate members of the squadron cast murderous glances at Major Bridger as they made their way from the flight line to the soccer field.

◆ ◆ ◆

G.O. stopped by the mess hall to check on Locker on his way to the soccer field, but the staff sergeant on duty said he was at sick bay. G.O. thought, as he stopped like the fabled Atalanta and picked up an apple on the way out of the chow hall, *I bet he's already at the party.* When G.O. arrived, most of the crew were gathered inside a makeshift pavilion that some disgruntled Seabee was ordered to erect. The melodious voices of the Four Tops wafted through the area as a few of the crew tried to sing-along with the Sugar Bear.

"Damn, Bugman, you have to sing? You ruinin' the harmony, my brother."

"Fuck you, Bear. You know I can't sing this shit. How come you don't play any Hank Williams or Johnny Cash?"

"Oo-o-h-h," the Bear replied, "they would take away my membership in the NAACP if I were to let somebody with cow shit in his voice sing on a black man's tape deck, you understand what I'm saying, Bugman?" The Bear laughed as he went through a series of intricate maneuvers as he slapped hands with the only other African American in the squadron.

"Yeah, well I know that's another *ratio* statement from someone who claims he don't like discriminatin' peoples."

"It ain't no *ray-shull* statement, my Tennessee brother. It just that a black man never could listen to his music around you white dudes before, you see, now he can."

"Well, how 'bout playing something different?"

"OK, how do you like this one?"

The Supremes were cranked up to full volume as they started with "Stop! In the Name of Love." And everyone joined in, except for Major Bridger who just kept giving everyone the stink eye.

After going to the trailer for his second beer, G.O. looked around and noticed that most of the officers had already left. Colonel Blue was walking around and actually saying good-bye to different members of the squadron. G.O. sat at a picnic table with several of the short time crew chiefs and listened to them grouse about having to stand in formation every day.

"Yeah, that crazy Bridger can stand out in the fucken sun, but I got work I been needin' to do on my bird for over a week."

"Yeah, the next thing you know, he'll want everybody in clean flight suits every morning."

"Has anybody told Major Motherfucker that this is a fucken war?"

"You're right, he acts like he's back in the states. If he'd been here during Tet, somebody would've fragged his ass."

"You got that right," they all agreed.

Then they all looked suspiciously toward G.O. as if he might report them to Major Bridger.

"Yeah, Hill, you poor dumb bastards will have to put up with his shit now. Me, I'm outa here in seven days and a wake-up.'

"Yeah, Hill, he will have y'all washing your birds so they smell good."

"He's so dumb he probably doesn't know that you can't wash that smell out."

"He ought to get a whiff of one of Chucky D.'s Hawaiian sunsets."

They all had a great Laugh. About this time one of the short-timers looked around and asked, "Hey, where's the beer trailer?"

While they had been talking, Major Bridger had waited until Colonel Blue and the sergeant major left, then told everyone the party was over. The major then climbed into the jeep and drove off with what remained of the beer in the trailer. Instant revolution. Tempers flared at the thought of a party ending after two beers. The lifers tried to keep everyone calm and even suggested going over to the E club to have a few more brews. When they finally decided they weren't getting anywhere with the group, they started wandering away, back to their quarters. Soon, only the revolutionaries were left at the pavilion. G.O. didn't really consider himself a revolutionary but he did think of himself a part of the group. No, it was more than that. G.O. felt like he had *earned* his right to be part of this very select group of warriors.

"Well, what the fuck is up with that?"

"Now we know who the Walrus is."

"Walrus? What are you talking about?"

"You know like in the Beatle's song, 'I Am the Walrus,' Major Bridger is the Walrus."

"Oh, yeah? So, tell me, professor, how is Major Bridger the Walrus?"

G.O. listened with intense interest as the professor explained, "Well, Lennon allegedly took the title from Lewis Carroll's poem, "The Walrus and the Carpenter" from Carroll's book, *Through the Looking-Glass.* So, anyway, in the poem, the Walrus invites all these oysters to a party and when they show up he devours them. The Walrus was a predator. He didn't give a shit about the oysters; all he cared about was what they could do for him. Therefore, I say to you, Bridger equals Walrus, *comprende stupido*?"

"Yeah, I get it. And from now on Major Bridger is the Walrus...goo, goo, g'joob!"

They all laughed. G.O. laughed along with them, not really knowing why. He wasn't quite ready to give up on the Walrus, as unpleasant a lifer as he had ever come across.

◆ ◆ ◆

Walking back to the barracks, G.O. heard a jeep coming up behind him and instinctively glanced back as he moved to the side of the road. It was the Bugman. Driving the Walrus's jeep. And pulling a trailer full of iced-down beer.

"Christ on a fucken crutch, Bugman, what have you done?"

"Well, I was walking through Officer's Country and guess what I found parked in front of Major Bridger's hooch?"

"Let me guess...a Shetland pony?"

"No, man, I found this jeep full of beer..."

"I know you found this jeep parked there, dumb ass. I was being facetious."

"Oh. You wanna go for a ride. I was headed to the barracks to give the rest of the beer to the guys."

"What I think you had better do, is ditch the Walrus's jeep, and pray that no one has seen you driving around in it."

"OK, but first, let's drop the beer off at the barracks, and then I promise I'll ditch the jeep."

G.O. second-guessed himself and got in with the Bugman and popped a beer as they headed for the barracks. No sooner had they distributed the beer than Sergeant Poppycock Emetic, the NCOIC (Non-Commissioned Officer in Charge) of the toolroom whom everyone called PC, came up and wanted to know if Major Bridger was in the barracks. Apparently, he had seen the jeep parked out front. G.O. and Bugman sent him to the back of the barracks, and while Sergeant PC was chasing the proverbial goose, the two desperadoes made their escape.

"Damn, that was close, Bugman. Let's get rid of this jeep and trailer before we end up in a Conex box."

"OK, but I'll tell you what...that fucken lifer, PC, better not turn us in."

"Dude, listen to me...let's get rid of the jeep. We will worry about getting caught later."

The two decided it would be best to park the jeep outside HMM-265's headquarters...in a spot reserved for Major Bridger. Only fitting. Imagine his surprise when he got to work the next day.

◆ ◆ ◆

The next morning, G.O. and the Bugman were told to report to the sergeant major's office. On their way in, Sergeant PC was on his way out. *Oh shit,* G.O. thought, *this does not bode well for the two of us.* As they walked up to the sergeant major's door, G.O. pounded on the door the customary three times and then in his best gravelly Marine Corps voice growled, "Sir, Corporal Hill and Lance Corporal York reporting as ordered, sir!"

Then from within, came the booming voice of Gunny G., "Enter, you fucken morons!"

G.O. and the Bugman marched in and stood at attention in front of the sergeant major's desk. Gunny G. sat next to the sergeant major and just glowered at the two, daring either one to speak.

"All right, we know what happened. Now which of you wants to go first?" the Gunny said, knowing only part of the tale and hoping for the rest of the story.

"Gunny, if I may?"

"Go on, Hill."

Before G.O. could stop himself, he decided to take the rap for both of them. "It was all my idea, Gunny."

"Go on."

"Well, after Major Bridger drove off with the beer, some of the guys were still wanting to party. I remarked that if I knew where he had driven off to, I would go and pick up the beer. So, the Bugman, sorry Gunny, Lance Corporal York, says he knows where the major went. So we walked over to Officer Country, found the jeep and the beer, and drove back to the barracks. After we dropped off the beer, we parked the jeep at headquarters so Major Bridger would find it this morning."

As G.O. stood there at a very nervous attention, the Gunny and Sergeant Major were whispering back and forth, but G.O. could not hear anything they were saying. Finally, the Gunny looked up and said, "Lance Corporal York, you are being transferred to HMH-463 at Marble Mountain. So, pack up your gear son, you're on the next flight out of here."

"Corporal Hill, the sergeant major thinks it best for you to report to the mess hall for thirty days' mess duty. I, personally, think you should be busted down to e-nothing and be sent to Long Binh for a little jail time. Do you remember our little discussion about decision making when you first arrived, Hill? Don't answer that; it was a rhetorical question, dumbass. So, you are to report for mess duty when you leave here, understand? And every day you are there, I want you to think about the decisions you will make in the future."

"Yes, sir...thank you, sir!"

As the two left the sergeant major's office, Bugman said, "Damn, son, what got into you? Taking the fall for us like that? Are you out of your mind?"

"I don't know, Bugman, why don't we just leave it at...I lost my mind. Good luck to you on those fifty-threes. I hear they are mystical aircraft."

"Well, good luck to you to G.O., I just hate having to miss Billy Graham. He's going to be here during Christmas, you know."

Well, hell, G.O. thought, *at least there's one good thing about mess duty, no Billy-fucken-Graham.*

♦ ♦ ♦

After G.O. and the Bugman had left, Gunny G. shook his head and told the sergeant major, "Well, Phil, thanks. I owe you one. This war is one terrible fucken disaster when kids like those two are thrown into a situation that they don't have a clue about. Back in the World both of them would have been busted and then spent time in the brig, but here, we need crew chiefs. But not just any kind of crew chief, we need hard-charging young warriors. I just hope those two idiots live long enough to make it back and if anything does happen to them...I pray that they behave like Marines. What's that, Phil? Right, I agree, Hill has a lot of potential, and like you I have no idea why he lied for Lance Corporal York. If York knew that Major Bridger was sitting in the shitter and watched him drive off with his jeep, he'd probably have a mild cardiac arrest." They both guffawed. "OK, Phil let me see those pictures you took of the Pale-Blue Flycatcher when you and Colonel Blue were down in Da Nang."

♦ ♦ ♦

Later that day a grenade went off in a bunker located outside of Sergeant P.C. Emetic's barracks room. PC jumped up so quickly when he heard the blast, he busted his head on the metal bed he in which he slept. Later, he would be awarded a Purple Heart for injuries sustained during a mortar barrage. Investigators said the mortar round must have somehow bounced into the bunker before exploding. Twenty minutes after the 'incident,' a CH-46 left Hue-Phu Bai for Marble Mountain carrying the Bugman.

Chapter Nineteen

Ly Cu Chi

Ly Cu Chi was born out of wedlock. Her mother had been seventeen and her father, a French civil servant in Hue City. When her mother became pregnant, her father was recalled to France. After Cu Chi was born, the family had insisted that she be given up for adoption, but her mother would not hear of it. Instead, her mother chose to marry a farmer in a small village not far from Hue.

She bore the farmer several children, but her favorite was always little Chrysanthemum, much to the farmer's dismay. It seemed as though each day the farmer found a reason to chastise little Cu Chi for various and unexplained reasons. In 1954, when Cu Chi was ten years old, her stepfather went to fight with Ho Chi Minh and the Viet Minh forces at Dien Bien Phu. The battle ended French domination in Vietnam, but it also took the life of Cu Chi's stepfather and left her mother to raise a family of six boys and one girl.

The children were too young to properly run the farm, so Cu Chi's mother was left with one alternative: to sell the farm and beg forgiveness from her family in Hue. The family would accept Cu Chi's mother and siblings but not her. Her mother was forced to make a decision. She sold Cu Chi to an elderly scholar in Saigon who was in need of a bright young assistant. Her mother did not know the elderly scholar was a procurer of women for a notorious brothel in Saigon.

The brothel was called the White House and was located close to the Rue Catinat where the new Caravelle Hotel was being erected directly across the square from the Continental Palace. Ly was given to the brothel's most popular courtesan, Ho Bich, as a servant and to learn the trade of prostitution. Ho Bich wished to be called Madam Jade when being addressed by others in the brothel. Anytime Cu Chi forgot, Madam Jade beat her severely with a bamboo cane as a gentle reminder. Cu Chi was made to sit in a hidden room and watch as Madam Jade entertained her visitors.

As the years slowly passed, the young women of the White House could not help but notice that Cu Chi was becoming more beautiful as each day passed. Madam Jade became more resentful as each day passed and never missed an opportunity to beat Cu Chi. However, Madame Jade had the foresight to only take the stick to Cu Chi's back where the marks would not show. Madame Jade was also smart enough to keep Cu Chi out of Mr. Troung's sight, the owner of the brothel.

Madame Jade knew that if Mr. Troung laid eyes upon Cu Chi, she would lose her servant, and in all likelihood, Cu Chi would become the most popular courtesan in the White House. It was at this time that Cu Chi's only friend at the White House, Hung Kim, an older courtesan, plotted with her a way that she might be brought to Mr. Troung's attention.

"Are you sure this is not poison, Madame Kim?"

"Oh, yes, child…these are just some local herbs that, when mixed with Madame Jade's tea, will make her very sick…hee, hee, hee…very, very sick. When she is sick, she will call you for help. This is when you must run and find Mr. Troung. Mr. Troung will call for me to help, and while I am helping poor little Jade…he will not be able to take his eyes off of you!"

Later in the day, it had gone as Hung Kim had planned. Mr. Troung became angry at Madame Jade for hiding such a precious jewel as Cu Chi from his sight and threatened to beat her severely with her very own cane. This was an act that Cu Chi had not bargained for but nonetheless anticipated with glee. Madame Jade was retching so violently that Mr. Troung finally relented on beating her until she regained her senses. However,

Kim was right about Mr. Troung; he could not keep his eyes off of Cu Chi. Ly could not help but notice that Mr. Troung's little *chim* seemed to be growing in his pants.

Mr. Troung would have Ly Cu Chi, but not before he capitalized on her virginity. As fate would have it, the new Hotel Caravelle would be opening on Christmas Eve 1959, and there would be men who would pay ten or even fifteen thousand piastres (P's) for Ly Cu Chi's virginity!

Yes, he would have her, but after he became a wealthy man. The opening was still a month away, and there was still much to do in preparation for the "auction." Each day began with Ly Cu Chi sitting naked in front of a full-length mirror while Hung Kim brushed her hair and talked about the many different types of men she had known. Cu Chi was a most striking seventeen-year-old Vietnamese woman. She had retained many of the French genes that had been passed on to her, and she possessed a commingling of the best traits of the Vietnamese and the French.

Most faces are not symmetrical; some may have one ear lower than another, or one eye may be a different shape. Sometimes the differences are so slight that they are not noticeable, like one cheek being slightly larger than the other. Ly Cu Chi's face possessed a perfect lateral symmetry and a very healthy appearance. Cu Chi's skin contained the small pores of Asian women but the light skin and healthy glow of the Northern European. Her eyes were more rounded than most Vietnamese, and her nose tended to be more pug, button-like, than the broad fleshy noses of most Asian women. Her lips were full but not too thick, and she exuded an animal magnetism that both men and women were drawn to, like moths to the flame. But Ly Cu Chi was much more than a beautiful, petite Eurasian woman. She was endowed with remarkable feminine intuition and could look into the hearts of others and know their true feelings and desires. Cu Chi was genuinely bewitching.

"You must never find fault with the man, Cu Chi. You must only praise him."

"Even if there is nothing praiseworthy?"

"Yes, especially if there is nothing praiseworthy. Many of the least praiseworthy men I have known became very benevolent benefactors to the courtesans who pleased them most. Sometimes you do not need to speak at all, just listen. You can communicate many things to a man by a slight adjustment in a facial feature."

"What do you mean, Kim-san?"

"When he tells you that you are beautiful, no matter how boring or how many times you may have heard it…a look of modest surprise will tell him that this is the first time anyone has ever paid you this compliment. By not speaking, the man must interpret the look. If done properly, he will interpret that he is the first to pay you this obvious compliment. Here, let us practice before this looking glass."

"Ly Cu Chi…you are so beautiful…" Hung Kim said, mocking Mr. Troung. While Cu Chi turned her chin slightly up and to the right and opened her eyes slightly wider and pouted her lips.

"Ey-e-i-i, child…too much!" Kim said as she whacked Cu Chi playfully with the hairbrush. "The movements must be more subtle. You seduce with the looks. You do not frighten the man!" On and on they practiced, day after day, until Cu Chi had mastered the art of nonverbal facial communications.

As well as her instructions in the courtesan arts, she was tutored daily by Master Ma. Master Ma was the stereotypical Asian tutor. He had a white goatee with a wispy white Confucian mustache. With Master Ma, Cu Chi practiced her French, read Vietnamese, Chinese, and French poetry, and she studied philosophy. She loved her French lessons most. The French Cu Chi learned from her mother when she was a little girl on the farm was quite a bit different than the French spoken in the elegant salons of Paris. Most of all she loved Master Ma. When she tried to use her newly acquired feminine strategies on him, he merely smiled and shook his tired old head, and he would say, "I have already experienced Nirvana, child, please to answer question." On the first of December, Master Ma and Hung Kim announced that Ly Cu Chi was ready.

◆ ◆ ◆

Mr. Troung could not believe his good fortune. Indubitably the gods favored him. Ly Cu Chi's virginity had been sold to a French businessman who was staying at the Hotel Caravelle during its grand opening.

◆ ◆ ◆

Andre Dubonnet was on the board of Air France and was one of its largest coinvestors. Mr. Dubonnet had paid fifty-thousand P (piastres) for the pleasure of deflowering Ly Cu Chi. Andre Dubonnet was sixty-two years old, with a full head of gray hair combed back in the fashion of the 1920s. Andre was a French flying ace and had flown a Spad during the First World War. During the 1920s he competed on the Olympic bobsledding team, and he spent time racing cars, and at sixty-two, Mr. Dubonnet, in the prime of his life, was smitten with a seventeen-year-old girl. Later, in Dubonnet's suite, a nervous Cu Chi had removed her clothes and sat on the bed with Mr. Dubonnet. He leaned down and kissed her gently on the lips. This she was not expecting. She had never seen Ho Bich kiss a client. But it was most pleasant. She was quite surprised by her new feelings. Hung Kim had told her many times not to envision being pleasured by a man, that her job was to give pleasure to the man.

Andre gently lifted her face to his and stared at her while she puzzled over which nuanced facial expression she should be using, she could only stare back into his haunting blue eyes. Eyes that had seen so much. He leaned down for another kiss, one that she was anticipating. She saw his eyes close and his lips part. She parted her lips as Andre drew her to him. Then she felt his tongue slip delicately and knowingly into her mouth. She reached her small arms around him and gently caressed his back as she drew imaginary feathery pictures there with her nails. Soon, he had lifted her in his strong arms and laid her gently on the bed.

Andre removed his clothes and climbed into bed beside her. His kisses became warmer as he moved to her petite breasts. She felt her head filling with the heat of passion and could no longer control her body as she writhed beneath his gentle kisses. Slowly, he moved downward to her stomach, gently kissing. Hung Kim had not prepared her for this passion.

Charles L. Templeton

As Andre's heated breath fell gently on her engorged *am vat*, she was ready to scream. Then his tongue darted into her secret place and softly caressed her hooded lady as she released a primal moan. She had never experienced such ecstasy.

◆ ◆ ◆

They had spent the night exploring each other's bodies and experiencing every kind of sex that she thought Mr. Dubonnet would enjoy. Losing her virginity was not as problematic as Hung Kim had explained and much more pleasurable than she expected. She had even offered him entry into the Chrysanthemum Gate, which he had thoroughly enjoyed although it was so painful for her.

She had dressed and was waiting for Mr. Troung's knock at the door. Mr. Troung would teach her the barbarous and obscene perspectives on sex. Ly Cu Chi would become the most sought-after courtesan at the White House. As the war in the south started heating up in the early 1960s and more American advisors came to Vietnam, the Hotel Caravelle filled with journalists, photographers, and many high-ranking soldiers. The Americans did not appreciate the courtesans as much as the French or Vietnamese. They just wanted whores. Something to stick their little chims in. But they paid very well. In fact, so well that Ly Cu Chi and Hung Kim were slowly accumulating enough money to buy their freedom from Mr. Troung.

In 1965 a bomb went off in the Caravelle that destroyed three floors. Mr. Troung and one of the younger courtesans had been killed in the blast. Cu Chi and Kim both felt pity for the young courtesan. This was an opportunity for Cu Chi and Kim to leave Saigon and go to Hue City. In Hue City, they opened the Congress, an infamous brothel that covered an entire city block. There was a club for black Americans on one street, one for white soldiers on another side road, one for Vietnamese, and of course, one for officers. Each night the girls rotated clubs. If a specific girl was called for, she could just walk through a few hallways to get to the club where she had been requested.

During the Tet Offensive in 1968, the Congress was leveled along with Ly Cu Chi. Hung Kim had been in a neighboring village visiting relatives. When she returned, she was devastated. She and some of the girls who survived moved into an abandoned French villa next to the Congress. Hung Kim visited with a Marine colonel that Ly Cu Chi had entertained on occasion and as a result, was able to procure a job as the head mama-san at the Marine Air Facility at Hue-Phu Bai. Kim's post allowed her to hire any of the former courtesans who chose to work in a different profession. Hung Kim was also able to talk the Catholic Church into opening the Ly Cu Chi Orphanage where the old Congress had previously stood. Hung Kim and the former courtesans of the Congress provided the necessary funds to keep the orphanage running.

Chapter Twenty

Our Lady of Hue

G.O. had been on mess duty for almost one week. He had developed a routine where he awoke each morning at 3:30 a.m., took care of his morning ablutions, and was in the mess hall by 4:00 a.m. He was usually back in the barracks by 8:00 p.m. in the evenings. After the first week, he had managed to stay up until 10:00 or 11:00 in the evenings. God, how he yearned to be flying.

About once every three or four days, G.O. had noticed something strange when he went to shave. Someone had taken a red marker and drawn a line from G.O.'s left ear, across his throat, to his right ear. *Damnedest thing,* G.O. thought as he stood shaving in front of the mirror in the showers. *You would think you could feel someone drawing on you with a marker.* G.O. had relentlessly tried to catch the culprit but always fell into a deep slumber before the phantom butcher came calling. As he and Locker walked toward the mess hall, he told Locker about the mysterious red line on his throat every morning.

Locker chuckled and told G.O., "Oh man, I should've told you. You know Jack, the Indian? Redfeather? Yeah, well when he drinks too much he will sneak around the barracks pretending to cut the white man's throat. Jack calls it 'counting coup.' Anyway, it wasn't a problem when the Bugman was here. When Jackson got drunk, the Bugman would just tie his hands and feet to his bunk. But now, sounds like he's on the warpath again. I guess we'll just have to start tying his ass up again."

"What you mean 'we,' white man?"

"You are doing it again, Hill."

"Doing what?"

"Stereotyping people, dumbass! *What'cha mean 'we' white man? What the hell is that*, if it's not making fun of Redfeather and American indians?"

"Hey, Locker man, I didn't mean to make fun of anyone, especially not Redfeather. I just like the way he talks."

"You mean like, *imitation is the sincerest form of flattery*?"

"Yeah, that's what I'm trying to say."

"That dog won't hunt, Hill. Have you ever thought that Redfeather speaks that way because he is making fun of the way white men portrayed Indians in the movies? Maybe he is making fun of the way the white man makes fun of him?"

"Not so sure I follow that logic, Locker."

"Redfeather is a master of subtlety and parody, Hill. If you would sit down and get to know him, you would know he sailed solo to Hawaii when he was fourteen and has sailed some of the toughest passages of ocean in the world. He is a potential qualifier for the Olympics. Now, do you think a man that has sailed the seven seas and is a master mariner talks like a movie Indian?"

"Well, er, ah..."

"Don't answer that. Hill. It was rhetorical. I'm just saying that you need to visit with Redfeather, get to know him. Then, you will know that his humor is aimed at the movie industry for creating the stereotype of the American Indian. The way Redfeather speaks in public, Hill, is a parody of a parody. And, if you get to know him, he might quit counting coup on you."

As the two walked into the chow hall, they went their separate ways, Locker to his grill and G.O. to the food preparation area. Locker spent his morning frying eggs to order in the Officers' mess while G.O. went to the pot shack, which he thought was appropriately named.

The pot shack was where all metal cooking pots and pans came to be cleaned and steamed. Some really inventive Seabee had rigged up a steam-cleaning machine that would make Rube Goldberg extremely proud. G.O. had two PFCs that worked for him in the pot shack. When they weren't patching holes in helicopters or painting them, they were used as door gunners on various missions. Seemed to G.O. that everybody wanted to fly.

When they finally got the steam machine cranked up, they would begin on the pots the night cooking crew left piled outside. The pot shack was actually just a screened-in shed. When the steam started pouring out of the place, the two PFCs would light up a doobie of questionable origin and proceed to stay high most of the day. No one ever came to the pot shack. It was filled with heated water vapor most of the day. G.O. found that he became mentally challenged when he got high early in the day, so he usually maintained until quitting time when he too would have a toke or three on some very potent Vietnamese herb. He also found that he could actually function the next day. When he went to the E club and drank too much, the next day was absolute hell, as he walked around in a lethargic comatose state. Yes, the herb was a blessing. All hail the herb.

When the two PFCs had loaded up a serving cart with pots and pans and anything else the cooks had sent to be cleaned, he would push it through the chow hall to the food prep area. Along the way, he would stop and swap insults with his squadron mates and catch up on the latest scuttlebutt. Sugar Bear was sitting at a table with, Scrotum, Barf, and Andrew Jackson Redfeather.

"G.O., man, how you like flying them shiny pots and pans around the mess hall on that raggedy-assed cart?" the Bear queried.

"It's a little slow on takeoff, Sir Bear, but it hovers like a dream."

About this time Pogo walked up and said, "Can I have your froot?" Pogo had been sent to mess duty the day after G.O. When the new CO, Colonel Van Meter, finally arrived the day after the now notorious party, the first thing he noticed was that someone had painted "I Like Dope" on the tops of all the shitters. Gunny G.'s powers of deduction led him to believe the culprit might be the same person he assigned to paint the shitters.

"Wha-tha-fuk-issup-witch-yew? Yew makin' sum homebrew?"

"No, the froot is for the chow hall mama-san."

Pogo now had the entire table interested. "Why would the mama-san want our fruit, Pogo? There's way too much for her to eat."

"No, no, no! G.O., she doesn't want to eat thees froots. She takes them to the orfanse."

"Orfanse, you mean orphans?"

"Oui, oui, oui! Orphans, yes. She takes the froots to the orphans."

Jack handed Pogo an apple off his tray and mumbled something unintelligible.

"Wha' da fuk, Jackson? You not fallin' for this crap, are ya? That ol' bitch is probably sellin' dem apples out in the ville. She ain't gettin' mine."

"Well, what do you think G.O.? You work with her every day," the Barf Man asked.

"I don't know guys, she's always taking scraps and puttin' them in a bag. I haven't really talked to her as much as Pogo. Pogo and the mama-san speak French to each other quite a bit. What do you think, Pogs?"

"I think she is good person. She takes care of meeny, meeny orfanse in the city."

"You mean she lives in Hue?"

"Yes, in Hue City."

"Well, if Pogo trusts her, so do I," the Barf Man said as he handed over a banana.

"Well, you know I was saving this orange for my mid-morning snack, but seeing how it's goin' to the orphans, she can have it," Bear said as he handed over the orange.

Jack looked at the Scrotum. Scrotum shrugged and handed over his apple. "Fuh-gedda-boud-it."

Pogo took the contraband to the mama-san and she smiled, put her hands together, and started nodding her head up and down toward the crew at the table as Pogo returned.

G.O. smiled. "Well, aren't you a bunch of tough fucken Marines. I can just see you guys throwing apples at the V.C., maybe you should call yourselves the 'Apple Core.'"

"Fuck you, G.O., them orphans didn't start this fucken war."

"Yeah, well, their brothers and daddies and maybe some of their mamas are running around in the bush trying to figure out a way to shoot your dumb asses out of the sky."

"You is a cynic, Hill, plain and simple...an old-fashioned, self-righteous cynic. 'Ye of little faith' is what my granddaddy would have said. She a old woman, Hill, give her some mercy. We gonna have to call you the Party Pooper."

"Yeah, da Poopa' for short," chimed in the Scrotum.

"I kinda like 'Killjoy,'" the Barf Man offered.

"I got it. How 'bout 'Tight-Fisted Tex'?"

As G.O. started mentally working on the epic put-down, Redfeather spoke.

"Wakan Tanka not make children responsible for white man's shadow."

"Well, I'll be damned. Chief Redfeather speaks," Barf Man said.

They all stared at Jackson for a brief moment. Finally, G.O. said, "Oh hell, come with me Pogo, and I'll get you a whole tubful of fruit."

"O-o-oh, o-o-oh, G.O., you is part of de 'Apple Core' now, my brother!" the Bear said as he pointed at G.O. and the crew broke up as G.O. and Pogo walked back toward the scullery and Mama-san.

◆ ◆ ◆

Pogo started talking to the ancient Vietnamese woman who was in charge of all the women that worked in the chow hall. Everyone simply referred to her as Mama-san. Mama-san probably wasn't over the age of forty, but with her sun-damaged skin and betel nut–stained teeth, she looked to be over seventy, or according to G.O., ancient. In fact, every older woman in Vietnam was referred to as Mama-san. She was somewhat stooped, hard of hearing, and moved as if she had an anvil strapped to her ass but she always had a smile for Pogo. As they talked G.O. went to one of the large walk-in food storage lockers in the food preparation area. He came out carrying a box of unopened apples when he was stopped by one of the staff sergeant cooks in charge of the chow hall.

"Hey, where you headed with that box of apples, Marine."

"Out to the chow line. Looks like they're running low, Staff Sergeant Bitebach."

"Well, well, breakfast is almost over so put 'em back where you found 'em."

"Yes, Sergeant! But there were a couple of pilots waiting for these."

"You didn't say they was for the officer's chow line."

"Oh, I didn't think it would make a difference, staff sergeant."

"Well, from now on let me do the thinking, Corporal. I want you to take more apples over to the officer's mess ASAP. Now move it."

"Yes, Sergeant!"

G.O. found a wide-eyed Pogo and even wider-eyed Mama-san as he came running with a crate of apples. "Hurry up and tell me where to put these, Pogo." Pogo spoke rapidly to Mama-san, and she directed both of them to an old two-wheel pushcart. G.O. put the crate on the push cart and Mama-san threw an old moth-eaten blanket over it but not before G.O. saw the contents of the cart. There were half-eaten apples, bruised bananas, and rotting oranges. *Jeez,* G.O. thought, *no wonder she has Pogo asking for fresh fruit.*

"Pogo, ask Mama-san if we can visit the orphanage she takes this fruit to in Hue."

"Yes, yes, you may visit. Would be much honored," Mama-san said.

A startled G.O. said, "Damn, you speak English!"

"Yes, I speke gud Ingrish, taught by nuns in Hue."

"Why didn't you speak English in the chow hall?"

"Not like talk fat cooks."

"Well, you do have a strong point there, Mama-san." And G.O. rendered his idea of a bow with his hands clasped before his face.

◆ ◆ ◆

"Let me get this right, Hill. You want to borrow a jeep, load it with food and supplies, and drive into Hue City with Pogo riding shotgun, and deliver the goods to an orphanage? You are one crazy fucken boot. That's the most hair-brained scheme I've heard in my twenty-seven years in the corps."

"But, Gunny, if there ain't no orphanage, we'll turn around and come back and then we'll know Mama-san is running a scam on the mess hall. On the positive side, if there is an orphanage, then our squadron will get great publicity in the *Stars and Stripes* for being involved in a charitable activity as part of the 'Winning Hearts and Minds' program," G.O. explained.

"How are you, a know-nothing boot corporal, gonna get an article in the *Stars and Stripes*? I can't even do that."

"Guy I went to boot camp with writes the column on 'Winning Hearts and Minds' for the paper, and his office is based in Hue. I already talked to him, and he said he would be there with a photographer if we could pull this off."

"I don't know, Hill." When Gunny G. started thinking out loud, G.O. knew he had a chance. "My gut tells me this ought to be run up the chain of command, but since we have a new CO, it will be unquestionably low on his priority list. With the luck you've been having, some other squadron will hear about it, then take all the credit. Right now, we could use some positive publicity, and if it works, then I'm sure the CO will want to become more involved in the project.

"Another maxim of the Marine Corps, Hill, never stand in front of an officer at a photo shoot. OK, numbnuts, you have my tentative approval, based on the following guidelines. Both you peckerwoods will carry sidearms and Pogo will carry a fully loaded M-16. You will leave in the morning after you load up the jeep, and you will return before dark. Both of you. If that little French pastry tries to go AWOL, I will hold you personally responsible, Hill. Am I making myself clear?"

"Yes, sir!"

"Yes, sir, meaning that you will put a bullet in that fucker if he tries to desert?"

"Yes, sir. Is it OK if I just shoot him in the leg?"

"OK, Hill, I'll call Staff Sergeant Bitebach over at the mess hall and tell him to fix you guys up in the morning. That dumb fucker will probably want something in return so don't be surprised when you get back in the air that you have some company that smells bad enough to knock a dog off a gut wagon. And one last thing, Hill, when you gonna get around to telling me about the naked man in your car back in North Carolina?"

"Just as soon as we get back from Hue City tomorrow, Gunny. I promise."

◆ ◆ ◆

Early the next morning, G.O. and Pogo, went to the armory and checked out their weapons. After G.O. explained to Pogo how to hold an M-16 and which end the bullet came out of, they walked over to the mess hall. Gunny G. was there visiting with Staff Sergeant Bitebach. Locker came out carrying a box of fruit. "Hey, Gunny," G.O. said, "how about letting Locker ride shotgun? Pogo doesn't know which end of the gun to hold."

"You don't know when to stop asking questions, do you, Hill?"

"Well, it would help if I thought someone was riding with me that wasn't afraid to shoot back. Just in case we got into a scrape."

"It's up to Sergeant Bitebach, Hill."

Staff Sergeant Bitebach looked at the three and said, "It won't be any great loss to the mess hall, Gunny. He can go."

After the trio secured the supplies under a tarp on the back of the jeep, Gallo climbed up on the tarp and faced to the rear of the vehicle. Pogo rode shotgun and Hill drove. As they left the mess hall, Gunny G. said, "Well, Bitebach, I hope to shit in your mess gear there's an orphanage in Hue."

"Me too, Gunny, me too," Bitebach responded.

◆ ◆ ◆

The three arrived in Hue without incident, and so found Mama-san's residence. *Residence? It's a fucken mansion,* Hill thought. Next door to

Mama-san's house was the orphanage. It looked like a bombed-out factory of some sort with a large parklike area in front and surrounded by a decorative wrought iron fence. Pogo and Hill went to the door of Mamasan's and left Locker to guard the jeep. They were greeted by an ecstatic Mama-san. "Come in, come in," she kept saying over and over.

"We need to deliver the supplies to the orphans first, Mama-san."

"OK, we go now, then you come back house?" She led the way down the steps to the jeep. Mama-san rode shotgun, and Pogo climbed on the back with Gallo. They drove around the block to the entrance, upon their arrival they were met by at least fifty children. They were singing "God Bless America." G.O. glanced over at Mama-san and felt ashamed at the thoughts he had been having all morning. G.O.'s friend from boot camp was there with a photographer, and they were taking photos as promised. All of a sudden they heard a horn beeping and looked up to see two more jeeps entering the compound followed by a six-by truck. The priest who had been conducting the singing had the children stop and get ready to begin again.

The first jeep contained the new CO, Colonel Van Meter, Major Bridger, and two Marine guards. The second jeep held the sergeant major and Gunny G. and two more Marine guards. As they pulled to a stop, the photographer and Hill's friend ran to greet them, and the children began singing "God Bless America" again. The Gunny came over to Hill and Mama-san during the mayhem. "Sorry about this, Hill. Word got out somehow and the CO wanted to make a big splash. On the positive side, like you said, it will be good for the squadron."

"More importantly, Gunny, these kids will have a lot more support now."

"You're right about that. Look at the smile on the CO's face."

G.O. looked over at the CO. "One ear, he only has one fucken ear!"

"Shut the fuck up, Hill!" the Gunny exclaimed. "He is very conscious of missing an ear, but let me tell you something, he can hear a mouse pissing on cotton with his good ear, son, so shut the fuck up!"

A young Vietnamese girl ran up to the colonel and pointed at her missing left arm and then at his ear. One of the nuns finally intervened and told the colonel that the little girl was trying to explain how much they were alike.

The colonel reached down and picked her up and raised his left arm as she raised her right arm in a brief symbolic moment of triumph, as the flashbulbs popped.

"Boy, if that don't make the piss dribble down your leg, nothing will," the Gunny said.

G.O. looked quizzically at the Gunny. *He really is touched. And I don't feel a thing. Maybe the Bear was right; I'm just a cynic. I believe that grandstanding bastard colonel will forget about that little girl the minute they quit taking pictures.*

◆ ◆ ◆

G.O., Pogo, and Locker managed to slip back to the mansion with Mama-san while the party continued at the orphanage. Mama-san took them to her kitchen and seated them at a small table as she began scurrying around to fix them some tea. The three sat at the table watching her scoot busily around the kitchen, when they heard someone knocking at the front door. Mama-san went to the door. They discerned the unmistakable voice of Gunny G. They walked into the kitchen together.

"Well, here you fuck-ups are. Been looking all over for you. The priest has talked Colonel Van Meter into building a new school next to the or-phanage." The Gunny sat next to G.O. "So, I have a proposition for you boys, that is, if you would like to get off mess duty. I volunteered you three to be labor for the Seabees when they begin construction on the school. As soon as the school is completed, you two can go back to flying"—the Gunny nodded at Hill and Gallo—"and you"—he looked at a wide-eyed Pogo—"will be my permanent orderly."

"Love to do it, Gunny, thanks," Hill responded.

"Count me in," echoed Gallo.

"What iz theze 'perment order-lee'?" queried Daniell.

"That, my young French fry, is that you will do…whatever the fuck I tell you to do, *comprenez-vous*?"

Pogo had this mystified look on his face, then came the aha moment. "Oh, oui, monsieur Gunny! Oui, oui, oui!"

"Don't get carried away with that *little piggy going to market* shit, Private...you will be working your ass off."

Mama-san brought tea to the table, then asked politely to be excused for a moment. She had only been out of the room for a moment as the group sat thinking the best way to entice the Seabees into constructing the orphans a new school. It was a quiet respite as they sat and smoked and waited for Mama-san to return. Then they heard a knock. They looked at each other.

"Was that the door?" the Gunny whispered.

"I don't think so," G.O. responded quietly. "It sounded like it came from the floor."

They all looked at the oriental rug on the floor. Then came two knocks. G.O. eased his pistol out of his holster at the same time the Gunny did. Locker looked over at them then he followed suit. Pogo was frozen with this look of horror on his face. Then the Gunny stamped on the floor twice. When he did a trap door that was hidden by the Oriental rug was suddenly raised, and there were two Vietnamese with AK-47s pointed at them. The next minute of yelling and screaming, in both Vietnamese and English, seemed to take place in a heartbeat. As they held their guns on each other, Pogo held his hands above his head. Mama-san heard the commotion and came running into the room screaming in Vietnamese and French and making the put-your-weapons-down-now motion with her hands.

G.O. was the first to lower his weapon, then Locker. Then with all eyes on the Gunny, he started to lower his .45. The two Vietnamese in the trapdoor followed suit. The standoff seemed to last forever. G.O. could hear his heart pounding in his ears. *Jeez,* Hill thought, *is this how it ends? Shot by two Viet Cong that came through a trap door in Mama-san's mansion?*

Mama-san spent a few minutes trying to explain that her grandson, Hung Dong, had been away for three years and entreated everyone present to remain calm and to treat her kitchen as neutral territory. Hung pulled his friend Xin Loi from the trap door and introduced him first to Mama-san, then Mama-san introduced him to the Gunny. While the Gunny and Xin Loi stared at each other, Mama-san brought in more chairs and brought teacups for Hung Dong and Xin Loi. When the two Vietnamese placed their weapons on the floor, everyone relaxed a little.

Jeez, G.O. mused, *is this shit real? Am I really in a room in a mansion with two Viet Cong? Or is this a dream? Am I crazy or just on some unexplainable mystical journey? I can just see myself writing home about this shit:*

◆ ◆ ◆

Dear Folks,

Today I had tea with two of the most delightful Viet Cong. You would have loved the sitting room, Mom. It was decorated with some of the finest, and somewhat surprising, oriental rugs. We sat and played mahjongg and just had a grand old time in one of the loveliest French villas in Hue City. This, of course, was after we delivered supplies to Buddhist orphans in a Catholic orphanage. Well, must close now, there is a tapestry on the wall that was supposedly made in North Vietnam in the art village of Dong Ho, and I am just dying to see what's behind it.

Your son,

George

◆ ◆ ◆

Yeah, that about sums up this absurd, lunatic experience. Unless, of course, there is more to come. It just feels so weird.

◆ ◆ ◆

"I feel like a cat trying to shit a peach seed," the Gunny said. G.O. and Locker laughed, and Pogo just stared wide-eyed.

"What is 'peach-a-seed'?" Xin asked.

"Well," the Gunny began, "a peach is a fruit that grows in the USA, and it has a seed about this big," the Gunny demonstrated by holding his thumb and forefinger together, "so the cat would naturally be worried when it went to take a crap."

Xin and Hung exchanged a few words. Hung smiled and nodded. Xin said, "Similar to monkey shitting coconut?"

"Yeah, you catch on pretty quick, quicker than the little French fucker sitting in the corner all wide-eyed and spooked."

"You are-a French?" Xin asked Pogo. Pogo nodded in the affirmative. Xin let out with several questions in French. Soon, Pogo and Xin were in some kind of deep philosophical conversation. Then Mama-san came to the table with an unusual looking bottle.

"This is-a 'ruou thouc,' it is-a very good medicine. Make-a everybody feeling-a better. You try, General Gunny?"

The Gunny just stared wide-eyed like everyone else. Inside the bottle was a python that had a small green snake clutched in its jaws. G.O. thought, *I know what that poor bastard feels like. Ain't no winners in Vietnam. Danny D. told me I would see some strange shit if I lived long enough. I suppose he was right.*

Xin Loi picked the bottle up and poured a small amount into one of the empty cups on the table. He took a small sip, then exclaimed, "This is very good, thank you so much, Mama-san!"

Then he poured a small cup for the rest of the crew.

G.O. and Locker looked at each other as they sipped. Then their eyes bulged, and both their complexions became bright red. Then the smoke poured from their ears.

G.O. smacked his lips and said, "Now that is some impressive rice wine."

The Gunny picked up his cup and took a mouthful. He squinted one eye closed as he swished the brew around in his mouth and then swallowed. "Ah-h-h-h," he sighed, "that is some mighty fine python piss, yes, sir!" He was not about to tell the boots and the two Victor Charlies that it tasted like lacquer remover with a hint of Agent Orange and burned like basketful full of chili peppers on the way down.

Pogo just sat and sipped and nodded occasionally. So much for the fabled French taste in wines.

By three o'clock in the afternoon, the Gunny was slurring his words and had his arm draped around Xin Loi's neck. The Gunny was also wearing Xin Loi's NVA-issued pith helmet. Xin Loi was trying to dig the python out of the wine bottle with some chopsticks. Pogo had passed out on the floor and somehow managed to keep this surprised Charles Boyer look on his face. Only Frenchmen could do that.

G.O. and Locker were showing Hung Dong how to light farts through the screen door that led into the kitchen from outside. Every time G.O. would light one of Locker's farts through the screen, it would turn this beautiful emerald green with a hint of lilac purple. G.O. thought the colors might have been partly due to the galvanized screen door. Once he put his Zippo a little too close to Locker's ass and burned off most of the hair on his ass. Accident of War. Collateral damage. Hung Dong could not stop laughing at the "Yanquis." Then Hung asked if he could light one of his farts through the screen. Hung had backed his bare ass up to the screen and was getting ready to cut loose with a monster Viet Cong fart. G.O. had the Zippo ready and fired up.

"Well, I'll be diddly-dog-damned!"

They all looked up. It was the sergeant major. Standing with hands on hips. Hung farted this beautiful Tibetan sunset that burned the wallpaper on the other side of the room.

Chapter Twenty One

Writing on the Wall

"Well, all I can tell you boys is that you better be damned glad Mama-san had another bottle of that 'Royal Phouc' or whatever the hell it was called, or we would all be looking through the slats of a Conex box," the Gunny remarked as they drove out of Hue City on a hectic traffic day.

"Yeah, but who would've thought that she had another bottle of rice wine with two pin-striped tit-babblers in it? I thought the sergeant major was going to wet his britches. I've never seen a man so crazy about birds," Locker quipped.

"Well, I'm kinda thankful he showed up when he did," G.O. chimed in. "I had a bad feeling about how that party was going to end."

"Well, like my friend Billy says, 'all's well that ends well,' and that ended pretty well. I'm just glad he let the two slopes di-di back to wherever it was that they came from. I mean that was some party...did you catch the look on the sergeant major's face when G.O. lit up Hung's blast-furnace fart and scorched the wallpaper across the room? I wonder what that boy had been eating? Phew-w-w-w!"

G.O. and Locker were riding shotgun in the back of the empty jeep while Pogo slept in the front passenger seat. They all had a good laugh over the impromptu meeting with the two V.C. "I guess you boys will respect the fact that you cannot now, or evermore, tell this story to any living human being...because you will put your credibility at risk, both the sergeant major and I will deny this incident ever happened. And if word leaks out, the only children's school you two will be working on...will be on the Island with No Name."

"Gunny, who would believe this story besides Locker?" G.O. said as he cast a suspicious eye at Locker.

Locker fired back, "Dude, you are not still talking about the guy that took his grandmother to Mexico are you?"

Gunny G. said, "Oh hell, I know that old saw. A good friend of mine from Tucson told me that story, said the body was stolen before they crossed the border into Nogales."

"Oh no, Gunny, it was Tijuana!" Locker said with a puzzled look on his face.

G.O. and the Gunny laughed uproariously as they arrived back at the squadron compound.

"You ain't forgettin' you owe me a story about a naked man, are ya, Hill?"

"No, Gunny, not at all. Once we get back to base and I get cleaned up, I'll come over to the line shack and explain everything."

♦ ♦ ♦

"It's Christmas Eve?" G.O said quizzically.

"Yes, it is fucken Christmas Eve and you numbnuts need to know that the CO has ordered that no one is to fire their weapons at midnight. But it's not just you guys; the grunts have been given this order also. Last year it looked like the Fourth of July." The Gunny was speaking to the crew chiefs and other line personnel.

"I don't fucken care if you douche bags sit up all fucken night singing 'Kum Ba Yah' and swappin' spit in the shower, you will *not*, under any circumstances, fire your fucken weapons! You understand what I'm saying, Duck?"

"Yes, Gunny...you don't want us touching our guns," the Duck said as he ran his hand over his empty tooled-leather holster.

"Or any gun, you fucken halfwit!"

"Line personnel…" They all came to attention. "Dismissed."

◆　◆　◆

G.O. and Locker had showered and walked over to where the Army Huey Squadron had built an outdoor theater. On the way over they smoked a doobie that Pogo had sacrificed to them if they promised never to take him to Hue City again. The movie playing was called *Two for the Road.* They sat on a Huey blade through about thirty minutes of the movie and just drooled on themselves. G.O. could not figure out why the troops were laughing. Locker said, "Dude, let's quit this scene!"

When they returned to the barracks the usual group was gathered on the bunker outside. Sitting on top of the bunker, sipping beers, and passing a joint around that looked like a cigar. One of the Bear's specials. Rolled between the legs of two young Vietnamese virgins. One of the metalsmiths from the metal shop that G.O. thought was an all right guy, was playing a beat up acoustical guitar and singing some old folk tunes. It was a mellow kind of music, but G.O. was really into the vibrations of the strings. With his senses heightened, it was like he could feel the rhythms of his body change to meet those being plucked and strummed by the young musician from the metal shop. G.O. stretched out on the sandbags and propped a couple under his head for comfort. Every so often they could hear hymns being sung at the Billy Graham rally. It made for an interesting mix.

"You comfy, Tex?"

"Yeah, Bear, very comfy."

"Well, here, take a hit off this fine Cambodian Red, my man, and you will feel no pain."

G.O. took a deep hit, held it, and slowly released the smoke. The metalsmith started playing "Boots of Spanish Leather" by Bob Dylan.

G.O. thought back to his last night with Proo and smiled. *When I get home,* he thought. Suddenly, his thoughts switched to Dupree being shot up. G.O. could see and feel the aircraft he was in being blown apart, and he could visualize Danny's calf flopping around in slow motion.

G.O. felt his heart beat faster and could hear the blood rushing and pounding in his ears. *Jeez,* Hill thought, *what the fuck is this shit laced with?* Suddenly, G.O. could see colors! Here it was at 2300 hours (11:00 p.m.), dark as truck-stop coffee, and G.O. was seeing colors. This was way past cool for G.O. "Hey, Sugar Bear," he said as the Bear looked over at him, "are you seeing colors?"

"G.O., my man, I believe you is high. Exactly what color am I?"

"Oh, man you are this beautiful shade of amber with like this radiant cinnamon surrounding you."

"Well, well, well, we got us a brother that can see aw-ruh's."

The Barf Man chimed in, "What's an aw-ruh, Bear?"

"You know, it's like a light that shines out yo' head."

"You mean like a halo?" Duck offered.

"Yeah, like a halo, 'cept it's an aw-ruh."

"Oh, now I know," said the Gerber Baby. "Aura."

"I believe that is what I been sayin', my corn-fed friend, aw-ruh."

"Hey, G.O.," Blaze chimed in, "what color is Metalsmith Bob's aura?"

G.O. looked over at Bob, "Oh man, Bob has this kind of gray cloud over his head with these turquoise edges. I mean the turquoise keeps flashing, like a blinking light in the fog."

Like my fucken brain, G.O. thought. *It's like all these lightning bugs caught in different colored Jellos moving in slow motion...oh-h-h-h Shit! Now the fireflies are dancing with these harmonica playing pygmies, no that's Bob on the harmonica. Shit, G.O., get yourself together man.*

G.O. started crying. "Hey, man, what is up with the tears?" Gerbs asked.

"I don't know, man, it's like I can't remember the last time I cried...but it feels ethereal, you know, man, like not of this world? And I can't seem to stop."

"Hey, look, it's a shooting star!" Duck cried.

"You may be the dumbest Marine I have ever met, Duckling. Shootin' stars don't start from the ground and go up. That was a tracer round some grunt fired off because it's Christmas," Bear amended.

Suddenly, the sky was full of tracer rounds, purples, oranges, reds, and yellows. They even fired off star cluster flares from their mortars. The young, stoned Marines lay on top of the sandbag bunker and enjoyed the show.

I wonder if Billy G. is enjoying this magnificent light show? Hill reflected, as a last tear slipped down his cheek.

◆ ◆ ◆

Christmas Day found G.O. and Locker in Hue City filling up sandbags and building a bunker, while the Seabees looked over a bombed out building next to the orphanage. Of course, G.O. and Locker didn't have to exert a lot of effort, because the good priest had provided them with some students to help out. The kids would hold the sandbags open, and G.O. and Locker would fill them and seal them. Soon the kids had a conga line going and were stacking the sandbags where G.O. and Locker had instructed them. It usually took two students to carry one sandbag, but they completed most of the bunker by the end of the day. The Seabees were really impressed with the effort of the Marines and the children.

By the end of the first week, most of the squadron had made an appearance at the construction site and took part in whatever the Seabees asked of them. Wherever G.O. and Locker went, there was a gaggle of Vietnamese children following them around. It was like having two Pied Pipers on the work site. Today, Colonel Van Meter was visiting with Major Bridger, and they were being followed by some photographers and writers for the *Stars and Stripes* and who knew what else.

The squadron had taken to calling Colonel Van Meter "Colonel Van Gogh" because of his missing ear. But not within his hearing or the hearing of any officer or lifer. "Would you look at the publicity hound," Bear said as he picked up a sack of mortar. "He gonna end up General Van Gogh."

G.O. and Locker both laughed, then twenty Vietnamese children laughed. The colonel looked their way and then said something to Major Bridger. Major Bridger approached Hill and Gallo.

"Colonel wants to know if you could have the children follow him around while the photographers and writers are here?"

"Sure, sir, no problem," Locker said. Then he turned and asked the priest to convey the major's request to the children and that if they complied, the colonel would have a special treat for them. The Walrus gave Locker the stink eye. The children jumped up and down and clapped and screamed their approval. They all ran to the colonel and began hugging his legs and grabbing for his hands.

"Problem solved," Locker said.

At the end of each day, usually around 1500 (3:00 p.m.), the Seabees packed up and left for the day. Locker and Hill would drive back to the squadron and report to the Gunny. There was always more to do. The War did not stop for orphans. There were maintenance schedules to be completed. Change out an engine. Change out a rotor head. Change out rotor blades. Or the one G.O. hated the most, change out a transmission. Usually, they would work into the night trying to keep at least ten of their twenty-two helicopters in the UP condition, or flyable, by Vietnam standards. In the states, only two birds would have met the up status, Bear's and Duck's. It was like they were involved in this unhealthy competition to see whose aircraft could acquire the most flying time.

♦ ♦ ♦

G.O. loved working with both the Bear and the Duck. They understood their aircraft and kept ahead of the maintenance requirements. The Duck was quiet and went about his aircraft in a professional and organized manner. He was scientific and technical in his methods. If he wanted you to do something, he was very specific in his instructions. The Bear, on the other hand, was a much better teacher. G.O. thought he knew everything there was to know about the CH-46D but was finding out that his knowledge just scratched the surface.

The Bear had G.O. greasing the main rotor shaft, which required some acrobatic positions. "You know, Bear, I have changed out more engines in one week than I did in a year back in the states."

"Shit, this ain't nothing, Hill. Wait till our squadron has to pull an operation with those fucken Mud Marines. They'll have us working twenty-four seven, son."

"Jeez, what are we doing now?"

"It's different when you are getting shot at all day, Hill, and then working all night so you can go get shot at the next day, you follow?"

"Do you grease this rotor shaft every day?"

"No, 'bout once a week, though. I don't want to be in one of these things if the rotor shaft seizes up, so I like to keep it well lubricated, my brother. You know, you take care of your airplane, it will take care of you, even if you get an inept pilot. You want to make sure that your head knows what your hands are doing and that your hands are trained to carry out what your head wants. But if your heart ain't involved, it don't matter how smart you are or what your hands can do. It ain't gonna work."

"So I have to love my helicopter?"

"No, you doofus Texas fuck, it's an attitude. If you care about what you are doing it will show. But ain't nothing wrong with loving your helicopter, you the one that keeps it flying. If you don't love to fly, then your helicopter will reflect that. But I wouldn't start talking to it. They might send your ass to the Island with No Name."

"So, when I do get my own aircraft, I should work on it with care."

"Man, I know you're trying to understand me, but you making it too hard. When you are working on the aircraft, anybody's aircraft, you are working on yourself. Think about the knowledge you possess that allows you to work on this bird and the different skills your hands have developed as a result. You do it long enough, and your hands begin to think for themselves. Think about the first time you tried to grease that number four aft fitting? You remember how hard it was to get your big ol' hands around the rotor shaft and then fit the grease-gun nozzle on the fitting and then hold it on with one hand while you pumped the grease in with the other hand? Probably can't remember that can you? But now, easy-peasy lemon-squeezy, right, Hill?

"Do you ever stop to think about the different folks who dreamed up the concept of a helicopter? How about the folks who machined the parts and then the folks who built the components that go into one of these birds? It is genuinely mind-manifesting, Hill. It is a soulful trip, my man. My African ancestors believed that their ancestors were keeping an eye on them and that the spirits of the dead could be both beneficial and mischievous. So in my culture, the African American culture, Hill, we venerate our ancestors. Maybe some of the spirits of those who created this helicopter reside in this bird.

"I pay homage to those spirits every day, Hill, by how I care for this aircraft. I know this is all some crazy philosophical shit to you...*but I care.* It is a privilege for me to work on this aircraft and when it flies, I honor everyone who has had or will ever have anything to do with this aircraft. And when I'm gone, there will be a part of me, my spirit, that is attached to every aircraft I have ever worked. So you'd be a lucky motherfucker to crew one of my airplanes, That's what I'm talkin' about, brother!"

"I think I'm getting it."

"Shit, Hill," Bear said and looked askance at Hill, "let me put it another way. See, I saw you and Locker working on that new school with the Seabees. Shit, them kids was followin' you around like you was the Pied Piper or something. Now, I know what you is gonna say, 'They was followin' Locker, too.' Yeah well, I happen to know Locker was givin' them kids chewing gum; that's why they was following him around. But you, Hill, is a natural teacher. You never yell at them kids, and you don't have to show them how to do anything but one time. And you got that big ol' shit-eatin' Texas grin for every damn one of those kids. You don't play favorites, Hill. Now, ax yourself, why is you so good with them? It's because you are compassionate, Señor Hill, because you really are compassionate. Now, if I could just get you to care as much about learnin' as you do teachin', you might make a decent mech."

G.O. didn't know how to respond. So he just kept quiet. Lomax, the one-eyed cockroach, looked out of the engine compartment, blew his nose and sighed.

Chapter Twenty Two

Holy Helo

G.O. and Locker walked into the line shack covered in the remnant filth of a day working for the Seabees. The Gunny set his coffee down on the counter and looked at the dirty duo. "Well, for crying out loud. If it ain't the Bobbsey Twins back from a day of making mud pies with the Seabees."

"Well, I want to be Bert, so that means that Locker has to be Nan," G.O. responded.

"What the fuck are you talking about, Hill? Who is Bert, and who is Nan?" the Gunny quizzed.

"The Bobbsey Twins, Gunny. Or at least the oldest pair. They had a younger pair of siblings that were fraternal twins also, Flossie and Freddie, but Locker doesn't look anything like Flossie."

"Goddamnit, Hill, we're not here to talk about the fucken Bobbsey twins. That was just a finger of speech, for cryin' out loud. You sure there were two sets of twins? Don't answer that, numbnuts. I'll find out on my own. They ain't Greek, are they? Never mind, you fucken halfwit, we are here to talk about why you two come into my line shack looking like forty miles of bad road between Ozark and East Jesus. From this time forward, when you return to base from working on the orphan school, you will shit, shower, and shave before reporting to this line shack. Am I making myself clear?"

"Yes, Gunny, perfectly clear," the duo chimed.

Sniggers and laughter from the quality control area. The Gunny gave the QC folks his shut-the-fuck-up stare. They went back to work furtively trying to sniff themselves as the Gunny barked, "Some of you could try using a little deodorant yourselves." He turned back to Hill and Gallo. "Well, clear out and report back here looking like Marines."

◆ ◆ ◆

Hill and Gallo walked into the shower and one of the crew chiefs due to rotate home, Ryan Sanchez, was the only other person there.

"My shit is gone tomorrow, hombres. I have officially made it out of Vietnam, and my shit ain't ever coming back."

"You know you're going to miss us, Sanchez," Hill quipped.

Sanchez pulled a giant economy-size tube of Prell off the shelf and started squirting it on his crotch and working up a lather. "What the hell you doing, dude?" Locker asked.

"I am getting Señor Johnson super clean before I leave tomorrow, *pinche gringos*, so he will be ready for action when he gets home. Of course, you pussy white boys don't have a clue about what I'm talking about, do you?"

"Well, all I can say is, you won't have to worry about Señor Johnson having dandruff," G.O. said as he climbed under one of the showerheads and began scrubbing all manner of filth off his body.

"Yeah, and your pubes will look 'radiantly alive' and possess that 'rich, silky look'!" Locker read from the Prell tube.

"Yeah, you two gringos won't be laughing when I'm back in the world humping little Rosarita while she screaming my name, 'Oh, Ry-yan, Ry-yan!'"

Locker pitched the tube of Prell back to Sanchez. After they left the shower, Sanchez was still in there scrubbing and singing, scrubbing and singing. *Must be nice to be a short-timer,* Hill thought.

After they had finished cleaning up, they reported back to the line shack. "OK, you two numbnuts, here's the word," the Gunny began. "The sergeant major has seen fit to give you two a reprieve. Also, most of our experienced crew chiefs have rotated back to the States over the past three weeks, and we need some warm bodies to keep these big green motherfuckers flying." G.O. and Locker couldn't help but smile. "So, you Gallo will go back to flying *Surf City* and you, Hill, will get Dupree's old aircraft, *Groundz for Divorce*. The sergeant major wanted me to make it very clear to you two numbskulls that you are on temporarily permanent probationary status."

"Wait up Gunny, what is 'temporarily permanent'?"

"Goddamnit, Hill! That's what the sergeant major said it was. You want to go ask the sergeant major what he meant, you dumb Commie fuck? Or do you wish to go flying for God, country, and Marine Corps?"

"I wish to go flying, Gunnery Sergeant!"

The Gunny set his coffee cup down and looked at Hill. "What? You can't say for God, country, and the Marine Corps? You are starting to seriously piss me off, Hill."

"I wish to go flying for God, country, and the Marine Corps, Gunny!"

"That's a little better. I was beginning to think you was an atheist Commie bastard."

"Communists *are* atheists, Gunny."

"Now you are catching on, Hill. The only good Commie is a dead Commie!"

"What about the Buddhist Commies?"

"Do Buddhist believe in Jesus, Hill?"

"No, Gunny."

"Then them orange-robed dipshits are atheist fucken Commies! Now, Hill, I want you to look at my coffee cup sitting on the counter."

"OK, what am I looking for?"

"You ain't looking for nothing. You are looking because I told you to!"

"Right, Gunny."

"Now, do you think the coffee cup is *permanent*?"

"Are we having some kind of Socratic dialogue?"

"What the fuck is up with you, Hill? When the Gunny asks you a question, you answer; you don't get to respond with a question, clear?"

"Clear, Gunny. Negative, the coffee cup is not permanent."

"Right you are, son. Is anything permanent?"

"Well...Jesus...maybe?"

"Goddamnit, Hill we ain't talking about Jesus or any other concept that might exist in our minds. We are talking about physical things."

"Right, Gunny. Then I would conclude that nothing is permanent."

"Goddamn, but you are one smart Marine. So, if nothing is permanent, it would be temporary, correct?'

G.O. couldn't help but smile. "Yes Gunny, it would be temporarily permanent."

"You goddamn right it is, Hill, unless the sergeant major changes his mind tomorrow. Now, are you going to keep the name of your aircraft, *Groundz for Divorce,* or do you want to change it to something more to your liking, say, *The Bobbsey Twins Go Flying,* or how about *Ain't Nothing Permanent*?"

G.O. grinned at the Gunny and said, "I believe I'll keep her as *Groundz,* Gunny."

"I swear to God, Hill, the longer you are around me, the smarter you get. Tomorrow morning you two idiots have Holy Helo duty."

G.O. had figured out by this time that he was not asking any more questions, so Locker stepped into the fray. "What's the Holy Helo, Gunny?"

"Locker, finally coming up to bat, huh? I was wondering when you were going to come out of the dugout, son. You and Hill will fly the Sky Pilot around to different firebases so that he may hold religious services for the troops. I suppose you have met Commander Ticonderoga, the navy chaplain?"

"Yes, Gunny," Both Hill and Gallo replied.

"Well, that's very good, my young boot crew chiefs. Your aircraft will fly lead, Locker, and which means exactly what, Hill?"

"That *Groundz* will be the chase aircraft."

"Ding-ding-ding, you got one right! You will fly chase. Your gunner will be the Gerber Baby, Gallo, and yours will be a newbie, Hill, PFC Delmonico."

"Is Delmonico a mech, Gunny?"

"No, Hill, he is in charge of the parachute shop."

G.O had forgotten that every Marine squadron had a parachute shop, even helicopter squadrons that didn't carry parachutes. Bureaucratic consistency at its finest.

◆ ◆ ◆

Early the next morning, Hill met PFC Delmonico on the flight line. Delmonico was a slight young man, maybe a 130 pounds, dark hair and dark eyes, with a wispy mustache. Delmonico had a ready smile for G.O.

"First thing you have to do, Private, is tell me what name you want me to call you. I'm not gonna walk around all day using a four-cylinder word."

"My friends call me Joey."

"Like a fucken baby kangaroo? Well, for fuck's sake! Joey, it is. Next on the list, Joey, you need to bring two fifty-caliber machine guns out to the aircraft with three cans of ammo for each and have them mounted by the time I get back from our briefing."

"Where do I get them, Corporal Hill?"

"You will pick them up at the armory, my young boot gunner, which is that building at the end of the flight line," G.O. said while pointing at a building four hundred meters away. "One more thing, Joey...call me G.O. We will get the bird ready for preflight when I return."

◆ ◆ ◆

G.O was telling Locker about the dwarf that was going to be his door gunner today, as they strolled back to their aircraft.

"Yeah, Locker, bet he doesn't weigh a hundred and thirty pounds soaking wet. I want to get back and give him a hand mounting the fifties. I don't think he will be able to lift them."

"I'll give you a hand, G.O. I may have to fly with Joe Parachute someday."

As they walked up to the aircraft, they noticed that both fifties were mounted and the aircraft was opened up and ready for preflighting.

"Well, I'll be damned," G.O. said, casting a perplexed look at Locker. Joey was sitting on the ramp of the helicopter, grinning.

"Well done, Joey, how did you manage to get the aircraft ready so quickly?" G.O. asked.

"Well, the armorer is getting ready to go on leave, so I told him I would sew him a canvas garment bag if he helped me with getting the guns to the aircraft and mounted. He was more than willing to help."

"Well, this, my young friend, is Locker Gallo, his aircraft is *Surf City,* and if you are genuinely fortunate, you will never have to fly with him."

"Shit, Joey, don't listen to him...you are welcome onboard *Surf City* anytime.*"

Joey Delmonico grinned, and G.O. and Locker both finally noticed he was missing four of his upper front teeth.

"Jeez, Joey, what happened to your teeth?"

"Oh, I thought it would be best if I took them out before we went flying."

"That's a good idea, but next time, give me a little warning. Also, you might want to leave them in until the pilot lights the fires," G.O. cautioned.

Locker asked, "Where are you from, Joey?"

"I'm from South Florida...the Miami area."

"How'd you lose those teeth?"

"Well, that's a long story..."

"You boys ready to go flyin'?" It was Captain D'Amato.

"Yes, sir!" they responded.

"Well, I'll be flying *Surf,* and Lieutenant Abramovitz will be aircraft commander of *Groundz,* so let's get these babies preflighted and fired up. And when the Padre gets here, send him over to *Surf City.* You ready to go, Gallo?"

"Yes, sir."

Both aircraft were turning and burning when the Padre finally showed up. G.O. was standing outside the aircraft as the Padre and his assistant approached him.

"Are we flying with you today, crew chief?" the chaplain yelled above the rotor wash and the jet engines.

"No, sir. You will be ridin' on *Surf City* today, right over there, Chaplain," G.O. yelled and directed the chaplain toward Locker's aircraft. "Good luck, sir."

"I don't need any luck, son. Jesus is riding with me."

◆ ◆ ◆

The crews flew in and out of several firebases during the morning: the Rockpile, LZ Baldy, LZ Witch's Tit, and several others. Around noon they flew into Vandegrift Combat Base and refueled while the pilots and the chaplain went to lunch with the Mud Marines. During the latter part of the afternoon, they were flying to LZ Azrael. Azrael was located in one of the valleys where two smaller rivers conjoined to form a substantial river, the Song Cam Lo. The LZ was cut into the jungle along the point between the two smaller rivers. As G.O. and Joey circled the LZ, *Surf City* spiraled in and set down. G.O could make out the Padre and his assistant making for the tree line. *Surf City* lifted off, and both helicopters circled above the mountains while the Padre conducted three five-minute services, Catholic, Protestant, and Jewish.

As they were flying up the river valley Lieutenant Abramovitz called back to G.O, "Crew chief...you need to come up here and take a look at this."

"Roger that, sir." G.O. climbed into the hatchway that led to the cockpit and could not believe his eyes. They were looking at a perfectly circular rainbow above the river and between the two mountain ridges. *Can't get rid of Danny D.*, Hill thought. *Here's another one of those strange things, like the albino water buffalo, I never would have believed. Yep, Danny was right. You see some weird shit in Vietnam.*

"That is awesome, Lieutenant! I've never seen a circular rainbow before now," G.O. said.

"It is a phenomenon, Crew Chief...I think Captain D'Amato intends for us to fly through the center of the rainbow. Do you have a camera?"

"Negative, sir."

"How about you, Lieutenant Masterson. Camera?" Lieutenant Masterson, the copilot (known as the Batman—pilots are so creative) pulled out his trusty Pentax. "Very good, Batman...try to get a before-and-after shot...*National Geographic* will eat this shit up."

"They would really like it if it had tits."

"Who said that?"

"That was private Delmonico, sir...doesn't know about radio discipline."

"Well, goddamnit, Delmonico, you might be on to something...wish I'd thought of that...tits on a rainbow!"

After they had flown through the rainbow, the copilot handed G.O. his Pentax so he could snap some photos out of the aft end of the 46. While G.O. was taking some pictures, the aircraft received a call from LZ Azrael that the Sky Pilot was ready to be removed from the LZ. *Groundz* made a slow turn with the lead aircraft as they headed back to LZ Azrael. As *Groundz* circled above the LZ, *Surf City* made its slow descent into the valley. When *Surf City* touched down, the Padre and his assistant came out of the tree line and hustled over to the aircraft. As fast as a navy commander can hustle. The Padre stopped on the ramp and made the Sign of the Cross to the Marines, then turned and went inside the aircraft. G.O. saw the aircraft lift off then heard the unmistakable pops of the AK-47. Then he heard Captain D'Amato over the radio. "We are taking fire...I say again...we are taking fire." As *Surf City* cleared the LZ, the grunts started pounding the hillsides with automatic weapons and mortars.

Captain D'Amato was on the radio again, "This is Highboy One Eight, and we have taken fire at LZ Azrael...we will try to make it to Vandy...are you reading?"

"Roger," Lieutenant Abramovitz replied. "Read you five by...ETA Vandy fifteen mikes...we are on your starboard aft side, Highboy One Eight"

G.O. saw smoke streaming from the port side engine on *Surf City*. "Sir...I have smoke pouring from the port side engine of *Surf City*."

Lieutenant Abramovitz called it into Captain D'Amato. A harrowing fifteen minutes later, the crippled *Surf City* limped into Vandy on one engine, taxied to a revetment, and shut down. *Groundz* taxied to the revetment next to *Surf City* and shut down.

When the crew of *Groundz* walked over to Locker's aircraft, they were all outside walking around, doing damage assessment. "Jeez," Hill said. "You took a lot of rounds, my man."

Locker looked at G.O. and said, "Yeah, I just get my wings back, and now I'm grounded again."

"Only temporarily permanently grounded, Gallo. Looks like you and Gerbs will get to babysit until the recovery team gets here with a new engine. You know, the nights are so enchanting at Vandy. Why, there are mortar attacks...and rocket attacks...and parachute flares going off all night long..."

"Thanks, Hill." Locker fumed as Chucky D. walked over.

"Well, y'all know the routine, Locker. You and the Gerber Baby will babysit your aircraft until the recovery team arrives. The rest of us will fly back on *Groundz*."

As they loaded up to head back to Phu Bai, G.O. looked over at one depressed Padre and said, "Don't take it so hard, Chaplain. I guess Jesus got on the wrong airplane this morning."

Chapter Twenty Three

The Highway Men

As G.O. and Private Delmonico walked into the line shack, the Gunny roared, "Goddamnit, Hill, I give you and Gallo a fucken milk run, and you two douchebags try to get the Padre zapped. Did your mama have any children that lived? And who is this numbnuts with no front teeth standing here beside you, shaking like a fucken leaf? Goddamnit, son, quit sha- kin'…you look like a Baptist in a whorehouse. You fly with this magnet ass, and you are gonna take some rounds."

"Oh, this is Private Delmonico, Gunny, from Miami. He's in charge of our parachute shop and was a door gunner on my aircraft today, and he was outstanding."

"No puke?"

"Roger that, negative regurgitation."

"Delmonico? What kind of fucken name is that? Sounds like a steak house. You a fucken wetback?"

"No, Gunny, I'm Italian."

"You are from Miami, and you're Eye-talian? You in the fucken mafia, son?"

"No, Gunny."

"Anybody you know in the mafia ever sell stolen goods?"

"Er, ah, not that I know of, Gunny."

"Just what I thought, you're a fucken mafioso, probably selling the squadron's parachutes to some lowlife underwear maker in South Florida. You selling our parachutes, you little toothless mafioso?'

"No, Gunny, I wouldn't sell off the parachutes…"

"Well, I'll be keeping an eye on you, Private Serpico."

"It's Delmonico, Gunny."

'Well, don't just stand there, Serpico, go somewhere and put your fucken teeth back in. The squirrels in QC are getting hard-ons." Evil looks from the QC personnel. "I'll inform the recovery team, and we'll get a bird scheduled back to Vandy in the morning. Not so fast, Hill, I am sending you and Private Serpico here down to Marble Mountain to pick up an engine for *Surf City*. We are out of spares right now."

"What about the scavenger aircraft in the hangar?" G.O. asked.

"When will you learn *not* to question your dear old Gunny? The C.O. has Sugar Bear putting it back together, and the Bear is supposed to test flight it tomorrow with Captain D'Amato. Now if you have no further questions, I suggest you two get ready to fly down to Marble Mountain."

G.O. thought he had sparred with the Gunny long enough, so he walked out into the hangar area, when he heard the Bear singing, "Can't get enough of that Sugar Crisp…"

G.O. walked up the ramp at the back of the helicopter as the Bear kept working in the flight control compartment.

"Fi, fi, fo, fum, I smells a dumb-ass Tex-i-unn."

"Hey, Bear, what's up?"

"What does it look like, I'm putting this jigsaw puzzle back together. Ain't nobody kept track of which parts that have been removed from this bird, so I have to check every nut and bolt on the damn thing."

"I thought this was your groove, man?"

"My groove? You didn't just say 'my groove,' did you? I suppose you wanted to say that working on aircraft was my expertise and that you have come to acknowledge my mechanical gifts."

"Yeah, that's it, that's what I wanted to say. You need any help?"

"No, G.O., I don't need any help. This baby is close to turning and burning. We're going to drag her out of the hangar later and turn her up.

You might want to be there for that. If she doesn't eat herself up in the revetment, you will know for sure that I am the master."

"You are the acknowledged 46 guru, oh great one. And as much as I would like to stay and watch a helicopter blow up, the Gunny's got us flying down to Marble Mountain to pick up an engine."

"Sheee-it, man. You get all the gravy. Story of my life, the black man work his ass off, and the white man just out playing in the sun. Well, it ain't always gonna be this way, my brother; things is changing. Next thing you know, I'll be Sergeant Bear. Then I'll be in the gravy. You hearin' me? Life will be a hand job with a velvet glove…milk and honey, G.O. The Bear gonna be fat. First thing I'm gonna do is put you back on mess duty just so you know who's boss, then I'm gonna give you every shitty job I can find. How you like that, Hill?"

"How about we walk outside the hangar and light up this doobie?" G.O. said as he held up a joint.

"Tryin' to influence me with a little bit of herb? Well, that works for me. Let's go." The two strolled out of the hangar and found a quiet spot beside a bunker and lit up. As they were sitting there enjoying some exquisite Laotian herb, Sanchez came walking up. Ryan Sanchez was not a small Latino man. He stood about six feet tall and had piercing green eyes and dark hair. He slipped into a barrio dialect when he became excited, but most of the time G.O. thought he might have attended Southern Cal. He was proud to tell anyone who asked that he was a tenth-generation American and that his family had been in California before the American Revolution.

"*Que pasa?*" Sanchez said as he reached for the J.

"*Que pasa* your fucken self, Sanchez man, what are you still doing here? You were supposed to leave today."

"Well, I had to go to sick bay and the doc he take one look at my poor *peni*, and he say, 'You must stay here until your pecker returns to its natural state!' So, I tell him my 'natural state' is California, he say, 'You ain't leaving Vietnam until your pecker looks normal!'"

"What happened to your johnson, man?" Bear asked.

"I washed it with an extra-large tube of Prell, and the next morning my crotch look like the Sahara Desert. The Hammer of Thor now looks like a baby chicken. It was itching me some-ting terrible, homes. So I went to sick bay."

"What did Doc do for you?"

"Oh he gave me a jar of Vaseline, and he tell me to rub it in three times a day until my little *pipi* turn back to normal. It's not so bad...I like having doctor's orders to rub the *Martillo de tor*," Sanchez said as he made movements like he was masturbating.

"Yeah, well don't go rubbing too fast. Marine Corp frown on that shit." The Bear laughed.

◆ ◆ ◆

After G.O. and Delmonico secured *Groundz* for the night at the Marble Mountain Air Facility, they walked over to the 53 Squadron that the Bugman had been assigned. The Bugman gave them a tour of the aircraft and then took them to the hooch where he and some of his squadron members lived. Later, G.O., the Bugman, Delmonico, and another 53 crew chief named Henry, but everyone called him Stick Shift, all went to the E club. G.O. filled the Bugman in on what had been happening back at Hue-Phu Bai since the Bugman had left. Finally, G.O. got around to asking Bugman if he was the one who fragged the bunker and scared the crap out of Sergeant P.C. Emetic.

"Hell, no, that wasn't me, Hill. If I was going to use a grenade, I would have put it under that motherfucker's bed. I wouldn't have just *tried* to scare him like he was some dumb eight-year-old. I wasn't brought up that way, Hill," Bugman said as he stared icily at G.O. "I was brought up that if somebody did something to you, you did it back worse. You break their legs or arms, or you put a round in them or burn their damn house down. But you don't leave any witnesses. And I was taught if you call somebody a pig-stealing son of a bitch, you better damn well produce a pig."

"Nobody's calling you anything, man. Lighten up. You don't have to be so defensive."

"Shit, I know you don't mean nothin', Hill, us southern boys have to stick together...am I right?" Bugman said as he smiled a wild-eyed, toothless grin.

G.O. didn't know how to reply. If he said he thought the Bugman was nuts, he might end up with a grenade under his pillow, and if he agreed, he was putting himself in the same boat he had been trying so desperately to escape. The SS *Bigot*. There was, however, some security in going with the flow and agreeing with shit you felt abhorrent about. Yet, something was keeping G.O.'s mouth closed, and he could not fathom the cause. *This is going to be a three-joint problem,* Hill thought. *Better to fight another day.* So G.O. responded the only way his heart would let him. "Goddamn, Bugman, it's hotter than a two-peckered goat in this place. Let's take our beers and go outside."

"Hell no, Hill...all them pot smokers is outside. You don't wanna go out there; everybody will think you're a goddamn peacenik," Bugman responded.

"Well, let's go back to the hooch, then. We sit can outside on the bunker and have a few more brews before we turn in. What d'ya say?"

"Yeah, this fucken place is way too loud," Stick Shift offered.

So the crew reluctantly retired from the MMAF E club.

◆ ◆ ◆

As the four of them were headed back to the hooch, they were stopped by a Marine who wanted a light for his cigarette. He looked and sounded as though he might be Hispanic. Suddenly, they were surrounded by a group of eight more Marines. One of them shoved G.O. in the back, then he heard Bugman yell, "Run!" So he started running trying to follow Bugman, Stick Shift, and Delmonico in the dark.

When they got back to the hooch, Bugman went to his locker, pulled out his M-16, and said, "Who's going with me?"

"Where you going, man?"

"I'm going after them fucken greasers. They've been rolling Marines coming out of the club since I've been here, but this is the first time I've been jumped."

"Hold on, man. How do you know they are greasers?" G.O. asked.

"Because they run around in gangs like that, and I heard them yelling at us in Spanish as we ran away. I tell you, those motherfuckers aren't getting away with that shit, not as long as I have a weapon."

"I say we take the beers out to the bunker. Drink a few and make a plan. I don't like just running off after those fuckers willy-nilly, Bugman," Stick Shift said. "We can always set up an ambush later, but that's going to take some plannin'."

"Well, you pussies can sit around drinkin' beer and makin' plans, but I'm going after them. See y'all later," Bugman said as he left the hooch.

◆ ◆ ◆

As the crew lay on the bunker drinking beer and visiting, Stick Shift told the story about why the E club was so hot. When the Seabees set out to build the first E club at MMAF they had located the club on a point that jutted out into the South China Sea. "Well, they had the foundation poured when the MMAF C.O. says, 'Oh no, boys, you can't put the E club there! Why, them insurgent communist guerrillas from the North might decide to invade from the sea. You must build it over there,' he tells them. So the Seabees, in their seven seas wisdom, packed up all their gear and left. So, flash forward to the new commander. He sees the foundation and says, 'Hey, that would be a great spot for my quarters, nice cool breezes off the South China Sea from three directions and it already has a foundation.' But the wily Seabees tells the C.O., 'We will build your quarters as soon as we build an E club. Where would you like that placed?' So the C.O. scratches his ass for a spell, and he says, 'Well, fellers, it needs to be someplace where they don't want to linger for long.' So now the Seabees are stumped 'cause who in their right minds would want to linger in this fucken country for any length of time? So, they finally decide to put it down by where they burn the shit to keep the gooners from spreading it on their rice. Well, flash forward again, new C.O. has the shit-burning pits moved 'cause no one is going to the E club, and the Seabees had already told him no way in hell were they moving the E club again. So, that's pretty much the story of the E club. It might be hotter than hell in there, but at least you don't have to put up with burning shit."

G.O. looked at Stick Shift. He was red-headed like Barf, only he had more brown and black in his hair. He had an easy smile and a quiet laugh, and he was missing one of his canines. He had a small scar across the bridge of his nose and another above his left eye, but they only added to his stoic demeanor. *Stick Shift Henry looks a lot older than the rest of us,* G.O. thought. "Damn, Stick, how long you been here?" he asked.

"Since '65. It'll be four years in April."

G.O. and Joey D. were dumbstruck. "Well, if you don't mind me asking, why are you still only a corporal?"

"I don't mind…seems like every time I go on R and R, I get busted for gettin' a little crazy. Something just comes over me, don't know why, just does. Anyway, I'm thinkin' this war is over for me, so I'm headin' back to the world in April."

"Shit, seems like everyone I meet has less time to serve than me," G.O. said.

"That ought to tell you something, cowboy," Stick replied.

"Where you from, Stick? You sound like the Bugman."

"I'm from Philadelphia, Tennessee, and Bugs is from Loudon, Tennessee, about six miles away. We never knew one another until we met here in Vietnam, though."

Bugman came walking up to the bunker. "Couldn't find the bastards… somebody throw me a beer."

"Well, hell, son," G.O. said. "They probably heard that ol' 'Daniel Boone' York was out lookin' for them"—he pitched the Bugman a beer— "so they skedaddled."

"Yeah, well this shit ain't over," the Bugman replied as he climbed up on the bunker.

Bugman looked at Joey D., who had his teeth out and a big drunken smile on his face, "Damn, son, you from Tennessee?"

"No," Joey said, "Florida." Bugman frowned and was about to say something when the first rocket exploded.

G.O. heard a piercing scream. "Incoming!" The Marines left the top of the bunker and ran inside as the rockets continued to explode. Soon the bunker was packed with Marines. As they sat in the darkness listening to the muted explosions, a voice came out of the dark. "Damn, it sounds like those rockets are falling on the army side."

"Yeah, it does," several others commented.

"Well, hell, let's get out of here," Bugman said. "We got beer on top." The crew was much faster exiting than entering. As they lay on top of the bunker watching the explosions go off on the other side of the MMAF runway, it wasn't long before they ran out of beer.

"Oh, hell," Stick Shift said, "we are out of beer."

"We got anything else to drink?" Bugman asked.

"I've got some gin, but I don't have anything to mix it with," Joey D. said.

"How'd you get that?" G.O. asked.

"I made one of the Boeing engineers a canvas garment bag with his name on it, and he gave me a quart of gin."

"Well, hell, you para-pukes is good for somethin'," Bugman said. "Let's go to the mess hall and see if they have any orange juice."

"The mess hall is closed, Bugs," Stick responded.

"That's OK, I have a key," Bugman said. So the crew left the bunker in search of the mystical mess hall.

Later, the crew sat on the floor in the mess hall by one of the walk-in coolers. They could not find any OJ on the premises, so they were drinking gin and chocolate milk. The gin-and-chocolate-milk combination was a shade north of unpalatable, but being Marines, they managed to choke it down. *Har-r-r-r.* They were all inebriated by this time. Stumbling, commode-hugging, gloriously drunk. The crew had long passed the organic chemist's mock alcohol sugars, jocose and morose, and had entered the bellicose state. Hammered. Their minds were still working but only barely. Any coordination between their thoughts and being able to express them had become next to impossible. After talking in tongues to one another for about five minutes, they had managed to agree that the Marble Mountain commanding officer should somehow be punished for not looking out for his men by placing the E club next to the old shit-burning pits. As the group struggled to their feet, G.O. thought, *Where're my feet? I know they are down there, but why can't I feel them? Shit, this room is moving...no, I'm moving...but where're my feet? I'll be OK, I'll just follow the guys and try not to fall. Damn, they are all glassy-eyed drunk. Jeez, I hope I don't look like them. Why do they have those stupid smiles on their faces? Fuck, I'm smilin' too! Why? 'Cause this is some funny shit!* G.O. started an uncontrollable laugh.

"What the fuck is so funny, Hill?" Bugman wanted to know.

"You and Joey D. look like fucken brothers," Hill said. "You know like those retards without any teeth you see down south sellin' watermelons on the side of the road."

Stick Shift started laughing, too. "He's right, Bugs, y'all do resemble each other a bit."

"Well, fuck you and the Shetland pony you rode in on, Hill," Bugman replied. "And you, Stick, I can't believe somebody from Tennessee would stick up for somebody from Texas. With the exception of that traitorous bastard, Davy Mother-fucken-Crockett, but then the greasers took care of him, didn't they?"

The crew had miraculously found a bulldozer, and Stick had managed to get it started. As they rumbled toward where they believed the CO's house to be located, they managed to get one of the treads securely mired in a slough that they would not have been able to see if they had been stone sober. Stick and Joey D. passed out on the dozer, while G.O. and the Bugman managed to pass out on a soft patch of sandy earth close by.

Lomax, the one-eyed cockroach, clinging to the exhaust stack, shook his head, sighed, and said, "This is a fucken train wreck, so much for your decision-making skills, Hill."

Chapter Twenty Four

An Egregious Shit Sandwich

G.O. moved. It hurt. It hurt all over. The pain was so excruciatingly intense, he could not discover its source. For a moment he thought he was blind, for his eyes simply would not open. This caused him to jerk suddenly and a violent pain shot from one temple to the other. G.O. lay perfectly still, his breathing shallow, trying to reduce the pain he felt in his head. He finally managed to open one eye to a slit. He reached up to remove the eye discharges that had collected there during the night and discovered all manner of nastiness caked to his eyelid. There was sand and mud as well as the normal discharges and no small amount of fly shit.

He closed his eyes and began removing the caked-on filth. It was then he noticed that his ears and nose were also caked with dried mud and sand. He operated slowly and methodically until the orifices in his skull had been cleaned as well as he could manage. He slowly opened one eye and could see slits of light. As his senses started coming back, he realized at last where he was.

He was inside a large metal container. Alternating metal strips about two inches wide had been cut out of the sides of the container. The source of the slits of light. The box was metal and about eight feet by eight feet by twenty feet. This type of metal box was used for shipping all manner of supplies to Vietnam, and the logistical term for them was Container Express, shortened to Conex by the military. G.O. looked around the box and saw Stick, Bugman, and Joey. *Jeez,* G.O. wondered, *how did we get here?* As hard as he tried, he could not remember much past getting on the dozer. At some point, G.O. knew, he had entered into a coma.

Oh, Christ, G.O. thought, *we are going to miss a flight if we can't get out of here. I wonder if the Marines still shoot people for that kinda shit... or worse...the Island with No Name?* He put his eye up close to one of the slits. He could see that they were in a compound surrounded by barbed wire with rolled concertina wire at both the top and bottom. There was only one other Conex box inside the wire, but he could not tell if anyone was inside. G.O. was about ready to try and wake Delmonico up when he heard this loud *clankety-clank-clank* banging on the outside of his present quarters. The inside of G.O.'s head exploded like a kettle drum. The others woke with a shock, G.O. knew what waking easy had been like, and he felt sorry for the awakening these poor bastards were getting. Then he heard the unmistakable voice of Gunny G.

"Rise and shine, goddamnit, rise and fucken shine!" the Gunny shouted as he beat on the outside of the Conex box with a metal pipe. The Gunny at HMH-463 had notified Gunny G. that two of his crewmen had been locked up with two from HMM-265. He hopped the first flight down, which happened to be Bear's test flight on the squadron's scavenger bird. "Goddamnit, Hill, I should leave you two dumbasses locked up for the duration, but Gallo is waiting for an engine at Vandegrift, you forget about that, Hill?"

A Marine guard with an SP armband, the Marine equivalent of a policeman, opened the Conex box. "Well, come on, you two, we haven't got all day!" G.O. and Joey started walking toward the hatch, followed by the Bugman and Stick Shift. "Not so fast, you two, Gunny Farquhar said you two needed to fill sandbags for the rest of the week and sweat out some of that alcohol. He said he would be around later in the week."

"Yeah, well, I wasn't ready to leave anyway," the Bugman intoned.

"I'll be sure and tell him that," Gunny G. responded.

The Gunny maintained as neutral a demeanor of pissed-offedness as possible as they climbed into the jeep the Gunny had borrowed. As the trio headed away from the brig toward the flight line, the Gunny said, "I've got to stop by the mess hall and get something to eat. I will drop you two off outside the showers, and I want you looking and smelling better when I come to pick you up, got it?"

"Got it, Gunny," G.O. responded. Delmonico was still in shock.

"Where are your fucken teeth, Delmonico?"

"I don't remember, Gunny..."

"Well, the Marine Corps ain't buyin' you any new ones, ass-wipe, so you better get used to eatin' soft foods!"

Well, that's more like the Gunny, G.O. thought. "Oh, hell, I remember now, Joey, you gave them to me last night so you wouldn't lose them." With that said, G.O. reached into the lower pocket on his flight suit pant leg and pulled out Joey's bridge. It was caked with mud and sand. Joey was delighted to have his teeth back, as he grinned from ear-to-ear, but he wasn't about to put them in his mouth.

◆ ◆ ◆

"Well, well, well...you two clean up real nice, and I'm glad you have your teeth back in, Delmonico. I thought on the way to the flight line you could fill me on what happened last night, Hill, the only thing in the SP report was that you were all four passed out on or near a bulldozer, and the engine was still running," the Gunny said as Hill and Delmonico climbed into the jeep.

"Sure, Gunny, but before I get started, what's in the sack?"

"I thought you boys might be hungry after a night in the Conex box, so I had the cook make up some egg sandwiches and throw in a couple of chocolate milks..."

G.O. leaned over the passenger side of the jeep, and Delmonico leaned out the back of the vehicle as they began spewing multiple ejections. The Gunny grinned inwardly to himself.

◆ ◆ ◆

The Sugar Bear had just finished his strawberry milkshake, and Chucky D. had finished his chocolate milkshake at the Seabee Materials Center in Da Nang. They had also just completed the first leg of the test flight for Bear's scavenger bird. The Seabees had added a club to the facility that was air-conditioned and served up milkshakes and cheeseburgers. It was a true respite from the war in Vietnam. For a few moments, you could pretend you were back in the world, and the Bear and Chucky D. were certainly savoring the moment. Anytime Captain D'Amato had to test flight an aircraft, this was always his first choice as a destination.

For test flights, usually only a pilot and crew chief went flying, and the crew chief regularly flew left seat during these procedures. The materials center was located just south of the Da Nang Water Treatment Facility, and the Seabees had built a landing pad that would accommodate four CH-46s. The Bear and Chucky D. finished their stateside repast and left the club for the Bear's new aircraft the *Couchay Express.* The Bear had named his aircraft after a novel he had picked up from special services by author John Dos Passos.

After Chucky D. lit the fires and had the blades turning, the Bear came up the ramp and headed for the cockpit. *Damn, I hope he don't fart in the cockpit again,* Bear thought. *I thought I was for sure gonna gag last time.* Captain D'Amato and the Bear went through the preflight checklist then Captain D'Amato called the tower at Da Nang Air Base for clearance since the Fast Movers were in constant motion around the Da Nang AB.

"Highboy One three...you are cleared to depart north...be advised do not climb above three zero zero feet before reaching Da Nang Bay.'

"Roger that tower...cleared to depart north..."

Then to Bear, "Well, Crew Chief, it looks like we have to fly directly over the excrement treatment facility, so get ready to hold your breath." The Bear looked at Chucky D., then smiled and thought, *It could be worse.*

It was. As they were climbing out of the Seabee Materials Center, the *Couchay Express* lost power as both engines came offline. Captain D'Amato barely got off a Mayday before they belly-flopped into the middle of the largest sediment pool in the water treatment facility. They created the proverbial tidal wave of shit as the CH-46 settled into the decomposing putrescence.

Chucky D. looked at Bear and said in his best Oliver Hardy voice, "Well, this is another fine mess you've gotten us into, Crew Chief."

◆ ◆ ◆

The Gunny dropped the double yo's at *Groundz,* and left to return the jeep to his friend, Gunny Farquhar, in HMH-463. Fortunately for Hill and Delmonico, the pilots, Abramovitz and Masterson, had not yet arrived.

"You get the top unbuttoned for the pilots, Joey. I'll take care of everything down here."

"Roger, that," Joey responded. But before Joey could climb up the stub wing of the CH-46, a jeep came roaring up with Gunny G., Lieutenant Abramovitz, Lieutenant Masterson, and another Gunny G.O. did not recognize but assumed to be Gunny Farquhar. Gunny G. and the pilots hopped out of the jeep and approached Hill.

"This thing ready to fly, Hill?"

"She was when we shut her down yesterday, Gunny."

"Very well," Lieutenant Abramovitz said, "we'll skip the preflight and light the fires." Abramovitz and Masterson headed up to the cockpit. G.O. stopped the Gunny on the ramp.

"What's the hurry, Gunny?"

"Well, it seems like your friend, Bear, and Captain D'Amato hard-landed the scavenger bird in the Da Nang water treatment facility about thirty minutes ago. So, we are going to pick them up, fly this spare engine back to Vandy, and then, powers greater than you and me will decide what we do next, *comprende,* dumbass?"

"Understood, Gunny," G.O. replied as he put his hard hat on and connected to the aircraft intercom system.

◆ ◆ ◆

"Why you smilin', Hill? You think this shit is funny?" the Bear asked as the crew of *Groundz* flew back to Hue-Phu Bai. "Or do I just you remind you of home?"

"Well, you do kinda smell like a feedlot that was close to my house," G.O. replied. "Seems like you could have washed some of that shit off before you came onboard my aircraft."

"The Seabees turned water hoses on us after we climbed out of the holding tank. I mean, we had shit up to our thighs. Captain D'Amato kept thinking they was gonna send a boat out to get us. Can you imagine? I mean, he one of the smartest pilots in the squadron, and he think they gonna send a boat out in a tank full of shit to rescue his ass. Then he keep talking like that fat motherfucker in them old movies back in the states. You know the one that run with the skinny guy?"

"Oliver Hardy?" G.O. chuckled.

"Yeah, that's the one. Shit ain't funny, Hill...it ain't funny...*Another fine mess you've gotten us into, Crew Chief.*"

"What do you think happened?"

"Shit, I don't know and won't know till I get the *Coushay* back to Hue and have a look under the hood, my brother. But I can tell you one thing, Hill," Bear postulated, "they better not try to pin this shit on the black man...that's what I'm talkin' about!"

"I hear you, Bear," G.O. replied, and for the first time in his life bumped fists with a black man.

◆ ◆ ◆

At Hue-Phu Bai, they dropped off Captain D'Amato, Gunny G., and the Sugar Bear and loaded up the recovery team and flew them to Vandy to recover *Surf City.* When they arrived, there was one pissed-off Gallo awaiting them.

"Where the hell you guys been, Hill? I thought you would return yesterday," Gallo ejected.

"Hey, slow down, Kemosabe...The world doesn't revolve around your ass. We got here as fast as humanly possible, old son. What's your problem, anyway? You didn't enjoy your quiet evening at Vandegrift Combat Base?"

"Quiet's ass, G.O. There were mortars and rockets and flares all fucken night long and the fucken grunts…they shoot at anything that moves or that they think might move. Shit, I didn't sleep all night long…but the Gerber Baby…that fucker could sleep through anything."

"War is hell, my friend, but trust me, it beats spending the night in a Conex box."

Locker cocked his left eyebrow and said, "Tell me more…"

Chapter Twenty Five

On the Road to Shambala

G.O. and Locker walked into the line shack at Hue-Phu Bai to be met by an overwrought Gunny G. "You two magpies get ready to go flying again. We are headed to Da Nang in thirty minutes to retrieve Easy Pickin's one-three."

"Jeez, Gunny, I thought they would use one of those flying cranes to bring it back?" Hill interjected.

"You, Corporal Hill, are about five pubic hairs away from the Island with No Name. Why do you insist on questioning decisions the Marine Corps is so happy to make for you? If I tell you to prepare to fly, what is the correct response, Corporal Numbnuts?"

"Aye-aye, Gunny!"

"Correct, Hill. Any more questions?"

"No, Gunny." Hill and Gallo made a quick exit from the line shack.

♦ ♦ ♦

As G.O. and Locker prepped *Groundz* for flight, they saw the Sugar Bear approaching. In his left hand he had a folder, and in his right hand he carried his Seabag. "Damn, Bear, you going on vacation?"

The Bear looked at G.O. and Locker for a moment trying to decide what to say. "No, you retarded assholes...I'm being transferred to a real

189

squadron, HMH 463 at Marble Mountain. If you look closely, it's Sergeant Lee from now on."

Locker and G.O. looked at the chevrons pinned to the Sugar Bear's collar. They were Sergeant's stripes. G.O. never knew the Bear's last name was Lee.

"Well, damn, Bear, man. Why the transfer? Are they saying it was your fault the *Coushay Express* wiped out in the sediment pool at Da Nang?" Gallo inquired.

"No, Locker, the Gunny said they are not saying I was to blame, they just needed somebody to blame. So the first black man they could think of was yours truly." Bear laughed, then sniggered. "I guess they was feelin' some of that white guilt shit 'cause they also promoted me to Sergeant before transferrin' me. Why y'all got them long looks on your faces? You know how the Corps is, don't matter how bad you fuck up if they like you…But if the powers that be don't care for you…well, you know, it could be worse, it could be *much* worse. This time the black man got treated like one of you white boys." The Bear laughed again. "Shee-it, Hill, you the one better be lookin' over your shoulder."

"Bear? I never knew your name was Lee," G.O. intoned.

"That's right, Hill. Lee is my given name. Marcellus Euripides Lee. My friends back in Motown called me Melee, you know like M-E for my initials and Lee, my last name, combine 'em and you get *Melee*. 'Cause they knew I would kick their asses if they called me Marcellus. I didn't let no one know my middle name, not even my teachers…you dig?"

"I'll be sure to let the Bugman know," G.O. teased.

"Uh-huh, you do that, Hill. You do, and they will never find all your body parts. Say, Hill…what do G.O. stand for? I never hear anybody call you by anything 'cept your initials."

"The G stands for George, and you'll just have to guess what the O stands for."

"C'mon, man…I told you my name. What do the O stand for?"

"Would you believe…Octavius?"

"No shit?"

"No shit."

"Well, was yo' mama fond of them eight-legged creatures, the Octo-pud-i-aye? Or are you putting one over on the black man?"

"You will have to find this one out for yourself, Bear."

"Well, you know I will, Hill. But right now I can't wait to see the Bugman. One thing I am looking forward to is ordering that dumb Tennessee redneck around like he was fresh outa boot camp," Bear said, and all three started laughing.

"I would like to be a fly on the wall when that happens," G.O. said.

Lomax, the one-eyed cockroach, looked out from under the crew chief's jump seat, shook his head and thought, *You had your chance at the E club, Georgie.*

◆ ◆ ◆

After they arrived at MMAF, they were met by two jeeps and a deuce and a half truck. In the back of the deuce and a half was a tow bar for the helicopter. G.O's and Locker's eyebrows shot up as the Gunny told the crew to mount up. By now, G.O. was afraid to ask any more questions. "Hill, you drive and I'll ride shotgun in the first jeep. Locker, you will drive the jeep behind the Deuce and the Gerber Baby will ride shotgun for you. Let's ride, boys."

The road was crowded with vehicles of every kind on the drive from MMAF to the Da Nang Water Treatment Facility. There were carts, old French and Chinese automobiles, bicycles, and every type of motorbike imaginable on the roads. The exhaust fumes created a noxious soup that attacked all of the crew's senses at once. Before they had traveled a mile, G.O.'s nose was running and his eyes watered. His throat was scorched.

G.O. had his left hand on the wheel, and his right hand was on the gear shift. G.O. felt a tug on his left wrist and looked over in time to see a young Vietnamese on the back of a Vespa motor scooter with an outstretched arm. The Vietnamese had hooked his finger underneath G.O.'s flexible Seiko wristband and then jerked. G.O.'s arm left the steering wheel as the watch band broke and the motor scooter sped off between a fish-oil burning bus and several automobiles. G.O. rubbed his wrist with his right hand as the Gunny said, "See, Hill, that's why you always wear your watch on your right hand..." As the Gunny held up his right hand to show G.O. his watch, another bike sped up on the Gunny's side of the jeep and sped off with the Gunny's watch before he could complete his sentence. "Well, I'll be goddamned...the little slanty-eyed motherfucker got mine, too!" The Gunny and Hill laughed at their misfortune all the way to the water treatment facility.

◆ ◆ ◆

Nearing the water treatment facility, they saw three Vietnamese children sharing a smoke on the back of a cart being pulled by a Water Buffalo.

> The first time I saw
> a preschool kid
> smoking a cigarette I
> just stood and stared
>
> Mama-sans squatting
> to pee along the road
> never drew a second glance
> But a child casually smoking
> was hard for me to unsee
>
> For a month I had a
> reoccurring dream of
> a smoking toddler a
> circus performer eating glass
> and a ward filled with
>
> Thalidomide babies
> But after about
> four weeks the dream
> became a memory of
> a dream of a memory

The *Coushay Express,* also known as Echo Papa one-three, was parked outside the Seabee Materials Center. The aircraft was covered in the foul-smelling sediment from above the stub wings to the ground. G.O. looked at the Gunny and asked, "What's the plan, Gunny G.?"

"The plan, Hill, is for you boys to get Easy Pickin's one three hooked to the back of that deuce and a half while the Gunny goes into the materials center and has a strawberry malt...when you boys are finished, you may join me, or you can stand around out here and attract flies."

"Aye-aye, Gunny," the magpies chirped.

♦ ♦ ♦

At their base camp in the mountains above the A Shau Valley, Xin Loi and Hung Dong shared a private moment over tea. Hung had received a letter from Mr. Cua from the village of Dong Ho in the North. His wives had all had babies, three beautiful boys, and Mr. Cua sent updates of the wives and children. On this occasion, Mr. Cua had provided photos. Hung had named the boys Hung Cua, Hung Loi, and Hung Tuan. Xin Loi had been flattered when Hung wanted to name one of his sons after him.

"Ah-h-h, friend Hung...little Hung Loi is definitely the best-looking son you have! The other two are so scrawny...maybe you should leave them in the jungle?"

"Bah, do not talk nonsense! They are all three beautiful...look at the arms on Hung Cua...and Hung Tuan...have you ever seen such clever eyes on a baby? They will grow up to be fine young men and will study art with Mr. Cua and me."

"So no more children?" Xin asked.

"Oh, who said that? The Fat Rhino has not retired. The only thing that prevents more Hung children being born is me being here in the South with you and this stupid Iguana. Once we are back in Dong Ho, I will try to make it the most prolific village in Vietnam."

"I'm sure you will, Dong, I am sure you will. Why do you keep that insipid creature with you?"

"You mean Darwin, my pet Iguana? Because he is a symbol of good fortune, friend Loi. And his third eye saved us from an American ambush. What about you, Loi? Is there a woman in your future?"

"Well, now that you mention it, your grandmother, Hung Kim, introduced me to one of the Vietnamese girls that work for her at Hue-Phu Bai. She was quite lovely, and she was so easy to talk to. I think I should like to see her again, that is, when your grandmother isn't entertaining American Marines."

"Now that was crazy, Xin Loi. Who would ever believe such a tale? I can't wait to tell Mr. Cua about it. He may be able to explain it to me."

"What do you mean, Dong?"

"Well, they seemed like good men, just like you and me. But yet, we go out each day and try to kill each other, like it is some kind of game we play with no winners. Only those who live and those who die. And while we are trying to kill each other, they are trying to build a school for the Vietnamese orphans. It makes no sense to me. Like the Albino Water Buffalo we saw before our scout platoon was destroyed almost two years ago."

"Oh, so you believe in omens, now?"

"If you see a sign, Xin Loi, and do not heed the sign, then the fault lies with you. And if you do not understand the sign, you should find someone to help you understand the sign. Mr. Cua helps me to understand the signs."

"And what would Mr. Cua say about the color of your farts being set on fire as they passed through a screen door?"

"That is not funny, Loi...not funny. I still have several large blisters on my beautiful ass." Both Xin Loi and Hung Dong could not help but laugh about their bizarre meeting with the American Marines."

"Well, it is my night to take the scout platoon out, so I must leave you now to think about your family and your beautiful sons. May they be blessed with gas as powerful as their father!"

Hung threw his one of his sandals at Xin Loi as he fled down the tunnel laughing.

• • •

After they had finished their malts, the Gunny explained that they would be moving Easy Pickin's one-three to the navy dock in Da Nang harbor. The navy would then load the aircraft aboard one the navy's helicopter carriers, the USS *Iwo Jima*. The Gunny went on to explain that the squadron would be onloading aboard the *Iwo* during the coming week for an operation with the ROK (Republic of Korea) Marines. The Gunny concluded that the ROKs were the "toughest little bastards" he had ever had to deal with. "Hell, they could be US Marines, if they was a little taller."

"What about General Krulak?" Joey Delmonico asked.

The Gunny looked at Joey, who was barely passing five foot two inches. "What about him...Private? Surely, you do not think General Krulak is too short to be a Marine?"

"Oh no, Gunny, that's not what I meant at all...I mean General Krulak is a Marine's Marine...and, uh, he's short...like the ROKs."

"You goddamn right he's a Marine's Marine, but I wouldn't go comparing him to a gook."

"I wasn't comparing—"

"Hell, Joey, Dude, you need to give it up, man. Talk about something you know, like parachutes," Gallo offered. "Forget about finding a Marine you can look down on." The rest of the crew sniggered.

On the drive back to MMAF, the crew did not suffer any significant setbacks. As soon as they arrived, the Gunny had G.O. and Locker tow the aircraft over to HMH 463 where Gunny Farquhar had promised they could wash down the helicopter. They were met by Sergeant Lee.

"Welcome to the four hundred and sixty-third's carwash, gentlemen. Now if you will stand back out of the way, Lance Corporal Bugman will demonstrate the proper way to high-pressure wash a CH-46 aircraft."

The Bugman came out carrying what looked to be a firehose. He was wearing just his jungle trousers. No shoes and no shirt. He did not look happy to see G.O. or Locker. The Bugman released a valve on the hose, and water started spraying the aircraft.

"Now, if you gentlemen will step into my office?" the Bear said as he led them through the back of the hangar to the line shack. When they reached the line shack, several Marines, of various enlisted ranks, came up to the Bear with questions. They all addressed him as Sergeant Lee. G.O. and Locker were impressed.

"OK, Bear, man. Tell us how you got that redneck, Bugman, to wash down the aircraft?"

"O-o-o-h, now that's a good story. When I found out he was locked up, I axed Gunny Farquhar if he would let me get him out. So, I told the Bugman he had to do everything I told him for a week, then he could have his plane back."

"He agreed to that?" asked an astonished Locker Gallo.

"It was either agree or lay in that shit hole till Gunny decided to release him. Now, what would you do?"

"Why do you have him washing the aircraft?" G.O. asked. "I thought he was a pretty good mechanic."

"He a damn good mechanic. But he a redneck. These other pecker-woods see him taking orders from a black man make my job a lot easier. Sheee-it! Hill, it don' matter how much I know or how smart I am or how much rank I have, I can't scrape this black off my ass. Hell, if I want to be able to share my gifts and talents, the very essence of my goddamned being, with the goddamned Corps, then I have to earn the white man's respect, they don't just give that shit to black folks. Some white mutha-fucker makes sergeant, hell, everybody supposed to provide that mutha-fucker their undivided attention. Me, I have to earn that shit."

Bear stopped in mid-rant and let out a laugh, "Hah! Hah! Hah! You boys put me up here on my black soapbox and got me preachin' to the choir. Anyway, when I get through makin' his doofus, -a,-um, Tennessee ass wash every goddamn aircraft in the squadron and then give him his aircraft back in a couple of days...well, I think he will be most apprecia-tive. And I don't believe I will have any trouble with these other chili-eatin' goobers. That's what I'm talkin' about."

"Let's hope so," Locker said.

About this time a corporal they did not know walked into the line shack. "Excuse me, Sergeant Lee, is there a Corporal Hill and a Lance Corporal Gallo here?"

"That's us. What do you need?"

"There's a Gunny outside in a Deuce and a half looking for you guys."

Locker and Hill climbed into the deuce and a half. "What's up Gunny?"

"The C.O. wants us to make a liquor run while we are here at Marble, so we are driving to the liquor warehouse at Da Nang. When we get there, you let the Gunny do the talking, y'all are just there to carry the cases of liquor, understand?"

"Understood, Gunny!" the duo quipped. As they left Marble and headed to Da Nang, G.O. looked at the Gunny's wrist and saw that he was sporting a new watch with a leather wristband. *Good luck on stealing that one,* G.O. thought. "Nice-looking watch, Gunny."

"Oh yeah. Almost forgot," the Gunny dug around in his pocket and came up with a watch for G.O. It, too, had a leather watchband. He pitched it to Hill.

"Well, jeez! Thanks, Gunny, you didn't have to do that!"

"Goddamnit, Hill, I know what I have to do and what I don't have to do. I don't need some draft-dodging commie bastard to tell me that. I figured if I left it to you, you'd be late to everything and blame it on not knowing the time. So just shut the hell up and quit trying to be nice. Marines ain't nice, *comprende*?"

"Understood, Gunny." G.O. was smiling as he fastened his new time-piece to his wrist while Locker playfully elbowed him in the ribs.

After the Marine guards had passed them into the warehouse com-pound and given them directions to the liquor warehouse, they were met by mayhem. Vietnamese workers scurrying around like they were under a rocket attack. The women were crying and screaming and pointing. The men were shouting and pointing.

In front of them was an industrial forklift and on the forks raised about fourteen feet in the air was a fabled outdoor three-hole toilet. Inside the three-holer, an ancient mama-san shouted in Vietnamese and shook her fist at the forklift operator. Whenever the operator started to lower the outhouse, he would make it bounce up and down. The human waste that filled the fifty-gallon drums would slosh around and splash up on the mama-san.

Then there would be more wailing and shouting from all the Vietnamese. After about five minutes of riding the shithouse tilt-a-whirl, the forklift operator finally set the three-holer back on the ground. An excrement-coated mama-san burst through the screen door shouting in Vietnamese. The workers all scurried away with the mama-san in tow.

The forklift operator climbed down and put on his jungle blouse. The Gunny came to attention as did Locker and G.O. "Sorry, Lieutenant, didn't know your rank, sir."

"Relax, Gunnery Sergeant, we're not that formal around here. You got here for the end of the show...how did you like it? That old bitch has been..." Eyes suddenly wide, the lieutenant continued, "Locker, is that you? Well, I'll be damned, Locker Gallo, didn't expect to see you here. Damn, we got some catching up to do. Relax, Locker, it's me, Howie! You can go back to being a Marine if my boss shows up, but that's not likely. Well, damn!"

"Howie, let me introduce you to G.O. Hill and Gunny Peabody, but we call him Gunny G. You catchin' any waves over at China Beach?"

"Naw, the waves around here ain't much, except right before a typhoon. Then there are some bitches that roll. Here, follow me and we'll get a drink and visit for a while."

The crew walked into what appeared to be an office. On one desk was a nameplate that read, 'Lt. Howard Patterson' and on the other desk a nameplate read, 'SSgt. Elwood Jefferson.' Staff Sergeant Jefferson never looked up as the crew walked in.

"Elwood, goddamnit! Let me introduce you to a friend from back in the States. This is Locker Gallo. We used to take our sticks up to Steamer Lane in Northern Cali and catch some bitchin' waves.

"Shit, Elwood, if I ever get you on a stick I'm gonna write a book about it, *Black Men I've Met While Surfin'*." Howie laughed and the others did too, although it was more of a nervous laughter as Elwood stood at his desk and held out his massive black hand.

"Nice to meet you, Sergeant," Locker said. The Gunny and G.O. followed suit.

"Yeah, Elwood here used to play roundball for one of the junior colleges in LA before he blew out a knee. He finished at UCLA with a degree in accounting, which comes in real handy in this shit hole." Lieutenant Patterson reached into a cooler by his desk and offered beers to the crew. The only refusal came from Staff Sergeant Jefferson. "So what brings you boys to Da Nang?"

The Gunny explained that they had been sent down by the C.O. to pick up several cases of booze for the O club in Hue-Phu Bai. Howie talked it over with Staff Sergeant Jefferson, and then Elwood left the office.

"He's gonna fix you guys up. I told him to put in an extra case of bourbon for you, Gunny, and a couple cases of beer for you, Locker. What do you like to drink, Hill?"

"Oh, he likes gin and chocolate milk," Gallo said.

"C'mon, man. You know I like beer."

"Shit, son, sounds like a hint of cow shit in your voice. Where you from, Hill?"

"I'm from Texas, Lieutenant…er, ah, Howie."

"That's all right, Hill. Call me whatever makes you comfortable. You didn't grow up with me like Locker. So what's your poison?"

"Beer is fine, sir."

The lieutenant walked over to the door and shouted at Staff Sergeant Jefferson, "Put two more cases of beer on the truck, Elwood."

Chapter Twenty Six

Nowhere Man

The Hue Phu-Bai line shack was a hive of activity, in spite of the nasty weather, as the Marines of HMM-265 prepared to board the *Iwo Jima* at the end of the week. After preflighting his aircraft, *Groundz,* G.O. reported to the Gunny in the squadron line shack. The first person he ran into was Locker. "Hey, Gallo, what's happening?"

Before Gallo could respond, the Gunny roared, "Where the fuck you been, Hill?"

"Preflighting my aircraft, Gunny."

"Did it ever enter your pea-sized brain that you might want to check in here first and look at the duty roster? Goddamnit, what is happening to my beloved corps?"

"Well, I think…"

"Don't answer that, Corporal Numbnuts, and how many times have I told you…"

Everyone within hearing distance of the Gunny responded, "If the Marine Corps wanted you to think…they would have issued you a brain!"

"Well, I'll be goddamned, if this bunch ain't gettin' smarter by the minute! Why is everyone standing around listening to a private conversation? If you don't have anything to do, there are plenty of boxes that need to be carried out to the flight line…"

As the Gunny went into a fifteen-minute tirade in the line shack, Marines of every rank scurried out of his way trying to look busier than the Marine next to him. G.O. noticed a sour-looking Marine sitting on a seabag.

His bullet-shaped head looked ready to explode at any moment. He had pale-brown skin, like the sandy soil in a fallow field, and he had small freckles lining the cheekbones under his eyes. His eyes were a translucent mahogany lined with yellow, with very little white exposed. His hair was short, wavy, and red. His wide nostrils were set above a perpetual frown. Under his bottom lip grew a small tuft of red hair that he kept stroking with his left hand. His green T-shirt was stretched tightly across muscles that looked to have been chiseled by Polykleitos. *That son of a bitch gives me the fantods,* G.O. thought. *Damn, he looks like he might go off on you at any moment. Cain and Abel personified.*

"Damn, Hill, quit eye-fucking the new mech and introduce yourself," the Gunny roared. "Corporal George Hill, this is Private Pernicious Bonebreaker. I think Mrs. Bonebreaker gets the Most Creative Mother award this year, if not the Most Creative then certainly the Most Intuitive. Private Bonebreaker comes to us from the Pendleton Brig, where he was serving time for assault and battery on seven squids. After he broke the jaw of one of his handlers, the Marine Corps thought he might do some good in the 'Nam. Private Bonebreaker and I have already had a heart-to-heart; his next fuck-up will get him an all-expenses paid vacation to the Long Binh Jail, and if he is fortunate, he will avoid spending the rest of his miserable life in Portsmouth."

"Now, Hill, Bonebreaker will join me and you and Lance Corporal Sullivan on recovery detail until we go aboard ship, then he will be assigned to *Surf City* as Gallo's first mech. Don't even say it, Hill...Gallo was here before you, so he gets the first available mech. Now I want you two limp-dicked fuckers to inventory the recovery vehicle and make sure we have all the tools we need if we have to make a pick up in the field. *Comprende*, Hill?"

"Understood, Gunny." Hill grinned at the light duty. "Let's go, Pernicious!" G.O reached down to pick up Bonebreaker's seabag. "Shit, son, what you got in here? This bag weighs a ton!"

"Books."

"Books? Well, I'll be damned."

As G.O. and Pernicious made their way into the hangar, looking for the Gerber Baby, Bonebreaker turned his demented gaze on Hill and said, "Don't call me Pernicious. That was my drugged-out crazy mama's idea of a joke."

"Exactly what name would you like to be called, Private?"

"It would be best if you called me Hakim, Corporal. Then when others hear you, they will do it naturally."

"Why Hakim, Hakim?"

"It was the name given me by Elijah Muhammad and the Nation of Islam when I became a Muslim."

"You mean like Muhammad Ali and Malcolm X?"

"Yes, praise be to Allah!"

"Well, hell, Ali is banned from boxing, and Malcolm X was assassinated…so tell me again why you want to be a Muslim?"

"Ain't always gonna be this way, Brother Hill. One day the black man is gonna rise up and take his rightful place in the world, and anybody try to deny him will be dealt a swift and terrible justice," Hakim replied menacingly as his eyes started to turn red.

Oh, shit, G.O. thought. *Changing the subject just might keep me from receiving an ass-whuppin'.*

"Does the Gunny know you changed your name?"

"He know. He don't care; he livin' in the white man's world. So he gonna call me the white man name my momma gave me. But then she up and killed herself on drugs one night when I was just eight years old. Had to go and live with my uncle and auntie in Chicago. They were both Garveyites, believed in everything Marcus Garvey had to say. The next thing I know, I'm enrolled in a Muslim school. Every day I was told how beautiful I was, how smart I was, and that I could do anything I wanted. Things I never heard in a whitey's schools. I never heard the word *nigger,*

Hill, till I turned sixteen! You believe that shit? So, Hill, tell me, if you had been in my shoes, what would you have done?"

G.O. looked at Hakim and immediately noticed that his eyes had gone from menacing to inquiring. *Sheee-it,* Hill thought, *the man's eyes are like a traffic light. Red is stop before I pounce, yellow is caution motherfucker, and mahogany, mahogany? It means let's talk."*

"Honestly? If I belonged to a culture that had been enslaved for four hundred years and not allowed to become part of society, even after emancipation. If nothing I accomplished would allow me to be called a man. If people rejected me because of the color of my skin. I suppose I would be angry, too. And I would want to take revenge on the culture that had done this to me and refused to make it right. So. yeah, I would probably join a culture that respected me as a human being...as a man."

"Well, sheee-it, my brother, you startin' to sound like a white H. Rap or a blue-eyed Stokely. White folks like you might be spared when the revolution comes..." Then cutting his eyes at G.O. and offering up a wolfish grin with his vampire-like canines exposed, he said, "But I kinda doubt it!"

◆ ◆ ◆

The recovery vehicle was a large rectangular metal box, about four feet wide and six feet long, with a depth of about three feet. With four tires and a handle, it looked like an overgrown Radio Flyer. Gerber Baby had the vehicle open and the tools needed to recover a helicopter from the field spread out on the hangar floor.

"We got everything we need, Gerbs?" Hill asked.

"Yep, it's all here according to the inventory list. Who's the FNG?"

"Oh, this is Private Hakim, Gerbs."

"Welcome aboard, Hakim."

Hakim just nodded and gave the Gerber Baby a desultory look. Eyes on yellow.

"All right, you two, pack up, and I'll let the Gunny know."

◆ ◆ ◆

"Goddamnit, Fantan! I just knew if I put you on the recovery team some dipshit pilot would augur in one of my goddamn aircraft. Shit, should have had you carrying boxes all day and saved myself this grief, you magnet-assed, androgynous douchebag-looking boot!"

The Gunny ranted at Hill while the recovery team rode *Surf City* out to the crash site to recover the Duck's aircraft, *Pandora's Box*. The crew of the *Pandora* had already been picked up and flown back to Hue-Phu Bai. The mission of the recovery team was to remove the rotor blades and rig a harness so either a CH-53 or a Sky Crane could pick the aircraft up and return her to base. The Gunny and Hakim were both in their camouflaged Jungle Utilities and sporting flak jackets and steel pots, while G.O. and the Gerber baby wore their flight suits and bush hats. All of the crew carried side arms and M-16s. On the back of the Gunny's flak jacket was an inscription, *John Wayne is dead!*

Gallo came back to the Gunny and told him that they would circle the rice paddy where *Pandora's Box* had hard landed, and the pilot would try to offload the recovery team as close as possible. As they circled the rice paddy, G.O. was happy to see that a platoon of grunts had established a defensive perimeter around the aircraft and that the paddy was dry. If the weather would hold, they could have the aircraft ready to be picked up before nightfall. *Surf City* swooped into the rice paddy and offloaded the crew. As they departed, G.O. could not help but grin as Locker mooned them from the crew's hatchway.

"Hill, get your crew to start taking off the rotor blades and loading them in the cargo bay. I'm gonna check in with the grunts."

"Ooh-rah, Gunny!" Hill replied. "OK, you heard the man. Gerbs you make sure the rotor brake is off. I'll unfasten the blades, Hakim you'll shake 'em loose. When we get them loose, you hand your end down to Gerbs, then you climb down and help Gerbs walk the blades into the aircraft."

◆ ◆ ◆

Gunny G. walked over to an area intersected by a corner of two of the rice paddy dikes, occupied by a radioman, a sergeant and a lieutenant. "Well, hell, I presume you are in charge of this clusterfuck, Lieutenant?"

"That's an affirmative, Gunny," replied a rather emaciated figure who held his hand out toward the Gunny, "so you can address me as 'sir' or as 'Lieutenant Stein.'"

Damn, the Gunny thought, *this sumbitch could be Ichabod Crane's lost twin.*

"Let's see," the Gunny pondered as he rubbed his chin, "Stein... Stein...You related to any of the Steins in Arizona, Lieutenant? There was a shitload of 'em in Sedona, musta been a Stein pissin' behind every adobe gift shop."

"Wot, there's Steins in Arizona? You gotta be fucken wid me, Gunny... I'm from Brooklyn. Besides, whoever heard of a Jew in his right mind living in Arizona?"

"Hope to shit in your mess gear, Lieutenant, but legend has it that them Arizona Steins is part of the lost tribe of Israel and a whole pea pot–load of 'em are directly descended from the Hopi Indians."

"Jewish Indians?"

"Yep, got noses just like yours, Lieutenant, meaning no disrespect, sir."

While the Gunny was having his conversation with the lieutenant, G.O. and his crew had removed one forward rotor blade and had started on the second, when all hell broke loose. Automatic weapons fire started coming from a tree line about two hundred meters away from the rice paddy. G.O. and Hakim jumped off the fuselage as enemy rounds pinged into the helicopter. All three Marines ran to the nearest paddy dike. The radio operator had called up a nearby firebase for artillery support, and the lieutenant was on the horn. As he fumbled with his map to find the co-ordinates to give to the artillery support, the Gunny calmly reached over and took his map book from him.

"Hell, Lieutenant, there ain't no firebase close enough to lob a few rounds on the gooners, besides there's a village behind that tree line that would definitely be exposed to artillery fire. What we need is a fast mover to drop some napalm on that tree line. In the meantime, you might want to get a thumper on that tree line!"

The lieutenant looked at the Gunny through hollow eyes and told the radio operator to get air support on the horn.

◆ ◆ ◆

In the tree line, an anxious Hung Dong crawled over to his Lieutenant, Xin Loi, who was directing fire for his scout patrol. "Xin, I think it may be time to di-di! We have been firing steadily at the downed helicopter for fifteen minutes, and their grenade launcher is finding our range."

"We will leave, comrade, when we hear the American jets. We will have plenty of time to get back to the safety of our tunnels."

"Did you notice that one of the Marines on the helicopter looked like one of the Marines we met at Grandmother Hung Kim's in Hue City?"

"It is part of the sorrow of war, friend Dong. Do not become sentimental on me, I need you in this fight!"

"Listen, Xin…Is that the sound of a jet approaching?"

"Yes, my friend, now is the time to di-di. Pass the word!"

◆ ◆ ◆

G.O. and the Gerber Baby were snug in the bosom of the rice paddy berm with looks of utter amazement on their faces as they watched Hakim unload one M16 5.56 mm magazine after another at the tree line. Screaming vile words and epithets at Sir Charles while he did so. "Why you little yellow motherfuckers shooting at a black man?" Bam, bam, bam. "I'll kill all you little motherfuckers!" Bam, bam, bam, bam. "C'mon, you little ying-yang-talking motherfuckers. I'll kill all y'all bitches!" Bam, bam, bam. G.O. looked at the Gerbs. The Gerbs tilted his head to one side and gave a palms up shrug. Suddenly, the tree line was lit up by 20 mm cannon fire from a F-100, followed by rockets, followed by a searing blast of napalm. G.O and Gerbs were still behind the berm while Hakim and all the grunts shouted and waved their M 16s at the passing fast mover. "Fry, you little motherfuckers...*fry!*" Hakim yelled.

◆ ◆ ◆

Lieutenant Stein put together a patrol to reconnoiter the tree line and the ville and put his platoon sergeant in charge. Hakim begged the lieutenant to let him go along, but the Gunny adamantly refused. "Your dumb Chicago A-rab talkin' horse's ass would probably get somebody killed. Now get your ass up on that helicopter, Private Bonebreaker, and start shakin' those blades for Hill. You really startin' to make my blood boil, son! You readin' me?"

"Loud and clear, Gunny!" Hill intoned and grabbed Hakim by the arm. "Let's go, man."

As Hill and Hakim approached the downed aircraft, Hakim said, "That damn Gunny don't like black men!"

"Now that's where you are wrong, Hakim," G.O. said as he turned and faced Hakim. "The Gunny cannot tolerate fuck-ups, and you came to our squadron with a less-than-stellar reputation. Therefore, Hakim, he is just waiting for you to exhibit that you're squared away and that you are going to pull your weight in this squadron, *comprende, amigo*?"

"I ain't got to prove nothing to no white motherfucker! And if I did everything the Gunny wanted, that motherfucker would just come up with some reason why I didn't do it right. Shit, I been around white folks enough to know what they think about black people." Eyes glowing red at G.O.

"Shit, Hakim, I thought you grew up in a home where people told you how pretty you was!" G.O. grinned.

"That don't mean I don't know what crackers think."

"Yeah, what am I thinking right now?"

"You thinkin' you gonna send my ass up on that helicopter first to see if they any VC snipers left hidin' in that tree line."

"Damn, the Gunny's wrong about you. You are one smart Marine!" Grin to smile.

Hakim smirked then started up the stub wing and onto the fuselage.

◆ ◆ ◆

As night began to creep over the paddy, G.O., the Gerbs, and Hakim walked up to where the Gunny, the lieutenant, and his radio operator were sitting.

"Hey, Gunny, we've got the rotor blades stored and the harness sling rigged up. We gonna be able to get out of here?"

"Afraid not, boys," the Gunny looked at Hakim. "It's getting dark, and they won't be able to get a Sky Crane out here until morning. You boys can grab something to eat and then sleep in *Pandora's Box* or, if you prefer, camp out with the grunts. Me, I'm staying inside. It looks as though a weather front is moving in our direction, I shit you not!"

"Lieutenant, you mind if I ax you a question?" Hakim interjected.

The lieutenant looked at Hakim and cocked a bushy eyebrow. "Go ahead, private."

"Did the recon patrol find any dead gooks...sir?"

"Now that is a fascinating question, Private. Sergeant, would you care to share your intel with the private, here?"

"Not at all, sir. We found nothing...nada...diddly-squat. No VC or NVA...alive or dead. Same for the villagers and the livestock...nothing. It's like everything just disappeared. Kinda spooky, don't you think, Private?"

Hakim shook his head as he walked away. The lieutenant said, "Your *schwarze* commando seems like a real hard charger, Gunny. Did you check him out during the firefight?"

"I got a look at that crazy motherfucker...er...beggin' your pardon, Lieutenant. Could be he's a real warrior, or it could be he's just an angry young Marine," the Gunny replied as he watched Hakim swagger over to a group of young black Marines and strike up a conversation.

◆ ◆ ◆

Later, in the downed aircraft, Hill asked Gerbs if he brought any C-rations in the recovery vehicle. Gerbs said they weren't on the inventory and that he thought they would be back at Hue-Phu Bai by now. After checking with grunts, they found out that they weren't expecting to be out in the field overnight, either. The Gunny told them to suck it up; they could go without one stinking meal. At midnight the rain started. The Gunny woke up and said, "Well, at least I'll have water for my coffee in the morning!"

That morning found the Marines shrouded in a heavy mist. Sometime during the night the mist tiptoed in and erased the landscape around the helicopter. The Gunny awoke to the smell of fresh coffee. G.O. and the Gerber Baby had rigged a makeshift firebox on the rear ramp of the 46 with an empty toolbox and a couple of cans of Sterno. On top of the jury-rigged contraption sat the Gunny's mess kit tin cup.

The Gunny stumbled down the fuselage between the neatly stacked rotor blades and roared, "Well, I'll be goddamned! You two tits on a nun are good for something! Where's that fucken Bonebreaker? Sumbitch go AWOL on us?" The Gunny picked up the scalding hot coffee and took a gulp. "Damn, that's good!"

"Hakim found a group of black Mud Marines and camped out with them last night, Gunny," the Gerbs replied.

"Hakim? Ha-fucken-keem? When did Private Bonebreaker change his name? You don't get to change your name in my goddamned Marine Corps! Who does that diddy-bopping ass-wipe from Chicago think he is? Muhammad Ali? Well, you two better start explaining before I have that motherfucker locked up and shipped off to the Island with No Name."

"Well…uh…Gunny, it's like this," G.O. started as he threw an embarrassed glance at the innocent Gerbs. "Private Bonebreaker grew up in Chicago with an aunt and uncle and they…uh…sent him to a uh…black Muslim school and uh…seems like he was pretty smart, so they gave him the name Hakim…he said they would give him a surname when he returned from the corps. He also said his mother gave him his slave name as a joke and he has only had to live with that name in the white man's world."

Well, shit, the Gunny thought, *that could explain some of Bonebreaker's anger...a mother's stupidity.*

The Gunny's thoughts were interrupted when out of the mist Lieutenant Stein strolled up to the back of the helicopter and said, "Hey, can I join this pahty?"

"Sure, Lieutenant, come on in, hope you brought your own cup," Gunny G. replied.

"Just got off the horn with our base camp, Gunny, no crane and no resupply till this weathah cleahs."

"Well, if you ain't the life of the party, Lieutenant! Hell, I guess we just hunker down and wait for the weather to dissipate and try to conserve what little food and water we have. Say, Lieutenant, if you don't mind my asking, what did you do before joining the corps?"

"Funny you should ask. I was a student of the Talmud."

"What the hell is a Talmud?"

"You wouldn't understand, Gunny. You have a non-Jewish brain. You don't think like a Jew."

"How would I know if you don't tell me, Lieutenant? It's not like we don't have some time on our hands."

"OK, Gunny, I'll give it a shot. So, two Marines come on the back of this helicoptah. One has a dirty face and one has a clean face. Which one goes to wash his face?"

The Gunny and G.O. looked at each other pensively like it was some kind of trick question, when the Gerbs blurted out, "Oh, that's an easy one, the one with the dirty face!"

"So you would think, Lance Corporal, so you would think, but I told you, you do not think like a Jew. The one with the clean face would go wash up. He would see the one with the dirty face and think his face was dirty also. While the Marine with the dirty face would see the clean one and think his was clean already."

"Well, hell, Lieutenant, one question don't prove nothing. Give us another one," a disgruntled Gunny asked.

"Oy vey! OK, OK, one more. So two Marines come into the back of this helicoptah. One is clean and one is dirty. Which one washes up?"

The Gerber Baby looked at the Lieutenant, with one eye squinted and said, "I think I've heard this one before, so I'll say the one with the clean face." G.O. and the Gunny looked at the Gerbs and nodded their approval.

"Buz-zz-z-z! Wrong again! When they looked in the mirrah, the Marine with the clean face saw that it wasn't necessary for him to wash up, while the Marine with the dirty face saw that his face was dirty, so he cleaned up."

"Now wait just a goddamned minute, Lieutenant. Where did this fucken mirror come from?

"What? I told you...you have a non-Jewish mind. Jews are taught to think about all the possibilities. You will never be able to think like a Jew, Sorry, Gunny."

"All right, Lieutenant, how 'bout just one more?" the Gunny asked.

"Well, one more, but that's all. Final. *Finis.* No more! OK, two Marines walk onto the back of a helicoptah. One is dirty and one is clean. Which one cleans up?"

Triple groan from the three not-so-wise Marines.

The Gunny studied the lieutenant for a moment, then asked, "First, Lieutenant, tell me how it is *possible* that two Marines could come onto the back of this helicopter after being in a rice paddy and one of them is clean?"

"Now you are thinking like a Jew, Gunny," the lieutenant praised.

G.O. looked at a perplexed Gerber Baby and shook his head and then smiled as he thought about Chucky D. telling the Bear, *Well, if this ain't another fine mess you've gotten us into, Crew Chief.*

◆ ◆ ◆

For the next two days, the crew lived like zombies in an old science fiction movie as they moved mechanically about the aircraft and around the rice paddy and were involved in thousands of meaningless tasks trying to keep their minds off their hunger.

The hunger that gnawed at their minds more than their empty bellies. There was no let-up from the intermittent rain and constant mist that kept them isolated on a small island in the middle of Vietnam. With the rain, came an unusual temperature drop. G.O. shivered as he cleaned his M-16 for the fifty-seventh time and listened to another shower clattering off the helicopter as the storm picked up in intensity. The grunts had been taking turns coming into the helicopter to sleep and trying to dry out before going back on duty. The circle of life. Another futile Marine enterprise. G.O did not think he would ever be dry again. *What was that like?* G.O thought, *Being warm and dry?*

◆ ◆ ◆

Shem lay in the warm straw in the stall where they kept Esther and Mordecai, the only pigs on the ark. "Goddamnit, Shem!" *Roared Noah, who resembled an upset Gunny G.,* "I sent you down here to clean out the pig shit, not to sleep with them! Do you know what the good book says about men that lie with animals, meshuggener?"

"I'm not fucken the pigs, Abba. I was just getting some rest from all the shit I've had to clean up this week. What? A man can't take a break?"

"Break...shmake, we'll take a break when God tells us, not before! I've never had a break in my life. I used to walk seven miles to yeshiva..."

"Yeah, I know, I know already...uphill both ways!"

"Don't be such a putz...get this shit cleaned up and then come to dinner. Your wife has made us a nice potato soup, huh?"

"Oy vey! How far can one potato go?"

◆ ◆ ◆

G.O.'s daydream was harshly interrupted by Gunny G. "Goddamnit, Hill, how many times are you gonna clean that piece? It won't have no grooves left in the barrel when you're finished!"

"Gives me something to do, Gunny. Besides, it's better than being outside with the Mud Marines waiting for Charlie to surprise you."

"Well, I got news for you, son. Charlie ain't coming out in this weather to fuck with us. He's holed up in some tunnel between here and Hanoi having a nice warm bowl of rice smothered in nuoc mam."

"Jesus, Gunny!"

"That sacrilegious, Hill, it's not Jesus, Gunny...it's Jesus H. Christ!"

"That's not what I meant..."

"Well then, say what the fuck you mean, Hill! You are the most undexterous Marine I know when it comes to putting simple words together!"

"What I meant was that I am doing everything I can to keep my mind off food, and you created this image in my mind of this huge bowl of steaming rice covered in fish sauce, and I could smell it and feel its warmth and literally taste it, and I was overcome by this overwhelming hunger again! It's driving me nuts, Gunny."

"You're startin' to lose it, Marine. I think a night on perimeter duty might clear your mind," the Gunny said as he looked deep into G.O.'s hollow eyes.

G.O. put on his bush hat and then pulled on his poncho liner. He picked up his M-16 and shoved in a fully loaded magazine. As he started out of the aircraft, he looked over and said, "Thanks, Gunny. This might help." As G.O. left the aircraft, the rain had started to let up again. As he slogged his way toward the berm through the mire of a rain-soaked rice paddy, in a mist so thick he could not see the end of his weapon, the light rain continued to spit on his hands and slap sideways into his face. As he came to the berm, up out of the large puddles forming in the paddy, he was met by the business end of an M-16.

"Damn, motherfucker, you always make so much noise at night?" whispered an apparition somewhere in front of him.

G.O. could barely distinguish the dark shadow that lay on the rice paddy dike in front of him. "Just didn't want you to mistake me for Sir Charles," G.O. whispered back.

"Ain't no mistakin' you air wing pogues for Charlie. I just don't want him knowing where I am, you dig?"

"Yeah, I dig," G.O. responded as he began to burrow in.

About 3:00 a.m., G.O. felt someone or something poking him lightly in the ribs and instantly awoke. "What is it?" G.O. queried.

"We've got some kind of movement out front. I'm going to look for Sergeant O'Rourke. You stay here and monitor the situation until I get back, you copy?"

"Yeah, I copy...but hey, don't be gone too long."

"You air wing pogues...I swear..." the voice replied as G.O watched the grunt scurry into the thick, dark mist. The rain had dissipated but G.O. was soaked through to the bone. This was one of the darkest darks G.O. could remember. Darker than any of the caves and caverns he explored in Southwest Texas as a youth. G.O.'s senses were on high alert. The quiet was almost deafening. The strong smell of the pungent wet earth filled his nostrils. G.O's mind raced as he strained to see through the mist. Then he heard what he thought was a very faint shuffling noise. Some movement.

Then a whisper. "You hear that, Hill?"

"Jesus, Hakim! How long you been here?"

"'Bout five minutes, now why don't you get yourself real quiet and we'll see if we can't locate that gooner, Hill."

Moments later, they heard a similar shuffling noise, like Sir Charles was making his way across the paddy. Hakim took off his flak jacket and bandoliers and set his M-16 down next to Hill. He took his K-Bar knife from its sheath and held the point close to G.O.'s right eye. "Now, Hill, I'm going out there and taking care of Mr. Charlie, and when I come back, I don't want you shooting at my pretty black ass. So here's what we are going to do. We gonna have a password. When you hear me coming back, you say, 'Red,' my response will be 'Rider.' If you don't hear 'Rider,' feel free to shoot that motherfucker."

"Don't you think we should wait for Sergeant O'Rourke and the lieutenant?"

"Hell, no, Hill, they'll just debate about what we ought to do, and by then Charlie might be gone. You just stay here and chill, my white friend. I'll be right back. We cool?"

"Cool."

Hakim placed the K-Bar in his mouth and slid silently down the opposite side of the berm into the dark black night. G.O. heard movement on both his left and right. It was the Gunny and Lieutenant Stein.

"What the hell is up, Hill?" the Gunny asked.

"Well, we heard movement out front, and one of the grunts left to find the lieutenant, and in the meantime Hakim, er, I mean, Private Bonebreaker left the perimeter to reconnoiter the area."

"*What?* I'll have his ass sent to the Island with No Name, if the dinks don't get him first."

All three lay on the berm and stared intensely into the dark misty night straining to hear any sound other than the pounding of their own hearts. Then a muffled scream, not quite human, broke the silence. Within moments, G.O. heard movement, then called out the password, "Red!"

Hakim replied, just inches away, "Rider...motherfucker!" and crawled over the berm, pulling what looked like a small body.

"Well, I'll be goddamned, Hakim. You bagged one of those little slant-eyed bastards."

"Shit, Gunny...beggin' your pardon, Lieutenant...that ain't a gook... It's a pig!"

"Well, I'll be..."

"A pig, you killed a fucken pig?" the lieutenant asked rhetorically.

"Yeah, Lieutenant, I thought it was a pig when I heard it rootin' around out there. Shit, y'all didn't think I was dumb enough to go after one of them little Vietnamese people on a night like this, did you? So I just sneaked up on him like I did G.O just then, and I slit his fucken throat," Hakim said.

"You slit his fucken throat?" a wide-eyed Lieutenant asked.

"Ear to ear, Lieutenant." A delighted Hakim beamed.

"You slit his fucken throat," declared the Lieutenant.

G.O. thought, *Must be some of that Jewish thinking going on.*

"Why did you go after the pig?" the Gunny asked.

"Because everybody here about to go crazy 'cause they so damn hungry, so I thought, 'Hey, some bacon and ham sound real good to me!' How about you, Gunny?"

"Sounds good to me…Private Hakim!" the Gunny responded. "Sounds real good to me."

◆ ◆ ◆

The Gunny found a grunt from Blytheville, Arkansas, who had skills in hog butchering. A Private Nutter. Nutter referred to his hometown as "Blahville," but other than talking like he had a mouth full of cotton balls, he used his K-Bar on the pig like a skilled surgeon. Soon, the grunts had the pig's carcass tied to a spit and roasting over an open pit. Thank goodness for jet fuel. An hour later the smell of roasting pork inundated the paddy. Farewell, Porky. Hello, salivation. Some hours later, Private Nutter started carving and sending portions of pork to the grunts. "Where's Private Hockem? I got a special cut for 'im."

"He's back on the line. Says Muslims don't eat pork."

"Well, hell, that's just more for the rest of us," chimed in the Gerber baby.

"How about you, Lieutenant?"

"No, I can't eat this pork either, Private Nuttah. It's not koshah."

"I can't believe y'all won't eat any of this fine pork, Lieutenant. It's your loss."

The lieutenant walked away into the mist.

◆ ◆ ◆

The crew was greeted the next morning by clear skies and sunshine. The weather had moved on to the mountains. The lieutenant approached the Gunny with a grin on his face and a greasy chin with the remnants of charred pork quite visible.

"We received word Gunny, a Sky Crane is on the way to extract this helicoptah, and your squadron is sending an aircraft to pick up your crew."

"Thanks, Lieutenant Stein. Can't say it's been my best three days in Vietnam, but it certainly hasn't been the worst." The Gunny looked at the lieutenant's chin. "I see you might possibly have set aside some of your dietary laws and had a taste of that pig?"

"What? Is it not possible that God put that pig there for all of us to share?"

The Gunny smiled. "Well, that is one possibility, Lieutenant. Yes, that is definitely one possibility."

Chapter Twenty Seven

Redemption

The cargo area of the Scrotum's aircraft began to fill up with an acrid sulfurous funk. Another one of Chucky D.'s famous fart bouquets. Captain D'Amato's infamous calling card. Sphincter on the loose. "Must've been eatin' some musical bananas," the Gunny quipped. "Sounded like he was fartin' Beethoven's *Fifth*." The entire crew sought any ventilation available thinking it might relieve the burning sensation in their nostrils. The Scrotum just sat on the crew chief's jump seat and grinned.

"Look at that dumb ass, sitting there grinning like he was at the Rose Parade," the Gerber Baby shouted above the rotor wash.

"Well," G.O. responded, "it is the Scrotum, probably thinks he's back home in South Philly."

Hakim just sat and glared. Yellow eyes.

After recovering *Pandora's Box*, the crew had returned to Hue-Phu Bai. They were debriefed, packed and on their way out to the USS *Iwo Jima*. The *Iwo Jima* was relatively new, a helicopter carrier, commissioned in 1961, whose primary function was to serve as an amphibious assault platform. As the Scrotum's helicopter, *Alpha Mike Foxtrot* or *AMF,* approached the *Iwo*, the crew stared out of the plexiglass portals at her sleek beauty steaming through the South China Sea. After the *AMF* touched down on the flight deck the crew picked up their gear and started down the ramp where they were met by Locker Gallo and newly promoted Staff

Sergeant P.C. Emetic. While Staff Sergeant Emetic left to direct the Gunny to his quarters, Locker led the crew to theirs. On the way to their quarters one level below the flight deck and to the rear of the fo'c's'le, they heard a bosun's pipe over the ship's public address system followed by the announcement, "Sweepers, sweepers, man your brooms."

"The fuck was that?" G.O. asked as he bumped his head on the first passageway he tried to duck through.

"Don't worry about it, dude. It's routine. They sweep this motherfucker about every fifteen minutes. And when they're not sweeping, they're going to general quarters or some other Navy bullshit."

As the Gerber Baby, G.O., and Hakim entered the squadron's enlisted quarters they received a standard Marine Corps welcome.

"Shit, just like you, Hill, show up after all the work's done," Duck Butter proclaimed as he looked from a cribbage board.

"You wouldn't know what work was if it came up and bit you in your pink ass, Duck," Locker responded.

Metalsmith Bob came through the hatchway carrying two large duffle bags shouting, "Mail call, Marines, mail call...come get your Dear Johns and overdue car payments. Mail call." Bob threw the overstuffed seabags on the table where moments before the Duck and Jack had been playing cribbage. The Marines gathered around as Bob distributed the mail.

> *Mail call is my daily*
> *reminder of who I*
> *am in real life My*
> *parents grandparents*
> *loved ones have no real*
> *idea what I am like as*
> *a Marine what my life*
> *is like as a Marine*
> *So their letters are*
> *always upbeat missives*
> *sent to the guy they*
> *knew The guy who was*

the real me The guy now
just wearing someone
else's Marine uniform

Those who received mail were subjected to some of Bob's irreverent comments. "Yo, Chief, you know a chick named Bitsy Matthews? What's your tribe gonna think when they find out you got a white squaw?" Then Bob would sail the envelope to the appropriate addressee. In the case of a package, Bob would act like he was weighing it, then hold it up to his head and make a guess as to its contents. "I believe Blaze has received some clean underwear from Ma and Pa Dawson from back in rattlesnake country. They have been designed in the signature style of Looney Tunes featuring the iconic Bugs Bunny, Daffy Duck, Porky Pig, no wait a minute, G.O. and his crew ate Porky...I see clearly now...it's Tweety Bird...*I thought I thaw a puddy cat.*"

◆　◆　◆

Locker and G.O. sat on the floor by Pogo's rack waiting for him to open a care package he had received from France.

"Dude, like hurry up," Locker complained.

"Yeah, Pogs, don't take all damn day," G.O. added.

"I must read the letter first. It is from my grandfather," Pogo responded in his most understandable English to date.

G.O. understood the Pogs feelings. He had a letter from Danny Dupree he was anxious to read. It would wait until later when he had some time alone.

After the letter had been read aloud to G.O. and Locker in French then loosely translated into English, Pogo opened his package with care. The first item he pulled out was a bottle of red wine. G.O. and Locker sat and stared in amazement.

"You best hide that wine, Pogo. You are not supposed to have wine aboard ship."

"G.O. is right, Pogo."

"Where can I hide thees wine, *mes amis*? There are four bottles."

G.O. and Locker thought it over for a minute, then Locker said, "How about in Joey D.'s parachute shop?"

"Good idea, Locker, Joey won't mind and it will be safe there. What do you think Pogo, you trust Joey?

"Yes, I think I trust Joey."

Pogo continued to unload his goodies. There were crackers, cheeses, a small rusted can of truffles, and a can of foie gras. *"Fooey grass*? What the hell is *fooey grass*, Pogs?"

"It ees not footy grass, G.O., it is *fahh grhaa…fooahh grhaa.*"

"OK, OK…fraa graa."

"No, no, no…not fraa graa…fooahh grhaa," corrected a frustrated Pogo. "You put the foie gras on a crackaire and you have a small bite, then you have a sip of the wine. Then maybe a taste of the cheese. Then you have another sip of the wine. You are so…what is the word?…not civil."

"Whatchatalkinbout, Pogo? I seen G.O. sit down to pee before. Hell, my little 'possum-looking friend, that's civil in anybody's country."

Pogo's eyes were wide open as he looked from G.O. to Locker then back again. Both hands went up in front of him as if to say, *Stop, I've had enough*.

Staff Sergeant P.C. Emetic came through the hatch. "Listen up, Marines! There will be a formation on the hangar deck at eighteen hundred hours. Jungle utilities will be the dress of the day. Ready crews will not muster. The ready flight crews will be Corporal Dawson and his first mech, Private Hunter. Also Corporal Abandonato and Lance Corporal Sullivan. Any questions? Then I will see you on the hangar deck."

◆ ◆ ◆

G.O. was rummaging through his seabag looking for a set of jungle utilities when he noticed Hakim sitting on the floor with a smile on his face. *Hakim smiling? George Wallace must've croaked.* "Hakim, what up? You get some good news?"

"Yes, I have a letter from the Nation of Islam. I have been given a surname...El-Hashim. My name is now Hakim El-Hashim."

"I thought you didn't do drugs, man."

"The name has nothing to do with drugs, my ignorant white Christian friend. El-Hashim was the great-grandfather of the prophet Muhammad."

"Why do you always bring race into the discussion? I may be ignorant, and I once was a semidevout Christian, but do I look white to you? I'm a beautiful Vietnamese tanned Marine." This brought a laugh from Hakim.

"You want to let the Gunny know about this right away so he can get the ball rolling on having your name legally changed."

Hakim shook his head from side to side. "Still the white-fucken-man's privileged-assed world."

"Privileged-assed white men got nothing to do with it. Getting paid has got everything to do with it, you dig?"

"I dig, Brother Hill. I'll go see the Gunny." Hakim stood and left the compartment.

◆ ◆ ◆

Major Bridger called the squadron to attention on the hangar deck. After a thirty minute tongue lashing by the major about the disgusting condition of the air crews, the helicopters, and morale, Colonel Van Meter took over. More of the same. Gunny G. read off the list of promotions, Poppycock Emetic to staff sergeant, Locker Gallo to corporal, Joey Delmonico to lance corporal, and Hakim El-Hashim meritoriously promoted to lance corporal. G.O could not believe his ears. *Did the Gunny call him Hakim El-Hashim?* After the formation, G.O. went to find Hakim and congratulate him on his promotion, but he had already disappeared.

G.O did catch the Gunny headed for the toolroom. "Gunny, got a minute?"

"Not if you're gonna ask about Lance Corporal El-Hashim, numbnuts. It wasn't my idea."

"Well, I don't know whose idea it was, but I think it was a damn good one."

"Goddamnit, Hill, how many times do I have to tell you—"

"I know Gunny, if the Marine Corps wanted me to think, they would have issued me a brain. I'm just saying I approve of the decision."

"Really, Hill? You approve. Tell it to the chaplain. He might actually give a shit. Trust me, nobody above the rank of corporal gives a shit about your approval."

"I stand corrected, Gunny. So who approved it?"

"Jesus, Mary, and cuckolded Joseph, it is none of your business... zero...nada. *Comprende*, Hill?"

"Understood, Gunny."

As Hill turned to go, the Gunny stopped him, "Goddamnit, son, wait a minute. Did you hear what Major Bridger said at the formation, or were you off in the Twilight Zone?"

"Uh...well...honestly? Twilight Zone, Gunny."

"Just as I thought. I'll tell you what, Hill, you get your aircraft cleaned up and in pristine condition before we pull this operation with the ROK Marines and I will tell you the whole story. The conditions are that you cannot, under any circumstances, reveal why you are taking such wonderful care of *Groundz* or ever let anyone know where you heard the story, *capisce*?"

"Aye-aye, Gunny."

"You goddamn right, aye-aye, if you don't wanna end up on the Island with No Name."

The Gunny turned to go into the toolroom. G.O. left to head up to the flight deck. The first thing he noticed was Hakim on a stepladder cleaning the pilot's windscreen on *Surf City.* He shook his head as he continued down the flight deck to *Groundz.*

Chapter Twenty Eight

No Balls, No Blue Chips

For the next two days, G.O. and the rest of HMM-265, spent all of their time ferrying ROK Marines and U.S. Marines aboard the *Iwo Jima*, and other support vessels that comprised Special Landing Force Alpha. G.O. and Joey D. were on standby along with the Duck and the Gerber Baby. The *Iwo was* so congested that they spent most of their time on the flight deck.

"Let's go get some chow, G.O.," Joey said.

"Do you really want to go down and stand in that damn line? Hell, it wraps halfway around the hangar deck."

"The Gunny said we were supposed to go to the front of the line if we had standby duty."

G.O. gave Joey D. his most sympathetic look. "You really want to cut in line in front of a bunch of black grunts that are looking for a reason to whip your skinny white ass?"

"No, I'm just hungry."

"Actually, Joey, I'm so damn hungry I could eat the ass end out of a cow, provided there was enough sautéed onions on it. I just wanted to make sure you were up to the challenge."

♦ ♦ ♦

On their way to the hangar deck, they picked up the Duck and the Gerbs. G.O thought, *There's strength in numbers.* When they arrived, they saw a line waiting to get into chow hall extending halfway around the hangar deck. "Well, here goes nothing," G.O. said.

"No balls, no blue chips," the Duck replied.

G.O. noticed that Hakim was with the group of black Marines at the front of the chow line. "Hakim, we're on standby, any chance of us going to the head of the line?"

"Hakim is not in charge my white brother," answered one of the grunts. "We just making sure all the black brothers is fed before those damn gook Marines get to the chow hall and eat everything in sight, you dig? So you white motherfuckers is gonna have to wait," he said as he adjusted his sunglasses. "You know, dig down deep and find some of that patience you forced the black man to have for the last two hundred years."

Locker Gallo came sauntering across the hangar deck. "Well, fuck, fuck, fuck, fuck, fuckity fuck," he exclaimed.

All eyes turned to Locker. Sunglasses looked at him and said, "The fuck is wrong witch'yew, cracker?"

"Nothing, my brother, I was just trying to catch up on the conversation."

For a moment there was complete silence on the hangar deck. Proverbial pin-drop silence. Mouse pissing on a cotton ball silence. Hakim started laughing followed by the grunts, then nervous laughter from G.O. and his crew. "My brothers, this crazy white motherfucker is my crew chief. Let these boys through…their shit is clean. When you're up to your necks in them little yellow men, who you think is gonna come get you?"

Sunglasses smiled this big toothy grin and extended his right arm to the side as if to say, go right ahead. *Gold tooth! The motherfucker has a gold tooth, I don't believe this shit,* Hill thought. As they walked by, Sunglasses said, "You boys don't abuse this privilege and don't ever let me hear you say the black man ain't never done nothing for you."

As the five of them were sitting around the table on the mess deck finishing up their meals, Locker asked, "There's a movie on the hangar deck tonight, you guys going?"

"We're all on standby," Duck replied. "I don't want to get halfway into a movie, then be called to the flight deck."

"How about you, G.O.?"

"What's playing? If it's John Wayne, count me out. I can't stand his gung-ho shit."

"You lucked out, dude. It's *Bonnie and Clyde.* About a couple of bank robbers from your part of the country."

"Sounds good to me, who's in it?"

"Fuck, man, I don't know, do I look like the president of the Screen Actors Guild?"

"What's a Screen Actors Guild?" Gerbs asked.

"Talking to you is like talking to a really bitchin' but mildly retarded brick surfboard."

"Aw, c'mon, Locker, man, I'll go to the movies with you...don't get your damper down," G.O. said.

"What's a damper?" Gerbs asked.

All four looked at the Gerber Baby for a moment, then resumed their conversation about the pros and cons of bank robbing. While they talked, the mess deck filled up with ROK Marines. What was previously a mess deck filled with the English language and all its lovely nuances, became rife with beautiful singsong Korean conversations.

Locker surveyed the mess deck with a look of absolute disgust. "This gobbledy-gook is driving me crazy, who wants to go to the fantail for a smoke?"

"I'll go," Hill responded. "You had better stay with the aircraft, Joey. I'll be up later."

"I think Gerbs and I will head up to the ready room to see what's shakin'," Duck answered.

♦ ♦ ♦

Hill and Gallo stumbled through the hatchway bathed in a red glow onto the fantail. They were greeted by absolute darkness and the melodic strains of Muddy Waters singing, *Got My Mojo Working.* G.O. noticed the pungent odor of marijuana wafting up his nostrils while he waited for his night vision to engage. *Welcome to the Fantail Bar and Grill.* He could make out several pairs of eyes staring in his direction. *Shit, I hope those aren't vampire bats staring in my direction.* He could also make out the red glow of the doobie as it was passed.

"Well, fuck, fuck, fuckity-fuck," Locker intoned. "You brothers ain't getting high before an operation are you?"

"Well, if it ain't that crazy-assed white boy from the hangar deck," responded one of the fantail group that G.O. thought sounded like Sunglasses. "Why don't you boys partake of some of this fine herb wid us?"

"Thought you might never ask," Locker responded as he took the joint and inhaled deeply. He passed it over to G.O.

"Naw, man. I can't tonight…I'm on standby."

"Well, shit, now…You a CID, white boy? 'Cause if you is, you might have an accident. I mean. white boys have fallen off the back of a ship before, know what I mean?"

Morbid quiet. Fear gripped G.O. Eyes blinking in the night. Staring. Locker held the joint out to Hill. "One toke won't hurt anything. I suppose," Hill said as he took the joint.

"Brutha know how to stay outa the pool don't he?" Sunglasses quipped, which immediately started a palm-slapping fist-bumping ritual.

"Yeah, this ain't no kinda night to be swimming with the sharks."

"You think they like a little cranberry sauce with they white meat?"

"You got outa being shark bait tonight, white boy."

"Go on and laugh," Hill said. "What you brothers don't know is that I'm carrying the Marine Corps' latest version of shark repellant. Won't no sharks come near me."

"What the hell you talkin' about, white boy?"

"Right here," Hill said as he patted one of the pockets on his flight suit. "It's made out of female shark ovaries and octopus ink. When the shark gets close he goes crazy…'cause he doesn't know whether to fuck you or eat you."

More silence. Then laughter. Sunglasses slapped hands with Hill, "You one crazy white boy, how you like your new reality?"

Before Hill could answer, the *Iwo*'s PA came on, "The movie on the hangar deck will commence in five minutes. The movie will commence in five minutes. Tonight's movie is *Bonnie and Clyde*."

"Let's di-di, Hill."

"Y'all coming to the movie?"

"Any black folks in that movie?"

"I don't know."

"Hah, that's a reality that gonna change too, Brother Hill. Yeah, that's what I'm talkin' about."

When they reached the hangar deck, it was packed. "Jeez," Locker said, "this place is packed with ROK Marines and sailors. None of 'em speak English, what the fuck they doing here?"

"Shit man, they came to enjoy the flicks, lose themselves for a while, just like us. Hey look up there, Gallo, it's Pogo." Pogo was sitting on the admiral's launch that was stored on the hangar deck. "Let's go."

Hill and Locker climbed up on the Admiral's launch and sat down by the Pogs. "Nice seats, my little french-fried friend, how much you have to pay for loggia seating?"

Pogo stared open-eyed at Hill and Gallo.

"He's just fucken with you Pogs, but how did you score this fine piazza?"

"Oh, the navy chief say I could sit in this launch if I polish the brass while I am here."

G.O. looked at Locker then back to Pogo and said, "Well, you made a fine deal. Next time, you might want to check with us first."

The movie started and G.O., Locker, and the Pogs sat in their semi-drug-induced comas and stared at the screen, enjoying *Foggy Mountain Breakdown*.

Fifteen minutes into the movie, Locker looked over at Hill and said, "This shit is in gookese...Nobody said anything about the movie being in ching-wah."

"Keep it down, Locker. We happen to be surrounded if you haven't noticed. Besides, the English translations are on the bottom of the screen."

"I didn't come to the fucken movies to read, *compadre*. I must quit this scene, you dig? I'm headed back to the fantail. You coming?"

G.O. was high. Gloriously and introspectively high. "Think I'll stay and finish the flick." G.O. loved the harmonious sounds of the Korean language. He thought they were more suitable to the action on the screen than the English words scrolling across the bottom. When Bonnie told W.C. Moss that she and Clyde robbed banks and asked if W.C wanted to come along, W.C. did not have to say a word. His facial expressions and body movements provided a delightful moment that told G.O. all he needed to know. W.C. was going on this adventure.

"All flight deck personnel report to the flight deck. All flight crew personnel report to their helicopters. Standby aircraft will launch in fifteen minutes," boomed the ship's PA.

◆ ◆ ◆

Xin Loi and Hung Dong had finished making themselves comfortable in their new quarters located in a myriad of tunnels that had been dug below one of South Vietnam's barrier islands. Hung was putting Darwin's bamboo cage under his bunk and then released him. The iguana moved slowly out of his cage, starting his examination of his new surroundings.

"Darwin is getting fat like his owner."

"What? This is all muscle," Hung said as he pounded on his stomach. "And Darwin can still jump in the air and take a banana out of your hand, and if you are not quick...he may decapitate a digit or two."

"He's getting to be roasting size, Hung."

"Do not joke like that, Xin. Darwin is my third eye. I could no more part with him than I could...the fat rhino."

"Well, if you keep feeding him lotus blossoms and bananas, he will eventually be bigger than you."

"I noticed chrysanthemums growing on the island this morning, maybe I will change Darwin's diet," Dong mused. Then he added. "It was very nice of the Comrade Colonel to send the entire scout platoon to this beautiful island for R and R."

"Maybe he thought they needed some reinforcements, Dong," Xin replied.

"You are always so negative, Xin. Well, you are not going to ruin my vacation. I plan to lay in the sun, swim in the ocean, and eat all the fish *you* can catch."

"It may be as you say, but it is hard to lay on the beach when you must run and hide whenever you hear an American aircraft."

"Phah! They will just think we are some of the locals...you have been in the jungle way too long, Xin. You must learn when to relax. How about a nice game of *tam cuc*?"

"You and your card games," Xin said shaking his head, "maybe later. Now I must go see the garrison commander and discuss our duties while we are here. I just have a terrible feeling about this place."

"Well, then, I will write a letter to my three wives and check on how my sons are progressing."

"As a blessing to their mothers, may your sons not be burdened with their father's gas." Xin laughed as he exited their quarters ahead of one of Hung's sandals.

◆ ◆ ◆

When G.O. arrived at *Groundz*, Joey was on the aircraft securing the pre-flight panels while Lieutenants Abramovitz and Kelly were climbing off the port stub wing.

"Nice you could join us, Crew Chief. We didn't take you away from your studies, did we?"

"No, sir. The only thing I was studying was Miss Dunaway's boda-cious ta-tas."

"They show her tits?"

"No, sir. But they *are* worth studying."

"This thing ready to fly, Hill?"

"It was before you two started climbing around on it, Lieutenant."

"Well, there's a recon team with wounded, on a karst promontory at the end of the island, and we are going to try a night extract."

"A karst promontory?"

"It just a big hill, Hill. Don't get your panties in a bunch over this. You ever done a night extract before?"

"No, sir."

"It should be a piece of cake if we can land, if we have to use the hoist cable, life might be considerably more difficult. Copy?"

"Copy, sir."

"Well, we've kicked the tires, so let's light the fires."

"Roger that, sir."

♦ ♦ ♦

Since *Pandora's Box* was sitting on the hangar deck, being used for spare parts, Duck and Gerbs were flying *What, Me Worry?* The aircraft had a picture of Alfred E. Neuman painted on the side with a Tommy gun in his hands shooting holes in his feet. *How apropos,* Hill thought. *The Duck and the Gerbs, not an ounce of anxiety between the two.*

"This is Highboy one-niner," Lieutenant Abramovitz called on the radio, "we have the island in sight and are dropping down to fifteen hundred feet for a closer look…I say again, we are dropping down to one five zero zero feet."

"Copy that Highboy one-niner," came the reply. "Highboy two-three will maintain chase altitude at thirty-five hundred feet."

Shit, Hill thought. *Major Arclight Bridger, the Walrus, is flying* Worry. *Well, at least Gerbs and Duck will be safe. That son of a bitch won't drop below the effective range of the AK-47.*

Hill stood nervously by the crew chief's jump seat straining to find the strobe lights the recon team had set up as Joey searched from the port side.

Lieutenant Kelly came on the intercom. "I have two strobes on the far end of the island."

"Copy that, I have them in sight...OK, Crew Chief, I want you and Joey on those fifties. We will fly around that end of the island while I make contact with the grunts. Copy," Lieutenant Abramovitz said.

"Copy that, sir," Hill responded.

The lieutenant engaged his radio, "This is Highboy one-niner...we have the strobes in sight...are descending to recon suitable extraction point."

"Copy that one-niner, two-three will maintain chase altitude."

As *Groundz* descended and began to circle the promontory, they received another radio call. "This is the Candyman and the Healer...we are in your area of operations and are flying two fully loaded Cobras...looking to blow some shit up...could you use some fire support?"

"Just when I was beginning to think Jesus didn't love me anymore... my prayers are answered," Lieutenant Abramovitz replied.

"Gentlemen, radio discipline is a sign of professionalism," snapped Major Bridger from on high.

"Who the fuck was that?"

"That would be our chase plane, Candyman."

"Chase plane? Hell, we thought that was a satellite."

"That's enough, gentlemen, maintain radio discipline!"

"Copy that."

"Copy that."

"This is Romeo Sierra three-four...we have visual on your helicopter. We have marked the side of the hill with three strobes...I say again, three strobes...you should be able to land inside the perimeter of the strobes."

"This is Highboy one-niner...copy. We are descending to strobes...be on your toes crew chief."

As they were maneuvering the back of the helicopter to the edge of the hill, Sir Charles opened fire on them.

G.O. was fascinated as he watched different hued tracer rounds crisscross in front of his fifty. He depressed the butterfly trigger and started returning fire to the areas from which he thought the rounds were emanating.

"This is one-niner, we are taking heavy small arms fire..."

"Roger that, one-niner, the cavalry is here...and all hell's about to break loose in Georgia, boys!" The Cobra gunships started making gun runs at treetop level. G.O. stopped firing for fear of hitting one of them. The Cobra gun runs served to take the enemy fire away from them and redirect it toward the Cobras. The Cobras' miniguns shredded the area surrounding the grunts' perimeter.

As the Cobras continued to fly circular patterns around the extract point, Lieutenant Abramovitz set the back of the aircraft on the hillside and dropped the ramp. Hill raced to the back of the helicopter and tried to find the recon team.

One of the team rushed up to Hill and said he needed help getting the wounded on board.

"Sir, this is Hill...the grunts need help with the wounded, so I'm disconnecting and leaving the aircraft...you've got it, Joey..." Hill disconnected from the ICS and saw Joey at the front of the helicopter give him a thumbs up.

Hill and the grunt raced to a stand of trees not twenty meters away.

"How many wounded?"

The grunt looked perplexed, "All of 'em.'

"Well, shit, why didn't you say so? Can any of you stand?"

Two of the grunts stood.

"OK, here's what we are going to do...you two standing are going to defend, while Private...what's your fucken name, anyway?"

"Jackson, sir."

"While Private Jackson and I transport the wounded to the helicopter, got it?"

"Got it."

After Hill and Jackson had moved the four severely wounded to the helicopter and retrieved the two walking wounded, Joey leaned down and shouted, "You made it just in time, the Cobras ran out of firepower and had to di-di." Joey informed the pilots that the grunts were on board and *Groundz* lifted off and started climbing as the enemy tracer rounds tried to find her in the night.

Hill saw Jackson hunched over one of the grunts lying on the deck of the helicopter. "Hey, Jackson, you need some help?"

"Yeah, start checking these guys and make sure we've got the bleeding stopped…"

Hill walked to the back of the aircraft and stopped at a grunt lying on his poncho. It was the young Marine that he and Danny D. had given lemon-lime Kool-Aid to when they had resupplied the Rockpile. He remembered he had one blue eye and one green. His face was covered in a gooey ooze. He reached down and started removing the mucus when Jackson walked over.

"Don't bother about him. He's dead."

Chapter Twenty Nine

Dulce et Decorum est

G.O. stared into his coffee mug and watched a gnat trying to escape, but all Hill could see was a young Marine with one blue eye and one green.

"OK," the Gunny sighed, "let me get this straight. You picked up seven members of a recon team under heavy fire, flew them to Da Nang, then flew back to the *Iwo,* and not one fucken ding in your bird?"

G.O. looked at the helpless gnat and thought, *Sorry, old pard*, and took a healthy swig, wondering if the gnat might fly out of his ass later. "That's about the size of it, Gunny."

"Unbelievable...I've read about shit like this in *Ripley's Believe it or Fucken Not*, but this is the first time I have actually seen it."

"If it hadn't been for those two Cobra pilots, Gunny, our whole crew would be pushin' up daisies on that stupid fucken island."

"I got news for you, son...ain't nobody gonna live forever. And if you asked those eighty-year-old ex-grunts in the nursing homes with tubes stuck in every orifice in their bodies how they would like to go out, I'm pretty confident they would prefer to go out in a blaze of glory fighting for their country. There are worse ways to die, Hill, and dying without dignity in a bed full of your own piss and shit is one of them."

G.O. looked up from his coffee cup and saw the Gunny staring at him with disdain in his eyes. *Why is he looking at me like that? Because I'm afraid to die or because I don't want to die in this fucken war? What does he know that I don't?* "You're right, Gunny," G.O said with a slight nod.

> *I don't want to die*
> *in this fucken war*
> *This war is not worthy*
> *of my death It's not*
> *worthy of my life*
> *It's a fucken war*
> *I don't want to die*

"You can bet your *sweet bippy* I'm more right than wrong."

"Now tell me, where was the chase plane while you guys were extracting the grunts?"

"I don't know, Gunny. We were way too busy with the grunts."

The Gunny put on his best stern, I'm-all-business, Cary-Grant look. "Well, Major Bridger recommended that Lieutenant Abramovitz be transferred for flying his aircraft into an untenable zone under heavy enemy fire."

"What? You gotta be shittin' me? Sorry about that, Gunny. What I meant to say is, that is *not* how it happened…we weren't taking any fire until we were ready to touch down."

"It don't matter, Hill. Captain Abramovitz is leaving today on the Marble Mountain shuttle aircraft. He chose that Cobra squadron that bailed your dumb asses out last night."

"Captain?"

"That's right, Hill…Captain. The colonel didn't want to transfer him under unwarranted negative circumstances but felt like the transfer must be made, understand?"

"Uh-h-h, not really, Gunny."

"It was his executive officer's recommendation. He had no choice."

"Right, but then he slapped Major Bridger in the face by promoting the lieutenant to captain. Wouldn't that piss off the major?"

"It did. But the C.O. gave the major what he's been asking for since we came aboard ship, his own personal CH-46 gunship."

"A 46 gunship?"

"That's right, the metalsmiths are working on it right now. It will have four fifty-caliber machine guns, two to a side, and an M60 stinger on the aft ramp."

"I'll be…What's the mission of this so-called gunship?"

"It will supply close air fire support missions for the squadron, so we don't have to worry about having a Cobra in the area when the *fit hits the shan*. And take that sorry fucken helpless look off your face; it's not Groundz. The designated gunship is Easy Pickings Seven, *The Randy Rabbit*. Dawson's aircraft."

Hill reached into his flight suit for a cigarette and felt Danny D.'s letter, which he had yet to open. He pulled it out and looked at it. The Gunny eyed him curiously, "You get a Dear John from Peggy Sue, Hill?"

"No, Gunny, it's a letter from Dupree. He's back stateside now."

"Well, let's read it, mullet-head, before the ink fades."

It dawned on G.O. that the Gunny never received any mail. He opened the envelope and took out the letter along with a photograph of Danny D. sitting at a blackjack table with his piss cutter (overseas cap) on sideways.

Hey, Numbnuts,

I hope you haven't got your ass in a sling since I'm no longer there to take care of your boot ass. As you can see by the photo, I'm in Vegas as I am writing this. This is a great fucken town, Hill, I shit you not. It is like one round-the-clock party. I came here with another Marine and a navy corpsman, but they disappeared after the first night. We checked into this great hotel and casino, the Desert Inn, and proceeded to get shit faced. We walked down the strip and found a liquor store and thought we would stop and get a bottle. There was a bum standing outside and wanted to know if we had any money to spare or if we would get him a bottle. Well, shit, we were drunk you know? So we got him a bottle of cheap-ass scotch and gave it to him. Well, after the motherfucker gets through crying, he upends the scotch and downs half the bottle, I shit you not. Then he just keels over dead. Right there on the street. As you would say, "Deader than Cooter Brown's pecker." Well, we di-di'd the hell out of there I'll tell you. And here I thought the albino water buffalo was the strangest thing I would ever see. I tell you, Hill, the world is a fucken mess.

Speaking of messes, the chow here is out-fucken-standing. Just like the booze and the gambling, you can eat, drink and gamble anytime you feel like it. And the women, for crying out loud, if they put a tent over Vegas you would have the largest whorehouse in the world. And these are not your run of the mill whores, Hill, these women are gorgeous, and I haven't met one yet that couldn't suck a golf ball through a paper straw. I can't wait to get back to Rhode Island so my pecker can have a little R and R.

So, anyway, I wake up this morning, and I'm like dead broke. So I'm at the desk trying to find out how to get my folks to wire me some money when this ugly old fucker walks up and stands next to me. I mean this guy is in a robe and house shoes and looks like hell. He had this long white hair that hadn't been cut in like years and these really long, nasty yellow fingernails. I tell you, he looked like something out of The Night of the Living Dead. *So the guy at the desk likes to shit a brick, and he starts all of this, "Oh, yes, sir, Mr. Hughes" shit. Next thing you know, my bill has been paid, and I have a first class ticket to Boston on TWA, all thanks to this Hughes character. I tell you, Hill, life just gets curiouser and curiouser.*

So, I'm off to the airport in twenty minutes. If your dumb ass makes it back to the world, we will have to meet up in Vegas, but right now I hear a blackjack table calling my name.

Semper Fi, motherfucker,

Gunz

"See, Hill, there are worse ways to die."

"I wasn't thinking about that old bum outside the liquor store, Gunny...I was thinking about the women."

"Hell, by the time you get back to the world you'll have forgotten what a pussy looks like. You'll probably just wanna throw rocks at it."

G.O. smiled at the Gunny. "They're some things you just don't forget, Gunny. Hell, every time the wind blows, I get a hard-on."

The Gunny leaned back and stared wistfully at the overhead. Then abruptly sat up and stared at G.O. "Speaking of forgetting…I almost forgot to tell you how Bonebreaker got his new name. Well, it seems that… *that* Lieutenant Stein, that Ichabod Crane–looking fucker we spent some time with in the mud, was impressed with Private Bonebreaker, and next thing ya know, he runs into Lieutenant Abramovitz in the O club at Marble. Well, by the time Stein gets through telling the story of 'Butcher's Paddy,' you would have thought that Bonebreaker was John-fucken-Daddy-Daddy-Wayne his own damn self. So Stein tells him how Bonebreaker wants his name to be Hakim. So Abramovitz takes the story to the skipper along with how much positive publicity the Marine Corps will get out of this with the African American community back in the states. And you know how much the skipper loves publicity. So Bonebreaker is now officially Lance Corporal Hakim El-Hashim. End of story."

G.O. knew that wasn't the whole story. He knew that the Gunny had to give his approval before the CO would make such a move.

"That's all, Hill. Send that damn skivvy-folder in when you leave so I can hear his side of this story, and for chrissakes tell him to put his damn teeth in."

"Aye-aye, Gunny." Hill performed an about-face and left the toolroom, looking for Delmonico.

◆ ◆ ◆

After Joey was debriefed by the Gunny, he and Hill went up to Officer Country. They eventually found Captain Abramovitz's compartment that he shared with Lieutenant Kelly. G.O. pounded on the hatch.

From inside the compartment, Captain Abramovitz called, "Enter."

"And just what brings you two magnet asses up to Officers' Country?"

"We just came to tell the captain goodbye and that it was a pleasure to share an aircraft with you, even though you ain't very good at maintaining radio discipline, sir!" G.O. responded as he and Joey D. stood at attention.

This brought a grin to Captain Abramovitz's face. "Relax, boys, you're not talking to Major Bridger. I guess you're going to have to break in a new rotor head now that my talents have finally been recognized."

"No, sir, it's like the Gunny says, 'You either have it, or you don't, it ain't something you can buy or teach,' and you got it, sir."

"Well, thanks, men, but you need to know, I felt like I was shitting razor blades last night and the only thing that kept me from leaving was waiting on you two numbnuts getting all the Marines on board."

"Well, sir, I appreciate you not leaving me out there, but what we really came for was to present you with this new garment bag Joey made. He spent all morning in the parachute shop sewing this thing together. He had to go back and redo your name tag 'cause he misspelled your name, but he finally got it right." G.O. said with a big grin on his face.

Joey stepped forward and handed the captain the garment bag. This prompted Lieutenant Kelly to get up off his rack and check out Captain Abramovitz's new piece of luggage.

"Well, damn, son, this is gorgeous...thank you, men. Every time I look at this bag, I'll think of you two scraggily-assed Marines, and the night we flew together in the friendly skies of Southeast Asia."

"Thank you, sir...see you on the flight deck."

"See you on the flight deck, Marines."

◆ ◆ ◆

The next morning found G.O. and the crew chiefs and pilots of HMM-265 in the ready room being briefed on the assault that was to take place the next day. Colonel Van Meter had turned the briefing over to Major Bridger.

"The ROK Marines will be landing on the northern end of Barrier Island in an amphibious assault, and our squadron will offload the First Battalion of the Twenty Sixth Marine Regiment at the southern end of the island as a blocking force. Our insertion will be supervised by the overwatch helicopter, the *Randy Rabbit*, being flown by Lieutenant Rinehart and me. Should any trouble arise, we will be like the mama hen, and you will be our chicks."

Oh shit, Hill thought, *lousy metaphor.* Then it started. Quietly, at first, then becoming louder throughout the ready room. "Peep...peep, peep...peep."

"All right, you clowns, that's enough, not another goddamn peep! This is serious shit and could save lives, so pay attention."

I need a T-shirt like that, Hill thought. *'Serious shit saves lives' or maybe 'Assholes I have met while yachting' or maybe one that rhymes like, 'Don't make a peep when the bullshit be deep.'*

"Now, before you are dismissed, Colonel Van Meter would like a word...Skipper?" Major Bridger invited the colonel to the podium and then waddled his walrus-looking ass into the shadows.

The colonel sauntered to the front of the squadron then turned his head slightly to the left to hide his missing ear. "Boys," he began. G.O. glanced at Hakim and watched as his eyes began to glow red. "It has come to my attention that there has been a lot of unnecessary radio chatter during operations. I would like for you to remember one of our squadron's most sacred maxims while flying, 'Radio discipline—"

He got no further when the entire ready room replied, "Is a sign of professionalism! Oooh rahhh!"

Small creases appeared at the edges of the colonel's eyes, "Well done, gentlemen...you are dismissed."

"No, no, no, G.O...you must sip each wine, like so. First, you must smell zee wine, then you swirl zee wine, then you sip zee wine. You swish zee wine around in your mouth so that zee palate is bathed in zee wine. Then you swallow. You do not just guzzle zee wine. Were you born in zee *toilette extérieure? Phah! Americaines!*" Pogo ended his oenology lecture to the crew gathered in Joey D.'s parachute shop. Pogo, G.O., Locker, Blaze, the Gerber Baby, and Joey D. were gloriously semi-intoxicated.

G.O. looked at Pogo through herb- and wine-glazed eyes and said, "I resemble that remark." A loud pounding on the parachute shop's metal door followed.

Joey replied, "Who's there? I'm swamped and don't have time for idle conversation."

"Hey, open up, you fucken fucks! I know you in dere!"

"Hey, man, open up. It's the Scrotum." Joey opened the hatch, and there stood Scrotum, Redfeather, and Wacky Wayne. Each carried a bottle of the water of life. *Aqua vitae. Uisge beatha.*

"Welcome, my sage friends, let the party begin."

"Damn, Scrotum, have you showered since we've been aboard ship?"

"Fuck you, Locker. I neva' shower before an operation, bad luck."

"It's bad luck if they smell you comin' too, dude."

"Yeah, well fuck you too, you little toothless fuck."

"Hey, man, leave the toothless fuck alone. It's his shop we are partyin' in."

"Oh, yeah, right...so what are youse talkin' about?"

"Two greatest syllables in the English language, Scrotum, my man."

"Oh yeah, what would dat be?"

"*Pussy*...but for you we can change the topic to penis."

"Whachew talkin' 'bout, Locker? I gotta a goil back in the world."

"Really, got any pictures of her?"

"Yeah, she just sent me a fresh batch," Scrotum said as he pulled an envelope from his flight suit and pulled out some Polaroid photographs.

G.O. grabbed one and let a low whistle as he looked at a thoroughly nude blonde stretched out on a bed. A full frontal. *In toto.* "Damn, old son, she's...uh...umm...ah...naked. Here, Chief, want to see Scrotum's naked girlfriend?"

Chief took the photo from Hill. "Me see her before...she has eagle tattooed on her bottom."

Quiet descended on the parachute shop. Scrotum stared daggers at Redfeather. "How you know dat, Chief?"

"You show me picture of her ass last week."

"Oh, yeah...forgot about dat. So I'm in the head earlier..."

"No one wants to hear about how many times you masturbate during the day, Scrotum."

"No, for real, dis is a good story. So, I'm standin' dere takin' a leak, and I see dis cockaroach trying to get outa da urinal. I'm thinkin', everybody in the squadron has been takin' shots at da poor guy. So, I feelin' generous, ya know, so I get a paper towel and reach down a grab da cockaroach and set 'im on da floor. So then Wacky Wayne walks in, sees da cockaroach, and squashes 'im flat."

"Is there a point to this story or are you just pissin' in the wind?"

"You don't need a point to have a point, G.O. It's just a fucken story, for crying out loud. But if you need a point, how about this…it's better to stay where you're safe being pissed on, than to get out in the world and get squished."

"Naw, it's more simple than that…it's keep your hands out of the fucken urinal."

"Also, don't squash cockroaches unless you're wearing shoes."

"Enlightening point, Wacky."

"Actually, you all have valid points, but it reminds me of the Prime Directive."

"Holy shit, the Gerbs speaks."

"What is theese *Prime Directiff*?"

"Shit, Pogs, you never watched *Star Trek*? Tell him, Gerbs."

"Well, it's a rule that prevents members of the United Federation of Planets from interfering in the internal development of alien civilizations. Because even well-intentioned interference can inflict unanticipated harm. Like Scrotum's empathy for the cockroach ended up killing the little fucker."

"Like white man civilizing the Indians."

"Or like Uncle Sam-U-Ell wantin' to help the po' Vietnamese out of the shitter?"

"Bingo."

"Speaking of roaches…anybody want a hit off this exquisite *Bleu de Hue* spliff?"

"Me smokum."

"Hell, Chief, you'd smoke a corduroy peach, if you thought you could light it."

"You betchum."

Lomax, the one-eyed cockroach, hidden in folds of parachute silk that lay crumpled in the corner of the parachute shop, gazed through the funky haze at the Saturnalia and reflected on his lost love, Archibella. A tear fell carelessly from his good eye as he thought about his last tryst with her before she was squished by Wacky Wayne. He thought, It's hard to be a cacarootch.

Chapter Thirty

Operation Corduroy Peach

Eighteen helicopters were turning and burning on the flight deck of the USS *Iwo Jima*. The Republic of Korea (ROK) Marines had been offloaded earlier on various amphibious craft to start their assault on the barrier island south of Danang. The Marines of the First Battalion, Twenty-Sixth Marine Regiment were designated as the blocking force and would be inserted by HMM-265. At a signal from operations, the first wave of 1/26 started boarding the helicopters like so many recalcitrant BBs being drawn across a table by a powerful magnet. G.O. stood at the starboard hatch, behind the cockpit, and felt the rotor wash on his face. At that moment, he sensed the divine spark that had driven human beings for thousands of years. His heart pumping gallons of adrenaline into every fiber of his being. He felt invincible. *Goddamn*, G.O. thought, *what a rush...*Sambhogakaya, *motherfucker...Jeezus, Mary, and Cotton-Eyed Joseph...that looks like Mr. Peepers gettin' on board* Interstellar Overdrive.

The Marines came on board and stacked their equipment on the deck in front of them as they took their seats. The last Marine on board gave him a thumbs-up. He triggered the ramp to close and notified the pilot, "Sir, we have twelve grunts on board, and the aircraft is secured."

"Roger that, Crew Chief, now if the LSO can just get this circle jerk unfucked, we can be on our merry way."

The LSO signaled, and the *Randy Rabbit* lifted off, followed by *96 Tears* and the *Ace of Spades*. One of the navy deck crew signaled for the chocks to be removed from *Groundz* and for the pilot to taxi forward toward the LSO. G.O. sat on the crew chief's jump seat and scanned the faces of the grunts. He did a double take when eyes landed on a black Marine with sunglasses. He gave the grunt a left-handed salute which was returned by a wide, toothy grin and the autonomous one-fingered crucifix. G.O. returned the smile and thought, *I just might have to fuck with the grunts once we're airborne. Groundz* joined the helicopter formation at fifteen hundred feet as they circled the *Iwo* waiting for the rest of the squadron to join them before heading inland. While they circled, he stared out the hatch and used his pistol grip to lower and then raise the aft ramp. Out of the corner of his eye, he could see the grunts getting nervous and were animatedly talking with each other. Finally, one of the grunts leaned over and grabbed G.O. by the arm and said, "Sir, we think something's wrong back there, the ramp keeps going up and down." G.O. glanced at the back of the aircraft and then abruptly stood and started climbing over the grunts equipment making his way toward the back of the helicopter. When he was at the rear of the aircraft, he dropped the starboard engine door, pulled a rag from his flight suit, and took down two cans of beans and frankfurters. Closed the engine compartment and started back to the front of the aircraft. He handed one of the cans to Joey and began to open the other with the P-38 he kept on the chain with his dog tags.

"Damn, Crew Chief, I believe I smell some beans and frankfurters," Captain D'Amato called over the ICS.

"You would be correct, sir." *Oh God, please don't let him ask for my beans and frankfurters. He hasn't farted once today.* "Would you like to share mine, sir?"

"Thought you would never ask, son. Pass those beanie-weenies on up here. You have the aircraft, Lieutenant."

"I have the aircraft, sir."

G.O. stepped into the cockpit hatchway and offered his lunch to Captain D'Amato. He looked out the windscreen as the last bird was preparing to launch. It was Lance Corporal's Huntz's aircraft, *Interstellar*

Overdrive. As it was lifting off, it suddenly flipped on its side and crashed into the deck of the *Iwo* and rolled into the South China Sea. *Hokey smokes*, he thought as he watched sailors scrambling to avoid flying rotor blades. Radio chatter picked up voluminously. "This is Major Bridger, gentlemen...remember radio discipline...we have been instructed to continue with the operation...let the navy take care of Echo Papa One Five. Maintain your formation we are headed inland."

"What happened, Captain?" Lieutenant Masterson asked.

"Jeez, Easy Pickings One Five just went down in the South China Sea. I've never seen anything like it."

"What do you think happened, Crew Chief?"

Like I know, for fuck's sake. "I really don't have a clue, sir...Who was the pilot?"

"I think Captain Sifuentes was the HAC and Lieutenant Triton was the copilot."

"I think I saw Mr. Peepers board when we were waiting for take-off."

"Really? The reporter from the *Post*? Well, hell, I hope he lives to tell about it."

"Aye-aye, sir...I hope they all do." G.O. received his first inkling that the beans and frankfurters might possibly have been rancid when the first repulsive vapors invaded his nose. *Jesus, that son of a bitch is at it again,* he thought as he covered his face with the oil rag he carried in his flight suit. *Safer to sniff hydraulic fluid with a hint of jet fuel than Chucky D.'s grody ass fumes.* G.O., in a moment of divine revelation, noticed that the Marines close to the cockpit were actually starting to turn a shade of green. *Oh shit, just what I need. A helicopter full of puking Marines.*

"This is Highboy six two...we are five mikes out from our designated LZ...I say again, we are five mikes out from our designated LZ...the LZ can accommodate three 46s at a time...Highboy one niner, Highboy two three, and Highboy one eight will drop to fifteen hundred feet and make the first approach...the rest of the squadron will continue to circle at thirty-five hundred feet until the first three aircraft offload and clear the LZ... copy."

"Highboy one niner copy," Captain D'Amato responded. "OK, Crew Chief...we will be one of the first aircraft to land...I want you and Delmonico on those guns...and I want the grunts off this aircraft as quickly as possible."

"Copy that, sir." *You don't have to worry about the grunts wanting off this aircraft.*

◆ ◆ ◆

Xin Loi and Hung Dong lay hidden in the trees at the edge of a field of elephant grass. They had been following a Marine recon patrol for several days as the Marines explored the island.

"What are these Yankee imperialists up to, Xin?"

"If we knew, Hung, we could report to the Comrade Colonel then di-di back to our scout platoon and leave this so-called *paradise.*"

"Well, it was a veritable paradise until the Ddang Kong landed on it this morning."

"Why do you insist on calling the Koreans *peanuts*? They are uncompromising soldiers, as are we."

"It may be as you say, but they are smaller than we are, you must admit."

"Yes, but if a Ddang Kong bullet kills you, you will be just as dead as if a gigantic American had fired it."

"Pah, you know the Ddang Kong can't shoot straight...they have slanty eyes."

Xin Loi inspected Hung Dong's face for any sign of sarcasm, then slowly shook his head. Xin looked up as he heard helicopters in the distance.

◆ ◆ ◆

G.O. stood by the stub wing and swapped war stories with a *grape,* the colorful name given to the aviation fuel handlers because they wore bright-purple jerseys, as *Groundz* was hot refueled on board the *Iwo.* He was happy. Giddy. Farting rainbows. All of the crew members and grunts had been extracted from the water within fifteen minutes of *Interstellar* going down. He couldn't wait to ask C.C. about his "Poseidon adventure."

"We are refueled and ready for our next hop, sir."

"Roger that, Crew Chief...get the aircraft buttoned up...we've got another mission."

As *Groundz lifted off,* G.O. experienced a minor panic attack. *Surely, two helicopters wouldn't crash on the same boat on the same day? Surely.*

"Where are we headed, sir?"

"We're off to pick up a recon team, Crew Chief."

Oh, shit, Hill thought, *can't those guys find their own damn way home?*

"You'd think, since they're a recon team, they could find their own way home, wouldn't you, Crew Chief?"

"Yes, sir."

"Can you believe everyone on board the *Interstellar* survived? That was unbelievable...Lucky bastards...and now they get thirty days' leave."

"Thirty days' leave...no shit? For crashing in the ocean?"

Their conversation was interrupted by a radio call. "This is Highboy one eight...we are on your starboard wing...we will be your dedicated chase plane today on this mission."

"Roger that, one eight...I have you on our starboard wing...proceeding to extract point."

"Copy that."

Well, good, G.O. thought. *Locker and Gerbs are back there in* Surf City.

◆ ◆ ◆

"This is Romeo two six. We have two choppers in sight and are popping smoke now."

"Roger that, two six...we have purple smoke in sight."

"Roger...purple smoke."

"OK, Crew Chief, I want you and Delmonico on those guns..." Captain D'Amato said as he dropped the collective stick and started his descent toward the smoke. The spot they were headed for was an open area covered in elephant grass. The grass itself was over six feet in height. As they touched down, the pilot was pulling up on the collective, and G.O. felt his whole body being pulled to the deck. Like being on a roller coaster, going from being weightless one moment to feeling like you weigh a thousand pounds the next. As the ramp dropped, G.O. ran to the back of the aircraft to usher the grunts on board. A gunnery sergeant stopped next to G.O. as they counted heads.

The Gunny looked at G.O and yelled above the roar of the helicopter, "We have one missing...you can't leave yet!"

"Sir," G.O. informed the pilot, "the Gunny of this recon team says one of his chicks is missing and that we can't leave yet."

"You tell that Gunny that he's *not* the helicopter commander, and if his Marine doesn't show in the next minute, we are hauling ass...we are not going to be a sitting duck for Sir Charles."

"You got one minute, Gunny," G.O yelled.

The Gunny drew a .45 automatic from his holster, pointed it at G.O.'s hard hat, and said, "We don't leave until my man is onboard!"

G.O.'s pucker factor hit 9.7. His ass cheeks slammed together so hard he was sure it could be heard in Danang. Tighter than a rusted lug nut on a '55 Chevy. Invincibility vanished, but the adrenaline rush was back. *Come on, brain, don't fail me now.* "Gunny...after we leave, the chase plane will come down and look for your missing Marine, but we are leaving, so either fish or cut bait."

As they lifted off, the Gunny holstered his weapon and mumbled something about the parentage of the fucken air wing pukes he had to hitch a ride with.

After they were airborne once again, G.O. spotted *Surf City* headed for the LZ they had just left. He saw a Marine run up the ramp of Locker's helicopter.

"This is Highboy one eight...we have your missing Marine onboard... will return to your pos."

"Roger, one eight...Crew Chief...would you notify the Gunny."

"Roger that, sir."

G.O. walked over to the Gunny. "Your man has been picked up, Gunny, and we are headed back to the *Iwo*."

The Gunny gave him a look that suggested a smile, but to G.O. it looked like he had just finished a healthy dump and had run out of toilet paper. *Jesus, this motherfucker gives me the fantods, they must go to a special school on how to give people the undogondolated creeps.*

◆ ◆ ◆

G.O. and Locker were on the flight deck cracking up over their latest mission as the grapes were hot refueling their aircraft.

"So anyway." Locker was choking. "This grunt comes running up the ramp before we had even touched down. And would you believe it? His nickname was Hud. He was whiter than a fucken sheet, Hill, and covered in elephant grass. I'm picking grass off of him and trying to find out how he got separated from his recon team. So he says you landed on top of him and then dropped the ramp on his ass and had him pinned under your helicopter. He said he was screaming and yelling, but nobody could hear him. I swear the funniest goddamn thing I've ever heard since I've been in the 'Nam. That poor dumb fucker is probably still shittin' razor blades."

"Yeah, well it wasn't so funny when that fucken gunnery sergeant pulled a .45 on me."

Locker waved his hand in front of his face like there was a severe gnat problem in the South China Sea. "Seriously, man, you need to change your underwears. You're startin' to smell like Chucky D."

"Yeah, well go fuck yourself, Locker. You're not exactly a bottle of Chanel Number Five," G.O. replied as the grapes gave them the finished fueling signal. G.O. walked up the ramp and told the pilot they were ready to rock and roll.

Chapter Thirty One

The Wisdom of Wombats

Toward dusk, the helicopters of HMM-265 changed missions and began ferrying supplies to different firebases the Marines had set up as a blocking force on the island. G.O. appraised the recon team through the tinted visor that was part of his hard hat. It was the same team they had extracted earlier in the day. They had on their face paint, but it couldn't hide the scowl on the recon Gunny's face. *Motherfucker could make a freight train take a dirt road*, Hill thought. One particularly terrified Marine stood out to him. He had the word *HUD* in all caps written on the front of his boonie hat. *Well, hell,* he thought, *that must be the feather merchant we damn near squished in the elephant grass. If memory serves, Paul Newman possessed a little more savoir-faire than that doofus-looking little prick. Ah, shit.* G.O. got off of his jump seat and went to sit by Private Hud.

"Hey man, sorry we landed on your ass," G.O. yelled above the roar of the helicopter.

Hud looked at him wide-eyed for a moment. "Are you the guys that landed on me?"

"What? Do I f-f-f-fucking stutter? I just said it was us."

"Well, you scared the hell outa me...I felt like a cockroach being squished under the Jolly Green Giant's foot."

Lomax peered over the edge of a discarded beany weenie can and shook his head. As much as a cockroach can shake his head. You don't know the first thing about being squished.

G.O.'s conversation was interrupted by a call from the Chucky D. "Crew Chief...if we can't find a suitable place to land on Hill 162...designated Widow's Peak...the grunts will have to rappel down...copy?"

"Copy that, sir...will relay to the recon, Gunny."

"Gunny, the pilot wants you to know if there is not a suitable LZ, you will have to rappel down to the Widow's Peak."

The Gunny grabbed a handful of G.O.'s flight suit and pulled him nose to nose. Then, in a voice that sounded like it had been pushed through gravel and shit over a cliff by the devil, said, "Fish or cut bait...huh? I should've shot your dumb air-wing ass when I had the chance. You ain't nothing but a taxi, son. Now stand aside and let the real men do their fucken job."

G.O. managed to make it back to the jump seat without shitting himself. He examined the Widow's Peak through the hatch. At one end there was a ridge with very little vegetation and appeared to be suitable for landing.

"Crew Chief...we are going to try and set this bad girl down on that ridgeline...you and Delmonico get on those guns."

"Aye-aye, sir."

As soon as they dropped the ramp, the grunts were off, *Groundz* was lifting off, and Chucky was singing, "Would you like to fly in my beautiful balloon? Would you like to glide in my beautiful balloon?"

◆ ◆ ◆

Suddenly, G.O.'s hardhat was deluged with a plethora of radio chatter. "This is Highboy two three...we are taking fire from southeast of LZ Glasscock...I say again...we are taking fire at LZ Glasscock..."

"Stand down, two three...this is Highboy six two...the cavalry is on the way..."

G.O. thought, Worry *was taking fire from the bad guys, and Major Bridger is going to make a gun run in the* Randy Rabbit...*this ought to be good.*

"We're taking fire...I say again...we have been hit, goddamnit..."

G.O. could tell it was Major Bridger who had been hit, but he could not ascertain how serious it was.

"Goddamnit...we just lost our number one engine..."

"Oh, sweet Jesus...we're gonna crash..." G.O. heard Lieutenant Rinehardt scream over the radio.

"We're not crashing...you fucken Bible thumper...we just lost one engine, for crying out loud..."

"But sir, you said we lost the number one engine...look at the gauges...we've lost power on the number two engine..."

"Oh, fuck...we're gonna fucken crash...goddamnit! I only had three months left in country...this shit ain't right...tell my wife I was a good pilot...tell my children I was thinking about them...tell my girlfriend..."

Then from out of nowhere, in a voice that sounded similar to Chucky D.'s, G.O. heard, "Gentlemen...radio discipline is a sign of professionalism."

"Who said that?" Major Bridger squealed. "I will have your ass up on charges...we are about to augur in, goddamnit!"

"Crew Chief," Captain D'Amato called, "I think we'll mosey over to LZ Glasscock and see if we can be of any assistance."

"Roger that, sir."

◆ ◆ ◆

Major Bridger had found a secure stretch of white sandy beach to hard land the *Randy Rabbit.* The area was festooned with Seabees offloading cargo and using the beach as a staging area before the supplies were dispersed inland to the grunts. The *Rabbit* was buried up to its stub wings in the sand, while the crew stood solemnly by the aft ramp. Captain D'Amato eased *Groundz* down to land nearby. The crew of the *Rabbit* came up the ramp and sat down as Chucky D. lifted off and headed back to the *Iwo* as the sun was sinking in the South China Sea.

◆ ◆ ◆

G.O. and Delmonico sat in rapt attention in the para shop as Blaze told them about his harrowing adventures in the *Rabbit,* while Wacky added color commentary when appropriate.

"So, like I was sayin', *Worry* was dropping a cargo net full of ammo to the grunts when they started taking fire. So Major Bridger decides we're gonna make a gun run...at fifteen hundred feet! Can you believe that shit? We could barely see the fucken ground."

"Yeah, we could barely see the ground," Wacky parroted. The crew cocked their eyes at Wacky Wayne.

"That's right, Wayne," Blaze said and nodded at Wacky. "So, there we were swooping in at fifteen fucken hundred feet, with all four fifties and the stinger blazing away...We were shooting up rocks and trees and probably even the damn grunts 'cause we couldn't see shit."

"Yep, I was shooting at the sky..." Wayne offered. More cocked eyebrows.

"Like I was sayin', we were shooting up rocks and trees *and the sky* when Mr. Charles decides to shoot back, and the sons of bitches weren't using no slingshots, neither." All eyes turned to Wacky. He just sat with this faraway look in his eyes. So Blaze continued, "So anyway we start taking hits, the Walrus starts screaming, and Lieutenant Thesaurus starts praying, you know, like God's gonna come pull his ass out this nasty crack we're in. It feels like we still have power, so I'm headed back to drop the engine compartments when we lose all power, and the major is screaming at us to brace for impact. I mean, we fell outa the sky like a hot turd and didn't stop till the *Rabbit* hit the beach."

"Yep," Wayne said, "like a hot turd." Momentary stillness as the crew looked expectantly at Wayne to proceed.

"So after we burrow in, Major Bridger comes flying out of the cockpit, grabs up an M-16, and hits the hatch with the rifle across his body. Wham! He hits the hatch and falls back into the bird. But the major is undaunted, see...he climbs back on his feet...and hauls ass out of the hatch. The fucken Seabees are sitting around on stacks of cargo eatin' their C-rats and watching this fiasco unfold as the major is making tracks across the beach like there's a North Vietnamese regiment on his ass. Then he stops and catches his breath...sees we're in a secure area...then starts back toward the helicopter. Damnedest thing I've seen since I've been in the 'Nam. Then here come you dickheads to the rescue. Goddamn, I was happy to see your ugly faces."

"You know," Wacky slurred through drunken lips, "you guys really *are* ugly."

"Beauty is in the eyes of the beholder, numbnuts," Joey said as he poured shots of Southern Comfort all around. "I bet you didn't care how pretty we were when we were picking your dumbasses up."

"You got that right, Joey...you could've had one eye in the middle of your head, no legs, and speaking Korean, and we would've been happy as a pig in shit to see your sorry asses," Blaze said, as they all clinked canteen cups.

"You can't fly with no legs, Blaze."

They considered Wacky's logic for only a moment then replied, "Shut the fuck up, Wacky!"

Lomax, who had been engaged in licking the remains from the inside of the Southern Comfort lid thought, *OK, enough of the one-eyed jokes. I gots feelings, too.*

◆ ◆ ◆

After G.O. had returned to quarters, he thought he would stop by and check on Lance Corporal Huntz, who had gone over the side in *Interstellar Overdrive* earlier in the day. When he found his rack, C.C. was perusing the latest reading materials he had received in a care package from home. C.C. was a young Marine from Rochester, New York who usually kept pretty much to himself. *Interesting oxymoron*, Hill thought, *introverted Yankee.* C.C. was reading by flashlight as Hill kneeled by his rack, "Hey, pard, whatcha reading?"

"Hey, Hill, you scared the bejeezus outa me...oh, this is just some comix Ma and Pa Huntz sent me. You might enjoy this one," he said as he held up a copy of *Bat Lash.*

"No thanks, man. I just dropped by to hear about your adventures in the South China Sea."

"Shit, Hill, I had to tell this story at least six times today."

"Well hell, old son, they don't start making sense until you get to at least the seventh tellin'. Let me hear the story so I can decide if you will ever be accepted around the campfires down in Texas."

"Well, there's not a lot to tell, really. We were sitting on the flight deck waiting on the LSO give us the takeoff signal. When he gave it to us, Captain Sifuentes pulled up on the collective...the helicopter started leaning to the left...I think that's when the captain tried to sit her back down. Well, we bounced left and right...it was like the back of aircraft was turning to the left while the forward end was turning to the right. Well, the oscillations became more violent and the next thing I knew everything started moving in slow motion. Rotor blades went flying across the flight deck...sailors running for cover...and the bird slowly tipping over as we plunged overboard. We had no sooner hit the water than the grunts were scrabbling out of every available exit...and we hadn't even sunk yet. Well, the chopper filled up pretty fast as you might imagine. So I swam up to look in the cockpit and the pilots were already out, so I says to myself, *C.C., it's time to di-di.* So, I swam out of the crew's hatch and popped my Mae West and hit the surface. We bobbed around like corks for a little while, then three different launches pulled up and started hauling our asses out of the water. When we got back to the *Iwo*, the Pecker Checkers had blankets for us and little bottles of whiskey, like they serve on airplanes. The Commodore came down and shook all our hands and told us what a great job we were doing. That's it, man."

"Well, it ain't a bad story...but it could be better, if you had a Great White shark in it...or a Kracken...or maybe a Leviathan, you know. Yep, it would be a much better story if you had to pull out your K-Bar and kill a shark to save the rest of your crew, maybe even get you a shark's tooth necklace. You know, to make the story more believable. Shit, son, you could drink free all night long with that story."

"Yeah, but it wouldn't be the truth, would it?"

"Truth? You mean like you leaving out the part where you almost shit yourself when your helicopter start trying to tear itself in half? Or how about leaving out the fear and panic you felt when your bird hit the water? Or how about tellin' folks that you think they are so dumb they can't decipher the truth for themselves, that's the truth, too. And leaving out any part of the truth would just be lyin'...now wouldn't it?"

C.C. smiled at Hill. "Why do you southern goobers have such a convoluted way of readin' shit into a story that just ain't there?"

G.O. returned the smile. "Well, two reasons, really. You tell that story, like you just told it, back home, people are just gonna look at you and shake their heads and go, 'Ohhh, C.C, you poor thing, tsk, tsk.' So, if you're looking for sympathy, go on and tell it like that. But if you were to exaggerate a little, just a tiny bit...it might give them pause to think or maybe even empathize with your experience. But you do have to be careful, you don't wanna be too surreal or stretch the truth too much. You know, like adding something like, 'When I was underwater it dawned on me, you are either swimming for the light or sinking to the darkness.' You do that and someone will definitely call, 'Bull Shit!'. And the more important reason...most people wouldn't know the truth if it came up and hit them in the ass with a two by four. If I were to tell you that I got shit-faced with two NVA soldiers, would you believe it?"

"Possibly...that could've happened."

"How about if after getting blotto we started lighting our farts through a screen door?"

"I would probably call bullshit on that story."

"So you're saying half my story is true and half of it is false?"

"You're twisting. Again...that's not what I said. I am saying it was believable until you added that part about the farts; then it became unbelievable."

"Eureka! You're starting to get the hang of storytelling...even if the flatulence part were true, I would probably leave it out of the story; that ol' dog just won't hunt."

"So do I qualify to sit around the campfires and spin war stories with the good ol' boys down in Texas?"

"Well, I don't know if you're ready for that. I remember one time sitting around the fire, listening to the good ol' boys telling stories about how tough they were."

"What was your story?"

"Oh, I didn't have one. I just sat there and stirred the fire with my pecker."

As G.O. laughingly retreated from the exasperated C.C.'s rack, he felt a jungle boot sail perilously close to his head.

Chapter Thirty Two

The Complex Nomenclature of Death

Early the next morning, G.O. was sitting on the ramp of *Groundz,* catching some rays and waiting for the pilots to arrive, while Joey finished greasing the rotor shaft. He opened his eyes as he felt a shadow cross his face. "Hey, Barfman, long time, no see. What brings your freckled ass out into the sunshine?"

Barf gave G.O. his best Bucky Beaver grin. "I was just down in the toolroom, and they were talking about how C.C. saved those grunts yesterday when *Interstellar* went overboard."

"No shit?"

"No shit. The grunts said when they were being picked up by the navy, a Great White started circling. The grunts panicked and started thrashing in the water trying to climb aboard the launch. Well, C.C. stayed cool and when the shark swam by him…Bam! He smacked that sucker right on the nose. The shark di-di'd out of there and hasn't been seen since. Gunny said it was a 'whale of a tale,' whatever that means."

"It just means the Gunny was impressed. C.C. will probably get some kind of medal out of that deal."

Joey walked onto the ramp and added, "Yeah, like crossed boxing gloves with a shark's head in the middle with X's over his eyes."

G.O just shook his head. "Well, when you see the Great White Shark hunter, send him our way. I would like to hear this tale firsthand. And in the meantime, Barf, I suggest you get out of the sun before all of them freckles grow together and we have to start calling you Brother Barf."

Hill and Lieutenant Kelly were preflighting the helicopter while Joey D. and Lieutenant Chatterley observed. They had just finished inspecting the aft rotor head, and G.O. was buttoning up the access panels when they saw a lone helicopter approaching the *Iwo.*

"Hey, Slash," Lieutenant Kelly called to Lieutenant Chatterley, "That looks like the *Randy Rabbit.*"

The *Rabbit* came in and landed amidships close to the hangar deck elevator. G.O. noticed that the HAC was Captain D'Amato and flying in the left seat was the Gunny. *Well, I'll be,* he thought. *I wonder how they pulled that off? They couldn't have changed those engines out that fast.* After the *Rabbit* was secured, they waited for Captain D'Amato and Gunny G. to exit the aircraft.

"We wasn't expectin' no welcome home party…don't you have somethin' to do besides stand around and gawk at me and the captain, Hill?"

"We just wanted to hear about the misadventures of the *Randy Rabbit.* How in the world did y'all get the engines changed out so quick?"

"Didn't have to change out no engines, numbnuts. The Captain managed to fire up the number two engine, so we thought, what the hell, and flew her back on one engine. Easy peasy, butt-cheek squeezy."

"You mean the major didn't have to augur in?"

"Jesus, Mary, and Limp-Dicked Joseph, that ain't what I said, Hill. You weren't there, so you have no idea why the major made the decisions he made…in the heat of combat, I might add. We clear, Corporal Shit-for-Brains?"

"Clear, Gunny."

◆ ◆ ◆

"OK, Crew Chief...we are five mikes out from LZ Glasscock," Lieutenant Kelly told G.O. over the ICS.

"Roger that, sir," he replied as he left his jump seat and pulled the bolt back on his fifty. *Groundz* was picking up three Marine KIAs at the LZ. As the chopper dropped the aft ramp, the grunts started hauling the dead Marines into the aircraft on their ponchos. G.O. was at the back talking to a grunt sergeant while Joey stowed the bodies. "Thought this was a secure area, Sergeant?"

"Secure's ass. We're taking shit all night every night. These poor dumb spook bastards got it at a listening post late last evening. They were probably smoking weed and fist slappin' when Charlie sneaked in real close and turned their Claymores around. When the LP thought they heard the bad guys, they set off the claymores and boom! Blew their own dumb trouble-making asses up. It's just three less fuck-ups I have to deal with, know what I mean?"

As *Groundz* lifted out of LZ Glasscock, G.O. stood at his fifty and watched the grunts scurry from the dust kicked up by the rotor wash. He was lost in his thoughts. Undeniably upset with himself. *Why didn't I say something to that racist asshole? Why did I just stand there with my mouth open gawking at him like a fool? Goddamnit,* G.O. swore at himself, *that's the last time I stand by quietly and listen to some illiterate half-wit denigrate another human being without saying something. But what do you say to a racist? Oh, pardon me, sir, but I believe you are wrong. Or how about the Gunny's favorite: Did your mother have any children that lived? Shit,* he thought, *you got yourself a bona fide conundrum, old son.*

G.O. glanced at the three dead African American Marines lying on the deck of *Groundz* as they flew to Da Nang and Graves Registration. One of the Marines looked vaguely familiar. He went to the Marine and kneeled by him as Joey watched. The Marine's chest and neck had been shredded by hundreds of steel balls. *Damn, if you don't look like that Marine from the Iwo. Sunglasses? Yeah, that's it...I didn't recognize you because you don't have on your shades.* G.O. rifled through his flight suit and found his aviator Ray-Bans. He placed them gently over the vacant eyes that stared into the abyss. *Now you are looking righteous, my brother, and when you're marching down that highway paved with gold, you can hold your head high. And God will rise up and shout in a voice that all the heavens will hear, "Attention on deck! We have a Marine on board."* G.O. stood and rendered his best parade ground salute, while a lone tear worked its way down his cheek. *Too fucken little and way too fucken late.*

◆ ◆ ◆

The rest of the day was spent in the tedious boredom of flying resupply and troop transport to and from a variety of LZs on the island. After refueling, Lieutenant Kelly was directed to taxi over to one of the two spots for the standby helicopters and shut down. After the rotors stopped turning, the pilot and copilot emerged from the cockpit drenched in their own sweat, "OK, Crew Chief, I suggest you and Delmonico check in with the Gunny, then grab some chow. You never know when we might have to launch."

"Roger that, sir."

As the pilots walked down the flight deck, G.O. turned to Joey and said, "Why don't you get her unbuttoned, I'll go check in with the Gunny and meet you in the chow line."

"I'd rather stick pins in my eye than see the Gunny...I'll see you on the hangar deck."

G.O. gave Joey his best *I understand* grin and said, "Well, put your fucken teeth back in first. You don't want to arouse the squids," and walked down the ramp.

◆ ◆ ◆

When G.O. sauntered into the makeshift line shack in the tool room, the Gunny was screaming at two FNGs and the prodigal Marine, Ryan Sanchez. *What the hell is Sanchez doing back here? He was on his way back to the land of the round eyes the last time I saw him. He had completed his thirteen moons and was on his way home to marry his hometown sweetheart, little Rosarita. What the hell?*

The Gunny had the three of them standing tall in front of his desk. "Goddamnit, son, do not now or ever correct a gunnery sergeant in the goddamn Marine Corps. If I call you Miles Floppy-*anus*, then that's your fucken name...clear?"

"Clear, Gunny!"

"Miles? Did you mama really name you Miles?"

"Yessir!"

"Goddamnit, son, do I look like a sir? I am a gunnery sergeant in the United States Marine Corps, and you may call me Gunny. Are we clear?"

"Clear, Gunny!"

"Miles, my ass, she should've named you Inchworm...you look more like an Inchworm than a Miles to me. So from this time forward, you will be Private Inchworm, clear?"

"Yes, uh, Gunny!"

"And who is this other boot that flew in with you, Sanchez? He doesn't look any smarter than Private Inchworm."

"Gunny, this is Lance Corporal Wunderlich."

"Wonderdick and Floppyanus...well, if you boys ain't a pair of the numbest nuts I have ever laid these Marine-green peepers on. The next thing you know, Private Jack Mehoff is gonna show up in my fucken Marine Corps. Shit, Sanchez, get these sad bastards out of my sight and get 'em checked in. Be back here at eighteen-hundred thirty, and I'll find something for Tweedle-dum and Tweedle-dumber to do. What the fuck is my precious corps coming to?"

On their way out of the line shack, Hill grabbed Sanchez by the arm. "Hey, Sanchez, is that boot's name really Floppy-anus?"

"Hill, good to see you too, gringo," Sanchez replied with a half smirk on his face. "No, man, his name is Fallopianus, Miles Fallopianus. The Gunny was just fucken with him. Miles ain't a bad dude for a gringo. After I get these boots squared away, I'll stop by *Groundz* and tell you all about my little Rosarita and how the *Martillo del Thor* conquered half the women in Southern California."

"Sure thing, I like a good fantasy."

"Goddamnit, Hill, don't just stand there, come in here and tell me where you been hidin' out all day!" The Gunny gave G.O. his hard stare as he stood before the Gunny's spartan desk that contained only Captain D'Amato's coffee mug and three sets of orders in his outbox.

"Well, we started the day off haulin' dead fucken Marines out of LZ Glasscock," G.O. began before he was abruptly interrupted by the Gunny.

"Goddamnit, Hill, how many times do I have to tell you…don't call them dead fucken Marines! You call them dead fucken warriors, son. Those dead grunts you were haulin' to graves were part of the backbone of this man's corps and deserve a helluva lot more respect than you are giving them. Am I makin' myself clear?"

"Clear, Gunny!" G.O. responded as he stood a little taller.

The Gunny's eyes were piercing deep into G.O. *Shit,* G.O. thought, *what am I doing standing tall for this Alice in Wonderland–looking Gunnery Sergeant, hearing his shit about warriors? Shit, I'm a goddamn warrior too and he knows it, so why is he bustin' my chops? Starin' at me like some kinda werewolf motherfucker. Jesus, Mary, and Halitosis Joseph, I would rather be in Nee-fucken-pall than here.*

The Gunny's quick psychological evaluation of Hill made him feel less than secure about Hill's mental state. "You're probably wonderin' why I'm bustin' your chops about dead Marines. Hell, you'd rather be in Kat-man-fucken-du than standin' here listenin' to the wisdom of your dear old gunnery sergeant, am I right? Don't answer that, Corporal Numbnuts, that ain't never gonna be Sergeant Numbnuts if he don't get his shit together… it was rhetorical. Shit, son, we'd all rather be any place other than here, so all we can do is make the best of it, do our fucken jobs, and maybe, just maybe, we get home alive with all our body parts in working order and Mr. Happy standin' tall. So, you been flyin' all day and you're tired…tired of gettin' shot at…tired of gettin' shit on, and tired of hauling dead bodies. So, tell me why you think you can bring your tired ass into my line shack and crawl up my nose with your fucken Jane Fonda attitude. This ain't no goddamn movie, Hill. This shit is your reality. You following me, Marine?"

"Yes, Gunny, I'm following you."

"Anywhere?"

"Anywhere, Gunny!"

"Kat-man-fucken-do?"

"Kat-man-fucken-do, Gunny!"

"You and that little toothless mafioso fuck go get some chow and if you have time get a shower, son. You startin' to smell like the last rose of summer. And now for some good news...you will also be on standby tonight."

G.O. kept a primal groan hidden deep in his gut and looked at the Gunny with his best Basil Rathbone face. "Aye-aye...Gunny!" He executed a perfect about-face and started out of the toolroom.

He heard the Gunny say as he ducked through the hatchway, "Learn to roll with the punches, Hill, tomorrow is another-fucken-day!"

Yeah, Miss Scarlet, Hill thought, *if we live that long.*

♦ ♦ ♦

Hill went by the Ready Room on his way to the flight deck to try and discover who the ready pilots would be that night for *Groundz*. If they were called out tonight, *Groundz* would be the lead aircraft, and Locker's *Surf City* would be flying chase. G.O. drew Kelly and Chatterley again, while Locker had D'Amato and Bandini. *Well, at least I won't have to put up with Chucky D.'s god-awful farts all night,* G.O. chuckled to himself.

As G.O. walked up to the ramp, he slapped his hand on the side of his bird a couple of times and yelled out, "Anybody home?" Joey Delmonico, who had been asleep on one of the fold-out canvas seats jumped up and ricocheted off the bulkhead.

"Goddamnit, Hill, you scared the crap outa me!"

"What? I catch you playing pocket billiards, old stick?"

"No, I was just trying to get some rest...damn, I don't remember ever being this tired before."

"I thought you were going to meet me on the hangar deck. I've been looking all over for you."

Before Joey could respond, a bosun's pipe screeched over the ship's public address system followed by the announcement, "Now hear this, now hear this…standby aircrews report to your aircraft, standby aircrews report to your aircraft…prepare to launch in fifteen minutes…tonight's movie on the hangar deck will be *What's So Bad about Feeling Good?*, starring the gregarious George Peppard and the mesmerizing Mary Tyler Moore…that is all."

Chapter Thirty Three

Widow's Peak Salvation

G.O sat on the jump seat and stared at the lights reflecting off of *Surf City* as she chased *Groundz* through the total blackness of the night. Both aircraft were carrying sling loads of ammunition and other paraphernalia of death beneath them so they could be dropped onto the Widow's Peak. It seems as though the recon team they had inserted earlier in the day had been discovered and were currently the intended target of a massacre. An eerie feeling settled over G.O. He had forgotten how incomprehensibly black night-flying in Vietnam could be. There was such a thick cloud cover that it would be unlikely the Jade Rabbit would make an appearance tonight.

Hill thought, *God, if only we had a moon tonight, at least I would know up from down.* His thoughts were interrupted by the pilot, Lieutenant Kelly, as Kelly's voice came ringing through G.O's headset.

"Jesus, Mary, and Mind-Manifesting Joseph…crew chief, you need to come up here and see this…it looks like the Fourth of July on the Widow's Peak…Whoa, Nelly! Did you see those rockets, Slash?"

"Roger that…they are blowin' shit up tonight!"

G.O. arrived in the cockpit in time to see the phantasmagorical light show taking place above and around the Widow's Peak.

"Don't stare at those parachute flares too long, Crew Chief...you'll lose your night vision...and we are going to need you and Delmonico on those fifties."

"We really going to fly into that shit sandwich and drop this sling load...Sir?"

"You didn't really expect to live forever, did you, Crew Chief?"

"Well...no, sir..."

"Those are Marines on that hill, Crew Chief...and when we see an opportunity...why, we will just swoop in and drop this load and di-di back to the *Iwo*...we'll be made in the shade with a spade...so don't panic...flight mechanic."

"Wish I could rhyme...but I don't have the time...sir."

"I didn't know you Texas boys could rhyme...Stand-by...this is Highboy one niner...I say again, Highboy one niner...with a resupply for Yankee Lima four eight..."

While the pilot was communicating with the other aircraft in the vicinity and with the recon team, Hill grabbed Joey and told him to take a look out of the cockpit windscreen. Joey turned to G.O. with eyes like saucers, and said, "We are not really going to fly into that shit, are we?"

"What?" G.O. yelled above the rotor and jet engine noise. "You wanna live forever?"

"Fucken A...Mama Delmonico didn't raise me to die on some fucken no name hilltop in Vietnam...besides I have a garment bag to finish when we get back to the *Iwo.*"

"Your mama doesn't have to worry. That hill has a name, Joey; it's called the Widow's Peak, and you don't have to worry either. We'll be in and out about fifteen seconds."

"Yeah, just long enough to get shot full of holes."

That hill has a name to
separate it from all the
other hills that have their
own names or no name
It's just a hill What we
gave it is just a name

But it's hard to separate
the deaths on that hill
from all the other deaths
on all the other hills
And all the names of all
the dead on all the hills

◆ ◆ ◆

Xin Loi dived on top of Hung Dong and rolled him over as another boulder came flying over the ridge of the Widow's Peak and landed where Dong had been lying a moment before. Another string of parachute flares had been dropped, and both the Vietnamese lay perfectly frozen while their shadows danced in the swaying light.

"That was close, comrade Dong, the *beaucoup dien cai dau* Americans must be low on ammunition and are reduced to throwing rocks at us."

"That's just swell, Loi. What will you report to the commissar commander, 'Hung Dong was killed by a rock thrown by an Imperialist Yankee Dog.' Maybe I will be remembered as the 'Rock of Vietnam." That would bring a smile to my father-in-law's face! Tell me again, why are we attacking this totally unimportant hill? Are we trying to copy the Americans and throw away lives in a futile assault on a hill?"

"Careful, comrade, we are here because we are ordered to be here. Do not let your fears dominate you tonight. I need you."

The last of the parachute flares winked out, and once again they were engulfed in darkness. Then they heard a helicopter approaching the hill.

"I think the Americans are trying to bring in supplies to their rock-throwing compatriots...oh, you can get off me now, Dong...and pass the word...maintain fire discipline until the aircraft hovers."

"Very well, Loi," Dong replied as he slithered toward the other members of their scout platoon clinging to the side of the hill.

As the helicopter came in and hovered about twenty feet above the hill, Xin Loi could see the pilots' shadows reflected in the red glow of the instrument panels. Then as the sling beneath the helicopter was dropped, the Vietnamese opened up. The chopper's nose suddenly lifted in the air, and Loi could swear he saw a body fly out the back as the aircraft rolled and crashed down the other side of the ridge. Xin Loi signaled Dong to approach. "I think one of the Americans fell from the helicopter, comrade."

"Really? Do you think he might still live?"

"I think we should try to find him...dead or alive. Round up the scouts and we will begin our search. I will report to the comrade Colonel that we are searching for the American who fell from the sky. Listen...what is that noise?"

"It sounds like laughter, Loi...it is laughter! The Americans are laughing at us! We have to take this position now...we cannot be laughed at!"

"The Americans would like nothing better than for you to become angered and let your blind fury take you up the hill. So they could chop you to pieces. This is a trap, Dong; do not be fooled. Now di-di mau and bring the scouts!"

◆ ◆ ◆

FIVE MINUTES EARLIER

"OK, Crew Chief...you and Delmonico get on those guns we are beginning our approach..."

G.O. took a last look through the cockpit windscreen and saw the last flares winking out. The tracer rounds from the Vietnamese remained uninterrupted as they sought out the recon team on the Widow's Peak.

As they came over the recon's position, the pilot called out, "Crew Chief… you will have to pickle the load…I say again…you will have to manually pickle the load…the release mechanism in the cockpit is not working…"

G.O. left his fifty and dived for the hellhole to release the sling load. As he pickled the load and watched it fall away, all hell broke loose on *Groundz*. The helicopter suddenly pitched nose up as the engines screamed and G.O. found himself bouncing toward the aft ramp. Then he was free, falling through the night, as he left the sacred womb of his helicopter. As he fell toward the earth, he saw *Groundz* twist in the air and dive toward the side of the ridgeline. Then he felt like he was being slapped all over his body by two-by-fours as he fell through the scrub pines that grew on the sides of the ridge beneath the Widow's Peak. He landed on his back and continued to roll and slide another fifty feet until he came to rest in a creek.

Jesus, Mary, and Stuntman Joseph, Hill thought. *I'm alive! Maybe not…maybe I'm just dreamin' this shit. Oh Morpheus, please don't let this be a dream. Perhaps it's not Morpheus; maybe it's his sibling Pasithea. Fuck! There's just too damn many Greek dreamin' gods!* He tried to sit up and pain shot through his ribs. *Goddamn! I've got to be alive…you don't feel pain in dreams. Oh, fuck…where am I?* Shock settled on him as he continued to physically check himself out for broken body parts and any superficial wounds that would keep him from standing. He looked like a chimpanzee in a ragged flight suit searching for his lost banana.

He finally made it to a standing position. He had lost his .45 in the fall but still had his K-Bar. *Fuck, this is a swell predicament, I brought a knife to a gunfight…in fucken Vietnam. Well, if I climb back up this Mount Everest–looking hill, I can rejoin the fight and find out what happened to* Groundz *or I can follow this creek to the South China Sea and wait for daylight to seek help. If I get back up there, that crazy recon Gunny will probably just shoot my dumb air-wing ass. Nope, I think I'll take my chances and follow this silly ass looking creek. Besides, it's going down-hill. And like Granddaddy Hill always said, "Easier to roll shit downhill than up, just ask that crazy bastard, Sisyphus."* He had walked for what seemed like hours and realized what awful shape he was in since the fall.

The raging battle on the Widow's Peak seemed far away. The blasts were muted and the lights fading. *Rest. Yep, I hear you callin' my name, gentle Hypnos. It won't hurt nothin' for me to stop and rest for a minute.* The side of the creek that faced the mountain had formed a small bluff over the years, and he decided that if he sat down in one of the gullies that ran down the face of the bluff, he could rest for a while. He took his K-Bar out and sat back in the gully and was slowly devoured by the Z monster as the strains of "Rocky Raccoon" floated through the swirling kaleidoscopic ruminations of his mind…

He said, *"Rocky, you met your match"…And Rocky said, "Doc, it's only a scratch…And I'll be better, I'll be better doc as soon as I am able…"*

G.O. awoke. He opened his eyes slowly, so that they were barely slits. What had startled him? He could hear the sounds of insects reverberating in his ears and feel them on his skin. Was that what caused him to awaken? Then a bush moved. *Shit,* he thought, *that fucken bush just moved! Or am I just hallucinatin'? Fucken bugs are eatin' me alive. Fuck, it moved again! Shit, another one just moved! Goddamn, there's a whole pea pot full of moving bushes. Shit, Macbeth, it looks like Birnam Wood on a field trip to Dunsinane.* Then one of the bushes started moving toward him. Slowly. Ever so slowly. *Don't panic, G.O., make yourself invisible, yeah, that's the ticket, invisibility.* G.O. couldn't breathe. He could see the business end of an AK-47 pointed at him, as the bush moved closer. The bush had a face. *Fuck,* he thought, *I know that face…where have I seen him before?* Another Beatles' song, "I've Just Seen a Face," forced its way into his thoughts. The "bush" reached into his trousers and pulled out something shiny. *Oh, shit, he's gonna gut me! Shit, shit, shit!* Then the bush reached over and held the object out to G.O. and nodded for him to take it. *Well, I'll be damned…it's my lucky Zippo! But where did this Viet get my Zippo? Wait…that face…it's fucken Dong! The Viet Cong I met at Mama-san Hung's in Hue City when we were lighting our farts.* G.O wanted to jump up and down and hug the Viet Cong he had met in Hue, but Dong put his finger to lips for G.O. to remain quiet. Then he turned and moved back across the creek and rejoined the moveable forest.

As the shadows moved off down the creek, G.O. breathed a quiet sigh. He held his K-Bar in one hand and the Zippo his grandfather had given him in the other. He glanced down at the Zippo, and even though he could not see the inscription, he knew it by heart. *You never know when you are going to need a light.*

Chapter Thirty Four

You're Not in Kansas Anymore

G.O. lay in the spotless white sick bay rack, replaying the events of the previous night in his mind. As he lay there, he kept snap-flicking his Zippo and sliding his thumb down on the wheel to light the wick. He remembered an old *Alfred Hitchcock Presents* episode where a finger joint was wagered against being able to light a Zippo ten times in a row. Flick and light. Flick and light. He could not seem to get past seven. He figured by now all he would have on his left hand would be a thumb. Then he heard a knock on the hatch by his rack.

"I thought I would find your gold-brickin' ass hiding out somewhere," the Gunny announced as he stepped into the *Iwo's* sick bay. He looked at the cast on G.O.'s left foot. "Well, that looks like a Purple Heart."

"Not really, Gunny. I didn't break it till I was getting off the rescue chopper this morning...story of my fucken life."

The Gunny sat in the white painted metal chair next to G.O.'s rack and asked to borrow Hill's lighter. After he lit up, he looked at the bottom of the lighter and said, "Oddiz, what the hell kind of lighter is Oddiz? One of these squids sell you a knock-off Vietnamese lighter, Hill?"

"Turn it around, Gunny...yeah, that's it...see, it says *Zippo.*"

"It's all perception, son, depends on how you wanna look at it. Just like your little escapade last night. Right now I want to know what happened, from the time Lieutenant Kelly pickled the ammo sling until the

Duck Butter picked your lost ass up the next morning wandering down the beach. And don't leave anything out, you hear? I'll be the one who decides what gets left out and what stays in the afteraction report. Clear?"

"Clear, Gunny, but before I begin, can I have one of those Luckies?"

"Hell, son...you can't smoke in sick bay. It's against the fucken navy's rules," the Gunny said as he took a drag and blew a smoke ring toward the ceiling.

G.O looked askance at the Gunny and began his narration of the night's ordeal and his harrowing trek to the beach. When he had finished, the Gunny had filled up a coffee cup with Lucky Strike butts.

"Well, Jesus, Mary, and Handiclapped Joseph! That's a good tale, son, all except the part about Hung Dong returning your lucky Zippo. I told you that little escapade in Hue would never be mentioned again, and we sure as hell don't want to have to explain that shit to the colonel, do we? I think it would be better if we just said you had to flee a platoon of North Vietnamese regulars and were unable to return to the recon team on the Widow's Peak."

"Whatever you say, Gunny."

"Goddamn, son, but if you ain't getting smarter every day! Of course, it's whatever I say...hell, there'll probably be some medals in there for you boys!"

"What? You get a medal now for a dumb-ass stunt like fallin' out of a helicopter? I'll pass..."

"No, goddamnit! You don't get to pass...if the colonel wants you to have a medal, you will goddamn well accept it...with a cheery, 'Aye-aye, sir!' Clear?"

"Even if I don't deserve it?"

"Hell, son...and here I thought you were gettin' smarter...the fact is you're too damn honest to be very smart...deserve ain't got nuthin' to do with it! If an officer wants to pin a medal on your dumbass, you salute and say, 'Thank you, sir.' Then you haul ass to the nearest bar and let some feather merchant buy you drinks while you tell the tale of the Widow's Peak. Easy peasy, Vietnamezy! Am I gettin' through that woefully thick skull of yours?"

G.O. knew he was not going to untie the Gunny's Gordian Knot, especially since there were some strong feelings and emotions involved on both sides of this argument. Anecdoche nightmare. The Gunny was right about one thing though—even if it felt dishonest, it was the smart thing to do. Plus he had other demons gnawing away at the edges of mind that had to be dealt with, so he replied, "Yes, Gunny."

One of the realities G.O had not wanted to deal with concerned the crew of *Groundz*. It was easier for him to imagine that they were all fine than to believe that they might be possibly wounded or dead. He was just thankful he was alive and for some strange reason, felt guilty for it. *Shit, old son, G.O. told himself, you need to quit mopin' and start copin'...ha...I think Lieutenant Kelly would have liked that rhyme.* "So, Gunny, what happened to the crew of *Groundz*?"

"I was wondering when you were going to get around to that, Hill," the Gunny said as he gave G.O. his best Errol Flynn *Dawn Patrol* persona. "Kelly and Chatterley didn't make it. They were killed when *Groundz* augured into the side of the hill. Delmonico was thrown into the flight control compartment and had the left side of face smashed in, but he somehow managed to live through it. He was medevacked to Danang and is probably on his way to Japan to have his face reconstructed. And I hope they give him some new damned teeth, lucky little mafioso shit!

"It was a good thing you boys arrived when you did, the grunts had resorted to throwing rocks at Mr. Charles and the NVA regulars that were trying overrun their position. That recon team put up one hell of a fight, I'll tell ya. Eight of those fuckers kept over three hundred NVA at bay for the entire night. Of course, they had a little help from the air wing angels that kept dropping flares and bombs on the bad guys all night long. Not to mention a couple of doofus helicopter crews that flew into that nightmare to bring them an ammo supply.

"Anyway, the story goes that at one point, that crazy Recon Gunny started laughing. Not your typical kind of laughter but the sort of uncontrollable laughter you hear in an insane asylum. Next thing you know, all the grunts are howlin' like a bunch of schizos. Anyway, the Gunny told a captain in S-two that here they were, sitting on a hilltop, out of ammo, throwing rocks at the bad guys, when a helicopter swoops in and drops a load of ammo. Then the next thing he sees is a body come flying out the ass end of the helicopter, and it struck him as absurdly humorous. So, he started laughing. Evidently, it was contagious because then the rest of the grunts began laughing hysterically.

"As it turns out, all eight of the grunts and the corpsman sustained wounds. They were all medevacked to Danang along with Delmonico. Hell, Hill, I can't sit around and shoot the breeze with you for the rest of the day, I've got to get back to the hangar deck and make sure the troops ain't playing grab-ass.

"Before I go, here's the good news, Hill. The general has declared Operation Corduroy Peach a military success, and all troops are being withdrawn. The *Iwo,* along with HMM-Two Sixty-Five, will be headed to my favorite place on this planet, Subic Bay in the Philippines, where your dear old Gunny intends to retire when he's done with this man's corps. Oh, before I forget…you are promoted to sergeant along with Gallo, and El-Hashim is promoted to corporal."

G.O. looked at the Gunny and said, "You forgot something else, Gunny." He held out his hand. "My Oddiz."

"Well, hell, son, I didn't forget, I just wanted to see if you was payin' attention." He reached into his jungle trousers and handed G.O. his Zippo. "As Lieutenant Kelly might say, 'See you later, when your leg is straighter!'"

As the Gunny exited sick bay, G.O. watched as his shadow faded, flicked his Zippo, and ran his thumb down the wheel. When the wick caught fire, he gazed into the flame, totally mesmerized. Mind manifesting. His thoughts wandered back to sitting in an English class and listening to his teacher drone on about Edgar Allan Poe's *The Pit and the Pendulum. Why is death the only escape from our fears?* he thought. *Or is it? What do I fear most? Is it death? No. I didn't even think about it when I was falling through space. My life didn't flash before me. There wasn't some long dark tunnel with a light at the end of it and some old man in a fucken robe waving at me. All I saw was that doofus looking Joey holding on to his fifty so he wouldn't come tumbling after me. When I thought*

Hung Dong was going to slice me open, was I afraid? Scared shitless, maybe. But was I really looking forward to plunging eight inches of my K-Bar into his chest and letting his warm blood spill over my hand? What dark thing took control of me? That's what I fear. That part of me that can perform atrocious, execrable acts against another human being. Not that I can do horrific things to others…but that I am actually beginning to enjoy it. Is that my greatest fear? Losing my humanity. Have I already lost it?

The hypothetical conversation taking place in his head was interrupted when he heard Locker's voice in the hatchway. "You can stop cleaning your rifle, Hill. You have visitors!"

G.O. looked up, "Hey, Locker man! And you brought the brains of the outfit, Hakim! What brings y'all to sick bay? A dose of the clap?"

"I don't know nuthin' about no clap. You must be talkin' about Brother Gallo."

"G.O. doesn't have to worry about acquiring some exotic tropical disease. He always wears a raincoat."

"Did you two come to harass a wounded warrior or to be entertained by the quixotic rendition of the hero's misadventures on the Widow's Peak? Or the story the Marine Corps has dubbed, 'How One Gutsy Marine with a K-Bar Held Off a Platoon of Insurgent Communist Guerrillas,' soon to be made into a movie starring Sean Connery."

Hakim and Locker looked at each other and then turned their smirks on G.O. "In yo' dreams is Sean Connery gonna play you in the movie… who's gonna play Locker?"

"Oh, I was thinking Redford or Newman…"

"How about me? Ain't nobody pretty enough to play Hakim."

"Sidney Poitier? Maybe?"

"Yeah, he might work…I build a shapel…you build a shapel…"

Then Hill and El-Hashim together, "Ve build a shapel…"

"Enough already…listen, Hill, we didn't come up here to talk about making a movie out of your adventures. We came up to find out what happened. We all thought you were a dead man—except for Hakim. He said he knew you would make it…*'cause you were the luckiest white mother-fucker he ever met.*"

"Yep, that's why I want you to be my trainer."

"Trainer? For what?"

"Hakim has entered a boxing tournament the navy is putting on next week as we sail for the Philippines, and he wants us to be his trainers. You gonna be up for that, G.O.?"

"Hell, yeah! I used to follow my brother to different Golden Glove tournaments down in South Texas. I know all the underhanded tricks boxers use."

Hakim gave G.O. his best Poitier I-can't-believe-you-just-said-that-shit look and said, "We won't be using no dirty tricks, Hill."

"I didn't mean *we* were going to use them...what I meant was I know how to teach you to protect yourself from them being used on you."

"OK, you two, break it up, we don't start sparring until tomorrow. Why don't you tell us the story about how you fell out of a helicopter."

"Well, all right." G.O. leaned back on his pillow and began his story.

When he had finished, Locker asked to see the Zippo. G.O. handed it to him. "Well, damn...this is it...the one Hung used to light up that monster fart at Mama-san's house! Hakim is right, Hill. You are the *luckiest* white motherfucker I have ever met."

Chapter Thirty Five

Dien Cai Dau

The hangar deck on the *Iwo* was packed. All of the US and ROK Marines had been offloaded earlier in the week, and the *Iwo* was on a zig-zag course to Subic Bay. Still, the hangar deck was packed. There were even Marines and sailors standing on the elevator that ferried helicopters from the hangar deck to the flight deck. The sailors in attendance outnumbered the Marines about three to one and so far had won every bout in each weight division. A smoky, blue cigarette haze hung over the makeshift boxing arena erected by the navy. The final heavyweight bout featured Navy First Class Petty Officer, Raul "the Butcher" Carrera and HMM-Two Sixty-Five's own Hakim "the Hammer of Allah" El-Hashim. The five-foot-ten-inch Butcher weighed in at 283 overweight pounds and was currently the fleet champion. The six-foot-two-inch Hammer weighed in at a sleek 203 pounds.

The referee, who was also a navy chaplain, walked to the center of the ring, wearing his Naval Academy sweatshirt, with a megaphone in his right hand, to introduce the combatants. "In the blue corner, we have the current fleet champion, weighing in at two hundred eighty-three pounds, Raul 'the Butcher' Carrera!" The cheers were deafening. "In the red corner, representing the United States Marine Corps, weighing in at two hundred and three pounds, we have Hakim 'the Hammer of Allah' El-Hashim." The boos were deafening.

Shit, Hill thought. *This must be how Davy Crockett felt at the Alamo.*

The two boxers made their way to the center of the ring for final instructions from the ref. G.O. stayed in the corner with Pogo and Locker. Hakim came back to his corner, "You got any sage advice for me, Hill?"

"As a matter of fact, I do…stay away from that big motherfucker!"

"How 'bout you, Locker?"

"Stick and move, stick and move, and for crying out loud…stay away from that big motherfucker!"

"You got somethin' you wanna say, Frenchman?"

Pogo, eyes wide with amazement, looked at Hill then Locker, and finally Hakim. "Do not let these beeg mothairefuckaire mare-der you."

Hakim smiled at the three of them then turned at the bell to approach the center of the ring and begin the bout that would become known in Marine folklore as the Slaughter in the South China Sea.

During round one, Hakim danced away from most of Raul's punches and was only able to land the occasional jab. The most limp-wristed of all of Hakim's punches. A jab that would have sent King Kong to the land of Nod, just a little bit east of Eden. A jab that would drive a ten-penny nail through a brick wall. That would stop a freight train. And this was his weakest punch.

Toward the end of the round, Raul was finally able to trap Hakim against the ropes and deliver a series of powerful roundhouse punches to Hakim's ribs. G.O. could see Hakim visibly wince every time one of the punches landed.

G.O., Pogo, and Locker kept yelling for him to move off the ropes and tie him up until the bell mercifully rang, and the relieved seconds scurried about focusing their attention on Hakim. Pogo placed the stool in their corner while Locker jumped into the ring. G.O. handed the water bottle to Hakim, who washed his mouth out and spit the blood and filth into a bucket.

"You OK?" Locker prodded.

"Do I look OK? That big squid can punch, Brother Gallo. My jaw hurts, my ears hurt, and you don't even wanna know 'bout my ribs. I let him get me on the ropes, but that ain't gonna happen again…I got this! We only gone one round and he tired. He about to experience the wrath of the Hammer."

The bell rang. Round two. Hakim strode from his corner and began his dance. His feet rhythmically dancing on the canvas, while the Butcher came on like a wounded bull ready to land a knockout punch. Hakim would dance in and land a combination of punches then waltz away before Raul could counterpunch. Raul could only pursue then cover up when Hakim would bob and weave his way in close and land a flurry of devastating punches. The hangar deck had grown quiet as Hakim continued to hammer away at the Butcher. Raul's face was a piece of raw meat. Both eyes nearly swollen shut. Right eye bleeding. Cut lip. Barely standing toward the end of the round. Hakim was playing with him like a cat with a mouse.

G.O., Locker, and Pogo were all yelling at Hakim to finish him. Hakim, with a sadistic smile on his face, shuffled toward Raul. Raul brought both arms up in a defensive position, then stepped back and delivered a desperate underhanded Bolo punch to Hakim's groin as the bell sounded, ending the round. Hakim screamed in agony, "Ah-h-h-h-h-h!" and dropped to the canvas in a fetal position, both gloved hands grasping his crotch as he rolled on the floor, groaning in his pain. The referee was telling the judges to take points away from the Butcher as the sailors on the hangar deck went wild. They were glad to see the favorite finally land a punch. Even if it was below the belt. Pogo and Locker helped Hakim back to his corner.

Hakim was taking deep breaths through his nose and breathing out through his mouth. The referee walked to Hakim's corner. "I should remind you that if you retaliate against Chief Carrera, you will be disqualified. Do you understand?"

Hakim said not a word, just nodded approvingly.

"Damnit, Hakim, quit playing around, just finish the big bastard," Locker intoned.

"He is wounded and he's dangerous. You need to be careful, Hakim, but like Locker said, finish that big motherfucker!" G.O. prodded.

◆ ◆ ◆

David looked at the giant before him.

"Anyone have a hand grenade?"

Daniel handed David a rock.

"A rock?"

"We're out of hand grenades."

"But a fucken rock? Your mother should have thrown you to the lions, you fucken schlemiel!"

"Well, ya gotta do something, Dave, you're our champion."

"Champion? Right, like they're going to put a nice Jewish boy on a box of Wheaties? Schmuck!"

"Davy, look! There's Bathsheba!"

"Oy vey!"

"What are ya gonna do, Dave?"

"Hand me that sling. I think I'm going to need it!"

♦ ♦ ♦

As the bell sounded to begin the third and final round, Hakim sprang across the canvas and unleashed a flurry of powerful jackhammer blows against the Butcher. When Hakim finally took a step back, Raul "the Butcher" Carrera fell forward like a mighty oak and crashed upon the mat. Raul was down. The hangar deck grew still once more as the referee ushered Hakim to the nearest corner.

The ref came back to Raul and began his count. Raul managed to get to his knees by the count of six. Out of nowhere Hakim appeared and landed a roundhouse punch against the side of Raul's head. He went down for good. Lights out. Good night, sweet Butcher. The ref grabbed Hakim and dragged him to where the judges sat and disqualified him. Hakim jerked away from the ref and landed another roundhouse punch against the chaplain's glass jaw. The ref was down.

Hakim danced around the ring, screaming at the crowd as they bombarded him with trash and insults. Pogo and Locker had jumped into the ring and were attempting to bring him under control. The navy chiefs and

Marine NCOs were trying to break up sporadic outbreaks of violence and remove the sailors and Marines from the hangar deck.

G.O. stood at ringside and shook his head and thought, *You fucking fuck, Hakim!*

Lomax, the one-eyed cockroach, peered over the spit bucket, glanced around the ring, and had an entirely different thought. *I'm glad that Hakim's not fightin' for the North Vietnamese!*

◆ ◆ ◆

The fo'c's'le had been cleared and the room set up for a captain's mast. Hakim had been given the choice of a court-martial or a nonjudicial hearing, called a captain's mast throughout the corps. On the advice of the Gunny, Hakim chose the latter.

G.O. sat in the back of the makeshift courtroom with Gunny Peabody and a few other members of the squadron.

"Gunny, what do you think is gonna happen?" Hill whispered.

"Goddamnit, son, I don't know. It all depends on how bad the navy wants its pound of flesh."

"What does that mean, Gunny? The navy doesn't get to tell the Marine Corps what to do...do they?"

"Hell, no! But goddamnit, Hill, there comes a time where you have to handle things skillfully, if you know what I mean. You have to compromise on contentious matters. 'Specially when a holy man gets knocked out."

"So what's the best and worst that could happen?"

"The worst? That goddamn ill-tempered idiot could be burning body parts that fall off of diseased Marines on the Island with No Name for the rest of his miserable life. The best? Burning body parts on the Island with No Name. Hell, son, I don't know. You're the one with more questions than a goddamn rabbi in a whorehouse. What would you do to Hakim?"

Before G.O. could respond, the judges' tribunal entered the fo'c's'le through the starboard hatch. They were composed of Captain D'Amato and Lieutenants Radley and Masterson.

"All rise!" snapped a sergeant attached to the Marine detachment aboard the *Iwo*.

"Seats," Captain D'Amato said after taking his seat at the center of the judges' table.

"Will the accused please rise while Lieutenant Masterson reads the charges?"

Hakim and his advocate, Lieutenant Bandini, both stood to attention.

"Corporal Hakim El-Hashim, you are accused of conduct unbecoming a member of the United States Marine Corps during a boxing exhibition on 20 July 1969 and for assaulting a superior officer."

"Thank you, Lieutenant Masterson. How does the defendant plead?"

"The defendant pleads not guilty to the first count of conduct unbecoming to the United States Marine Corps and not guilty to the second count, assaulting a superior officer."

"Damn, Bandini, you may be the dumbest lawyer I have ever laid eyes on," Captain D'Amato quipped. "Hell, son, there were close to six hundred sailors and Marines on that hangar deck, and we all saw the same thing… Hakim punched that sailor when he was down on his knees and when the padre grabbed him by the arm…he decided to knock him out, too!"

"But the law demands," Captain D'Amato said, sighing, "that I ask you to present your evidence no matter how crazy the court thinks it is, so proceed, Bandini."

"Yes, sir! We have witnesses who will testify that Corporal El-Hashim entered into a state of *non compos mentis* after he was struck below the belt by Chief Carrera…"

"Oh, hell, Bandini, we don't have time to listen to all your witnesses. Especially the ship's psychiatrist, who thinks we all want to kill our daddies and fuck our mothers. No, what we want is to hear what Hakim has to say for himself before we send him off to the Island with No Name."

"But, sir—"

"But, Bandini, but? Is your cornbread cooked all the way through, Bandini? This court has ruled, now put a sock in it. We want to hear from the accused."

"So," Captain D'Amato continued, "Corporal El-Hashim, are you bat-shit crazy?"

"Sir, no, sir!"

"So why did you punch the Butcher when he was down?"

"Sir, after he hit me in the balls..."

Sniggers and guffaws erupted in the courtroom.

"Quiet in the courtroom!" Captain D'Amato yelled as he banged his gavel. "If there are any more outbursts like that, I will have this courtroom cleared.

"Now continue, Corporal El-Hashim. What happened after Chief Carrera punched you in your...er...ah...testicles?"

Hakim glared at the gathering in the courtroom before he turned again to face the tribunal.

"I was about to say, sir, after the Chief punched me in my er...ah...tes-tamentals, everything just went black...I don't remember a lot after that until Pogo and Locker started trying to get me out of the ring."

"So has this uncontrolled rage and anger surfaced at other times?"

"Only one time that I know of, sir. When I was out with the recovery team to bring back *Pandora's Box* and the Vietnamese opened up on us from a tree line. I lost it then. The Gunny said I emptied five magazines into that tree line, but I don't remember any of it, sir."

Captain D'Amato and Hakim stared at each other for a long moment.

"Very well, Lieutenant Bandini, that concludes the testimony. The tribunal will now retire to discuss our findings. We will return to render our judgment after doing so."

◆ ◆ ◆

"All rise!"

The courtroom stood to attention as the tribunal made its way back to their seats.

"Seats," Captain D'Amato declared. "The tribunal has met, and we are ready to render our findings. The accused will stand and face the tribunal.

"Corporal El-Hashim, this tribunal finds you partially not guilty on both counts."

"Partially not guilty?" Bandini blurted out.

"Goddamnit, Bandini, this is a captain's mast, not a fucken court martial, and this tribunal can come to any goddamn conclusion it wants, we clear?"

"Clear, sir!"

"It was our decision that anyone who climbs into a boxing ring has to be a wee bit crazy and that a punch to the gonads could cause a temporary mental blackout. However, you are still a Marine and will always be a Marine, so there is an expectation of conduct that is conducive to good order. Which means, in effect, Corporal El-Hashim, that even when you're nuttier than a fucken fruitcake, you will still act like a Marine!

"As a result of this finding, it is the decision of this tribunal that you will remain confined to quarters until the *Iwo* docks in Subic Bay, at which time you will be transferred HMM-three sixty-four operating out of Marble Mountain Air Field in the Republic of Vietnam. You are also fined one week of your base pay, and a letter of reprimand will be placed in your personnel file.

"It is the sincere hope of this tribunal that you get your anger under control, Corporal El-Hashim. You are one hell of a Marine, son, but you need to know that if the ship's chaplain didn't have a forgiving heart, you would be on your way to the Island with No Name."

Captain D'Amato rapped his gavel on the table. "This tribunal is now adjourned."

Lomax, the cockroach, looked at the Gunny from his vantage point at the rim of the trash receptacle placed by the tribunal's table. He could not believe his eye: under the Gunny's nose, which looked like it had been hammered by a blind blacksmith, there was the semblance of a smile.

Chapter Thirty Six

Asphodels

"Goddamnit, Hill, they should have sent his black ass to Portsmouth for life!" Locker fumed.

Several heads nodded in the affirmative.

"What, pray tell, should they have done with the rest of him?"

Several of the crew chiefs and mechanics were gathered around Locker's bunk in the Quonset hut that provided temporary quarters for HMM-265. They had been assigned temporary duty at Cubi Point Naval Air Station located next to the sprawling naval base at Subic Bay. It was their first liberty since reaching the Philippines. They were all dressed in their recently acquired civvies as they prepared for a night in Olongapo City. Hill and Locker continued to feud over the punishment of Hakim El-Hashim.

"Fuck you, Hill, you know exactly what I'm talking about. Hakim got away with punching out an officer because he's black. Pure and simple, dude. If it had been you or me, we'd be doing time on the Island with No Name."

Affirmative nods.

"Come on, Locker, man, Marine officers don't see black and white; all they see is green."

A few affirmative nods.

"Boy, you are a naive Texas simpleton. Hakim beat the system because he's black, Hill."

Affirmative nods.

"So, Locker, you think you're better than Hakim?"

"What's that got to do with anything? And no, Hill, I don't think I'm better than Hakim. He was my first mech and my friend, I thought, before he punched out the chaplain. I just think they should have put his dumb ass away."

Affirmative nods.

"If it had been me, would we be out celebratin', or would you want to see me behind bars?"

Locker stared at G.O. for a long moment. "I would want to see you busted to E-nothin' and locked up for the rest of your miserable life."

"So, you think Joey and I ought to still be rotting in that damned Conex box in Marble Mountain or burning body parts on the Island with No Name because we got drunk and stole a bulldozer? Or do you think maybe the Gunny made the right call?"

"Shit, Hill, I think the Gunny made the right call on that one. We're in the middle of a fucken war, if you hadn't noticed, and he needed all the warm bodies he could find to keep these flyin' death traps in the air."

"Oh, I get it. The Gunny's smarter than Chucky D.?"

"Don't try to trap me with your Socratic-style bullshit, Hill. You ain't changing my mind about that black Muslim Hakim."

"I get it now. It ain't about him being black; it's his religion you are opposed to?"

"I ain't going down that rabbit hole with you, Hill. Suffice it to say, Hakim was guilty and beat the rap, and that's wrong."

"Well, hell, Locker, I thought you might at least give Hakim some points for being on the receiving end of the same damn AK-47s that we were."

"Points don't matter, you dumb fucken Texas doofus! What I'm tryin' to tell you is that your Black Panther compadre, Hakim, lost his shit in the ring and should have been punished for it."

"Well, I can almost accept your logic, Locker, but I can't understand your hatred for Hakim. I guess you don't think being sent back to Vietnam is punishment? I mean, what's up with you, Locker? You know, you're startin' to sound like some of those redneck Klan fucks I knew back in Texas."

"Fuck you, Hill. You can't let anybody get away with breakin' the rules, no matter what color they are. It's just gonna cause chaos in the world when we get to make up our own rules as we go. And when society breaks down and the revolution between the white man and the black man finally comes, whose side you gonna be on, Hill?" Locker stormed.

G.O.'s eyes filled with sorrow as he stared at Locker. In his mind, the image of the three dead Marines he had picked up at LZ Glasscock came into focus. "There ain't gonna be the kind of revolution you're talkin' about, old son. The black folks are a lot more forgiving than we are. All they want is a little mercy and the same respect that everyone who calls themselves human being, should have. They don't ask a lot after four hundred years of being treated like they are less than human.

"The only revolution, Locker, if there is one, is going to be in how we view our new reality. Are we going to open our minds and try to look at things in a way we never thought about before, or are we going to keep looking at things the way we always have?"

"I ain't afraid of nothing, Hill. That's something you should know by now. Reality might change, but it ain't changin' me, and it sure as hell ain't changin' my mind. That fucken Hakim skated for one reason...he's black!"

"Hell, Locker, when did you go from laid-back California surfer dude to squadron bigot? I'm done here. Who's going to the Gunny's bar with me?"

◆ ◆ ◆

G.O, Pogo, Barf, and the Gerber Baby sat in the back of the colorful jeepney, the Maranatha, as it bounced and oscillated up a gravel road above Sierra Beach on the outskirts of Olongapo City. Along with them were Blaze, Scrotum, and Wacky Wayne.

"Fugedaboudit, Hill. It don' mean nuthin'," Scrotum said, trying to draw G.O.'s attention back to present.

"Sorry, man, it's just hard to get all the things Locker said off my mind."

"Don't be such a puss, Hill, you gotta roll with it, man."

"Yeah, I guess your right, Blaze. It could be worse…"

"That's right, we could all be shovelin' shit in the South China Sea!"

"Fucken A."

"Look, there's a picture of Jesus on the roof!" Wacky chimed.

"Well, Jesus, Mary, and Filipino Joseph, I believe you could be right, Wackorus."

All heads turned up to look at one of the many paintings on the roof of the Jeepney. All of the artwork was profoundly imbued with religious overtones while the trim had a distinctly Islamic geometrical design.

"Look, there are the three wise men…"

"You fucken doofus, that's the Beatles!"

"Where's Paul?"

"Paul is the walrus…"

Everyone in the jeepney was thrown to the floor when it began an abrupt slide before slamming into a eucalyptus tree. They had arrived at the Gunny's bar, the Mystic Foxhole Yacht Club.

As they piled out of the back of the Maranatha, Wacky looked up and said, "The Mystic Foxhole Yacht Club, what the fuck kinda name is that for a bar?"

"It's the Gunny's bar, go ask him, Wacko."

Before the crew stood a beautiful multilevel bamboo structure that soared up the side of the hill they had just traversed in the Jeepney. A flight of steps led up to the veranda that surrounded the bar on three sides with a beautiful view of Subic Bay.

The Gunny appeared at the top of the stairs holding a frosty San Miguel beer, decked out in a colorful Hawaiian floral shirt with giant parrots peeking out of the jungle scenery, cut-offs, and huarache sandals.

"Well, hell, glad to see you boys made it, where's the rest of the Hole-in-the-Wall Gang?"

"They're on the way, Gunny. They were still talking about Hakim when we left." G.O. scowled.

Eye rolls at G.O. Except for Wacky, who had a perplexed Jerry Lewis–look perpetually glued to his face.

"Well, get on in there and get yourselves something cool to drink and make sure you tightwads tip appropriately, or else you'll find one of these size-twelve Guatemalan ground grabbers somewhere between your bunghole and your throat. Not so fast, Hill. After you grab a chilly one, come see me out here on the veranda."

"Aye-aye, Gunny."

"Yo, Hill, you fucked now!"

"Yeah, just wait till I tell the Gunny you sleep with your underwear on backward, Scrotum."

"No one gonna believe that, Hill. Everybody knows I don't wear no underwears."

The group walked into the bar and came to an abrupt halt. The bar was lined with beautiful, young Filipina women. All they could do was stare. And drool. Lurker paradise. Eyeball orgy.

Finally, one of the Filipinas grabbed G.O. by the arm and started escorting him toward the bar. G.O. estimated her age to be between forty and 140. "You Marine funny. You neva' see woman before?"

"I've seen a few," G.O responded.

The Filipina matron looked at G.O. and grinned. "Then why your eyes so bugged out?" *Why does the oldest, most rode-hard, put up wet–looking woman in the bar pick me?*

"I could tell you...but then I would have to kill you."

"Oh, you sounda like Gunny G., now. He just beeg Teddy Bear. He all grumpy all time, but he just beeg softy."

"Yeah, how come you know so much about the Gunny?"

"Oh, me and Gunny been marry long time now."

"You're the Gunny's wife? No shit?"

"Hope to'a shit in your mess gear, Marine. Twenty fo' year now we marry."

"Well, fuck me!"

"Oh, no can fuck you, Marine, marry Gunny!"

"Uh, sorry, ma'am, that's not what I meant. I was just trying to say how surprised I am to know the Gunny's married. I bet you know where all the bodies are buried?"

"Oh, many body buried 'round here. Japanese kill many, many, many Filipinos."

G.O. and the Mama-san moved to a table to continue their discussion.

◆ ◆ ◆

"Hill, goddamnit! I thought you were coming back with more brewskis, and here you are chattin' up my fucken wife! What kind of lowlife fucken Marine are you, Hill? Tell me you are not trying to get into my Kapi's drawers!"

"Jeez, Gunny. Take it easy...Kapi and I were just having a talk. She was tellin' me how y'all met and all that...hell, Gunny you ought to write a book about your life, or should I call you *Pabig nungoy*."

"No, no, G.O., it pronounce *Pag-ibig ng Unggoy*."

"Goddamnit! Nobody calls me that but Kapi, numbnuts. And if I ever hear that word from you or anybody else in this squadron, I will personally knock the top of your head off and scoop what few brains you have out with a spoon. Are we clear?"

"How about Love Monkey?"

The Gunny reached across the table and grabbed G.O. by the throat as they both rolled on to the floor, while Kapi burst out laughing.

"You two so funny...same same all Marines! So funny!"

◆ ◆ ◆

G.O. and the Gunny stood by the Rube Goldberg–designed outdoor grill.

"Damn, Gunny that is one of the most interesting grills I've ever laid eyes on. Who built this contraption?" he said as he held a cold San Miguel close to his swollen jaw.

"Bob the metalsmith, down in the airframe shop. See, with this crank handle here, I can raise or lower the grill and can control the heat. Or I can lift it to put on more charcoal or wood. And with this crank over here, I can move the grill away from the coals altogether, so I don't burn myself when I take the food off.

"Now I suggest you quit trying to change the conversation and get back to the question I have been asking you since you first landed on my doorstep. Did you or did you not have a naked man in your car before you were shipped off to Vietnam?"

"It's a long story, Gunny…"

"Not so fast, Hill. You have used every trick known to man and even a couple of unconventional ones to try to avoid tellin' me this story. Well, no longer, my young friend. You are going to tell the story if it takes the rest of the night."

G.O. looked at the Gunny, and that night before Locker left for Vietnam came surging back into his memory. "Well, Gunny, it's like this. I had a friend back in the states who was leaving for Vietnam, so we decided to give the guy a going-away bash. We went to one of the local dives on the outskirts of Jacksonville and commenced to get shit-faced in a proficient military manner, as you would expect…ooh-rah?"

"Ooh-rah. Carry on."

"Well, these two Westpac widows come in, and we manage to introduce ourselves, and one thing leads to another, so we end up in their apartment. Well, not much happens. We drink. We laugh. Just having a good time you know? So my friend and his date go off to a bedroom. I'm thinking, play your cards right, G.O., and you may find the promised land tonight. Well, we hear all this screaming and laughing, and we jump off the sofa and run down the hall. There's my friend and his date standing in the shower with all their clothes on, just laughing and screamin'. So my date reaches in and turns the shower off and hands her friend a towel. They go off to the bedroom and dry off and change clothes. My date comes back and hands me a blanket and says, 'Here, Mr. Clean can wear this home.'

"So we are in the car headed back to base. My friend is wrapped up like Sitting Bull, and his clothes are lying in a wet puddle on the floor. It's three in the a.m., and we decide to stop for coffee. Well, every cop in Jacksonville is there, and two of them come over to the car and want to see my driver's license. So, I dig it out and hand it to the officer. While I'm doing that, the other one walks around to the other side of the car and asks my friend, 'Hey, boy, whatcha wearin'?' Being a sharp thinker and smooth talker, my friend replies. 'A blanket, dumb ass, what's it look like?' Well, for some strange reason the officer takes offense. The two of us end up in the house of detention. After a lengthy discussion with the desk sergeant, it became apparent that they did not have anything to charge us with, so they let us go.

"But what I'm really curious about, Gunny, is how did you even know about this story?"

"Sure, I'll tell you that…as soon as you tell me the name of your drunk friend."

"It was Locker, Gunny."

"Figures." Gunny cast a knowing look at Hill. "I heard it from a friend in the FBI who was doing a background check on you two, tryin' to find out if you might be material for HMX One."

"What's HMX One, Gunny?"

"The presidential helicopter squadron, doofus."

"For real?"

"For real, my young friend. I've been waiting to hear this story before I asked the CO to approve your orders. So, you'll be headed out of here on the next available flight."

"So having a naked man in my car won't keep me out of the presidential helicopter squadron?"

"Nope, if it won't keep you from being president, it won't keep you from being his crew chief."

♦ ♦ ♦

Another jeepney pulled to a halt in front of the bar, and Locker and his crew started piling out. There was Duck, Redfeather, Metalsmith Bob, C.C., Inchworm, and Wonderdick all hell-bent for the bar.

"Locker, you drunken commie bastard!" shrieked the Gunny. "Get your ass over here."

Locker separated himself from the stampede and began his casual surfer shuffle toward the Gunny, like he was strutting in front of a group of bikini-clad groupies huddled together on the beach at San Onofre. On the way, he threw G.O. the stink eye. G.O. stinked back.

The Gunny, being the adroit pseudopsychologist he was, couldn't help but notice the eyeball war going on around him.

"What's going on with you two? Normally, you two are so tight I have to pry you apart with a crowbar. Well?" the Gunny queried as his eyes rotated between the two. "Who's going first?"

Locker turned toward the Gunny. "We just have a disagreement, Gunny. It ain't no big thing."

"Well, Sergeant Gallo, I'll be the judge of that, so what's this disagreement about?"

"We disagreed about Hakim's punishment, Gunny."

"You gotta be fucken kidding me, you fucken halfwits! The goddamned Marine Corps has ruled on Hakim. You mullets don't get to disagree with the Marine Corps. You're not worthless fucken boots anymore, and you both know your opinions don't mean squat in this man's Marine Corps. So, this disagreement ends now, *comprende*?"

Hill and Gallo just stood and stared at each other. Neither blinked. Neither offered a hand. Eons seemed to pass.

"Well, hell, boys...there's only one way to settle this dispute. But first we eat and drink and make this night one we will never forget. So grab us some brewskis, Locker, and let's get started."

"Aye-aye, Gunny," Locker replied as he turned and headed into the bar.

Chapter Thirty Seven

Mystic Foxhole Yacht Club Bowl

It was late in the evening, and G.O. was beyond drunk. A steady rain was coming down. He sat at a table with Kapi, the Gunny, and two Filipinos who looked as though they had just taken a break from an old World War II movie production. Kapi had made them stash their AK-47s behind the bar when they arrived, but they still wore their ammunition bandoliers and an assortment of knives. The Gunny explained that the old man, Kapi's uncle, fought with the Huks against the Japanese, and now he and his son belonged to the New People's Army. They were all speaking Tagalog and chattering like geese on methamphetamines and getting louder by the minute. The older of the two had a patch over his right eye and a scar that ran down the right side of his face, from his eye to his lip. When he talked or smiled, he looked like Alice's Cheshire cat. *Jesus, Mary, and Joseph the Haberdasher, that guy would give Scrotum a run for his money in the looks department,* Hill thought. The younger guy looked as though he might weigh a hundred pounds soaking wet. A head full of black hair and a permanent scowl on his face. G.O. sensed the young one might be trouble. *Son of Patch? Psychopatch? Patchsquatch? I'll have to ask Kapi later.*

The bar had filled up, and there was a steady stream of Marines, squids, and Filipinas making their unsteady ways to and from the second floor. A Filipino cover band was playing Iron Butterfly's "In-A-Gadda-Da-Vida," and a bar full of inebriated patrons tried to sing along with the band. The cacophony of sounds was deafening. G.O. just sat there with a ridiculous grin on his face. He was going home. Soon.

The Gunny looked at G.O. through his own level-one state of intoxication. "So, Hill, you going to make nice with Gallo, or are we going to have to settle this the Marine Corps way?"

"I don't believe that's going to be possible, Gunny."

"You don't believe it's possible?" the Gunny mocked Hill. "You don't believe it's possible!" the Gunny screamed. "Fuck all that's holy and the horse you rode in on, Hill. I don't give a shit for what you believe or that commie-fuck-wave-rider, Gallo." While the Gunny screamed at Hill, Kapi did her best to translate to the two Filipinos at the table. "I don't give a good diddly goddamn if you believe in a beige Virgin Mary and a purple Baby Jesus or if God lives in a fucken tree, and when you die, you become just another fucken nut in the tree. Shit, Hill, everybody believes in somethin', but it don't mean a goddamn thing unless you believe in it, too. Hell, some people believe in strawberry colonics or walking around a labyrinth contemplating all the nuts hangin' in the fucken tree. There are others that rub crystals on their body parts and walk around with patchouli incense sticks protrudin' from their rectums, thinking it will bring them health, wealth, and happiness. Every fucker in the world is operating on a frequency we can't comprehend. Some of them sons o' bitches worship fucken cows, some think bird nests are a delicacy, some think you can stick a pin in a doll that looks like you, and you will feel the pain, old son. Now, I hear folks sayin', 'I'm not religious. I'm spiritual.' What the fuck does that mean, anyway? I'll tell you what it means. It means whatever works for them, Hill. Whatever gets them through the day. That's what people fucken believe. It might mean stickin' bones through their ta-tas and hangin' from the top of the teepee for a day, or maybe tyin' themselves in yogi knots and contemplatin' about what kind of rabbit food they're havin' for dinner. But what I really want to know, Hill, is what do you believe?"

It was uncomfortably quiet at the table as all eyes focused on G.O.

"You want to know what I think?" G.O. asked the Gunny.

"No, you fucken retard, I don't give a good goddamn what you think! I wanna know what you *believe*!"

"Oh, you want to know what I *believe*."

"Well, goddamn, I knew there was a brain floatin' around in that head of yours somewhere. So tell it, son, what do you believe? We ain't got all night."

G.O. looked down at the table and flicked his Zippo. He looked fixedly at the flame for a moment. Flipped the Zippo closed. As he stared at the eagle, globe, and anchor emblem on the lighter, he proceeded. "When we were stuck in that rice paddy for three days without food, I believe a bird's nest sautéed in garlic and butter would have tasted damn fine. But I don't believe I woulda told anybody about it. I don't have a clue about sticking an incense stick in my hind parts, but I know for a fact that the rectum makes an excellent launch site for bottle rockets. You just don't wanna squeeze your butt cheeks too tight, or you will end up with some major blisters. Lighting farts through screen doors produces some divine colors but I ain't sure if anybody's ready to make that part of their liturgy. I don't have a clue about my astrological sign, but I do know this is the Year of the Rooster on the Chinese calendar, and in the words of my grand-daddy, 'Don't fuck with the rooster!' I believe sex is highly overrated and making love, highly underrated. Yessir, *highly underrated*. I believe that a quart of Jack Daniels and some good Cambodian Red can have you talkin' in tongues quicker than the Holy Spirit. It will also help you under-stand why God treats mankind like a bunch of red-headed stepchildren, but you won't remember any of those deep insights the next morning because you have to get on with life. I believe when a man falls out the ass-end of a helicopter, he prays all the way to the ground. I believe if you fall off a horse, you should get right back on him, but even from where I'm from, we know when to quit flagellatin' a deceased equine. Something the good ol' United States hasn't figured out yet, or we wouldn't still be in this fucken war. I believe God has to be a fucken Marine, and on the eighth day when God said, 'Who will Follow me?' all the fish rose from the sea. I also believe God is pissed off because he ain't as omnipotent as a gunnery sergeant. He probably lays his head down on a humongous fluffy cloud every night, then cries like a little fucken baby, 'cause he got sent home from boot camp for tugging on his itty-bitty Holy Cannoli."

G.O. flicked his Zippo a couple of times and looked up at the Gunny. "Lastly, I believe some people's skulls are so fucken thick that the light will never penetrate, no matter how bright the light shines or how many holes are punched through the skull. I will not compromise my beliefs, Gunny, while Locker is allowed to remain entrenched in his ridiculous opinions about justice. Hell, it's just racism tied up in cute bows and ribbons, masqueradin' as justice. Hakim told me before he left that white men were going to have to face a new reality. My new reality required me to examine everything I was taught growing up. You know, like an inch being equal to five armadillo penises. I grew up believing that white folks were better than brown and black folks and that if you were born in the USA, you were better than anyone else on the planet. But I have had to reexamine all those beliefs and my own racism. And I believe compromising with racism, even subconscious racism, only serves to promote evil. So I guess we are going to have to settle this the Marine Corps way."

Suddenly, the Gunny was on his feet, standing on his chair, blowing a whistle and screaming for everyone to listen, "Quiet, goddamnit! Quiet! OK, listen up, cocksuckers." The Mystic Foxhole became improbably and remarkably quiet. Even the band stopped in the middle of the Beatles' tune, "It's Your Birthday." All eyes were on the Gunny, who continued to alternate between screaming and blowing on his obnoxious whistle. "Listen up...we have a dispute between two of my crew chiefs that has to be resolved. There is only one way to bring about a harmonious resolution to this dispute. We are going to have a fucken football game!" The bar erupted in wild cheering and glasses and bottles banging on tables. "Quiet!" the Gunny continued. "Sergeant Hill will captain one team, and Sergeant Gallo will captain the other. Since there's a turd-floater going on outside, the game will have to be played here in the bar. So let's start moving all the tables and chairs outside to the veranda."

As the shit-faced throng began moving tables and chairs outside, Kapi was going postal on the Gunny while Patch and Son of Patch looked on. After Kapi had calmed down, the Gunny sent her to the bar to fetch some bar towels. He immediately began tying the bar towels into an otherworldly object that vaguely resembled a football. Only if you did not look closely. The Gunny called the two captains together to pick out their respective teams. G.O. called his team the Palace Cowboys, and Locker went with Poop-Chute Packers. The Cowboys had to wrap black bar towels around their heads, and the Packers used white ones. The Packers won the toss and elected to receive. Kapi had all the Filipino working girls standing on the bamboo bar yelling for both teams. The Gunny blew his whistle, and it was game on.

G.O. lobbed the football down the bar. It ricocheted off the ceiling into the hands of Locker, who started screaming, "Wedge, wedge!"

The black towels descended on the Pack with G.O. screaming, "Somebody get that motherfucker!"

Pogo and two sailors about-faced and ran for the veranda.

Wonderdick and Redfeather led the wedge and took out Hill and Barf with full-on body blocks. Scrotum and Barf ran into the opening and delivered a bone-shattering tackle on Locker. As Locker went down, the contorted mass of Marines and sailors ended up in a pile on top of him. The Gunny blew the play dead as the two Huks ran and jumped on the top of the pile of squirming limbs.

As the pile started to unwind, the Gunny was giving the Huks an earful, as Kapi translated for him. "Goddamnit, you can't jump on the dog pile after the whistle has blown. That's a foul." Both Filipinos reached for their barong knives. The Gunny held his hands in front of him. "I'm going to overlook it this time, 'cause y'all don't know the fucken rules." Both Patch and Son began bowing to the Gunny.

"Goddamnit, Gunny, that ain't right. You ought to penalize those fucks for unsportsmanlike conduct or something," Locker fumed. The two Huks turned to face Locker, and their hands went to their knives. "On the other hand, neither of them know the rules, but at least tell them they can't just jump on the pile anymore."

"Ooh," Scrotum said. "Maybe, youse should change your name to Pussy Packas. Youse actin' like ya's packing one."

"Fuck you, Scrotum. Why don't you just shut the fuck up and play the game?"

"Gallo's right, everybody go huddle up," the Gunny offered. "First and ten on the thirty-five-yard line."

"Thirty-five-yard line?" G.O. queried. "With all due respect, how in the hell did you come up with that, Gunny?"

"It's my field, I am the ref, and I get to make all the calls. Any more questions, Sergeant Hill, fixin' to be Corporal Hill if he keeps asking his Gunny dumb-ass questions? We clear?"

"Clear, Gunny!"

In the Cowboys' huddle, G.O. said, "OK, guys, here's what we are gonna do...when Locker takes the snap, I want everyone and their mamas to hit him. Hard. I wanna hear him squeal."

"That don't seem fair, G.O.," Wacky said.

"Fair, if that motherfucker wanted fair he shouldn't have joined the Marine Corps!"

"G.O.'s got a point, Wacky," Blaze responded.

"OK, let's take him out! Ready...break!"

"Break!" The 'Pokes responded in unison, as the two Huks looked at each other and then at their teammates with utter bewilderment on their faces.

Locker brought his team to the line. The Packers were in a shotgun formation as Locker looked over the defense. He had Radley and Masterson wide left, and Duck was split out to the right. *This is great,* he thought. *No one is covering my receivers!*

Metalsmith Bob snapped the football back to Locker. Locker drew his arm back as the entire Cowboy defense converged on him. He was driven headfirst into the bamboo bar. As they started to unpile, G.O. could see the two Huks flying through the air and heard Locker scream at the bottom of the pile. When G.O. looked around, he could see Duck in the end zone doing the Monkey with the football. The Gunny was blowing his whistle and signaling touch down, with arms raised. Radley and Masterson rushed over to the Duck and lifted the conquering hero in the air. The ceiling fan, not recognizing the hero, immediately tried to decapitate him. All three of the end zone celebrators were knocked to the ground. As the pile untangled, the Packers ran to the end zone to participate in the touchdown dance-a-thon.

Locker, blood streaming from a cut left eyebrow, put his hand on G.O.'s shoulder. "See what happens when you come after me, Georgie?"

Hill slapped his hand away. "It ain't over yet, Locky."

◆ ◆ ◆

The game raged on as both teams battled back and forth, delivering vicious blows that caused the bar girls to put their hands over their eyes and screech in anguish. Colliding bodies smashed together onto the bamboo floor, collapsing into writhing piles, only to stagger to their feet and go at each other again. Blood and perspiration intermingled on the barroom floor, as the combatants hammered away at each other. All of their pent-up anger, frustration, and rage that had built up over the past months found the ideal outlet. The flying twelve-to-sixteen hours a day, the lack of sleep, and the constant uncertainty that gnaws away at your ability to control your fears, the profound enervation affecting the squadron, all found their release. Football.

To keep Patch and Son from piling on after every play, G.O. resorted to alternately giving them the ball when the 'Pokes had possession. After one violent play, Patch had to be carried to the bar in a state of semiconsciousness and laid out on the countertop while he recovered. All of the players felt like the Huk had received a fitting reward for his unsportsmanlike play.

G.O. offered to let Junior carry the ball on the next play. Junior didn't want the ball. No one on his team wanted the ball. They were exhausted, bleeding, aching, battered, and disfigured. The only player who appeared to be unfazed was Scrotum, but he always looked like he had just climbed out of an automobile wreck. G.O. looked deep into their eyes. There was no quit on this team.

"OK, quarterback sweep left...Ready, break!"

"Break!" The 'Pokes roared as they broke out of the huddle.

On the snap, G.O. caught the ball from center and started around the left end. He lowered his shoulder and hit C.C. in the chest, knocking him into the Duck. Redfeather grabbed his left arm, where G.O. held tightly to the ball and was swung into the bar. The Packers and 'Pokes both collapsed in a crushing mountain on top of him and Redfeather. They slammed into the bar with such impact that the bar girls and Patch fell onto the jumble of bodies. The Gunny was blowing his whistle. Kapi was screeching in Tagalog. G.O., pinned at the bottom of the mass, could only move his head to the right. When he turned, the most bodacious Filipina ta-ta hit him in the eye. *I believe I have died and gone to heaven*, he thought. *Good to know angels have ta-tas.*

"OK, this is the last play, goddamnit!" the Gunny roared.

"What's the score?" asked a perplexed Wacky.

The Gunny pulled a score sheet out of his pocket and said, "I have it at Packers, ninety-seven...and...Cowboys, ninety-seven."

"A tie? A goddamn tie?" shouted Locker.

"Yes, the score is tied, numbnuts! The Cowboys have one more play to break the tie."

"C'mon, Gunny, you're playing favorites!"

"Who the fuck said that? Speak up, goddamnit! That's what I thought...whoever said that doesn't have the balls to accuse me of favoritism! Goddamnit, it's my ball, my field, and my fucken rules! If you gutless mullets don't like it, you can take your sorry asses out of my bar. Now, what's it gonna be, Locker? You boys have enough juice left for one more play...or are you gonna quit?"

"I don't ever quit, Gunny!"

"That's right, bring it on, Hill," said Duck.

"No way you guys can score on the last play!" challenged the Inchworm.

"You betchum, Kemosabe," added Redfeather, as he winked at G.O.

The Cowboys went into their huddle. G.O. looked down the barroom floor. The makeshift end zone looked a mile away, even though it was only about fifty paces away. "Hey, Gunny," G.O. called. "Can we get a time-out?"

The Gunny blew his whistle and yelled, "Time-out...Cowboys...drink time, everybody!"

There was much cheering, applause, and good-natured bantering as the teams headed over to the bar. G.O. approached the Gunny. "Gunny, I was wondering, since this is our last play of the game, can we kick a field goal?"

"Are you out of your fucken mind, Hill? Even if we had a goalpost, who you got on your team that can kick a bag of rags, tied into a knot, sixty feet? Hell, son, that's a dumb-ass play. Just go out and run your best tricky-ass play. What have you got to lose? If you don't score, hell, the game's still tied, and you and Locker can both save face. If you score, you win. So fucken what? You're still gonna walk over there and shake Locker's hand, and hopefully you two will put your problems behind you."

"Hell, Gunny, I haven't had any problems with Locker since the first play of the game when Patch and his son dove feet-first on the pile. Now, it's just all about the game. Sure, I'm gonna walk over and shake his hand after this is over. But I would rather do it with a smile on my face.

"The goalposts shouldn't be that hard, Gunny. We can have two of the hookers...er...ah...working girls stand on chairs and form the uprights with their arms. As far as who can kick it that far, well, I've seen Pogo kick a beer can through a three-holer window from fifteen yards away. I figure a beer can don't weigh much more than that bag of rags, so do we get a shot?"

"Well, if that's what y'all want to do, you got my go-ahead."

"Thanks, Gunny," Hill replied as he went in search of Pogo.

G.O. found him and his squid sidekicks by the Gunny's exotic tropical fish tank. Pogo had a koi tail sticking out of his mouth. "Damn, old son, you having a bit of sushi?"

Pogo forced a swallow. "Oui, I am just a little 'ongry," said a wide-eyed Pogo.

"Well, come with me, Daniell. We need you on the next play."

"No, no, no, G.O., I do not know theese Americaine futbol. I cannot play."

"All you have to do is kick the ball!"

"I jus' kicks the boll?"

"That's right, you just kicks the fucken ball."

"I will kicks theese boll for you, G.O., *mon bon ami*."

♦ ♦ ♦

G.O. had explained to Daniell several times what a field goal was and how it was conducted. "All you have to do is kick it between the girls holding their arms up at the end of the bar," G.O. explained.

Pogo stood wide-eyed and shaking as G.O. knelt to take the snap from Barf. The bar girls looked to be a mile away. The 'Pokes were foot to foot, sweat and blood dripping from their determined faces as they prepared to take the charge from the equally resolute Pack.

Locker walked back and forth behind the defense shouting encouragement. "Free drinks and pussy all night for the son of a bitch that blocks this kick!"

The bar girls were chanting, "Brock that kick! Brock that kick!"

The Gunny blew his whistle to begin play.

Barf snapped the ball.

Locker came crashing through the line and dived to block the kick.

Pogo made the kick as Locker plowed into G.O.

It was too late. The ball was in the air as G.O and Locker crashed to the floor.

Epilogue

Washington, DC
20 February 1989

As G.O. sat on the Lincoln Memorial steps, he thought, *That was one helluva game.* He stood and stretched and gazed at the Wall one more time. *The Wall that heals, my ass.* As he stood there, he noticed a man in a faded field jacket and a camouflage boonie hat working the crowd. The man would walk up to an unsuspecting visitor and hold out his hand as he spoke quietly. The visitor would either reach into their pockets or shake their head and walk away. *Damn, he looks familiar.*

As G.O. nonchalantly made his way toward the Wall, he kept his focus on the man in the boonie hat. *As I live and breathe, it's the Bear!* he thought. "Bear, is that you?" he called. The Bear looked all around and then did a double-take as he recognized G.O. A huge smile broke out on the Bear's face. They walked toward each other and embraced in joyous reunion. Slapping each other on the back and talking simultaneously at the unlikely coincidence of the meeting.

"C'mon, G.O., let's get the hell outa here. People startin' to look at us hard, and you puttin' a cramp in my Wall gig."

"I definitely want to hear more about your 'Wall gig,'" G.O. replied.

"Oh, this is just a side hustle, G.O. It's not my real job."

"A side hustle?"

"Yeah, you know, all these people come down to the Wall to look for a loved one's name, or somebody they knew who was killed in the 'Nam. You know, I walk up and talk to them and ask if they can help out a vet. They gimme a little somethin', and they leave feelin' better than they did. You know, the Wall that heals. Been healin' me for a while now, and providin' me with a little pocket change." The Bear laughed.

As they walked and talked, G.O. found out that the Bear had spent twenty years in the corps and retired as a gunnery sergeant two years previously and now owned a bar in Anacostia. The Bear had kept in touch with many of their former squadron members and was filling G.O. in on their whereabouts when he got to Hakim.

"You remember that wild man y'all sent to my squadron from the Philippines?"

"You mean Hakim El-Hashim?"

"Yeah, he the one. Well, you know the brother had a few dents in his head, right? I mean that brother was at war with his demons. After he got back to the States, he couldn't find a job, much less keep one. So, he took to robbin' liquor stores. He was shot and killed in Chicago back in seventy-three. I think it might have been suicide by cop.

"Now, the Duck, he a whole 'nother story. He livin' the high life in Manhattan sellin' real estate. He come down here to visit 'bout once a year. He always got a new roommate. The boy is starved for love.

"And Danny D.? He working for the highway patrol...can you dig it? He still crazy. I meet him in Vegas after the New Year every year. You ever hear from any of the crew?"

"I get a postcard from Locker occasionally. He's usually in some exotic locale on a remote beach searching for that perfect wave. We haven't seen each other since we left Vietnam.

"I did run into Redfeather, though. Down in Cartagena, Columbia. He was the captain of some rich guy's yacht and spends all his time sailing around the Caribbean."

"How 'bout you, Hill? What have you been up to the last twenty years?"

"Oh, you know, a little of this...a little of that, just trying to keep my head above water."

The Bear laughed. "Who you tryin' to fool, Hill? This here's the Bear, son. You still searchin' for something, just like everybody who spent time in that hell. You happy, Hill?"

"Well, I'm not unhappy."

"Ooh, now! That sounds just like your dumb Texas ass. *I ain't happy and I ain't unhappy, guess I'm jus' a po' stepchild don't nobody care about, po' me, po' me,*" the Bear mimicked. "What you need, Brother Hill, is a night out with the Bear, and everything gonna be all right in the morning." The Bear and G.O. left the Wall with their arms around each other's shoulders. Neither looked back.

As they walked away people
would nod at them as if
they knew But the
farther they walked the
fewer nods they received
until they were out of the
shadow of that long wall

About the Author

Charles L. Templeton served as a Marine Corps helicopter crew chief in Vietnam from 1968 to 1969, during which he flew over 150 missions. He was promoted to sergeant and, upon his return home in 1969, received orders for the Presidential Helicopter Squadron, where he spent a year before leaving the service to pursue a career in education.

Templeton is currently on the Board of Directors at the Writers' Colony at Dairy Hollow and serves as the acquisitions Editor for their online magazine, *eMerge*. Charles wakes up everyday thankful for the gifts he has been given and looking forward to whatever adventures the day brings. Knowing that whatever happens, it beats *'Shovelin' shit in the South China Sea*.

A portion of the net proceeds from the sale of *Boot: A Sorta Novel of Vietnam* will go to the Writers' Colony at Dairy Hollow in Eureka Springs, AR. https://www.writerscolony.org/ and the Semper Fi Fund https://semperfifund.org/

Made in the USA
Middletown, DE
05 February 2021

33168894R00194